The dog whimpered.

Jendara risked a look over her shoulder and felt her stomach twist. The sea had arrived in the harbor. It raised itself above the beach, hoisting longships and sailboats up into its muddy mass with a nasty crashing crunch.

There was no time for shinnying up the column. Jendara grabbed the dog by its collar and flung it onto the porch roof. Then she jammed her belt knife into the column and pulled herself up. Her hand closed on the edge of the roof as the great wave hit the first row of houses.

Walls boomed and crumpled, wooden joints screeching as they ground together. Jendara hung for a second, and then Kran grabbed the back of her jacket. She came up onto the roof.

It wasn't high enough here. They had to get to the top of the building, the ridgeline with its finials—they could hang onto those.

"Up!" she shouted.

Kran was already moving. The next section of roof was much higher and steeper, and for a second she thought he wouldn't be able to get a grip on it, but he did. Oric was right behind him. He caught a shingle and dangled for second. Then the shingle broke free.

The boy hit the roof of the porch and slid down. Jendara lunged for him. Her fingers closed on his wrist and his weight hit the end of his arm with a crack. He screamed in pain and grabbed her with his other hand just as the wave smashed into the side of the meeting hall.

The water slammed down on Jendara . . .

THE PATHFINDER TALES LIBRARY

THE PATHFINDER TALES LIBRARY

STARSPAWN

Wendy N. Wagner

A TOM DOHERTY ASSOCIATES BOOK

New York

PATHFINDER TALES: STARSPAWN

Maps by Crystal Frasier

A Tor Book
Published by Tom Doherty Associates, LLC
175 Fifth Avenue
New York, NY 10010

www.tor-forge.com

The Library of Congress Cataloging-in-Publication Data is available upon request.

ISBN 978-0-7653-8433-1 (trade paperback)
ISBN 978-0-7653-8432-4 (e-book)

First Edition: August 2016

Printed in the United States of America

0 9 8 7 6 5 4 3 2 1

For my husband John, who refuses to let me give up, and keeps me smiling even when the stars aren't right.

Inner Sea Region

Story Locations

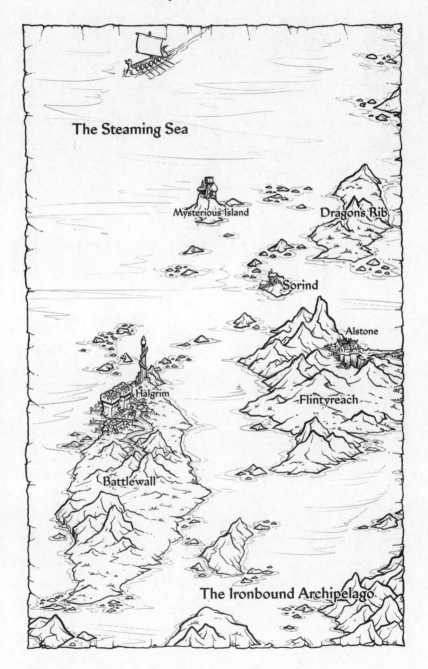

The Steaming Sea

Mysterious Island

Dragons Rib

Sorind

Alstone

Halgrim

Flintyreach

Battlewall

The Ironbound Archipelago

1

Harbor Wave

Jendara put down the file and checked the edge of her blade. She'd worked out the last of the nicks, but the sword could use a touch of the whetstone to bring out the edge. She reached for the bottle of oil at her elbow and paused. It was the kind of autumn morning in the Ironbound Archipelago that she loved. The smoke of her village's fires rose up in straight blue streaks, and the sound of children at play resounded in the crisp air.

"Ho, Jendara!"

She turned from her makeshift workbench, a split length of driftwood balanced on two fat stumps, already smiling. "Good morning, Boruc."

"No sign of the *Milady* yet?" The big man tucked his thumbs into his belt—nearly hidden under the bulge of his belly—and glanced out at the harbor.

"Not yet, but the tide only turned a few hours ago. The boatyards at Halgrim aren't *that* close."

"That captain husband of yours ought to hurry." Boruc grinned, and his teeth showed brightly against the red of his beard. A native islander like Jendara, he'd become one of her closest friends in the time since she'd returned to the archipelago. "Doesn't he know it's your birthday?"

"You remembered?" She laughed and got to her feet.

The ground moved beneath her in a sickening shudder.

She grabbed onto the workbench to steady herself. The earth jolted and jumped, and from the cottage behind her came the smashing of glass. A heavy yelm of thatch crashed down off the roof.

Her mind leaped to her son. "Kran!" She stumbled as the ground gave a last shake, then found her footing again. She sheathed the sword and broke into a run. "He went to the beach with Oric and that damn dog."

"You ain't got much time," Boruc warned.

Jendara knew it. She'd grown up on an island not that different from this one, and she'd spent her life on the sea—she'd seen what could happen after an earthquake. She scanned the horizon. It was probably too early for the ocean to rise up, but given the power of the shaking, the tsunami wouldn't be long.

A woman raced out into the street. "Fire! My house is on fire!"

Any other time, the rest of the village would have rushed to help her, but not now. People stumbled out of their houses, running uphill. Jendara could already see the tide turning in the harbor, the water pulling itself away from the shore like a blanket whipped back from a muddy bed.

"Kran!" she bellowed. The boy had brains. He knew he had to get away from the shore.

A man shoved her aside.

"Hey!"

"Gotta get uphill!" he shouted over his shoulder, and she saw the chicken clutched under his arm and the blue beads strung in his beard. The baker, Norg.

His wife ran behind him. "Get out of here, Jendara!"

"Kran!" Jendara shouted again. The boats at the piers were already high and dry.

"Jendara!" A tall man with sandy hair and beard—Morul—caught her by the arm. "Tell me the boys are already headed up to Boruc's house."

"I haven't found them yet." She caught the look of panic in his eyes. "I'll get the boys. You get Leyla to high ground!"

"She can't walk yet—the fever's got her knocked out."

"Then you better hurry!"

She broke away from him, her own fear climbing in her throat. Kran was a smart lad and levelheaded for a twelve-year-old. He should have made it up from the beach by now.

The crowds pressed against her and she found herself shoving aside old men, children—anyone that stood between her and her son. She could already see the ridge of water forming on the horizon. It didn't look like much right now, but she knew these waves to be deceptive. When it hit the island, it could be devastating.

Her boots slid on the mud of the beach. Were they down by the boats or over by the caves? The beach itself was empty, dotted with abandoned clam shovels and buckets.

"Kran!"

He couldn't answer, of course. That only made it all the worse. Her boy, her precious boy, was mute.

"Help!"

But Oric wasn't. Kran's best friend shrieked like a stuck pig, his voice bouncing off the rocks by the caves. Anger lit Jendara's blood on fire. Even on a good day, the caves were dangerous.

She raced toward the rocks.

And then skidded to a stop.

"Oh, shit."

She stared at the two boys on the nearest outcropping of rocks, unable to quite make sense of what was happening. Her son had Oric by the arm, but the other lad was clearly stuck between the two great rocks—a space she herself had passed through a dozen times collecting mussels.

"Help!" Oric screamed again. Kran looked over his shoulder, his eyes black circles in a too-white face. His little dog burst out of the gap between the rocks, whimpering. She was caught in something as well—some kind of thick, sparkly rope had wound itself around her chest, binding her to the stones.

Jendara scrambled up beside Kran. The ocean began to growl softly, the sound of all the rocks and debris it had sucked up now grinding along at the bottom of the sea bed. She could feel sweat prickling in her armpits.

The same tough rope had snared Oric, she saw. Jendara drew her sword. She'd never seen rope like this. It clung to the tow-headed boy with the stickiness of tar, and it shimmered with a pale purple-blue light. It reminded her of a spider's web—if the spider were the size of a small cottage.

She hacked through it, glad she'd sharpened her blade. The roaring was getting louder.

Kran jumped down beside the dog, pulling on its front legs.

"Cut the dog free," Jendara snapped at him.

He shook his head wildly and held up an empty hand.

"Where's your damned belt knife?"

"He must have left it at my house." Oric was nearly babbling. He wriggled and twitched as the words bubbled out. "We were whittling and then we needed mussels for your birthday dinner and—" He broke off at the fury in her eyes.

She seized the boy by the armpits and yanked him free of the rocks. A strip of skin ripped free of the back of her hand, stuck fast to the strange silk, and she hissed.

"Now run!" She slashed the binding on the dog and then sheathed her sword. "Get running, both of you!"

They slipped and slid on the mud. The dog raced past them. It might have been a half-sized, ugly thing, but it wasn't stupid.

Jendara risked a glance over her shoulder. The wave had picked up speed. It towered over the bay, a wall of mud and debris ready to crash down and swallow the island. They were never going to make it to the safety of the hilltop.

She put on a burst of speed to pass the boys. "To the meeting hall!" She stretched her hand behind her and caught Kran's sleeve.

The meeting hall was the largest and sturdiest building in the village, and stood on a knoll of rock above the main street. Decorative finials stuck up from each end of the high ridgeline of its shingled roof, while colorfully painted columns outlined a covered porch. She ran her hands over the green-and-blue surface of the nearest column. Kran wouldn't have any problem shinnying up it.

"On the roof," she ordered. He was up the column in a flash, and then immediately put out his hand to help his friend. Oric leaped onto the column but slid down again. He was bigger than Kran and less agile.

Jendara gave him a shove and let him scramble up onto her shoulders. His boot knocked into her head as he struggled up onto the roof.

The dog whimpered.

Jendara risked a look over her shoulder and felt her stomach twist. The sea had arrived in the harbor. It raised itself above the beach, hoisting longships and sailboats up into its muddy mass with a nasty crashing crunch.

There was no time for shinnying up the column. Jendara grabbed the dog by its collar and flung it onto the porch roof. Then she jammed her belt knife into the column and pulled herself up. Her hand closed on the edge of the roof as the great wave hit the first row of houses.

Walls boomed and crumpled, wooden joints screeching as they ground together. Jendara hung for a second, and then Kran grabbed the back of her jacket. She came up onto the roof.

It wasn't high enough here. They had to get to the top of the building, the ridgeline with its finials—they could hang onto those.

"Up!" she shouted.

Kran was already moving. The next section of roof was much higher and steeper, and for a second she thought he wouldn't be able to get a grip on it, but he did. Oric was right behind him. He caught a shingle and dangled for second. Then the shingle broke free.

The boy hit the roof of the porch and slid down. Jendara lunged for him. Her fingers closed on his wrist and his weight hit the end of his arm with a crack. He screamed in pain and grabbed her with his other hand just as the wave smashed into the side of the meeting hall.

The water slammed down on Jendara, driving out light and air and all sense of up or down. An incredible crackling and ripping resounded around her. For a second, she couldn't breathe.

Then with a powerful crunching, the porch roof ripped free of the meeting hall. Jendara gasped for air as she popped to the surface of the water.

The roof slid along the side of the meeting hall, riding the muddy mass of the wave. Oric clung to her, and she clung to the edge of the porch. If the roof broke apart or sank, the debris caught in the floodwater would crush them.

The wave drove them into the side of the next house. The walls had cracked and buckled against the power of the water. Wood groaned and snapped all around them. Over the powerful stink of mud and brine, the smell of smoke was choking. The earthquake had caused its own damage via fireplaces and woodstoves.

She looked around, desperate for her boy. She made out his silhouette on the still-intact ridgeline of the meeting hall and felt herself relax a little. If he was still all right, she could focus on saving herself and Oric.

"Jendara!" Oric's voice cracked with fear.

Jendara whipped her head around. A wall of debris was headed right for them: wood and rubble and a still-recognizable door, jutting out of the swirling water like a giant knife.

Jendara shoved against the broken house. She wasn't going to die pinned to a cottage, stabbed to death and buried in muck. She'd killed a giant and a troll and faced down a horde of barbarian shapeshifters. She had a family, a business, friends. Damn it, she wasn't going to drown!

The porch roof popped free of the broken house. The figure-head of a longship smashed into the wall where they'd been trapped, and with a groan, the house began to collapse on itself. The porch roof bobbed into the middle of the street. The water had carried them uphill, but it was still up to the bottoms of the windows, at least four feet high, and it would only get higher until the floodwaters withdrew.

Jendara searched for safety. They couldn't stay on this make-shift raft. Another wave would rip it apart or smash it into bits. Her eye caught the building on the far side of the street—the black-smith's. The only stone building in the village. Its porch wasn't much, but it was the best shelter she could see.

She grabbed a length of board floating beside her and poled hard. The road beneath her climbed the hill, and the current was fighting her now as the water pulled back for its next pounding wave. The raft shuddered as it moved slowly through the churning water.

She drove her pole between the slats of someone's garden fence. The support column for the blacksmith's overhanging roof was just a few feet away. Someplace nearby someone screamed for help, and her heart gave a squeeze.

But she couldn't help anyone if she didn't help herself first.

She jerked her chin at the porch, arms trembling to hold the roof-raft in place. "Get over there!"

Oric grabbed onto the fence with his good hand and jumped off the raft. The water was shoulder deep on him, but he didn't complain. He might not have Kran's stoicism, but he was still an islander through and through.

Jendara jumped off the raft. The water tugged the raft away in an instant, smashing it into a floating log. It sank immediately.

Here on the other side of the sturdy garden fence, there was a little less floating debris. A plow sluiced past, grinding against Jendara's side and bumping up against the fence with a heavy thud. She hoped the fence would hold a little longer.

Wading was hard. The water pulled her back with every step, and rocks and broken tree branches slammed against her chest and legs. Oric slipped and slid, then made it up onto the porch. Though the difference in height was slight, she thanked the ancestors as she followed him up onto the porch. There was less wreckage moving in the water, and the current wasn't as strong. She took hold of the porch column, then frowned.

Oric gripped the column with one arm, but the other hung uselessly at his side. He must have dislocated it when she'd grabbed him on the roof. If another big wave hit, he'd be gone.

She felt for her belt, the leather stiff in the saltwater. Cursing, she got it off and around the column. "Grab onto that," she ordered.

Then the next wave hit, and all she could do was cling to the column and the boy and try to protect her head as mud and smashed stonework and broken bits of everything battered them. She coughed and spluttered.

The next wave seemed a little smaller—or perhaps she was simply used to it. She lost count of them as they came, driving flotsam into the corners of the porch and dragging it back out into the street. A dead duck washed up against the pillar and floated in the eddy, its yellow feet sticking up in the air as the water spun it in a slow circle. Then it sank beneath the muck.

Between the waves, she stared at the roof of the meeting hall and watched Kran and the dog huddle in silent misery as the water slowly withdrew. He had never felt so far away, and she had never been so powerless to help him. She had thrown away her old life—a dangerous life, to be sure, spent serving bloodthirsty Besmara, the pirate goddess—to find someplace safe to finish bringing up her boy. Leave it to nature to prove her wrong.

Oric shivered beside her, and she risked letting go of the column to grip his shoulder. If only he hadn't gotten caught in that stuff down by the rocks, that strange silky rope like spider webbing. They would all be up at Boruc's house waiting for the water to recede, warm and dry and safe.

It was just bad luck, she supposed. As the Varisians might say, it was just a bad alignment of the stars, bringing misfortune down upon their entire village. She shivered and tightened her grip on the column.

The breeze strengthened, pushing aside a few clouds and inviting the sun to play on the surface of the floodwaters. They were receding, she realized. The houses on this stretch of the street were badly battered, and the ones closer to the beach were smashed and ruined, but at least the worst was over.

"I've got to get Kran," she told Oric. "You stay here."

"Don't leave me!"

"You'll be fine. The water's going down. And Kran's been alone this whole time."

"We would have all been out of here if he hadn't wanted to make you that stupid present," Oric grumbled.

Jendara shot him a stern look. "You'll be fine," she repeated. She took a careful step down from the porch. Something shifted beneath her feet and she gritted her teeth. There was no way to see what lay beneath the surface of the water—the stuff was as opaque as milk and as dark as garden soil. The worst might be over, but that didn't mean it was safe.

It was like capturing a rival pirate ship, she thought, setting her foot carefully before taking the next cautious step. They fought hard on the deck and you felt your blood boil as you cut your way forward, knowing every hand was set to kill you. But that was only the obvious danger. Down below was where the real nasty stuff waited: the injured happy to take someone to Pharasma's Boneyard when they went, the vicious cook devoted to his captain, the booby traps some loyal mate had set when all seemed lost.

Back in her pirate days, she'd seen plenty of her crewmates killed after the battle was ostensibly won, and she'd learned a thing or two. She kept her focus on the ground and the debris floating around her knees, and she moved slowly, even if every bit of her wanted to race back to the meeting hall and make sure Kran was all right.

Then she was there. The porch columns were slick with mud, and some stood at odd angles. She didn't trust them. She looked around for an alternate route.

To her left, Kran's dog barked.

She turned. The dog stood on the canted roof of the house beside the hall. At some point, a massive fir tree had toppled down on the broken house, and now lay at an angle, its top driven into the colorful wall of the meeting hall and its roots tangled in the wreckage below. The dog must have climbed down the tree.

"Smarter than you look," she grumbled. The yellow-and-white mutt wasn't the companion she would have picked for her boy. It wasn't a sturdy herding dog or a fine hound bred for hunting, just some stray he'd found by the docks, good for nothing but eating Jendara's venison. "Come here . . ." She tried to remember its name. "Fylga. Come."

The dog scrambled onto the tree trunk and began climbing back up to the roof of the meeting hall.

"Or maybe not." Jendara picked her way toward the base of the tree and gave it a shove. It felt solid.

In the distance, wood groaned and crumpled. Someone called for help again, the voice thin and tired. She had to get moving; people needed her.

"Kran!"

The boy peered over the roofline at her. He pointed at the tree and spread his hands questioningly.

"It's safe, I think. But hurry!"

He came down the tree cautiously, clinging to it like a bear cub. Jendara found herself reaching for him before he even made it to the halfway point. Her lip hurt from biting into it. The meeting hall could collapse, the tree could shift, the house could crumple more—

And then she had a hold of him and he was on the ground and she was squeezing him tight, tighter than she'd hugged him in years. He was twelve, after all. And he'd never been a cuddly boy, even when he'd been little.

He kissed her cheek and hugged her back. Then he pulled away, a smile spreading over his face. With his black hair hanging in wet clumps, that smile looked even whiter and broader than usual.

He pointed at the demolished house beside them, and it took Jendara a minute to make out what he saw in the midst of the broken beams and the sludge of mud. There was only the hint of colorful paint to remind her of the meeting hall's porch columns, one of which had been driven through the ruins of the house next door.

And there, jutting out of what had probably been a blue-and-green painted sea star, was the belt knife she'd stabbed into the wood as a handhold just before the wave had hit. Kran wrenched it free with a grunt, and handed it to her, beaming.

Maybe her stars weren't so badly aligned after all.

2

HOPE STAYS AFLOAT

She brought Kran to the relative safety of the blacksmith's porch. Waves still lapped at the bottom of the step, but the porch itself stood above the water. A good two inches of mud coated the stone, dotted with shards of glass and bits of broken lumber. Broken crab pots and smashed wooden pieces lay everywhere.

Oric sat on one, his face very pale. She remembered his hurt arm and felt a pang.

"Dara! Are you okay?"

She sagged with relief at the sound of Boruc's voice. "We're okay, but Oric's hurt," she called out.

"There's plenty of injured on their way to the farms. Let's get him to the healer so she can patch him up." The big man splashed his way toward them.

"Can you help Oric?" Jendara asked.

"I can walk," the boy snapped. "It's just my arm."

"Spoken like your father's boy." Boruc grinned. "None of our kin's ever been much for complaining. Give me a minute to catch my breath—had to clear a lot of rubble to get here."

Behind them, something crumpled and crashed. Probably a tree's roots giving out, Jendara thought, or a damaged house giving in to the pull of the outgoing current. The whole village could fall down into the sea with this kind of flooding. She thought of her own little cottage and wondered what condition she'd find it in.

"Help! Somebody help me!"

Boruc caught her eye. "Sounds like you're not the only one who got stuck down here. Want to lend a hand?"

Jendara nodded. She'd come to the island of Sorind to be part of a community, and helping out in an emergency was part of being a good neighbor. "Kran," she said. "You start clearing out a place for hurt people. We'll need places to sit and a spot big enough to lay someone down. Oric, you help as best you can, but take it easy till we get that arm bound up. I'll be back with more folks as I find them."

Kran gave her a mock-salute. Boruc paused a moment.

"I almost forgot why I started toward your house this morning. Happy birthday, Jendara." He held out a linen-wrapped package, it shape roughly triangular and about half as long as her arm.

Kran grinned knowingly. Jendara raised an eyebrow. "Were you in on this?"

The boy nodded. She unbound the length of linen and smiled at the beautiful creation in her hand. Boruc was a true artist, and though stone was his preferred medium, the work he'd put into this piece of wood and steel made it something outstanding.

"A new handaxe." She tested its balance in her hand. "It's amazing."

Her heart felt suddenly too big for her chest. The year before, she'd lost the handaxe that had belonged to her father—the only token she'd had left of her family, wiped out by raiders before Kran was born. In the time she'd spent on Sorind, Boruc had come to seem like a brother, part of the extended family she'd made for herself from crew and islanders.

The big man consented to a hug. "You'll probably get some good use out of it today."

He was right. The day crawled by as she shifted timbers, chopped open jammed and broken doors, and bandaged small wounds. Folks from the farms came down to lend a hand and bring lunch. The healer took Oric away to join his family, although he protested about leaving the repair work.

The tsunami had cruelly battered the island. Many of the houses on the higher ground in the village stood strong, needing only some surface level repairs—but a few were just gone, the island's clay soil washed out from under them. The town's gardens were ravaged, the livestock decimated. It would be years before the village fully recovered from the great wave.

After working most of the afternoon, Jendara and Kran finally headed toward their own home on the edge of town. Jendara had purposefully avoided looking in its direction all day. The roof of the house looked fine, but as they drew closer, she could see the massive driftwood log that had stove in the front wall of her house. Kran stopped beside the garden fence and stared.

"Well, shit." She kicked the fence, then kicked it again. "Shit!"

Kran tapped his chest as though his heart pained him. It probably did.

"I don't want to go in," Jendara admitted. She'd built this cottage herself, working with Boruc and his brother Morul to frame the building with wood they'd felled in the forest beyond Yul's farm. The *Milady*'s caulker, the green-haired gnome named Glayn, had helper her sew the curtains from fabric she and Kran had picked out on a trip to the mainland. The ship's first mate, Tam, had helped her build the boxes for the bees in the garden.

The bees were probably all dead now.

She walked up to cottage's splintered door, but found she could go no farther. After all the ruin and trouble she'd seen today, she was just too tired to think of clearing out the entrance of her own house.

She thought of the day of her wedding, only four or five months ago, when Vorrin had tried to carry her over this threshold, and instead knocked her head against the doorframe. She'd had a goose egg for a week.

She patted the frame with its ruined door. Their first home they'd had as a family, and she would have to rebuild most of the place.

"Could be worse," she said out loud. "Plenty of folks lost everything they had."

Kran tossed a smashed crate out of what had once been her potato patch and then made his way back to the garden fence. He paused to pet the dog and then climbed up to perch on the top fence rail. After a moment, she joined him. It was probably more comfortable than anything inside her soaked house.

Kran tapped her shoulder and pointed to the harbor. A tall ship glided across the water, its yellow-and-blue pennant snapping proudly from its tallest mast. The *Milady*. At least they'd have a dry place to sleep tonight.

Jendara watched from the beach as the dinghy approached. The four rowers stowed their oars, and the humans of the group began climbing out of the small craft to drag it onto the shore. Vorrin, her husband since early summer and her best friend for the past seven years, moved the fastest. Next to his massive first mate, he looked almost scrawny, and his neatly trimmed dark brown goatee stood as a contrast to the full beards the men of the islands wore. Even his hair, neatly clubbed back instead of left loose and decorated with sewn braids, marked his Chelish background.

Amid the humans, she saw Glayn the caulker, still clambering out of the dinghy. Despite his small size, the gnome immediately took his place with the others, working to get the boat ashore. Kran's yellow-and-white dog kicked up a spray of water as she raced to meet them.

Jendara waved at the group: her closest friends—her family, really—gone the past week to repair the *Milady*. The rest of the crew must be waiting on board the tall ship, worrying. The island had to look terrible from the harbor.

"Thank the gods you're all right!" Vorrin let go of the boat and ran to meet Jendara on the beach. He held her tight for a long moment. "We waited till it was safe to come into the harbor," he murmured. "I thought I'd die from the wait."

"It was pretty bad," she admitted. "The flood surge wiped out the cottage."

He leaned back to read her face. "Is it—is everything—?"

"The house is ruined. All the furniture soaked and smashed. I don't think anything's worth saving."

"Oh no." He reached out for Kran and gave him a hug. The boy didn't mind. Even before Vorrin and Jendara had married, Kran and Vorrin had been close. The man had always been there for the boy.

The others approached. Tam, a giant islander with wild yellow hair, beard, and eyebrows, called out: "Is it as bad at it looks, Dara?"

"Is our cottage ruined?" Glayn blurted. He and Tam had finally built a place on the island after years of bunking on board the ship. Glayn loved the little cottage.

Kran was already writing on his slate. *It's fine!*

"Wish we'd built as far up on the hill as you two," Jendara added. "A tree fell on one end and smashed up your roof a bit, but nothing like ours. We've got nothing."

Sarni, the newest and youngest crew member, not even twenty yet, patted Jendara on the shoulder. "I'm sorry about the cottage." She sounded unusually solemn. Though the girl had been a part of their crew for less than a year, she had grown as close to Jendara as a younger sibling.

Then Sarni grinned, brown eyes crinkling in her round face— her usual expression. Everything about the teenaged girl was cheery and compact and brown, like sea otter who had decided to join human company. "Tell her the good news, Vee!"

Vorrin sighed. He didn't care for his new nickname, and the young deckhand irritated him. But Jendara had taken Sarni under her wing after finding her running with a gang of vicious thieves raiding boats in Halgrim's harbor. Perhaps because Jendara had saved Sarni's life in that first meeting—or perhaps because Sarni knew that Jendara, too, had once run on the wrong side of the law—Sarni had been overeager to remold herself in Jendara's image ever since.

"It was amazing." Glayn beamed up at Jendara.

Tam nodded. "We only saw it for a moment—"

"You wouldn't believe how beautiful it was!" Sarni interjected.

"Hey," Jendara barked. "Shut up and give me the news straight."

"A new island," Vorrin explained. "It was unbelievable—we were on our way here, and the sea went crazy. Off to the west of us, the water looked like it was boiling. Orcas were racing to get by, leaping up in the air."

"That part was terrifying," Glayn interjected.

"I thought we were dead," Sarni added. "But Cap'n Vee wasn't scared."

"I nearly pissed myself," Vorrin corrected her. "Thirty-seven years at sea and I never saw anything like it."

"A new island?" Jendara shook her head.

"It just came up out of the sea," Tam explained. "Real slow at first. It sounded even stranger in his matter-of-fact delivery. He was an islander, born and bred, and took things in stride.

"What do you think made it come up?" Jendara asked. "The earthquake?"

"That had to have something to do with it," Glayn said. "Maybe it broke off of something at the bottom of the sea and floated to the top."

"Rocks don't float, Glayn," Tam noted.

"Pumice floats!" Glayn shot back.

"Maybe," Vorrin said, his dark eyebrows drawing together. He rubbed his neatly trimmed goatee, a sure sign he was thinking hard.

"All of this doesn't matter," Sarni blurted. "What matters is the gold!"

"Gold?" Jendara's voice was sharp.

Sarni nodded. "We saw it through the spyglass."

"I didn't dare get close to it. But we could see the entire surface was built up, like a city covered it. And it practically sparkled in the sun—we could see the gold shining on the tops of buildings," Vorrin explained. "It all looked really, really old."

A golden city on an island that had just popped up to the surface of the sea. If it had been inhabited by sea creatures, they were probably dead or desperately escaping back to the ocean. If it had been inhabited by air-breathing creatures—well, they certainly weren't going to still be around if the thing had been underwater.

"An abandoned city of gold."

"Hail, Jendara!" a voice called.

Jendara glanced up. Another dinghy approached from the *Milady*. Half the crew had stayed in Halgrim for the winter, taking on extra work at the shipyards or staying with family. The four in the approaching dinghy and the four on the beach were all long-time friends, teammates who'd been on board the ship since the day Vorrin inherited it. Glayn had been with her even before that, serving alongside Jendara during the dark pirating days. Every last one of them was worth three of the cottages she'd lost. The thought eased a little of the hurt of losing her possessions. Possessions could always be recovered if there was gold at hand.

And perhaps there *was* gold at hand. "You didn't see any other ships out there, did you? No one else was staking a claim on this new island?"

Kran looked from Vorrin to Jendara, a smile spreading across his face. He already knew what she was thinking.

Glayn chuckled. "If your house was ruined, your boy's going to need an all-new winter wardrobe. And a new bow, and a spear, and a new—"

Jendara cut him off. "If that island has as much gold as your story makes it sound, Kran can have his own *armory*."

"Are we headed back out?" a woman nearly as tall as Tam called from the second dinghy. It was Zuna, the *Milady*'s navigator. The sun winked off the tiny silver bells and glass beads woven into her many black braids. The dark-skinned woman and her comrades jumped out of the boat and began dragging it ashore.

Jendara and the others walked down to the meet this second group. Zuna put an arm around Kran. It had taken Zuna a few years to warm up to Jendara; the woman had served on too many merchant vessels to trust a pirate, repentant or not. But Zuna was dead loyal to Vorrin, and she'd learned to like Jendara well enough. Kran, no one could help but love.

Vorrin looked back at his ship. "We still have supplies on board from our trip to Halgrim, but not many. We'll need to lay in some stores before we commit to anything. It might not seem like it, but winter's coming. This warm streak won't last forever."

The group divided itself, long experience making instructions unnecessary. Three crew members hung back to ask Jendara about their kin in the village; they agreed to help get Vorrin restocked for the journey to the golden island, but were too concerned with Sorind's well-being to sign on for this kind of adventure. Jendara couldn't blame them. The *Milady* was a trading vessel. The crew, no matter how stouthearted, wasn't all cut out of adventuring cloth.

Jendara kissed Vorrin on the cheek and left him to finish settling up with the crew members who were staying. She hurried to catch up with Kran and the long-legged Zuna, looking the other woman in the eye. "You sure you're up for this?"

"If you're asking if I'm up for a chance to make a fortune scraping gold off an abandoned city that's been lost beneath the waves, then yes. I wouldn't mind being rich." Zuna broke eye contact and studied the ground, careful of debris underfoot.

Careful. That was how Jendara had always thought of the woman. She kept to herself most of the time, and had never misguided the ship in all her years of navigating. Jendara had never seen her worried or frightened. While the others had faced cannibals and skinwalkers last year, Zuna had broken her leg on a trip to the mainland and missed it all. Jendara wondered what she'd be like in a fight. No one could be that collected all the time.

"It might be dangerous," Jendara warned. "There's no way of knowing how long that island's been underwater."

Zuna stopped and glared. "If you want to mother someone, mother your son. I can take care of myself." She pivoted on her rope sandal and strode away.

"What's her problem?" Jendara snapped.

Kran patted her shoulder soothingly, then reached for his chalk. He paused and wrote: *Island sounds great.*

Jendara frowned at the slate. "Kran, you're not going."

What? He underlined the word twice.

"You heard what I said to Zuna. Parts of that island could still be flooded, not to mention who knows what kind of weird magic or critters might be on it. There's no way I'm letting you go."

He threw down his chalk so hard the tip broke off against his slate. It swung crazily on its cord. For a moment, she half-expected him to throw his slate off on the ground, the way he would have just a year ago, but instead he just stood glaring at her.

She folded her arms across her chest. "Let's go check on Oric."

His fingers curled into fists. He looked like he was ready to explode, but he didn't.

She walked up the hill without looking back at him. She couldn't take him with her, and she wouldn't cave, but no matter how well Kran knew it, he wouldn't let the matter go. He was going to be angry with her for a long time.

Jendara pasted a pleasant look on her face, smiling at villagers as she passed. But inside, she sagged with exhaustion. Raising a boy was like fighting a war, sometimes. And right now she wanted nothing but a bit of quiet and a pint of beer in her own little house.

In other words, she wanted the impossible.

Jendara stood at the deck rail as the morning wind blew sweet salt into her face. The trip to the island would take all morning and a good chunk of the afternoon; Zuna was planning a careful course that skirted the rocky shoals they'd seen off the northeast side of the island. The crew's energy ran high—Jendara could hear it in their voices as they called to each other in the sails. It was a skeleton staff without the three Sorinders, although Vorrin had pressed their old friend Boruc into assisting, and she could hear the big man singing someplace up in the rigging. He wasn't much of a salt, but it would be a short journey to this mysterious new island. They could manage the ship well enough with no weather.

She rubbed her eyes. She'd slept poorly, even though her and Vorrin's bed in the captain's cabin was comfortable enough. There had been a time when she and Kran were inseparable, more best buddies than parent and child, but over the last few years his temper and will had pulled them apart. Things had gotten quieter since Vorrin joined their little family, but in the last few weeks, there had been signs that the good times were coming to an end.

"You all right?" Vorrin set a hand on her shoulder.

"I don't like leaving Kran like this. I hate fighting with him."

"I know. But you were right to leave him behind. I tried to explain to him just how much Oric and Morul were going to need his help while we're gone, but I don't think it helped." Vorrin shrugged. "I don't know that much about being a father."

"You're the closest thing he's ever had," she reminded him. "His own's been gone a long time."

"I do my best." He sighed. "Jendara, do you feel good about this trip? About this island, I mean?"

"Sure. We just lost everything we own, outside of this boat. After crew pay and all the repairs on the *Milady*, we're flat broke. Anything that could make us a copper or two feels fine."

He set his elbow on the rail. "I don't know. I just can't help but wonder what makes a sunken island come up out of the sea like this. You haven't seen it yet, so you don't know. It's ancient. Just looking at it, you can tell. Whatever built that city, they lived a long, long time ago. Who knows what they were like?"

"We'll be careful." Jendara nodded to herself. "I'm sure everything will be just fine."

3

TALL CLIFFS AND SEA CAVES

Jendara adjusted the spyglass. "So that's our island."

It looked like a giant tree stump rising out of the sea—the sides some kind of dark stone that stood nearly vertical, the top mostly flat beneath the city structures. A trio of ridges at the center made several of the largest buildings stand tall above the others. The imposing structures gleamed in the sunshine, the pale stone and gold details blindingly bright between patches of scabrous seaweed.

At the base of the island, knobs of rock stuck out like a tree's roots bulging above the surface of the soil. Jendara scanned the waters around the lower rock formations for a safe place to tie up, but her attention kept wandering back to the top of the island.

She had visited a dozen cities on the mainland—even Absalom, the largest and most beautiful city of all the Inner Sea—but she'd never seen a city like this. The island itself wasn't large—about five miles across—but every inch of it supported some kind of building or statue, and most of them glinted with the sheen of gold.

She lowered the glass. "It's stunning."

"Incredibly," Vorrin said. "Let's make a full circuit to get the lay of it." He walked away toward the bow.

Jendara couldn't take her eyes from the city. The amount of treasure visible to even the naked eye was astonishing. It was hard to believe that all of this had been sitting quietly beneath the sea while her people's longships had been passing over it, none the wiser. If that earthquake hadn't brought it up to the surface, no one would have ever known it was there.

Of course, if there hadn't been an earthquake, the village of Sorind wouldn't be a mud flat right now, but that was beside the point. Now she was here, and so was all this treasure.

"Pretty amazing, isn't it?" Sarni bounded up to Jendara and gripped the railing. She bounced on her toes, too excited to contain all her energy. "Not much to a former pirate like you, I'm sure."

Jendara rolled her eyes. "Please. I was picking off merchant ships, not emptying the king's coffers. I bet most kingdom treasuries don't have as much gold in them as the top of this city."

Sarni laughed, nearly a giggle. Sometimes she seemed younger than her age, as if, since she'd missed out on having any real childhood, she was trying to get some of it back now. Jendara thought of Kran and was glad she'd gotten him away from her life of crime. Piracy was no life for a child.

"Hey, can I use your glass?"

Jendara handed it over and Sarni stared through it. She went quiet for a minute, then laughed again.

"Look at all those statues. That one over there has got to be as tall as the *Milady*." Sarni turned to grin at Jendara. "It's got a lot of seaweed on it, but I'm pretty sure it's got wings and tits." She went back to scanning the island. "Oh wait, those might be a pair of krakens. Tits are funnier."

Jendara rolled her eyes.

Sarni handed the spyglass back to Jendara, face suddenly serious. "I've never seen anything like this place.

"Well, it's old and it's in pretty rough shape. It's going to be an adventure for all of us."

Sarni shook her head. "It's not that. It's . . . all the gold and the decorations?" She turned to put the railing at her back and folded her arms around herself. "Can you imagine living like that? Even the palace in Halgrim ain't that fancy, not by half."

"Well, we're islanders. Everything we've got we had to pull out of the sea or grow ourselves. Takes a lot of work to get what you need, let alone fancy things."

"Ain't that right. Down by the harbor, where I grew up, nobody had shit." She shrugged. "Well, shit we had, but that was about it. If we got lucky, there was enough fish to eat and the ice sealed up the hole in the roof."

Jendara searched for the right answer. There had been hard times in her life—more than enough—but at least as a child, her family had been able to live off their land. Her clan had always been able to pull together during hard times, and no one had to suffer on their own.

"The first pair of shoes I ever had?" Sarni continued. "Stolen. My mama wouldn't steal, but I would, and it felt damn good not to be barefoot on the ice. Stealing was the only way I ever got anything."

Jendara put a hand on the young woman's shoulder. "That's behind you now, Sarni. You're not living on the docks and running with gangs. You've got us."

Sarni glanced back over her shoulder at the island. This side didn't look nearly as fancy as the south end. There were no golden towers, only boxy stone buildings packed in beside each other. Gold winked off what must have been window frames. "If we get rich, I want to help people. I don't know how, but I want to."

Jendara just smiled. That was why she'd taken in Sarni. Beneath the foul mouth and loud voice and the history of trouble, there was a warm, kind human. She had no doubt Sarni would use her funds from this mission to help the less fortunate.

Vorrin strode toward her. "We've almost made it completely around the island. Any thoughts on where we ought to try landing?"

Vorrin may have been the ship's captain, but he let Jendara take the lead on anything involving land. They made a good team together. Even before she'd fallen in love with the man, she'd liked working with him.

She thought for a moment. "I've seen signs of stairs and streets while looking over the city. To me, that suggests people with legs built this, not swimming folk. I'd guess this was all above the water at one time."

"So they had to have some kind way to load and unload ships."

"Probably. I mean, gold isn't exactly common in this part of the world. I imagine it came from someplace."

"And that means ships." He shook his head. "To the east, there are too many rocks for a ship to get close. At the north and the south, there's some good anchorage, but I don't know how anyone got up or down the sides of the island. I wouldn't want to try to climb them with ropes."

Jendara imagined what a long, muscle-eating climb that would be and rapped her left hand on the wooden deck rail. It was her private good luck ritual, a tiny nod to the ancestor spirits she'd witnessed firsthand last summer. She didn't keep a shipboard shrine or even make offerings to them, but she knew the ancestors were out there, watching over her people. The silver scar on her left hand was a mark they'd left behind when they'd driven out both a nasty spell and a tattoo devoted to the pirate goddess Besmara.

The thought made her stretch out her right hand. Jendara's remaining jolly roger tattoo, twin to the one the spirits had burned away, had faded over the years. The ink was beginning to seep into the white spaces, running the skull's teeth together into a solid bar of gray. Jendara wasn't troubled by the reminder of her old life, but she was glad all that was behind her.

But she didn't think they'd need to do any climbing. She'd already had another idea.

"There was a cave on the southern tip. Can we get a closer to it?" She caught the questioning expression forming on his face. "I thought I saw something down there. I might have an idea."

In a few minutes, they approached the southern end of the island with its glorious spires and fantastic statues. Seaweed and slime covered a great deal of it, but what showed nearly took Jendara's breath away. She might have grown up simply, but she could admire fancy when she saw it.

She lowered her attention to the rock wall just below the city. "There, starting at this tip of the island, and running a good ways along the west side. See that purple shiny stuff?"

Vorrin squinted. Without the spyglass, the glints of purple were mostly obscured by layers of algae and ropy weed.

"I think it's glass."

"Purple glass?"

"Sure," Sarni chimed in. "When glass gets old, it turns purple. We used to keep our eyes out for purple glass at the market. People pay more for old things."

Vorrin raised an eyebrow. "Why did you want to find old glass?"

"To steal." She smiled innocently.

Jendara nudged Sarni aside. "So those are windows, probably. Which means there have to be rooms, passages, even stairs inside the island." She nodded toward the sea cave. "Maybe I can get in through there."

"A sea cave? Sounds dangerous."

She folded her arms across her chest, eyes narrowing. "I think I can handle a little spelunking."

"Jendara!" Boruc waved his notebook at her. His boots thudded as he hurried their way.

"I don't mean to interrupt," he began, and she waved aside the apology. He opened the notebook, holding it toward her. She saw that charcoal smudged his nose. "Have you noticed the artwork?"

"It's pretty amazing, isn't it?"

"Yes. Even these columns are fantastic." He grabbed the stick of charcoal from behind his ear to jot a note in the notebook.

"Columns?"

"Sure." He shoved the notebook at her. He'd drawn in the cave mouth, and she looked from the paper to the cave, taking in the details. "They're overgrown, but you can see the chamfered capitals, the subtle ornamentation."

Boruc may as well have been speaking a foreign language, but his drawing in the notebook made sense. Now Jendara wondered how she'd missed the shapes of the columns outlining the cave.

"If they decorated that cave, that means they looked at it. A lot." She turned back to Vorrin. "I'm going in."

Vorrin opened his mouth, but Boruc was already nodding. "I'll come, too," he said. "This stonework is too good to miss."

The hairs on Jendara's arms prickled. The cave, the columns, the gold: this entire island was too good to miss. She couldn't wait to get in that cave and start exploring.

Jendara caught herself grinning as she rowed the dinghy toward the mouth of the cave. Without Vorrin to give her disapproving looks, she let the smile spread. It had been months since she'd done anything more exciting than negotiate a trading agreement, and while some of the craftspeople she knew drafted some severe contracts, it was work that called for wits and ledgers, not a sword. Now here she was, rowing toward a mysterious cave, a new handaxe in her belt and an unexplored island beckoning. It felt fantastic.

"Four fathoms here," Boruc said, dropping their sounding line back into the bottom of the dingy. "The *Milady* could sail right up to the cave."

"That'll be convenient if we're loading a lot of gold." Jendara craned to see over her shoulder at the oncoming island. But of course, this close all she could see was the steep cliff face.

Without the sight of the city on top, the island looked a little less otherworldly.

"Slow down now, we're almost in." Boruc reached for the lantern cached in the bottom of the boat and lit it with his flint striker. Jendara twisted around in her seat, no longer rowing but just letting the obliging current pull the vessel inside the great mouth of the cave.

"Merciful Desna," Boruc breathed.

Jendara stared around the space. Vast darkness surrounded them. Their little lantern cast a golden circle around the dinghy, but it was a firefly's glow inside the enormous blackness, and for a moment, direction became meaningless. The dinghy floated in a bubble of brightness like a star in a limitless sky. It would have been magical if not for the thin keening whistle resounding throughout the space. The wind, probably. The pitch of it made Jendara's ears feel strange.

She lowered her oars to slow the boat. "Can you make out anything? Rocks? Walls?"

Boruc put the light on the seat beside him and reached for the sounding line. The lead made a solemn plunking as it broke the surface of the water, and then silence prevailed—save for that faint whistle.

"Do you hear that?" Jendara asked.

"That wind? Damned annoying, ain't it?" He retrieved the sounding line. "Three and half fathoms. The *Milady* could sail all the way inside if Vorrin wanted."

He lifted the light again, and this time the flame reflected on something besides the deep waters of the grotto—something glossy off to Jendara's left. She began to row toward it.

"That a beach?" Boruc asked.

A broad shelf of pale stone stuck out into the water. About the width of the *Milady*, its damp surface glinting in the light of their lantern. A darker shape jutted out of it like a tongue.

"Could that be a pier?" Jendara asked.

"Can't see how wood could have survived being underwater all these years," Boruc protested.

But it *was* a pier. The way it stuck out from the stone beach, it had obviously been designed as a place for ships to tie up.

"Sometimes the saltwater preserves wood," she began, and stopped. She couldn't begin to explain away the mystery of this place. There was nothing ordinary about this island. It was covered by an actual city of gold, for the ancestors' sakes. For the first time, she wondered if it might be worth adding a wizard to her crew.

"You're thinking magic, ain't ya?"

Boruc knew her too well.

"Wish I knew more about magic." She turned the dinghy so it lined up with the strange pier. "But as my father would have said, 'If wishes were pigs, beggars still wouldn't have bacon.'"

"What does that mean?"

"You've got to think on it a bit." She looped the mooring rope over the nearest mooring cleat. Giving the rope a sharp tug, Jendara was pleased to feel the pier hold strong. "You stay in the boat while I take a quick look around."

Boruc didn't argue with her, but let her scramble up onto the pier alone. She held out her hand for the lantern and he hesitated a moment before passing it up. She wouldn't want to be left waiting alone in the dark, either.

"I'll just be a moment," she reassured him. She squatted down on the pier to rap on the decking. Still strong, but it sure didn't sound like anything she was familiar with. She scraped it with her fingernail. "I think it's bone," she called back to her friend. "Whale, maybe? That'd be big enough."

Whalebone. It made more sense than wood, she supposed. If the golden city covered the entire surface of the island, that didn't leave room for crops or forest. What they needed, they had to take from the sea.

There were plenty of ways to make a living from the sea. Just ask a former pirate.

She took a few careful steps forward. The pier groaned, a sad tenor counterpoint to the wind's whistling descant. But the structure held. She raised the lantern higher and tried to make out the beach ahead.

At first, she saw only darkness. She took a few more steps, still slowly, but more confidently, and then strode faster to reach the end of the pier. The beach proved to be reassuringly ordinary stone. Its surface looked smooth, but time had worn it down in places. Patches were still slick with water, and clumps of weed and foam floated in the deeper puddles. The white stone rose at a comfortable angle until it met a set of stone stairs, climbing into what looked like a long throat carved into the island itself.

The damp air felt a little cooler here, and she turned up the collar of her sheepskin jacket. She studied the staircase. Her lighting was limited, but it looked clear enough. A few clumps of what looked like seaweed dotted its broad stairs, but it was somehow free of the kind of debris that had buried Sorind during its brief time beneath water.

Of course, this island had been underwater. Maybe the mud and detritus had been flushed out when it drained.

She took a cautious step up, her free hand settling on the handle of her axe. The sea creatures that had lived here must have certainly been flushed out, too, she reassured herself. But it was good to be prepared.

"Jendara?" Boruc's voice was no more than a whisper in the darkness behind her.

She waved the lantern once, side to side, to reassure him, and took another halting step upward. While nearly wide enough for two people to walk side by side, the risers were ridiculously short and strangely deep. Whoever had built this place didn't have a stride like hers.

She craned her neck trying to make out the end of the strange staircase, but it snaked around a curve. It looked sturdy enough. No broken stone to warn of cave-ins ahead, and no debris piled up at the curve. If there was a better way to ascend to the gleaming city, she hadn't seen it.

Jendara ran back to the dock and hurried back on board the dinghy. Boruc snatched the lantern from her.

"Well?"

"Looks like there's a way up," she answered. "Let's get the others and find our fortune."

The wind's whistle grew louder as Jendara rowed toward daylight. She tried not to think of the sound as unfriendly, but found herself rowing faster anyway.

"I don't like it," Vorrin said. "We don't know what made this island sink in the past, we don't know what made it rise today—"

"The earthquake," Jendara scoffed. "It thrust up as the rock shifted."

"But what made it sink in the first place?" Zuna snapped.

Of course she'd be in agreement with Vorrin. It was the cautious route. Jendara flexed her fingers to keep from balling up her fists or folding her arms, both sure to irritate Vorrin.

"We haven't seen the island move an inch since we got here," she said in her most pleasant voice. "It took a serious earthquake to make it come up to the surface. We're smart and we're tough. We know how to be safe in there. If anything goes wrong, we'll get right back to the *Milady*. We're not idiots."

Vorrin sighed. "I don't know."

"Do you really think climbing those cliffs is any safer?" Jendara urged him. "We're all good climbers, but fully loaded with gold and treasure? I think it's worth the risk of exploring new territory to prevent a big fall."

"I guess," he agreed.

"Great. Boruc's gotten both dinghies ready for us. Let's just collect the last of our exploring gear and we can head out." Jendara turned, ready to head below for some more supplies, but Glayn caught her by the arm.

"Dara," he said, pitching his voice low. The gnome's face, usually all smiles, was nearly grim. "What makes you so sure the earthquake made the island come up?"

"It makes sense, doesn't it? Earthquakes can change whole landscapes."

"There've been other earthquakes," he reminded her. "Why didn't it show up the last time one rattled our bones?"

"Well, what else could have caused it?" She put her hands on her hips.

"What if the island caused the earthquake? Did you ever think about that?"

"No, and I'm not going to. It's crazy. The earthquake is the simplest, most logical explanation." She began heading down the stairs and looked back over her shoulder. The green-haired gnome was still frowning down at her. "Besides, explaining the mechanics of the thing isn't our problem. Let's just focus on grabbing whatever we can and getting out of here before anybody else realizes this island has shown up."

Jendara strode quickly toward the galley. She could understand Vorrin's caution and Glayn's concern, but she couldn't imagine turning back from that staircase inside the island. It might be a risk to explore it; it might not even be a viable path. But it was worth exploring. Weren't any of the others thinking what she was thinking? If the *outside* of the island was so full of treasure, what might the *inside* be like?

She lit the nearest lamp and then hurried between the two big tables, her sights set on the door to the storage room. She'd put a lot of extra rope and lamp oil in there. They'd need that, for certain.

A rustling made her stop as she reached for the latch. No longer caught up in her own thoughts, she could see that the storage room door was drawn shut, but the latch wasn't set. The rustling repeated, a little softer. Something was inside.

Or someone.

4

STOWAWAYS

Jendara readied her handaxe and threw open the door.

All hell broke loose. Barrels crashed. Someone gasped. Something hairy burst out at her at the same time a wood-splitting maul toppled out and smashed her toe.

She stumbled backward as the dog leaped past her, barking happily. She could hear shouting out in the hallway and her toe pounded, but everything was obscured by the hot mist of rage filling up her vision. There wasn't much light entering the storage room, but there was enough to see her son's pale face in the destruction he'd wrought within.

"Get out here right now!"

He crept over a bag of nails and a couple of small casks, cringing away from her. She caught him by the elbow and marched him to the nearest table.

"Sit down."

"Everything all right?" Glayn skidded to a stop. "Kran?"

"Looks like we've got a stowaway." Jendara glared down at the boy. "I ought to make you swim back to Sorind."

Fylga barked and jumped into the boy's lap. The boy pulled her close to his chest.

"What did you think you were doing? I told you that you couldn't come. So you just disobey me? Are you insane?!"

"Jendara." Vorrin hurried into the room and took her arm. "Can I have a word?"

"I'm not done here."

"Hey." He forced her to meet her eyes. "Come out in the hall and talk to me."

She spun around so fast her braid caught him in the face. Stomping out to the stairs leading topside, she waited for him with her jaw set.

"You don't want to yell at him like that," Vorrin said.

"Butt out." She raised a hand to stop whatever was about to come out of his mouth. "Kran's my son, Vorrin. I'm in charge of him, not you."

"We're a family," he snapped. "Don't forget that."

She drew a breath to snap back at him and caught a glimpse of Tam peering down the stairs. She swallowed her words and forced herself to search for another, quieter reply. "I told him to stay on Sorind. I made arrangements with Morul and Leyla. He can't go behind my back like that. He has to be punished."

"And he will." Vorrin leaned in closer. "Do you think it's good for the rest of the crew to hear you yelling like that? This island is bad enough without you sounding like you're coming unhinged. We're depending on you to lead us out there."

He was right, and she knew it. It made her even more furious at her son.

She shot Vorrin an angry look and went back into the dining area. Kran still sat on the chair, the dog on his lap. He put the dog down on the floor.

Jendara glared at the little beast. Kran had always been hard-headed, but the dog represented their longest, loudest battle. She'd tried to explain her logic. Kran stayed with friends part of the year while Jendara traveled; if he was going to get a dog, he ought to get a dog that earned its keep. A hunting dog or one that could pull a cart. She hated to see the little mutt tagging along behind him, an empty belly on stubby legs.

But Kran loved it. He wouldn't hear of getting rid of it. When she told him to give the dog away, he hid it in his bedroom and snuck food to it behind her back.

And Vorrin had encouraged him. The two of them drove her crazy sometimes.

She forced herself to take a deep breath before she kicked something.

"I'm not sure what I'm going to do with you," she said, her voice rough but quiet. "But you're in big trouble, boy."

Vorrin moved to stand beside her. At least he looked supportive.

"We're going ashore now. I don't know how long we'll be gone. You can have hardtack and some of the apples if you're hungry, but you're not to go on deck while we're gone."

"And I want this mess cleaned up," Vorrin added. "Fix the shelf in the storage room. Get everything back the way it was."

Kran gave a tiny nod, his expression pure misery. Another time, Jendara might have given him a pat on the shoulder, but not today. Couldn't he see that she made her decisions to keep him safe? He had to learn.

She loved the thought of exploring this island, but imagining her boy climbing around on it made her queasy.

She lit another lamp and went into the storage room to retrieve the adventuring supplies. Sometimes this motherhood business stank like a three-day-dead fish.

It was nearly an hour later before they made it up the long dark throat of the staircase and into the heart of the island. No one spoke as they climbed those stairs. Even with their lanterns, it was impossible to step into that darkness and not feel the weight of the stone around them, the weight of history pressing down on their flesh. Jendara kept listening for the stone to give way around her, despite her assertion that the place was safe. Safeish. At least safer than a hundred-foot climb up a rope.

When they emerged into some kind of great open space, she felt herself take a real breath again. Glayn patted her arm.

"It's the darkness," he said, kindly. "It makes things worse."

He was right. It wasn't exactly bright here at the top of the stairs, but a certain grayness permeated the space, as if sunshine filtered in somewhere nearby. She oriented herself toward it.

"Those windows must be this way," she said.

"I'll lead," Tam volunteered. She let him.

Just ahead, the space grew wider, as if the builders had intended this passageway to serve as a huge underground boulevard. The first of the windows started here: great purple slabs of glass that began above head height. Every other one curved up into the ceiling, forming skylights. Jendara had no idea how the glass could have survived its trip below the waves and then back above them. It was either a wonder of craftsmanship that had been lost to history, or there was powerful magical protection on those windows. Either way, their very existence spoke of a culture far more sophisticated than that of most in the Ironbound Archipelago.

"Look at this," Sarni called. She knelt beside the tumbled remains of what might have once been a kiosk and held something up. "What I can see beneath the muck looks gold."

Glayn hurried to her side. His eyes widened. As a lover of beauty—and having lived more than two hundred years—he'd seen plenty of good-looking loot. Sarni must have found something really nice.

"There are other hallways connecting with this one," Vorrin called out. Jendara peered into the darkness of the far side of the boulevard. The opening Vorrin had noticed looked wider than Sorind's main street. "This part of the island must have been full of people."

"Or not quite people," Jendara reminded him, thinking of the strange dimensions of the stairs in the staircase.

He nodded and retreated into the smaller hallway again. With a frown, Jendara went after him, her hand on her new axe. The second hallway was much gloomier than the boulevard with its purple windows. "What are you doing?"

"Just taking a quick look," he called back over his shoulder. "I wanted to get a sense of how big this all is. I think there's another staircase down here."

"Well, come back. I don't want us splitting up." She folded her arms across her chest as she waited for him to rejoin her. "You trying to get yourself hurt?"

He leaned in for a quick kiss. "You're irresistible when you're mad at me."

Rolling her eyes, she led him back toward the others. After Sarni's find, they were looking over the rubble rather more attentively.

"Look at this." Boruc pointed to the far wall where the light from the first window shone. "It looks like all of this was painted once."

"It's sparkly," Tam noted.

Boruc took a step backward, following the curve of the wall up to the ceiling. Jendara followed his gaze. She could see the faint sparkles that Tam had noticed, but she was far more interested in the blotches and patterns of the faded paint. They looked a little like human figures—bipedal, lumpen figures with eyes that winked in the light. She took a few steps down the great boulevard and glanced back at them. The eyes had followed her movement.

"There's more light up ahead," she said. "Let's keep moving."

As the boulevard made its way north, the sunlight grew brighter. Jendara's instincts urged her toward it. She wanted to rush but didn't dare. More of those fallen structures dotted the space, and here and there the flagstones in the floor had buckled, creating puddles and pools.

Tam looked back over his shoulder as they skirted the edge of one of the larger stretches of water. "I swear something was moving in there," he whispered.

"I wouldn't be surprised," she whispered back. "Stay well back from the water," she said, loud enough for the others to hear.

A soft *splish* came from the pool, but nothing emerged.

They walked cautiously for a few more minutes. Jendara paused to check another fallen structure. Built from stone, like the other one, this one had held up better—two walls remained, and Jendara plucked a gold coin from bits of broken shell heaped up in the corner.

"Mind if I sketch that?" Boruc held out his hand.

She let him add a quick drawing to his sketchbook, noticing as he drew that he'd put in the compass rose on the other page. She squinted. "You mapping this place?"

"Trying." He handed back the coin. "Art on it reminds me of the statues we saw from the ship."

Jendara held it up, looking carefully at the design stamped on the back. "Think those are tentacles?"

"Ayuh. Noticed them in the murals, too. I think."

"You all have got to see this," Tam called. "It's pretty amazing."

He stood in a pool of bright sunlight that came from the gap between two enormous doors made of the same stuff as the pier in the cave. Ornate designs had been carved into them, many of which were overlaid with gleaming gold leaf. What looked like an oversized church pew had been jammed between the doors, and now Sarni scurried up over the pew to enter the bright room beyond.

"All clear in here," she said. "No big puddles, even."

Boruc and Tam set their shoulders to the nearest door. Despite its size—at least twenty feet tall and probably half that wide—once it ground free of the debris in the frame, it moved easily, a work of inspiring engineering.

Several rows of the great pews still sat neatly in the center of the room, facing what must have once been a wall of glass. But unlike the windows in the boulevard, these had not fared well against waves and time. A few shards of green and red glass stuck out of the first pew, propelled by the ocean's power.

"It looks like a chapel," Glayn murmured.

Jendara nodded, lost for words. She stood in the center aisle and slowly turned in a circle. The other walls were dark blue, perhaps painted, perhaps some kind of stone, and golden stars stood out in complicated networks around the room. She caught one grouping that looked familiar and moved to stand in front of it. The stars weren't just gold paint: they had beaten out of metal and then fixed firmly on the wall. Tracings of the same glittery paint they'd seen outside connected the stars into constellations.

"That's The Dancer," she said, "but her arms aren't right. There are too many stars in her left hand."

"Stars shift," Zuna reminded her. "The oldest star charts aren't quite the same as ours today."

"Everything's stars here," Boruc pointed out. "They're even carved on the backs of the pews."

"The Star Chapel," Vorrin said. He smiled at Jendara. "Sounds promising."

Zuna moved behind Jendara's pew to explore the back wall. Very little sunlight entered that part of the chapel, and when Zuna knelt down, she was nearly invisible. "This is interesting," she called back over her shoulder. "There are recesses back here."

Glayn jogged over to join her. "Reminds me of the places where people leave their offerings—light candles and whatnot."

Zuna stepped back into the light, examining what she held. "And strange statues," she mused. "This was just sitting there. Do you think it's worth anything?" She held the statue out to Glayn.

He weighed in it his hand and turned it so the light played over it. The statue stood about eight inches tall, its base square, the whole thing vaguely columnar. Lumpen shapes stuck out around it. Barnacles and a few black mollusks obscured the statue's details—the first reminders of flooding they'd seen inside the chapel. Glayn pulled out his belt knife and scraped off one of the barnacles. "I think there's gold under all the garbage," he said. "You'll have to do a lot of cleaning," he warned her.

Zuna beamed. "Gold? Really? Gold!"

For the first time, Jendara felt like she was seeing the real Zuna. It was as if her reserve had scraped off with the barnacle. She took back the statue and studied it for a moment, the uncharacteristic smile fading as she looked at all the barnacles and corrosion.

Vorrin approached Jendara. "This is going well. We've been exploring for barely an hour and already half the crew's found gold."

"Speaking of which, we'd better look for a path to the surface before it gets much later." Jendara squeezed between Vorrin and a pew to stand in the doorway.

She shook her head. They'd been so distracted by the chapel with its sunshine and ornate doorway that no one had noticed the staircase only a few yards down the boulevard. This was no dark, enclosed stairwell but a wide, grand staircase built from pale stone. The railings must have once been embellished with carved details, but now mussels and chitons covered most every surface.

The mussels gave her pang. Hadn't Oric said they needed mussels for her birthday dinner? If Kran hadn't been such a generous soul, he wouldn't have gotten trapped on the beach with a tsunami rolling in. And now the little dunderhead had to pick a fight with her. She didn't want to be angry with him when he'd just done something sweet.

Jendara shook off the tender feeling. "I found the way topside." Without waiting for the others, she went toward the light-filled stairway.

By the time she was halfway up the stairs, the others had caught up.

"Six people could walk side by side without bumping into each other," Vorrin noted.

"Steps are the same awkward size," Tam grumbled.

"They're fine for me," Glayn said. "The folks that lived here must have had short legs."

"Stone's a little worn here at the top," Boruc pointed out. "It's awful slick, so be careful."

Jendara sidestepped the spot he'd noticed and stepped out onto the surface of the island. The tall buildings and statues that crowded the island cast dark shadows across the open space at the top of the stairs. At one time, the area must have been a large, enclosed plaza. The low heaps of white stone suggested the remains of walls, and one taller section still stood. She leaned against it, noticing that the spot had an unobstructed view of the sea to north and south. To her left she could make out the yellow-and-blue pennant snapping above the *Milady*'s mainsail, and to her right, the open sea stretched out in lonely peace.

Her eyes narrowed. Maybe not so lonely. She reached for the spyglass on her belt.

Off to the west, she could just make out the shape of a large black ship accompanied by several small, blocky vessels and a handful of canoelike boats. They were several hours out, but they were headed straight for the island.

"Vorrin," she called. "Come take a look."

He took the spyglass from her and scanned the horizon. His back stiffened. "What kind of ships do you think those are?"

She'd forgotten. He'd grown up on ships, but he was still a mainlander at heart. What she'd seen out here, he'd probably never had to deal with.

The rest of the crew came closer. Sarni's eyes were fixed on Jendara's face, her expression nervous. Tam had put his arm around Glayn.

"I'm not sure about the big black ship," Jendara admitted, "but the smaller ones probably belong to ulat-kini."

He shook his head. "Ulat-what?"

"Scum," Sarni spat. "They're thieving, kidnapping bastards that don't deserve to breathe."

Jendara glanced at the girl. There was a story behind that anger, she was sure of it. Jendara held out her hand for the spyglass, then slipped it back in its case. "Ulat-kini are trouble. They look part human, part fish, with a little frog thrown in. My father said they used to keep to themselves, out at sea, and that every now and then they'd come to raid little villages."

"Not just little villages," Sarni said. "We'd see them skulking around plenty on the edge of Halgrim."

"Now their raids are a lot more common," Jendara explained. "They can breed with humans. The human hybrid type don't breathe underwater like the others, so they build boats out of what they can find or steal. Real awkward vessels—that's why they're easy to recognize."

"I never saw an ulat-kini, myself." Tam scratched at his beard. "But I've heard plenty. If they're coming this way, we'd better move the *Milady* out of sight. They'll plunder anything they can get their webbed hands on."

"Shit." Jendara's eyes widened. "Kran!"

"We'd better get moving." Vorrin frowned. "Where's Zuna?"

The tall woman no longer stood behind Boruc at the edge of the stone plaza. She had vanished into the great city. Jendara felt a rush of impatient anger. *This* was what came of bringing someone with no experience on a raid. She should have never let Zuna off the ship.

"Everyone just be quiet," Glayn said. "Remember, she's got those bells in her hair."

The stupid bells. Jendara cocked her head, listening hard, mind racing. There hadn't been any noise, no gasping, no screaming—that had to mean Zuna was fine. She must have just wandered off. Jendara realized she was rubbing the ancestor's spot on the back of her hand and made herself stop.

Tam caught Jendara's eye, pointing between two precariously leaning buildings on the eastern side of the plaza. From a distance, the city had looked untouched, but up here Jendara could see how badly warped the structures were. Even the golden spires stood askew. She led the group forward, taking careful steps.

Then she saw Zuna a few yards ahead, hunkered down beside a massive fallen statue, furiously chipping at some detail. Jendara's lips tightened. One taste of success, and Zuna had turned treasure-mad.

"What do you think you're doing?" she snapped.

Zuna looked up, so focused on her find she missed the anger in Jendara's voice. "Rubies!" She held one up that was the size of her thumbnail.

"Wow!" Sarni hurried up beside her. "That's amazing!"

Boruc stooped. "There's gold inlay and little emeralds beneath the seaweed. It's got to be worth a fortune."

Jendara wanted to be angry, but pragmatism won over. She could talk to Zuna about the idiocy of leaving the group later. "All right, let's get it down to the cave. We can load it onto the *Milady* and get moving before those ulat-kini arrive."

She studied the statue more closely. It actually looked a bit like the columns down in the sea cave—she could see the flat top where it must have supported something at one time, and the broader base where it had met the ground. Upright, it would have towered over Tam or Zuna, the tallest members of their party. Mud and seaweed covered most of the sides, but she could see details of sea creatures in the gaps. What looked like a solid gold dolphin with sparkling emerald eyes caught her attention. It was nearly as long as her arm.

"I don't know how we'll get it down all those stairs," she admitted. "It's going to weigh a ton."

"Tam and I can sort it out," Boruc said. "I know a thing or two about hauling stone, remember?"

They began laying out their supply of rope, discussing the project animatedly.

Vorrin caught Jendara's eye. "That's just one statue. Think how much we could make if we put a little effort into it." He pointed out the next building. "I think that's a gold sea star above that doorway."

They walked closer, their boots slipping and splashing over the rough ground. Shells crunched beneath Jendara's feet. The creatures of the sea had made this island their home during its time beneath the waves.

Vorrin balanced on a fallen slab of rock and poked at the starfish ornament above the open doorway. Silhouetted against the darkness of the interior, he looked like a more heroic form of himself—something out of a story. "I think it's solid gold."

A noise like low mumbling made Jendara look away from him. She hurried to the corner of the building and peered around it.

A group of creatures walked in the narrow alley between the next two buildings, chanting in a glottal language. Their massive dorsal crests and bulging eyes spoke of some deep-sea progenitor, their thick limbs ending in webbed and clawed appendages that only vaguely resembled hands or feet. They moved on two legs like humans, but there the comparison stopped. And despite the presence of the ulat-kini ships she'd just sighted, these were no ulat-kini. They were some kind of fish-folk the likes of which she'd never seen.

She whipped back around the corner, hand going not for her handaxe, but for her sword.

"What's wrong?" Vorrin had the good sense to whisper.

"There's somebody else up here," she whispered, "and they've got us outnumbered."

5

THE WHITE DAGGER

Sword at the ready, Jendara risked a look around the corner. The creatures had paused in front of a doorway she hadn't noticed on the last glance. A few of them worked together to carry something heavy and bound in a net, but the others bunched up too closely for her to make out what they held. The leader of the group, a creature with a purple sea star dangling from an ornate circlet of woven seaweed on its brow, stepped aside. Two more of the fish-folk hurried forward to scrabble at the doorway. Jendara couldn't make out exactly what they were doing, but the soft scuff of rock on rock suggested prying open a difficult door. The pair disappeared inside the building.

She leaned back around the corner. "Get down," she hissed at Vorrin. "Don't go in front of the open door."

She took another glance and saw the other creatures making their way inside. Beckoning to Vorrin, Jendara crouched beside the open doorway on this side of the building. The creatures couldn't be seen, although their voices murmured faintly in the darkness.

"Get the others moving," she whispered. "I'll keep an eye on the fish-folk."

He opened his mouth and closed it, trusting her instincts. He crept away. Jendara hesitated a moment. She could just stay put, listening carefully. Or she could make her way into the building and get more information about the creatures. They didn't look like adventurers. Besides the big package, none of them had carried large weapons or any rope or tools.

She glanced over her shoulder at her crew. They had managed to move the column a few feet closer to the staircase, and now Vorrin was lending a hand. However they'd rigged it, the process was surprisingly quiet. Jendara peered into the dark building. She could just make out a faint blue glow in the depths of the place.

They needed to know more. She slipped inside.

Rubble filled a front room that might have been a foyer or something similar. No door closed it off from the next space, so Jendara kept low and crept forward. Sunshine lit the square of the doorway, leaving the rest of the chamber in darkness. There were no windows. The air felt thick and damp, and the smell of seaweed and dying shellfish hung heavily in the motionless air. The voices sounded louder up ahead.

Creeping cautiously, she felt more than saw that the room opened onto a hallway. To Jendara's left, a sliver of light revealed the door that the fish-folk had come through. The blue glow was stronger now, spilling out into the hallway ahead. Jendara moved a little faster. The creatures' chanting had built to an eerie bass rumbling she could feel in her chest.

Something squished beneath her boot and she slid sideways, just catching herself. She froze, certain she'd been heard, but the chanting continued uninterrupted. She moved closer.

The creatures, thirteen of them, stood in a circle outlined by glass bubbles—perhaps fishing floats—filled with a cold, aquamarine light. The creatures' hulking shapes looked even broader and more awkward up close. Their sloping faces with needlelike teeth reminded Jendara of the fish she'd seen brought up in the deepest of the deep sea nets. These were not creatures of light and air, but of the ocean's darkest trenches.

The leader fell to its knees, webbed hands uplifted. Its voice rose in pitch and volume, the tones piercing Jendara's ears.

Jendara stiffened. The package they'd been carrying lay in front of the creature, a soft-looking heap in the blue-tinged shadows, and now she noticed the neatly triangular dorsal fin pointing at the ceiling, the round, smooth forehead stretched toward her.

A dolphin. Its flipper gave a weak twitch, and Jendara bit her lip to stopper her rage. The cheerful animals had swum beside her ship too many times for her not to feel a sense of kinship with the one lying on the floor. It must be in torment above the water.

One of the fish-folk stepped forward, holding out a finely wrought dagger made entirely of some white material like bone or ivory. Jendara held her breath, admiring the blade's astonishing workmanship. The creature bowed low to the leader and backed away.

The chanting picked up speed. The leader raised the white dagger over its head and sang out a resounding tone. Then it plunged the dagger into the dolphin's side.

The dolphin jerked and twitched. It gave a tiny whistle and slapped its flipper on the ground. The leader of the fish-folk ripped the dagger from the animal's side and drove it down again.

Jendara turned away, hurrying back through the hallway toward the light. She didn't know what the fish-folk were or why they were here on this island, but she knew a sacrifice when she saw one. And whatever undersea gods these creatures worshiped, she doubted they would look kindly on land-dwellers like herself.

The crew had reached the top of the stairs. Sweat ran down Vorrin's face, and Boruc stood rubbing his back. Glayn hurried toward Jendara.

"What did you see?"

"Some kind of fish-men." She saw the look on Sarni's face and hurried to clarify. "Not ulat-kini—something I've never seen before."

"Do you think they're dangerous?" Vorrin asked.

"I'd bet on it. They're big, as tall as any of us, and they've got mean claws and teeth. The ones I saw were sacrificing a dolphin in some kind of ritual, so I'm guessing they're priests. I wouldn't want a run-in with one of their fighters."

"Let's get this downstairs, then," Vorrin ordered.

"And fast," Jendara suggested, taking a place at the ropes.

"Careful of the railings," Boruc warned. "Don't want to bring the stairs down on us."

"Right." Glayn took a place beside Jendara. "One . . . two . . ."

"Three."

They all pulled together. Jendara felt the column roll slowly onto the first step and sit solidly.

"Easy now," Tam said. "Get behind it and push just a little so it stays under control. One step at a time." Everyone shifted positions.

"One . . . two . . ."

"Three."

The column landed on the second step with a thud, just as Tam had planned, but Boruc's gasp warned her something wasn't right. For a second, she thought he would be fine, but the slick spot on the top stair, the very one he'd pointed out to her when they'd ascended, threw him off balance. He slid forward, his big boot striking the precariously balanced column.

"Boruc!"

She grabbed for his hand, catching him before he fell.

Glayn shouted as the rope went taut in his hands. The column broke free of their grip and bounced down hard, smashing into the steps, breaking off streamers of seaweed and bits of gold inlay. The stairs began to shake.

"Run!" Jendara bellowed.

They raced down the shaking stairs, slipping and skidding on the wet seaweed the column left behind it. A grumbling filled the air.

The column hit the railing and punched through, smashing down onto the ground below with a terrible crash. With a drawn-out screech, the flagstones gave way, blocks of stone tearing free of the shuddering staircase.

Jendara leaped down the last of the stairs and hit the ground running. Tam passed her, towing Glayn behind him. Jendara searched around wildly.

"Vorrin!"

The smashing of stone overpowered any response he might have made.

The crew came to a stop in the purple-lit boulevard, just past the entrance to the Star Chapel. They were somehow all there, from trembling Sarni to ash-pale Zuna. Vorrin reached for Jendara's hand and gripped it hard. She pulled him close to her side, whispering a prayer of gratitude to the ancestors that he had survived the destruction.

The grand staircase was no longer. Four or five stairs remained at its base, but the destruction of the railing had taken the middle of the stairway with it. Piles of broken white stone lay around the edge of a vast open pit.

Grit pattered down from the plaza above, the only sound besides their ragged breathing. Jendara spat out a mouthful of stone dust.

"Everyone all right?"

"Not a scratch," Vorrin said, his voice shaky. "A rock the size of a man came a hair's breadth from braining you, and you don't have a scratch."

Jendara rubbed her head absently. "I didn't notice. I was looking for you."

"Our fortune," Sarni whispered.

Jendara let go of Vorrin's hand and walked to the edge of the chasm where the stairs had been.

"Careful," Vorrin warned.

She considered stepping a little closer and pulled back her foot. There was no trusting this floor now. She rose up on her tiptoes to see better into the big hole.

"I think I see it," she said. The light from the stairwell barely penetrated the pit, but she could see bits of pale-colored stone down below. "There's another level, and the column's just sitting there. In pieces, of course."

Sarni's face lit up. "Maybe we can get it back!"

"I did see that other stairway," Vorrin pointed out.

Jendara's mind began spinning a plan. The column was only one floor down—it couldn't take them that long to find it. They'd get the column and retreat quietly.

"Let's get out of here before those fish-things come check out the noise," she said. "We'll hide the *Milady* from the ulat-kini and come up with a real plan."

"That's the spirit." Tam grinned at her. "I've always wanted to be rich."

The group began to hurry away from the pit and the Star Chapel. Vorrin waited for Jendara. He suddenly stooped and picked a rock up from the ground.

"For you," he said, holding out his find.

A ruby the size of his eye sat on his palm. Jendara gave him a kiss and slid the ruby into the bottom of her belt pouch.

For a moment she thought of the dolphin's blood, ruby red on the blade of the white dagger. She pushed away the vision.

"Come on," she said. "We've got to make sure our ship and our boy are all right."

The *Milady* sat untouched and cheerful in the afternoon sunshine. Jendara left the others to haul anchor and sort out ideas about finding and moving their fallen treasure; she was more concerned about the incoming ulat-kini and that black merchant ship.

She caught Sarni's eye. The teenager looked as bored by the conversation going on around her as Jendara would have been at her age. "Why don't you and I go do a little scouting?"

Jendara had Sarni ready the dinghy while she briefed Vorrin on her plan, pointedly ignoring Kran, who was sitting beside his stepfather. She still wanted to turn him over her knee and spank him like a toddler, but knew he'd outgrown that years ago. His punishment would come to her soon enough.

She offered Sarni a strip of jerky and settled into the dinghy, letting the girl row. Sarni moved the oars slowly, slipping them into the water with all the stealth the former thief could give them.

They kept close to the rocks jutting out from the base of the island as they headed north. The island was quiet, save for the soft whistling of the wind in the rocks. The sound was no less eerie out here than it had been in the sea cave.

"Let's move a little farther out from this headland," Jendara instructed. "But keep low."

They rounded the largest outcropping of weed-slicked rocks, and Jendara brought out her spyglass. She could see creatures moving in the water at the northern tip of the island, swimming between floating boxes and the ugly ulat-kini craft. The big black ship sat closer to the shore, partially obscured by the many rocks between it and Jendara's dinghy.

"Know your enemy like a friend," she murmured.

"What?"

"It's what my father would have said if he were here. He was a firm believer in the importance of scouting everything out in advance. If he'd been in charge of this operation, he probably would have found a way to climb to the highest spire and get an aerial view of the island before we ever set foot on the ground."

Sarni eased them a little closer.

"All right," Jendara whispered. "Let's stop here where we blend in with those rocks up ahead. Just be quiet." She brought the spyglass to her eye.

The ulat-kini had begun assembling a floating dock at the tip of the island. Jendara couldn't recognize the material they used. They unloaded it from the floating boxes, so it had to be light, but the structure they'd created seemed far more stable than a simple floating dock. Ulat-kini scurried across the platform without it noticeably dipping or swaying. The black ship sat beside the dock, its gangplank crawling with figures both ulat-kini and human. Or Jendara guessed them human, anyway. At this distance, even with the spyglass, it was hard to make out details besides the black robes and turbans. The mysterious crew shrouded even their faces in black scarves.

"What do you see?" Sarni whispered.

Jendara handed her the spyglass. "So far, they're just building a dock."

Sarni leaned forward as if the extra few inches could clarify her view. "They're bringing out some massive crates. Looks like they're full of more black stuff." She paused. "Now they're taking ladders out of the crates and putting them together. Black ladders."

"They're going to climb up to the top of the city." Jendara bit her lip. "Can I see that again?"

Sarni returned the glass. Jendara fixed it on the nearest small boat, an ugly scow built out of what was clearly flotsam. She'd never seen a more haphazard vessel. A group of ulat-kini stood on board, as well as one of the black-turbaned travelers. The ulat-kini looked normal for their kind. Each stood about Jendara's own height, with legs and arms very much like a human's, but they clearly depended on their long tails to help them balance upright—their broad, fishlike heads and spiny dorsal fins would otherwise overbalance them. They wore no clothes, although several wore simple belts woven from seaweed, and all were armed with tridents or clubs.

However, one of the ulat-kini wore an elaborate headpiece—not quite a crown, but more of a miter. The creature gestured broadly as it leaned toward the turbaned figure. Clearly they discussed something of great importance.

She had a feeling the group wasn't here for a simple treasure hunt. She thought of the fish-folk in that dark house in the city above. Did the island hold some religious significance to the people of the sea? And would that put the crew in more danger or less, should they encounter these creatures?

Her father would have encouraged a retreat and more scouting before moving on. Or else he'd have recommended a swift run for the treasure followed by a quicker retreat. But this was Jendara's call.

She could only trust her gut.

Jendara turned her attention to the ulat-kini on the floating dock. Two of the fish-men struggled to snap together two shorter sections of ladder. They weren't making much progress.

She frowned. "I don't understand why they're settling here on the north end of the island without even scouting out a better location, but I'm guessing it'll take them at least a day to get settled in."

And thus her mind was made up: the swift run with fast escape.

"Let's get back to the others and tell them we've got twenty-four hours, maybe, before we have to start worrying about ulat-kini trouble."

Sarni hesitated. "And the turbaned folk?"

Jendara glanced back at the ship. Her eyes widened. "The black ship is already raising anchor. That's good news, I think."

"If they don't head toward our cave."

"Good point." They waited a moment, watching the black ship. The big vessel began to slowly head north, away from the cave and the *Milady*. Jendara checked the sun. They had maybe two hours of daylight left. She beckoned for Sarni to begin rowing.

The girl rowed stealthily for a minute or two. She opened her mouth twice, but each time changed her mind before she managed to speak.

"Is something wrong?" Jendara looked closely at Sarni's face. She'd never seen the girl so withdrawn.

"No," Sarni answered.

Jendara raised her eyebrow. "Can't you at least *try* to sound like you mean that?"

Sarni gave a weak chuckle and looked down at her knees. "Look, you know I was raised by thieves. That's because ulat-kini took my mother when I was six." She went quiet.

"That's why you were so upset when we saw the ulat-kini this morning."

Sarni nodded. "I'd always heard the stories—ulat-kini, the scum of the sea. Parents used 'em to scare their little ones—'Don't go out at night, or the ulat-kini'll get you.'" She spat over the side of the dinghy. "Turns out the stories are true."

Jendara studied the girl as she rowed. Sarni had fixed her face in a tight, hard expression, arms moving in powerful strokes. Jendara knew that feeling—trying to overcome sadness with anger and action. Losing her own her family to a barbarian attack had been part of what led Jendara to piracy.

They reached the sea cave just as the *Milady* slipped inside, like a fish swimming into the mouth of a massive shark. Jendara rubbed the gray spot on the back of her hand. She hoped their hiding place was good enough to keep them safe from the ulat-kini and the other mysterious fish-folk. She'd been excited about taking her friends on an adventure, but this island was turning out to be more trouble than it was worth.

6

Lures and Bobbers

Jendara glanced back over her shoulder at the *Milady*, sitting quietly beside the bone pier. The last of the afternoon sunlight cast a soft glow behind the ship, the colors already shifting toward the oranges and golds of sunset. Jendara could just make out Sarni and Kran, who still stood at the railing beside the gangplank. Sarni put her arm around the boy and raised her other in a silent goodbye.

"Why Sarni?" Vorrin murmured in her ear. "Kran knows Boruc better, and as annoying as Sarni is, she can be surprisingly useful."

Jendara waved back at the pair at the railing and then led Vorrin away. The others had already entered the dark stairwell.

"Sarni's got too strong a personal connection to the ulat-kini." She paused to lower the flame on his lantern. "If we run into any, I want all of us at our sharpest."

"What if they find the ship?"

"I'm keeping my fingers crossed." Jendara urged Vorrin to go ahead of her on the stairs. "Besides, once it gets dark, the cave will blend in pretty well with the cliffs around it. I'm hoping it's safer than wandering around the bowels of the island."

They climbed the rest of the stairs in silence. The whistle of the wind, unpleasantly loud in the sea cave, faded as they moved upward. A mustiness replaced the smell of the sea.

The others waited for them at the top of the stairs. In this late hour, the boulevard was full of shadows. The sun still pierced the windows, but the purple skylights had gone dark, the light's angle too low to reach them. Somewhere in the distance, an occasional water droplet plinked.

Vorrin pointed toward a street-sized tunnel leading east off the boulevard. "That's the tunnel I checked out earlier, the one with the other staircase."

"Let me note that on my map," Boruc said, drawing out his notebook. His charcoal shushed across the page as they entered the new tunnel. Their lanterns were the only light in this space, and it felt much smaller than its actual size. Jendara didn't suffer from claustrophobia, but the dank and the dark pressed in uncomfortably around her.

Even by the lights of their small lanterns, it was obvious the city's creators had taken fewer pains decorating this corridor than the boulevard behind them: there were no signs of glitter, and only a small mural at the conjunction of the two tunnels. Most of the doors lining the hallway hung off their hinges or had been ripped away, presumably by the outrush of water during the island's return to the surface. The empty doorways looked like hollow eye sockets in a battered skull.

"Look." Boruc tucked his charcoal behind his ear and knelt down beside one doorway, where a pale stick had been trapped in the rubble. He gave a little grunt as he tugged it free. He studied it a second and then held it out to Jendara.

She held her lantern over it and frowned. It was no stick, but a long finger bone, much longer than a human's, and very slender. An ornate ring had fused to the bone, salts and other mineral deposits crusting the two into one inseparable whole. The creatures who had built this city had been human enough to enjoy decorating themselves, as well as their environment.

Jendara felt herself inadvertently spinning the thick gold band of her wedding ring with the tip of her thumb. "Think it's worth anything?"

He shrugged and stuck it in his belt pouch.

"Here's the staircase," Zuna said in a soft voice. She played her lamp over the mouth of the stairway, built very much in the fashion of the staircase leading to the beach. She pointed out a sconcelike structure built into the wall. The crumbling figure of some human-shaped being held the shelf of the sconce on its shoulders, and the shelf itself was carved in the shape of seven-pointed sea star. "Was there anything like this on the stairs leading into the cave?"

"I'm not sure," Vorrin admitted. "But these steps look more worn than the ones back there. Must have gotten a lot of traffic."

"I hope it'll take us underneath the purple boulevard," Tam said. "I'm ready to get our treasure and get out." He took the lead on the stairs, Zuna falling in behind him. The staircase curved a little, obscuring their figures in only a few steps.

"Careful as you go," Jendara called softly. "There could still be water down there."

They went quiet, everyone moving slowly. Jendara had a hunch she wasn't the only one thinking back to the way Boruc had slipped on the staircase leading up to the surface. If someone fell here, well—she touched the handle of her handaxe. There could be anything at the bottom of these stairs.

Then she rounded the curve and saw Zuna and Tam stepping down onto level ground.

"It's not flooded," Zuna announced, looking back over her shoulder at them. "But it looks like the water level's only recently fallen." She pointed to a damp line a few inches above the floor. Puddles still filled depressions in the floor, and the space smelled less like mildew and more like seaweed and fish slime. Dying barnacles and shellfish clung to the walls, and shriveled ribbons of weed hung from every surface like strands of dark hair.

Jendara moved to examine the nearest wall. She scraped a few of the barnacles away, revealing the stone below. The same gray as the stone making up the grotto, it looked plain and undecorated. She moved to brush away a long rope of weed.

Her hand passed right through. Jendara held up her lamp. "It looks like there's another hallway connecting right here." She ripped away a handful of the seaweed. "I'd say it runs roughly the same direction as the big boulevard, but it's hard to tell."

"Let's take it," Tam urged. He pushed back the weed and led them into the north-south corridor. "Looks like there's another tunnel coming up that goes east. This place is like a maze."

"It must have been spectacular when it was inhabited," Glayn breathed. "Even if the city only occupied the surface and these two levels, it would have been bigger than Halgrim."

Jendara grinned. "If they were still on our trading route, we'd be rich." Her smile faded as she remembered the bone in Boruc's belt pouch. Perhaps it was ill-advised to joke around when she stood in what was essentially a giant graveyard. She remembered her trip to the Forest of Souls on the Isle of Ancestors, just last autumn. Sometimes the dead remained near their remains.

She didn't much like ghosts, even those of her ancestors. Ghosts with no relation to her had to be even less pleasant.

"Ho, ho!" Boruc clapped his hands together. "Look what we've got here." He was a ways up the hallway, still in sight, but farther away than Jendara liked. The group moved to join him. He put his shoulder against a partially opened door in the wall and shoved.

"We're trying to hurry," she reminded him.

"Just a quick look. You see this image here?" He pointed to a blob of stonework that, while not covered in shellfish, was entirely meaningless to Jendara. "It's a chisel and hammer—this must have been a mason's workshop."

He set his shoulder to the door again, and with the crunch of shattering barnacles, the door ground open. Boruc stuck his head inside and immediately began pointing out delights like a kid at his first knife shop.

Glayn hurried behind him. "That's lovely."

Jendara stood in the doorway, her lips tight. Lantern light flickered gold across the slab of marble lying in the center of the room. Glayn circled the thing, brushing his fingers over the rounded shape—a whale, still just emerging from the pale stone. It was far from complete, but the smooth head and solemn eyes were remarkably true to life.

Boruc appeared from the back of the room, which was apparently built in an L-shape. "It's a real mess back here, but I found some nice pieces." He held up what appeared to be a jade figurine of a squid. "It's not even missing any of the tentacles."

"Let's get out of here," Jendara said. "We've got a load of treasure to haul, remember?"

Vorrin took the jade squid from Boruc. "This is good stuff, Dara. We should bring it, too."

"There are some fallen shelves over there that might have something good mixed in with the debris," Boruc said. "Give me a hand."

He and Vorrin went into the back of the room where it rounded a corner. Jendara scowled.

"Hey, captain's orders," Tam said with a shrug. "Why don't Glayn and I check the room next door? If there's one artist's workshop down here, there might be more."

"I'll go with Tam and Glayn," Zuna said, and then the trio headed out into the hall.

"You've got five minutes!" Jendara snapped at them. Then she followed after Boruc and Vorrin.

This leg of the room was longer and narrower, some kind of storage space, perhaps. Jendara's boots splashed as she picked her way through the debris. The water hadn't finished draining out of this enclosed space, and there were three or four inches of standing water. Boruc and Vorrin's splashing echoed in the little storage area.

She wriggled her toes and was glad she'd treated her boots with mink oil. "You'd better have found something really valuable," she growled.

"Oh, this is remarkable," Boruc murmured. He was only a few feet ahead of her, but she couldn't see anything beyond his broad shape. She raised her lantern and craned her neck.

"Where did they find such fine alabaster?" he cooed.

Jendara shook her head. She couldn't see anything, but the room smelled strange, sweet and musky somehow. Her eyes and nose itched.

"Nothing here," she heard Zuna call on the other side of the stone wall. It couldn't be very thick—Zuna sounded like she was practically in Jendara's ear.

Then Boruc shrieked. His lantern flew from his hand as something yanked him forward into the darkness.

"Boruc!" Jendara leaped forward and felt a strand of something slimy slap against her hand. She whipped her hand away.

Boruc's lantern rolled in a half-circle on a shelf just above the water, and came to a stop at the base of some kind of quivering, rustling mound of greenery. A tendril shot out at Jendara and just missed her.

"Jendara!" Vorrin shouted somewhere in the darkness.

The wall beside Jendara seemed to wriggle. The musky smell grew stronger and her head spun. "Vorrin?" She squinted into the darkness beyond the mass of rippling seaweed. "Get out of there. Run!"

"Help . . . me," Boruc gasped, his face appearing between the fronds of the slimy green creature.

She lunged to grab him but the creature wriggled aside, taking Boruc with it. Jendara skidded on the slimy floor, smashing against the wall. Her lantern crunched. Debris rained down around her. She covered her head with her arms and stumbled out of the rain of rock.

"Jendara!" Zuna shouted, and helped her to her feet. The wall between the rooms must have been thin and half-eroded for it to break so easily.

"Help Boruc!" Jendara shouted, pawing grit from her eyes. "Something grabbed him!"

Vorrin suddenly ran past Jendara, his eyes wide. A trickle of smoke followed him.

"Vorrin!" she shouted. But he ran past her as if deaf. She leaped to her feet. "Come back!"

He was already out in the hallway and Jendara charged after him, shouting for him. But Vorrin kept running deeper into the darkness. Jendara's wet boots skidded on the slick bodies of dying mollusks. She couldn't see a thing.

"Vorrin!" she shouted, but now she couldn't even hear his footfalls. She was alone in the dark, and she couldn't find the walls. Panic gripped her. Jendara forced herself to stop and think.

She shook her head, clearing it a little. At least that smell was gone. Her head felt strange from the stink of it. Even this seaweed-and-decaying-fish smell was better than that perfumed stench.

"Jendara!"

That sounded like Boruc's voice. "I'm coming!" she called back. Boruc. By the gods, she was glad he was all right. The others must have freed him from that seaweed creature's grasp.

The glow of a lantern appeared and she hurried toward it. "Boruc, are you all right?"

He coughed hard, waving a hand. Now that she was closer, she could see the purple welts around his neck and along his cheek. That seaweed creature had nearly strangled him. "Your lantern. When it broke, the thing caught fire and let me go."

"But why did Vorrin run away?"

A pair of lanterns appeared. "Dara?" Tam called. "You see Glayn anywhere?"

He and Zuna stopped beside Boruc. Smoke and dirt smeared both their faces.

"Something green came out of the wall just before you did, and Glayn ran after it," Zuna explained. "He looked strange, like he was under a spell or something."

"And Vorrin—it was like he couldn't hear me." Jendara looked around the group. "Do you think that thing lured them both away?"

"I've heard stories of this happening," Tam said slowly. "Things out at sea luring crews to their death with songs, or some kind of perfume."

"The smell!" Jendara jabbed her finger at Boruc's chest. "Did you smell something back there?"

"Yes . . . I think."

Jendara shook her head. "We've got to find them. Even if that plant thing doesn't strangle them, they could still get hurt in this place." She turned to face the darkness beyond. "I think Vorrin went this way. Come on."

They went in silence. Jendara took Boruc's lamp and led them down the corridor, cursing herself every step. She had been so sure that the island would be empty, its previous inhabitants sluiced out to sea or turning to jerky in the dry air. These underground tunnels with their pockets of trapped water defied all her expectations of an island topped by a city of gold. She should have scouted it out better before she'd ever allowed her husband or her crew to explore the place.

Her thumb worried at the thick band of her wedding ring. Vorrin was gone, and it was her fault. If she'd followed her father's rules, he'd still be here, but instead she'd let overconfidence and impatience get the better of her. She'd always been hotheaded. It was her worst trait.

They peered into every room they passed, but as they walked, the hallway took a slight corner and became even narrower, the doorways fewer and farther between. Most were closed, so overgrown it was nearly impossible to see them, let alone open them. The gloom and stench of dying shellfish was oppressive.

At least Sarni and Kran were back on the *Milady*, Jendara reminded herself. She didn't have to worry about them.

"Hold up." Tam caught her by the elbow and pointed up ahead. "There's something shiny over there." The usually cheerful man's voice was tense.

Jendara moved closer. "It's a lantern." She picked it up and quickly lit it. "One of them must have dropped theirs." She passed the spare back to Zuna.

"Oh no," Zuna said, raising the lantern higher. "That looks bad."

Just a few yards ahead, a neat square of darkness nearly filled the floor of the tunnel. A flagstone remained on either side of the pit, offering something like a safe path. It was as if the flagstones in the tunnel's center had simply been removed.

A faint cry sounded from far below.

Jendara rushed forward, dropping onto her belly beside the pit. "Vorrin?"

She could feel cold strands of seaweed beneath her, and bits of the stuff dangled over the edge of the pit. Her arm hairs rose up in prickles. The smooth edges of the hole; the camouflaging weed. This wasn't the work of time and water; someone had built this.

The voice and a flurry of splashing echoed in the darkness. Tam dropped to his hands and knees beside her. "Is it them?"

"I can't tell." She held out her lantern. Far below, the gold moon of its reflection played over a rippling pool.

"Dara!" Glayn's voice sounded very faint.

"Let's lower a torch," Zuna suggested. "Get a better look down there." She was already digging in her pack for supplies.

It was a good idea. Jendara smiled at the navigator. Maybe she had the stuff of an adventurer in her after all.

Jendara moved as close to the edge as she dared. "Are you all right? Is Vorrin down there?"

"We're fine. We found a rock to climb up on."

Jendara let out a breath. This far north, the water's chill could kill, even in summer.

"There." Zuna tied the last scrap of fabric around a bundle of candles and secured it to the line of rope she'd stashed in her pack. Then she tossed the makeshift torch over the side of the pit. It swung in a huge arc, its flickering flames lighting damp stone walls and, far below, a broad expanse of water. She lowered it slowly.

Jendara's stomach gave a lurch. She had no idea how Vorrin or Glayn had survived that fall. The water below had to be nearly forty feet down. She didn't like Vorrin's silence, either.

"Is Vorrin okay?"

Glayn didn't answer right away.

"Is Vorrin *okay*?"

"He's knocked out," Glayn admitted. "I can't tell how bad it is."

Jendara sat back on her heels, heart pounding, mind racing. "We've got to get them out of there."

Boruc knelt down beside her. "We don't have enough rope." He kept his voice low. "We'll need to make some kind of harness for Vorrin—he won't be able to climb."

"He's right," Zuna whispered. "We're going to have to go back for supplies."

Jendara stared at them for a long second. "All right. You go ahead, I'll stay here with them."

Glayn heard that. "No!"

"Hey, we're the rescue team," she called. "You don't get a say."

"No," he shouted again. "There are things up there. You can't split up. We'll be fine. You just hurry!"

"Things? What kind of things?" she asked, but no one answered. No one could.

Jendara scrubbed her palms over her face. The burst of energy she'd felt just moments ago was fading. The thought of leaving Vorrin and Glayn alone down there made her sick, but Glayn had a point. She had to protect her team if she was going to get Vorrin and Glayn out alive.

"We'll be back soon," she called. "We'll leave the torch, okay?"

"Okay," Glayn said. "Tam?"

"I'm here."

"I love you."

"I love you, too. Now shut up and stay alive so I can rescue you."

Jendara picked up her lantern, biting her lip. Vorrin would be fine. It would only take a few minutes to get to the ship and back now that they knew the way.

Vorrin would be fine.

7

OF DEEP ONES
AND DRY ONES

Zuna led them up the staircase, where they were all forced to slow. There was no running on these stairs with their awkwardly short risers. Their breathing rasped loudly in the narrow stairwell. It had been a long climb.

The sound of barking drew Jendara up short.

"Fylga," Boruc whispered.

It had to be. Jendara's heart sank. The dog sounded close at hand, perhaps in the purple boulevard.

"Why would they leave the ship?" Boruc spoke for them all.

Jendara freed her handaxe from her belt. "He wouldn't disobey me out here, not once he heard about the ulat-kini. Let's all be quiet."

The barking increased in volume, the tone thin and unhappy. Jendara hoped the dog wasn't badly hurt.

They crept out into the narrow hallway, and Jendara could see where it met the purple boulevard; a faint dimness lit the mouth of the hallway. Night had fallen while they'd explored the halls below, and they were no closer to leaving this island than they'd been when they first descended the stairs.

Fylga gave a frustrated growl. She had to be very close now.

Jendara waved for the group to stay back and then turned off her lantern. There was no telling what might be out there with the dog. She crept out into the boulevard, mindful of every step. The comforting bulk of a heap of rubble, probably one of the fallen kiosks, provided a bit of cover. From her right, the dog's barking came again. She peered over the rubble.

Nothing moved. Fylga's shape lay beside the biggest pool of water, her white patches bright in the gloom, but she was alone. Jendara darted toward the dog.

"Hey, girl," she whispered, dropping down beside the animal. This close, she could see what she'd missed before: the fine strands of a net entangling the dog. Fylga wagged her tail and pushed her cold nose into Jendara's palm. "I'll get you out," Jendara murmured. Where was Kran? Why wasn't Fylga with him?

Boruc ran out from behind the pile of broken rock and joined Jendara. He pulled his lantern from the cover of his jacket, turned down low. Shielding the light, he held it above the dog. "She's got a bad cut on this leg." He pulled a handkerchief from his pocket and bound it up quickly. "Where's Kran?"

"I don't *know*." Jendara hissed. "He—" With a grunt, she hacked at the net. "Look, whatever caught Fylga could still be out here."

A muffled shout from the direction of the Star Chapel underscored that thought. Jendara ripped the net off Fylga and the dog streaked toward the sound. Jendara raced after her.

A pallid twilight came from the doors of the Star Chapel, and Fylga ran straight into the room. Jendara had the presence of mind to stop and peer around the doorframe to take stock of the situation. She heard the heavy footfalls of her crew pounding behind her.

Three figures stood outlined against the windows, two of them the hulking fish-things she'd seen inside that structure on top of the city, the other slighter and shorter as it held off the first two with a nasty-looking trident. There was no sign of Kran, but Jendara readied her sword. She searched for Fylga.

A tiny sound came from the darkest corner of the room and she made out Fylga beside a shadowy humanoid shape.

Kran. Her son was in there.

Jendara charged.

Her blade bit into the largest fish creature's neck before it even noticed her, slicing through the vertebrae to crunch into its collarbone. The blade stuck fast. The creature went rigid, and then, with a hollow gurgling, slid onto the floor, Jendara's blade still trapped in its body. The second of the fish-folk spun to face her just as Tam stepped in, his sword slashing across its leathery face. Its eye spilled clear jelly, but it slashed at him as if it hadn't noticed he'd ripped open its face. Tam ducked under the blow.

Then blood bubbled out of its mouth as the trident burst through its chest. Jendara pulled free her sword and pivoted toward the last of the fish-faced creatures.

Kran jumped out of the shadows behind the thing, and at the last second Jendara checked her blow before it connected with creature and boy. Tam smashed the thing in the face with his fist, and the slender creature crumpled.

Kran stared at it, mouth wide open.

Jendara pulled him to her chest. "You're alive. You're alive."

Then she looked around. Her lungs felt suddenly as if someone were squeezing her ribs. "Where's Sarni?"

Zuna turned up the flame in her lantern and looked around the Star Chapel. The dead bodies of the fish-folk lay sprawled in the main aisle, and the smaller creature—an ulat-kini, Jendara realized, and only small in comparison with the much more powerfully built, silvery fish-folk—still lay motionless at Tam's feet, although it still breathed. Up close, Jendara could see the gills on its neck and faint fuzz of eyebrows over its almost-human eyes. It had to be one of the ulat-kini–human hybrids. Not that it made a difference, she reminded herself. It lived with the ulat-kini, and that made it an ulat-kini.

She looked away from the misshapen creature. Zuna's lantern caught the golden constellations and made them dance, as if the sky itself reeled around them.

"There's nobody else here," Zuna said. "Sarni's gone."

Sarni was really gone. Back at the *Milady*, Jendara got the story out of Kran while the others worked. He had fallen asleep shortly after they'd left and awakened from terrible nightmares to find himself alone. He'd gone out looking for Sarni after searching the entire ship. But he hadn't found any sign of her besides the lantern she'd left burning on the deck.

That detail made Jendara's spirits sink lower. She'd left express orders to keep the ship dark and to stay below, hoping that darkness and silence would protect the pair from the notice of anything searching the cave. Sarni would never disobey one of Jendara's orders—not unless an emergency called for it.

"Shit," she said, rubbing her forehead. Her head hurt.

"I still don't understand why we brought that thing back with us," Zuna complained. "Tam and I've got it tied tight in the storage room, but I don't like leaving it alone on the *Milady*."

"Me, neither," Jendara agreed, "but he's not going anywhere, not if Tam tied him." She shrugged. "Kran insists the ulat-kini saved him from those big fish things."

"I guess we can turn it loose after we leave," Zuna said. "I don't even care if we get more gold. We should find the captain and get out of here."

"It's not that easy. We have to find Sarni, too." Jendara got to her feet quickly. "I'm going to get a few things for Kran before we leave."

"Kran?" Zuna's black eyes flashed. "You're not taking him with us, are you?"

"I'm not leaving him here. Something *took* Sarni right off this deck. He's not safe."

Jendara threw open the door to their cabin and rummaged through the drawers beneath the built-in bed. She kept some spare gear on hand in case of emergencies. Kran would need something stouter than a dagger.

A foot scuff behind her made her spin around.

"Kran!" She smiled. "I was just getting you some gear. I'm not leaving you here after what happened to Sarni."

He took a tentative step toward her. His face, twisted with worry, looked younger than usual. He reached for his slate. *Sorry*, he wrote.

"For sneaking on board? I know."

He shook his head, moving his hand in a circle that indicated her, him, the ship, everything.

"Sarni going missing isn't your fault." She had a feeling he meant something more than that, but she wasn't quite sure what.

He bit his lip, tapped his chalk on his slate a few times, then wrote: *Dreamed it.*

"You dreamed something took Sarni?"

Kran moved his free hand in a wriggling gesture, snakelike.

"It was just a dream, Kran. I didn't find any scales or any sign that a sea snake got her—" He was shaking his head and already scribbling, so she broke off.

Octopus—squid? Had suckers.

She opened her mouth and closed it. Kran had barely been outside the galley. He hadn't seen all the statues with tentacles, all the strange wriggling art. She didn't like the fact that those images had somehow gotten into his dreams.

She sat back on her heels and tried a different tack. "Look, no one in our family has ever had any kind of prophetic dreams. I don't know why you had bad dreams, but that's all they were: dreams." She ruffled his hair. "It's a lot more likely that those fish-things took Sarni. And I'm not going to let them near you."

Kran made a faint attempt at a smile, proof he wasn't himself. Normally, an attempt to ruffle his hair resulted in a punch in the arm. He need a distraction, and fast.

Jendara pulled out a scabbard. "Can you get this on your belt?"

His mouth fell open as he recognized the shape. He patted his hand on his chest.

"Yes, you can use it. For now." She slid the blade from the sheath, admiring its edge. This long seax had been her first husband's go-to blade for close quarters, and his first masterwork weapon. "I gave it to your father as a wedding present."

She passed it to the boy and he secured in place on his right hip. Like his father, Kran was left-handed. The thought made her want to pull him close to her again, as she had back in the Star Chapel. Her mother had died when she'd been only a girl, her father and sister taken from her just when she was old enough to strike out on her own. Ikran had been murdered by a rival when Kran was only a little one. She wasn't going to lose any more of her loved ones: not here, not ever. A fire kindled in her chest.

She got to her feet. "Let's go find Vorrin."

The smell of scorched seaweed still clung to the damp walls of the hallway where Vorrin and Glayn had been lured away. The crew marched grimly past open doorways, no longer tempted by treasure or curiosity. With Sarni, Glayn, and Vorrin all missing, this island had proven itself filled with enemies. Every corner they turned could lead them into danger, whether from creatures or from rockfalls.

Jendara had made sure every member of the party was roped up to the others, and she'd had Tam check their lines before they set off. If they'd done that the last time they'd gone down to this level, Vorrin and Glayn would be safe right now. The rope got in the way sometimes, but it was worth the extra measure of safety.

"Just a little farther," she reassured Kran, her voice pitched low.

She felt more than saw him nod. They were only using three lanterns, the minimum she thought they could use for safe travel. She'd noticed that the ulat-kini and the fish-folk hadn't carried lanterns. Her crew needed light, but it made them a target for creatures with better dark vision.

"Here," Tam whispered.

The group gathered beside the pit, untying each other so they could set to work. Tam had already prepared a harness under good lighting in the *Milady*'s galley, and now he brought it out.

Jendara knelt at the edge of the opening. It felt like balancing on the mouth of some huge creature that could swallow her at a moment's notice. A cold waft of fish and seaweed came up from the pit, a fresher smell than the dead shellfish around them.

"Vorrin?" she called. She raised her voice a little. "Glayn?"

No one answered. Water droplets fell someplace, a lonely and plaintive sound.

She leaned over the edge, peering into the darkness below. Zuna's makeshift torch had gone out. "Someone give me a lantern."

She held it out, but its light failed to penetrate the depths of the space. On the water's surface, the flickering dot of her flame seemed to mock her. "Glayn?"

Only silence replied.

Throwing off her pack, she reached for the nearest coil of rope. "You've got to lower me down."

Zuna opened her mouth to speak, then paused. Finally, she nodded. "It's not a bad idea. You can take the harness."

Tam was already joining the coils of rope and tightening a loop around Jendara's waist. Zuna pressed the harness into Jendara's hand.

As they worked, Boruc lit another bundle of candles and began lowering it down. He passed the rope to Kran. "Hold it steady."

Boruc took a stance beside Jendara. The rough fibers rasped against her hands as she tossed the rope to him, who ran it once around himself before tossing the rest to Tam. They were big men and Zuna was tough. They would make sure she didn't fall.

Jendara hesitated on the edge of the open pit. The water looked very far below, the walls invisible in the darkness. There could be anything down there: rocks, beasts, more traps. Vorrin's dead and broken body, floating outside the circle of lantern light.

Her stomach roiled at the thought, and so she lowered herself over the edge, needing to see with her own eyes.

For a moment she swung helplessly, the rope slipping over the broken flooring before jerking tight, and then Boruc and Tam brought it under control. She began to move slowly toward the water. She still couldn't make out the walls of the pit or get any sense of how large the space around her was, but at least she knew down from up.

Beside her, the bundle of candles and rags spun around slowly, its light playing off the dull surface of the nearest wall. Jendara nodded to herself—the wall that formed the boundary of the hallway apparently continued down as one continuous slab of rock. It made structural sense, at least. The wall descended without adornment, a smooth face of damp stone that met the water without offering up doors or ledges for a pair of men to creep onto. Nothing but a few crumbling stones protruding like islands from the pool's surface.

"I don't see anything," she called up. "No Glayn, no Vorrin. No exits, no ledges." She paused. There was something, right at the waterline. She squinted. "Hold up a sec."

The makeshift torch flickered and then steadied, and Jendara saw the dark patch at the waterline again. This time, she noticed the ridge of neatly worked stone framing it off. If she hadn't given the staircases in the other hallways such a careful looking over, she might have overlooked it, but she was starting to understand the construction methods of the ancient builders. "There *is* an exit," she shouted. "A door, maybe even a staircase. I'm guessing Vorrin and Glayn swam for it. Bring me up!"

Slowly, she ascended. She scrabbled at the stone flooring a minute before she got her grip and pulled herself up. Tam and Boruc sat on the floor, looking tired. But Zuna was frowning.

"There's another possibility," she began. "We know someone made this pit trap. And what does a hunter do when she sets a trap?"

Jendara went still. "She brings home her prey." A muscle twitched in her cheek. "Someone took Vorrin and Glayn."

"Either the ulat-kini or those fish creatures," Boruc said.

Tam stood up. "I think we should go talk to the ulat-kini. Even if they don't have our folk, they might have more information about the fish-things. Being sea critters and all."

"Well, we know where to find them," Jendara said, voice grim.

The plan formed quickly while they re-roped themselves. Time was of the essence. Going back to interrogate their prisoner would add another hour to their search, and there was no guarantee the prisoner even spoke their language. He hadn't said a word to Kran, and he'd been too groggy to talk while they were tying him up. Their best bet was to get into the ulat-kini camp and find one of their translators. The creatures were known more for theft than trade, but a group this size probably had at least one trader with a smattering of Taldane, the main human tongue in the region.

Jendara had argued for heading back to the grotto and getting the dinghies to approach the camp from the water. From the sea, she knew she could find the docks and ladders she'd seen under construction. She didn't like the idea of wandering through the island's labyrinthine tunnels. They'd made little headway exploring the subsurface so far, and Vorrin and Glayn were depending on them.

But Tam and Boruc were certain the sea approach was a bad one, and she had to agree with their logic. One ulat-kini could easily tip or sink a small dinghy: on the water, the creatures had every advantage. The ulat-kini wouldn't expect a land approach, either.

"Besides," Boruc said, "we won't be exploring, opening doors, or digging around. We're in a tunnel that goes north. I say we just stick with the tunnel and see where it goes. It's not such a big island, really."

It made a certain kind of sense. Jendara stroked the gray dot on her left hand and wished the ancestor spirits were the kind of spirits that gave signs or sent comforting portents. She could only trust her gut to make the right choice, and her gut was all too invested in the outcome of this one. Vorrin had been in danger before, but not since they had married.

Finally, she nodded. "It's as good a plan as any." She sent a silent, fervent wish up to her father, should he be watching out for her, that this plan was the right one.

They moved at a steady pace for several minutes, each of them lost in their own thoughts. Boruc fell in step with Jendara. "I know this plan is a long shot."

"I believe in your plan, Boruc. Don't take my nervousness for doubts in you."

"I'm nervous, too," he said. The words were strange, coming from the big man's mouth. He and his brothers were three of a kind—tough, smart, hardy folk. They reminded her so strongly of her father that they could well have been her own brothers. Admitting fear or weakness went against their grain.

"It's this place," Tam said. Jendara started. She hadn't even realized he'd been listening. He, too, was an island native, and as close to family as Boruc. "It weighs on me. The rocks, the constant shrieking of the wind, the smells. Everything is old here, and long dead." A breeze stirred the flame of his lantern so it cast shadows across his face, turning his eyes to dark hollows.

"Not dead," Zuna said. "Can't you feel it? It *knows* we're here." She hesitated. "Not dead, but maybe sleeping."

The wind gave a wheezing laugh, as if it took pleasure in their discomfort. Jendara rubbed her ears. She wasn't cold, but the wind's chill bit at her flesh.

Kran tugged at her arm, cupping his hand to his ear.

She listened for a second, then shook her head. "All I hear is the wind."

He made an impatient hand gesture. The wind. Something about the wind.

"Why is there wind?" she asked. "We're underground."

Tam was nodding. "How does wind get into an underground tunnel? We've got to be near some kind of exit." He looked excited, but Boruc was already shaking his head.

"Doesn't mean anything. There could be a crack in the wall or a natural chimney. You see that all time in caves."

Fylga trotted ahead to a spot where the tunnel bent leftward at a steep angle. She scrabbled at the tunnel wall, sniffing. Kran stooped beside the dog, feeling the wall carefully. He beckoned to the crew.

In their lantern light, the crack running up the northern wall was apparent. It grew wider toward the top, and a cool breeze came through it.

Jendara pushed on the tunnel wall. "There must be a natural fold in the island's bedrock." She closed her eyes and tried to remember what the island had looked like when they made their way around it. "There were three big ridges," she mused, "each with its own steep valley."

She opened her eyes to see Zuna nodding. "I remember them. There were smaller buildings tucked down into the valley, nothing like the spires on the tops of the hills."

"So this must be the edge of one of the valleys, probably the northernmost one." Jendara decided. "The buildings at the north end of the island looked more humble than the ones at the southern tip."

"I'm not seeing how this helps," Zuna interjected. "Our tunnel bends and goes west here."

Jendara pulled her new axe from her belt. Boruc's eyes widened in horror, but she reversed the beautiful tool in her hand and began to tap the handle against the wall. Stone flaked from the edges of the crack. "We've seen how the other rock walls take a blow. Maybe we can break this one down."

"Even before it went under the sea, this side of the hill would have taken the brunt of the storm season," Boruc reasoned. "And after coming up out of the sea? It's got to be even weaker."

Tam fell in beside her, rapping his pommel against the wall. "It's chipping."

"This is too slow," Boruc grumbled. "Get out of the way."

Jendara looked up from her hammering to see Boruc backing up. He lowered his shoulder, aiming the pommel of his sword like a battering ram. Jendara pulled Tam out of his way.

Boruc charged. With a wonderful crash, rock burst outward and moonlight poured in. Zuna grabbed at the back of Boruc's shirt just in time to keep him from falling into open space. His arms windmilled as he teetered on the brink of a new cave mouth. Jendara caught his hand and helped pull him back inside.

"Merciful Desna," Tam whispered.

It had been one thing to be in the city this morning, surrounded by light and standing on the edge of a great expanse of majestic buildings. It was an entirely other thing to stand here in the heart of it, the moon's light beating down on the ancient ruins. The details of the buildings were obscured by heaps of drying seaweed, but the details didn't matter. It was the scope of the place. Every inch of land was covered by rubble or the remains of some kind of structure or statue.

Low, rectangular buildings, still mostly intact, ran down the hill's impossibly steep flanks. Broken plinths of stone bridged narrow gaps that must have once been alleys, and stone figurines stood beside almost every sagging or collapsed doorway. Jendara tried to imagine what it must have been like before it sank beneath the waves, and found her imagination not quite up to the task. By the look on Kran's face, he was struggling, too.

Jendara took a cautious step toward the hole Boruc had smashed in the wall. Directly to Jendara's right, the facade of a wide, templelike building jutted out of the cliff face, its columns still intact. Ornate stonework still showed in places where the masonry wasn't overgrown with sea life or worn down by the elements. She could see the tracings of what could only be carved tentacles coiling around the bases of each column, twining up toward the sky.

"Tentacles," she murmured. Kran gave her a sharp look.

"They must have worshiped the sea," Zuna mused.

"And the stars," Tam added. He pointed to their left, where a knot of shorter buildings somehow clung to the side of the steep hill. Most of them were badly damaged, but Jendara could still see the patterns of contrasting stones laid into their walls in the shapes of stars.

"It makes sense," Zuna said. "To any seafarer, the stars are their best guide."

"We could use a guide right about now," Boruc grumbled. "We may have found our way out of that tunnel, but how in all hells are we supposed to get over that?"

Jendara tried to recall the island's size and shape. "This is the northernmost valley," she said slowly, "so once we go over that hill in front of us, we'd be looking right down at the dock the ulat-kini were building."

Crossing the surface proved easier said than done. The group moved from ruin to ruin, testing the ground as they went. Sometimes they scrambled over fallen buildings; sometimes they circled around them. Jendara wished she could see inside some of the bigger ruins, but debris and seaweed choked any openings that still remained. They climbed and scrabbled their way across the city until the edge appeared and the worst of the debris flattened out.

Jendara picked up her pace, relieved to be on something like solid ground. She took a few quick steps and pulled ahead of Zuna and the others. They had nearly reached the ulat-kini.

Rubble shifted beneath her boots and Jendara felt herself sliding downhill. Her arms flailed and she caught the edge of a strange statue beside her. Stone and shells clattered over the edge of the cliff. A slab of stone, like some very worn and ancient roof tile, teetered on the drop-off and then slid over the brink. It fell a few feet and then caught on a thin lip of stone jutting out below.

Zuna and Tam arrived at the edge of the cliff, Boruc moving slowly behind them. Tam's face was pale. His fingers fumbled at the knots around his waist until Zuna took over for him.

"Glad we roped up," Zuna said. "There was a point there I might have lost Tam, otherwise."

Boruc pointed out a pair of black knobs jutting up over the cliff's edge, just a few feet to Jendara's right. "Do you think that's one of the ulat-kini's ladders?"

She shifted over a few steps, keeping her hand on the sturdy statue, to peer over the edge. "Looks like it." She gave the others a weak smile. "Nice of the ulat-kini to give us an easy way down to their camp."

Zuna joined her beside the ladder. "Looks solid." She crouched to look down at the water below while trying to stay hidden. "I don't see many ulat-kini. Not even any kind of guard around this ladder."

Jendara looked down. Far below, she could see the four ugly boats tied up at the dock, which was now quite a large floating platform supporting a few shabby tents. At the farthest end, what appeared to be a clothesline held up a load of perfectly ordinary linen.

"I don't think this is a raiding party. This looks like an entire community of ulat-kini." She looked at Tam. "Does that make sense to you?"

"I don't know. Maybe they're planning to settle this place?"

She turned her attention back to the camp. "Maybe." The camp looked quiet and unassuming beside the strange floating dock. "The black ship is gone. Maybe it was a cargo vessel hired to bring the platform stuff?"

"No point wondering," Boruc said. "We just have to get down there and see what we find." He took hold of the ladder and began his descent, Zuna right behind him.

He was right, of course. They had to get down there and find out what there was to be discovered. Jendara just hoped she'd find Vorrin, safe and well.

Because if he wasn't, there would be all hell to pay.

8

VOICES IN THE WIND

Darkness and shadow covered their descent into the ulat-kini camp. As Jendara's boots hit the ground, she sent a little thanks out to the ancestor spirits, wherever they might be. Then she crept forward toward a pair of ulat-kini sitting on two empty barrels. If they were sentries, they had failed at their job.

As Zuna crept to the right, Jendara stalked toward the ulat-kini on the left. It sat up a little straighter, looking around. Jendara knocked it out before it realized what it was even looking at. Its pallid body lay sprawled on the floating platform, an obscene mix of human, fish, and frog parts. Jendara resisted the urge to kick it over the side of the platform so she could stop looking at it; this mission called for silence.

The other creature, absorbed in the fishing net it held in its finny fingers, suddenly realized its friend had fallen on the ground in front of it. It jumped to its feet just as a gust of wind rifled Zuna's hair, sending her bells jingling. The creature spun around, eyes wide.

Tam leaped forward, driving his own forehead into the ulat-kini's. Its eyes rolled up in its head and its legs crumpled. Tam eased it to the ground.

"Damn it!" Jendara hissed. "Your stupid bells, Zuna."

Zuna looked ashamed. "I didn't think—"

Jendara raised a hand, silencing her. "Vorrin's life is on the line. Glayn's and Sarni's, too. You stay here and cover our back trail.

Kran, keep an eye on her. Tam, let's go check out the boats. Boruc, I'm counting on you to let us know if anyone heads our way."

Jendara shoved the spyglass into Zuna's chest and turned away, trying to get her anger under control. She should have thought about Zuna's hair before they'd ever left the *Milady*. How stupid were they all, sneaking around while forgetting about something as obvious as bells knotted into braids? Jendara's father wouldn't have forgotten. Jendara knew that much.

Tam and Jendara crept forward in single file. Where the narrow walkway of the pier joined the big black platform, they split up, sticking to the edges of the ulat-kini's floating base. Jendara reached the nearest tent and dropped to her belly. If she was going to be spotted, it would be here, where the ulat-kini were most heavily concentrated. She crawled forward, holding her breath.

The tent flap had been rolled up, revealing some messy bedding and a few worn-looking baskets. It was empty.

Relieved, Jendara looked more closely at the structure. It gave off a strong stink of fish slime and dried seaweed. Her nose crinkled. If the stories were right, and there were humans forced to live with these wretched fish-faced folk, there was a chance a human lived here, breathing in this stink and sleeping in that mess. She'd rather throw herself into the sea than live in such squalor.

A clatter of crockery made her stiffen. The sound came from the biggest of the ulat-kini boats, a tar-stained scow Jendara wouldn't trust to cross a quiet bay, let alone take out on the open sea. Someone had clearly patched up a junked ship, replacing broken bits with whatever they could find and doing a bad job of it. The walls of the cabin leaned awkwardly in several different directions, and the few painted boards all sported different faded colors.

She searched for Tam and saw him peering over the side of one of the other boats. She caught his eye and pointed out the scow. It was the only vessel with a real cabin, and it looked like it might be the only structure sturdy enough to hold a determined prisoner. Jendara drew her handaxe and stepped on board.

She pressed her ear to the wall of the cabin, listening hard. A ceramic clanking sounded again. Out of the corner of her eye, she saw Tam join her on board and slip around the far side of the cabin. Jendara's mouth felt suddenly dry. She glanced back over her shoulder at the base of the cliff. She couldn't see Kran or Zuna, but she couldn't see any ulat-kini approaching, either. Everything was silent except the faint buzz of a fly.

Slowly, she moved around to the front of the cabin. Tam already waited at the corner. He gave a tiny nod, urging Jendara on.

Jendara put her hand on the door, and it swung open.

She raised her axe and charged at the figure in the middle of the dimly lit space. The resident dropped to the ground with a gasp. Jendara froze.

"You're no ulat-kini."

The huddled figure on the floor raised a tearful and very human face. "Please don't hurt me."

Jendara looked around herself. A filthy wad of bedding lay heaped on the floor, a few dirty dishes beside it. A strong smell of urine permeated the room, as if a chamber pot had spilled and never been wiped up. It had all the earmarks of a prison, including the miasma of despair. But aside from Tam, Jendara, and this pathetic stranger, the cabin was empty. "Are you alone? Why wasn't the door locked? Are you all right?"

Tam put a hand on Jendara's shoulder. "Slow down, Jendara. Can't you see she's scared?" He squatted down to make eye contact with the captive. "It's all right. We're here to help."

The woman sat up. "Really?"

In this light, it was hard to tell how old she was—her hair could have been light brown or mostly gray; her round face, while not seamed with age, had the chapped skin of someone who spent a great deal of time in the elements. She rubbed at the tears on her cheeks with knobbed, swollen hands.

"Where are the other prisoners?" Jendara asked, keeping her voice soft. "A woman and a man, and a gnome with green hair. Have you seen them?"

The woman shook her head. "Haven't been any other prisoners. Just me. Yerka." She sniffed. "I've been here ten years."

Jendara and Tam exchanged looks. Ten years? It seemed impossible. The woman didn't look particularly unhealthy, and even her dress, although worn, was intact and whole. How could anyone live as an ulat-kini prisoner for so long and be so well?

And more importantly, how could she not know about the others? Jendara tried again.

"Have you heard anything strange? Anyone calling for help? Maybe they took the other prisoners on the black ship."

Yerka shook her head harder. "Nope. Nope. No one but black robes on the black ship. Too many secrets." Her eyes got bigger. "The black robes left yesterday. Gone, gone. Everyone went with them, except the air-breathers. Only the hybrids stayed here, waiting."

"Waiting for what?" Tam asked.

Jendara raised a hand. "Maybe you can tell us later." She turned to Tam. "Those guards are going to wake up any minute. If we want to get up that ladder, we've got to move."

He nodded and helped Yerka to her feet. Her plight seemed to touch the big man; he kept an arm around her shoulder as they led her out into the moonlight. The wind ruffled Yerka's hair and the woman cringed a little. Did they ever let her out of that horrible cabin? Jendara's left hand curled into a fist.

From one of the other boats, a voice shouted in surprise.

"We've got to run for it," Jendara warned. She broke into a run. Tam picked up his own pace, half-carrying Yerka down the dock toward the cliff.

"Who's this?" Boruc asked, rising from his hiding spot behind a pile of fishing nets. Zuna and Kran appeared from behind a rock.

"Later," Jendara gasped. "We'll never get up that ladder in time!"

"Ladder?" Yerka asked. "Why not just hide in a tunnel?" She pointed at the cliff face, where a dark opening spat a waterfall down into the sea.

"How do we get there?" Zuna snapped. "Even if we swam over there, it's a good fifteen feet above the water line."

"There's another ladder," Jendara realized. "Running behind the waterfall."

Tam slipped into the water and held out his arms to Yerka. "Can you swim?" he asked her.

Yerka plunged in. "It's so cold," she gasped.

"I hate this," Boruc grumbled as he joined them.

Zuna's eyes met Jendara's for a moment, her gaze clearly hostile. Jendara immediately regretted her boorish comment about Kran looking after her. Then Kran pushed between them, he and Fylga diving neatly into the water, and it was time for Zuna and Jendara to follow suit.

The sound of the waterfall drowned out everything as the group paddled toward the hidden ladder. Had the ulat-kini seen them get in the water, or would they assume the humans would take the land route? Jendara tried to peer through the curtain of spray as Tam helped Yerka get a grip on the ladder. But the world beyond was obscured. She could only hurry and follow Zuna up the ladder.

Jendara pulled herself up into the wet tunnel. The little stream gurgled past her, cold and smelling of dank things that had never seen the sun.

"This is much deeper beneath the city than we've been before. This could be two or three floors beneath the spot with the pit trap." Jendara reached for her pack and pulled out her lantern. It didn't feel too damp, thanks to the pack's well-oiled leather. Morul had tanned that hide, and Leyla had made the pack. They, and all of Sorind, felt suddenly very far away.

So was Vorrin. If the ulat-kini hadn't taken him, then he could be anywhere. There was no way to know where the fish creatures had made their base—she'd seen them on the surface of the island and down in the purple boulevard. They seemed to know the place already.

Jendara worked her flint striker and managed to get her lamp lit. She needed a new plan, and soon.

Boruc brushed his fingertips against the stony walls. "The craftsmanship is much less detailed," he pointed out. "It's rough, with no details around the tunnel mouth. I'd guess this is some kind of sewage tunnel."

Tam struggled to get his own lamp lit. "Makes sense," he agreed. He peered down the waterfall. "I think they missed us," he said, in a pleased tone. "There's no one in the water or on the ladder."

"Then let's hurry up," Jendara said, her mind already hurrying on ahead. "I want to know why Vorrin and Glayn and Sarni weren't in that camp, and I'm hoping our ulat-kini prisoner knows something."

She strode ahead of the group, holding her lantern high. Light might be dangerous, but seeing felt more important than being observed. Right now she might relish a run-in with a fish-creature. At least it might give her some kind of clue about the things.

Jendara's head nearly scraped the tunnel roof here, and Tam and Zuna had to hunch to fit. It felt like a sewer tunnel, supporting Boruc's idea. Luckily, any sewage foulness had long been washed away.

Tam touched her elbow. "Look." He pointed up ahead, where the tunnel had a kind of stair step in it, forcing the water to run in a foaming white fall. He stooped to look at the shallow bowl that looked to have formed over years of falling water, presumably before the city sank into the sea.

"Find something?" Jendara asked.

He held up a golden shape. "It's a little gold frog."

Jendara leaned in to have a closer look. "Looks like a charm from a bracelet or a necklace."

"Pretty," Yerka breathed. Her eyes had lit up, and for the first time, Jendara could see a hint of the woman Yerka must have been ten years ago.

Tam smiled at the woman. "You can have it, if you like." He held it out to her.

As she took it, Jendara realized Yerka's hand trembled. She looked harder at the woman. "Your teeth are chattering."

Zuna reached into her pack and found a woolly scarf. "It didn't get too damp in my pack. Your light clothes aren't much good wet."

Yerka brushed her palms down her stained linen skirt. "It's all I've got."

Jendara had to turn away. She'd never really thought about those stories, had never imagined how sad the stolen women's lives must be. To be kidnapped and forced to serve the slimy ulat-kini, let alone bearing their half-breed young—by the gods, she was looking forward to interrogating that ulat-kini down in the galley.

"Let's rope up and keep moving," she said. Her voice sounded thick. "Anyone have any water in their canteen?"

Jendara struggled to keep her eyes open, the play of shadow from her lantern and the constant darkness ahead making them heavier than they ought to feel. Her inner sense of time had abandoned her. They had been walking a long time in the twisting folds of the sewer tunnel. It had to be very late.

Her eyes sagged shut. An image of the night sky filled her mind's eye, the stars shifting wildly against the velvet of the heaven. A shrill keening split the air.

She jolted awake. Kran was shaking her arm. She blinked at him. "You okay?"

He pointed at her.

"Yeah, I'm fine. Just tired."

"Let me take the lead, Jendara," Tam said, already reaching for the knot at his waist.

She turned down her lantern and took the place behind him. To ration oil, only the front and rear walkers carried lit lanterns. They barely cast enough light for safety, but there was no way to know how long it would take to find the *Milady*.

"Hold up," Boruc called from the rear. "I think I've found a ladder."

He untied and explored for a second, and then they followed him up to the next level. It looked more like a passage than a tiny sewage tunnel, and while they still walked in a roped single file, at least they could all stand up straight. This level smelled different from the floors above, the smell of dead and dying fish less pervasive. The floor and walls were smoother. When the island had lain below the sea, this dark passage had been so far beneath that surface that it could offer the creatures of the sea little beyond shelter. Even kelp and shellfish needed sunlight to produce their food. Now and then, Jendara's boots crunched on the thin, desiccated arm of some dead sea star or still twitching creature for which she had no name. But despite the presence of these small life forms, in the dim gloom of the lanterns, the hallway was abandoned.

Occasionally the soft murmur of the wind penetrated the walls. There was no apparent source to it, no crack in the wall or adjoining tunnel, just a mysterious breeze. This wind's tone was different, more like a voice than the constant shriek of the wind in the *Milady*'s grotto. Since they'd entered this tunnel, her ears had been struggling to tell her companions' whispers from those of the wind.

"What did you say?" she asked for the fourth or fifth time in last half hour.

Boruc shook his head. "Too tired to talk. And too hungry. Is there any more of that hardtack?"

She passed him another oilcloth-wrapped bundle. She couldn't imagine eating any of it.

"Did you hear that?" Tam paused. "I think it came from that doorway."

They hadn't opened any doors or entered any of the rooms that stood open. But Tam pressed his ear to the closest one, listening hard.

"I didn't hear anything," Boruc said.

"I did," Yerka blurted. "It almost sounded like *her* name." She pointed at Jendara with a knobby finger.

Jendara moved to stand beside the door, her head cocked. Behind the stone slab, the wind's shriek sounded louder, its tones pitiful. "It's just the wind." She touched Tam's shoulder. "Do you want me to lead?"

Tam shook his head. "No, you deserve the break." He put his lantern down on the floor and rubbed his eyes. "It gets tense, walking by these doors. Who knows what's behind them?"

"Don't think about it," Jendara advised. "And keep your sword handy."

"Good idea." Tam reached for his lantern and stopped in mid-motion. "No, that wasn't just the wind. Listen!"

Jendara pressed her cheek against the stone.

"Please," someone called. "Please! Jendara!"

"Oh, ancestors," she breathed. "That's Sarni."

She kicked the door, but it didn't move. The others just stared at her. "Come on!" she shouted. "It's Sarni!"

Boruc put his shoulder to the door. The cords of his neck stood out as he pushed against it, harder and harder. He stopped to breathe. "It's not moving."

"Maybe the next one." Jendara pulled them forward to the next door, which wasn't quite closed. She drove her heel into the door and it ground open a few inches.

Tam leaned around her, holding up his lantern. "You see anything?"

Jendara squinted. "Maybe some old furniture." She shoved the door with her shoulder and felt it move another inch or two.

"Let me try," Tam said. He kicked the door, and it opened wide enough for Jendara to fit through.

She untied the rope at her waist. "Sarni!"

"What are you doing?" Boruc asked.

"Going in there." Jendara gave him a stern look. "If I'm not back in ten minutes, keep moving."

"Like hell," he grumbled, but she was already stepping inside the dark room.

"Sarni?" she called out again, but not even the wind answered her.

The lantern's light flickered over two heaping mounds of detritus that ran in parallel across the room. A gray silt covered everything, obscuring the details of what must have once been shelves full of someone's things. A metal bowl lay on its side in the center of the room, its surface showing only a little green patina.

Jendara picked it up. A border of long-legged sea stars ran around the rim, as clearly as if it had been made yesterday. Had any of her own possessions held up as well to the flooding of her home? If anyone looked inside her ruined cottage, what would they think of her, and would they wonder where she had gone?

The bowl was varnished bronze, worth no more than a few copper coins, but she tucked it in her pack anyway.

"Please," the wind sighed. "Please."

Her shoulders sagged. There was no one here. Sarni, wherever she was, was gone.

"Jendara!" There was a little pause, and then it repeated: "Jendara!"

"By the gods," Boruc said, now at Jendara's back despite her orders, "that's her."

Zuna strode past them. Standing at the edge of the circle of light, she laid her palm against the wall. "Here," she said, finally. "I think there's a crack funneling the sound to us."

Jendara played her light over the crack, which ran into the ceiling and disappeared. "The main walls are cut out of the island itself. They could be carrying the sound from anywhere."

Zuna rapped on the wall with her knuckles. "It's a thick one. You could be right."

"She could be anywhere," Jendara repeated. The words weren't as depressing as she had expected them to be. "Sarni!" she shouted. "We're looking for you!"

Zuna raised an eyebrow.

"Maybe my voice will carry up the crack," Jendara said. "I have to hope, anyway."

"We're on our way!" Boruc bellowed. His voice echoed in the little room. He made a rueful face at Jendara. "I'm a little louder than you."

"We need to keep moving," Tam said from the doorway. "Wherever Sarni is—wherever Vorrin and Glayn are—they're not here."

Jendara crossed to her friend. Even in the shadows, she could see the misery written on his face. Tam was always the first to laugh, the first to find some cheerful notion in a troubled situation. To see him so unhappy caught her like a fist in the belly. "We'll find Glayn and the others," she said. "Have faith."

He swallowed hard and only nodded in response.

Fylga gave a soft bark as if in agreement with Jendara. Jendara glanced down at the animal. It didn't look so ugly anymore; maybe she'd just gotten used to its odd looks. She pulled the next-to-last strip of jerky from her belt pouch and gave it to Kran. "Share it with Fylga." He grinned at her.

The group set out again. Tam let Zuna lead, and Jendara gave Boruc her lantern so he could take the end of the line. Thin, pained sounds followed them out of the room and down the hallway, and Jendara couldn't tell if they came from the wind or she still heard Sarni, wherever she was.

They walked in silence for several more minutes. The hallway showed no sign of ending. At this depth, the city's builders had cut a straight line through the island, ignoring the hills and valleys that affected the upper levels. They hadn't seen a cross-street in what felt like miles.

Zuna paused. "I'm going to turn down my lantern," she announced. "To conserve oil."

Boruc's flame lowered, too. The shadows pressed in closer. Jendara wished she dared light her own lamp and drive the gloom away, but she knew the time would come when they would be glad of their thrift. She tried to push aside the fear that perhaps they had missed the staircase to the next level, and that they would be trapped down here forever.

Zuna whispered: "I think there's a cross-tunnel."

Jendara stopped. "Should we explore it?"

From the darkness ahead came a crash.

9

WHERE THERE IS DARKNESS, LIGHT

At the intersection of tunnels ahead, a very small blue light bobbed. Then the spot of eerie luminescence paused. If it were anything with the ability to see in the dark, it was looking right at Jendara's crew.

"Turn up your lamps!" Jendara ordered, dropping into a crouch. She already gripped her handaxe, but now she raised it.

Zuna raised her lamp and Boruc followed suit, their lanterns blazing like day. Kran drew his seax, his stance as solid as a blooded warrior's.

Someone shouted and a figure lunged forward. Jendara caught the man by the arm. "Vorrin!"

"Dara?" He shielded his face with his arm. "I can't believe it's you."

Glayn stumbled forward. "You lot found us! And brought enough lights for an army."

Still shading his eyes, Vorrin hurried toward Jendara and crushed her in a hug made awkward by the rope tying her to the others. When he pulled away, he explained: "We were in total darkness until we found a patch of this strange seaweed." He held out the blue blob, which proved to be a ball of luminescent leaves.

Kran squeezed in to hug Vorrin while Tam and Glayn clasped each other tightly. Then Vorrin and Glayn exchanged glances. "There's a bit of a story," Vorrin said.

"Tell it while we walk," Zuna suggested. "We're almost out of lamp oil."

Vorrin reached for the lantern still clipped to his belt. "There's still oil in my lantern; the wick's just too wet to burn."

The others gladly refilled their lanterns, and Zuna turned up her light a bit. Since Vorrin and Glayn had already explored the length of the intersecting hallway, the group continued down the main corridor. Tam quickly introduced Yerka, and gave a brief recounting of their search for the missing men.

Jendara gave Vorrin's arm a squeeze just to reassure herself he was beside her. "So what happened?"

"I think we should keep our voices down," he warned. "We're not alone down here. We saw more of those fish-things."

"Just tell us the story," Boruc complained.

"When we fell into the pit trap," Vorrin said, "I got knocked out. We're lucky we both didn't die. I would have drowned if Glayn hadn't caught hold of my collar and hauled me out onto a rock."

"It was pure dark until you lowered that torch," Glayn added, "but then I could see there was some kind of opening on one wall."

"So Glayn told me to stay there and then he dove down underneath to see if the hole he'd seen in the wall was any kind of exit—"

"Which it was," Glayn cut in, "so I made him dive, too—"

"Thought I'd drown," Vorrin grumbled.

Even by the faint light of the lanterns, Jendara could see Glayn roll his eyes. "It wasn't that long of a swim, although it was all swimming down stairs."

Zuna stopped and turned to face the pair. "Wait. You swam *down* stairs? So we're under the place where you fell?"

"No, because there was another bit of stairs, back up." Glayn shrugged. "Didn't make sense to me, neither."

But Jendara saw the logic. "The pit trap room must have been built so it opened onto the sewage tunnels," she began, excited. "Maybe they used it as some kind of cellar." She forced herself to quiet back down. "This is good. This gives us a real sense of how deep this city is."

"You're right." Boruc rummaged in his pack for his sketch book. "Damp. Good thing I'm using charcoal and not ink." He untied himself from the group so he could sit down on the floor, and then began to draw furiously by the low light of his lantern. The rest of them stowed their rope. It might be safer to be tied together, but the break felt good.

"Anyway," Vorrin continued, "we came out into a long hallway, lit up a bit with patches of this glowing seaweed. On one side, a door stood open and one of those big fishy things sat on a pile of weedy stuff. I thought we'd have to fight him, but he was asleep. Damn lucky for us, too."

"We took some of the seaweed, and we've been walking down here for the last three or four hours. Thought we'd never find the way." For delivering such a pessimistic thought, Glayn certainly sounded happy. He clapped Tam on the elbow. "Thank the good gods we're together again."

"Come see." Boruc waved them over. "It's still rough, obviously, but it's a general overview of the four levels: three with big halls like streets, and then the smaller sewage tunnel underneath. Somehow the people who built this had all this space and still had the city aboveground." He tapped his charcoal pencil against his chin. "I can't imagine how it worked. Who would want to live down here when they had all that glory up there?"

Zuna shook her head. "Being in the dark all the time? It'd make me sick."

Jendara leaned close to Vorrin's ear. "You didn't kill that guard?"

His face grew serious. "If we'd killed him, it might have raised an alarm when somebody found him later. We could hear a bunch of them in one of the other rooms, croaking to each other. I get the feeling they're planning something. They built that pit trap for a reason, Dara."

"I feel like we stumbled into something over our heads. I wish we hadn't come here."

Vorrin went silent for a moment. "I didn't think it would be like this. I just thought—an easy little bit of exploration. Quick money. I didn't think it would be dangerous."

"Hey, we made this call together. Remember, this is a partnership. A team." She reached for his hand and squeezed it. She kept holding his hand as they walked, even if it meant she had only one hand free. She wasn't ready to let go of him quite yet.

"The floor drops here," Zuna warned. "It's only a few steps."

"Great," Glayn grumbled, "we're going back downstairs."

Boots splashed. "And it's wet," Zuna complained.

Jendara freed her hand reached for the flint striker in her belt pouch. Something about Glayn's description of the stairs he'd navigated leaving the pit trap room had stuck in her mind, and now she had a bad feeling. Castles and forts and other large facilities often had only a few rooms that were connected to the cellar and sewage lines. Bathrooms and kitchens were the happiest of such places. Prison cells and dungeons were another sort of place entirely.

She lit her lantern. "Oh, blessed ancestors," she breathed. She paused in the middle of the stairway and played the light over the wall. Great gashes had been scored in the stone.

"Do those look like claw marks to anyone else?" Boruc asked. He hoisted Fylga off the ground and tucked the damp dog under his arm.

The stairwell ended in short hallway that bent a few feet to the right, and then came to an end in an open doorway. Zuna paused at the base of the stairs, standing in knee-high water. "Water did real damage here."

No one had left the door open to the room beyond: the heavy iron door had rusted in its years below the ocean, and it had been too weak to hold up to the pressures when the island emerged from below. Broken-off shards of rust hung from the twisted hinges, but the rest of the door had gone to the hands of time.

"This is the first iron we've seen on this island," Jendara noted. She paused, in case any of her comrades had gotten the same notion she had. "Makes me think this might have been a dungeon."

Everyone turned to look at her. She shrugged and then joined Zuna at the doorway. What would an ancient dungeon look like? Would they find corroded implements of torture and the broken bits of thousand year-old skeletons, or would a civilization as mighty and intellectual as these star worshipers have only a few spartan prison cells?

"Let's keep moving," she said, and waded carefully into the room beyond.

The floor lay a few steps lower than the hallway's floor, and the water now stood chest deep. Kran's chin barely cleared the surface.

Jendara's teeth began to chatter. When the island had been submerged, this chamber might have lain hundreds of feet beneath the surface. No sunlight had warmed this water in years.

"Oh, it's cold," Zuna breathed.

"And it stinks like something died," Boruc grumbled.

Zuna held her lantern high above her head, casting light around the great open space. The room was a bit longer than the *Milady*, maybe fifty or sixty yards. The walls rose into darkness, the ceiling impossible to make out. If this was a prison, it could have held a great number of prisoners.

The lantern light glinted against the far wall. "Look." Glayn, at this depth forced to tread water, pointed to the reflection. "Bars."

Jendara squinted. The light wasn't strong enough to make out the details, but she thought Glayn was correct. "Looks like prison cells, maybe." She wondered why the bars of the little cells still gleamed like new when the main prison door had rotted out. They reminded her of the windows in the purple boulevard—perhaps the bars and the glass had all been magically or alchemically treated.

She took another step forward, sending out a wake of ripples across the murky water. Something bobbed on the surface and she pulled it toward her.

"That's not old at all." Glayn grabbed onto her arm to steady himself as he treaded water. He looked closer at the thing, a broken chunk of painted wood. "—*ermaid*," he read. He shook her head. "This is the bow of a fishing boat. The *Mermaid*. Never saw it, but it went missing a few months ago. Presumed sunk."

Boruc jerked his chin to the left, his arm still clamped tight around the dog. "Is that her crew?"

Jendara turned. Her lantern lit up the left side of the room. At first, she couldn't understand Boruc's question. Something big floated on the surface of the water, a moist heap of pale and quivering stuff. Then her stomach turned. "Merciful Desna," she breathed.

"Are those—" Yerka broke off. She clapped her hands over her mouth, her eyes filling with tears. "Tell me they're not."

Boruc took a step closer. "That's a boot. And a hand."

Jendara didn't want to make out those details. The waterlogged flesh was horrible enough. The cold had slowed decomposition, but nothing could stop the onset of decay, and these men had been dead a while.

"How'd they get down *here* if the *Mermaid* went down two months ago?" Glayn put some distance between himself and the bodies. "Bodies float, not sink."

"Something must have put them here," Jendara said, "the gods only know why."

Tam shook his head, eyes fixed on the corpses. "They're in too good of shape for something that's been in the sea. No crabs feasting on them. No fish nibbling on their flesh. Whatever brought them down here wanted to keep them fresh. Like hanging your venison in a cold house."

"We've got to get out of here," Vorrin said. "If this is something's larder, it's not going to appreciate visitors."

"I'm sure whatever cached these bodies was flushed out of here when the island came up to the surface," Glayn said. "I mean, I hope." His teeth chattered.

Jendara looked from him to Kran. The boy's lips had turned blue. "I hope as well as you, Glayn, but let's get moving anyway. It's damn cold."

Zuna waded forward. "I think there's a staircase going up over by those jail cells." She indicated the far wall with a wave of her lantern. A dark gap showed, overlaid by the same gleaming metal bars as the prison cells.

A bit of hope stirred in Jendara's chest. "If they went to the effort of protecting those bars from rust, then I'm guessing that staircase goes someplace more important than the lowest level of the island. I think we've found our way up."

"You can pick a lock, can't you, Jendara?" Vorrin sloshed past her.

"If it's not too tough a lock, yeah." She followed behind him, sliding her axe back into her belt as she went. She caught up with him and they waded to the steel grate blocking the staircase. He took her lantern and held it close while she tugged her belt pouch out of the water and felt around for the slim metal tools at the bottom. "My hands are pretty stiff," she warned. "This might take a while."

"Here." He took the leather strip out of his clubbed-back hair and used it to tie the lantern to the grate. "I've gotten pretty warm walking in this muck." He took her hands and rubbed them briskly.

She smiled at him, feeling some of the prison's grim atmosphere fall away from them. "Works every time."

He gave her fingers a little squeeze and she turned back to study the lock. The main lock was at chest height and looked easy enough. She probed inside the lock for a minute and heard it click open. She tugged on the gate. It jiggled, but stayed shut.

That meant a second lock, probably a bolt going into the floor—common enough in a prison. She jiggled the grate again and studied the resistance. The floor bolt must be just to the right of the doorframe.

She wanted to be right over it when she dove; she was going to waste enough air feeling around for the damn thing without having to search for it. She shifted over a few inches and felt something crunch beneath her boots. It wasn't the hollow, crisp crunch of an empty shell, but a more solid snap, and even before she looked down she knew what it was.

"There are skeletons in this," Tam called out. "I've got at least two shackled to the wall by the door we just came in."

"There's one here, too," Jendara announced. She could just make out the jumble of bones in the murk of the bottom. Human. Or if not human, humanish. She supposed she'd get to feel all of its details while she probed around in the muck.

"Hey, Boruc!" Tam sounded excited. "Remember that ring you found? The weird long finger inside? These things have the same kind of finger bones. Toes look long, too."

"Maybe you can sketch it," Vorrin said. He began to wade back toward the other entrance. "What about that second cell?"

Jendara breathed long and deep, then drew in several short sharp breaths beyond her normal limit. Overbreathing. The divers she knew claimed it could give you extra time underwater. If they were right, she'd be glad of it. One last sip of air, and then she forced herself beneath the water's surface.

The water was too shallow to use kicks to drive her to the bottom; she had to pull herself down with her arms, following the bars of the grate. Silt swirled around her face, obscuring almost everything. Her fingers tapped the bottom and she ran them along the bottom slab of steel that made up the grate. It had to be at least six inches wide and felt as slick as new metal. Whoever had built this place had been very concerned about something breaking out.

A clanking and crashing came from off to her left. Tam and Vorrin must have moved their investigation to the prison cells. She hoped they didn't stir up too much muck and send it in her direction.

The water cleared a bit and she saw the round dome of a skull just an inch in front of her nose. A bubble of surprise escaped her mouth. The side of the skull was stove in, and the crushed area matched the size and shape of a bar in the iron door. The creature who had died here must have been smashed against the bars of the prison when the ocean rushed inside.

Her fingers felt for the still-hidden bolt, her eyes unable to look away from the skull. The eye sockets seemed far too huge to be human, the brow bone above broader, the forehead slung back in a vaguely amphibian way. But the lower half of the skull bore a strong resemblance to a human's. She'd never seen a creature like it—not even the ulat-kini looked like this.

Her fingers closed on something heavy and round, sending up silt as they moved. She forced herself to concentrate on the latch, but the silt obscured everything. She squeezed her eyes shut to protect them and tried to envision the thing from just the information her fingers sent her. The burning in her lungs threatened to distract her.

Yes, she could visualize it: a flat disk, about two fingers wide, with a very small opening in its middle.

She made another pass around the thing's edge. It felt like a padlock. Grit and mud covered it despite the strange magic that otherwise protected the grate and its mechanisms—she couldn't see it at all, but it felt sturdy.

Jendara was going to need to breathe before she could get started on the padlock. Feeling for the nearest bar, she pulled herself up to the surface.

Spluttering and blinded for a moment, she almost didn't register the splashing from the other side of the room. She scrubbed the back of her hand across her eyes. "What's going on?"

"There's something big coming out of a crack in the floor!" Vorrin shouted. "Get that gate open now!"

She snapped her head around to see what he was talking about. Iron screeched as a swollen maroon claw closed around the bars dividing the first and second prison cell. Something huge and red was slowly pulling itself out of prison floor, the stone groaning and splintering around it.

Jendara turned back to the prison door and drew a deep breath.

"Jendara!" Tam shouted, one arm supporting Glayn as he waded desperately toward her. "Hurry!" The others were right behind him.

She plunged under the water, sliding her way down to the lock. With cold, stiff fingers, she slipped her pick inside. Grit ground inside the mechanism, and she hoped the ancestors heard her silent prayers not to let it jam.

The lock gave a little jerk and loosened. She pried at it. The corrosion held it tight. Her lungs burned: she'd forgotten to over-breathe. Cursing, Jendara pulled herself to the surface.

"Is it open?" Zuna shouted.

"Where's the creature?" Jendara gasped.

"Behind us!" Boruc said. "Tell me that lock's undone!"

"I can't get the lock off the bolt," Jendara explained. "Maybe if we shake the gate, it'll break down some of the corrosion."

"Okay—" Vorrin began.

Then something yanked him backward.

"Vorrin!" Jendara screamed. The water roiled behind her, foam obscuring man and beast.

She shoved past Tam. The pick fell into the water. She didn't give a damn. "Vorrin!

Jendara plunged beneath the surface. Silt and debris had turned the water to something like stew. She couldn't see a thing. The water even sounded like chaos. Something leathery struck her on the temple and she fought to get her feet back under her, feeling blindly around as she came out of the water to gasp for air.

Her hand closed on the leathery thing—Vorrin's boot, she knew its texture by heart—and she yanked hard. His motionless body collided with hers. "Help me!" she shouted.

Zuna reached for Vorrin and pulled him back toward the gate even as the creature drew itself up out of the water. Its red-and-purple mottled body hulked over Jendara, the shape of a crab but far larger—practically the size of an ogre. Its claw snapped shut just inches from Jendara's face. Its other forelimb sported a warped and twisted hand, gripping a stone knife.

A tremendous clang sounded behind her.

"Jendara! We got it open!"

"I'll close it behind me," she called. The creature's evil black eyes sparkled at her. She didn't stand a chance of fighting this thing in the water.

It lunged at her with its primitive blade. She caught the blow on the edge of her axe and the steel rang out. Its claw shot out and she ducked under the blow. Inside its defenses, she swung her axe and the creature screeched in pain as the blade bit into its misshapen hand.

She resisted a sudden urge to laugh. This was what she was made for—fighting her enemies face to face, not swimming around like a frightened little fish. She scored a crunching blow higher up on its arm.

"We're out!"

Beneath the water, the creature lashed out with one of its sturdy back legs, sweeping Jendara's feet out from under her. She went down, nearly inhaling water. In a fair fight, she could kill this thing, but not like this. She had to retreat. She got her footing and backed away.

She filled the air with blows as she made her way toward the doorway, chopping at the creature's claw as it snapped at her again and again. She wished she could risk drawing her sword, but didn't dare waste time wrestling it from the soaked leather of her scabbard. She felt behind her for the gate and nearly shouted out when her fingers hit it.

"Hurry!" Boruc shouted.

She threw herself backward. Boruc yanked on the gate just as the crab-thing's claw clamped shut around her ankle. The lantern tied to the gate clanged and clattered as their bodies shook the bars, and shadows flickered wildly.

"It's got me," Jendara grunted. The tough leather of her boot had kept the claw from biting into the flesh of her ankle, but now the gate ground into her leg, too. Hands closed on her shoulders, pulling her as if she were the rope in a vicious game of tug-of-war.

There wasn't enough room to swing her axe. She struck out with her free foot, but the creature hardly noticed. Then Boruc threw himself across her, his dagger driving down into the claw with a nasty crunch. The creature shrieked in pain and surprise.

Jendara slammed the gate shut behind her and dropped to fumble in the mud below for a second. The bolt. The crab-thing lashed out with its injured claw, the sharp tip of its pincer slashing across her forearm just as she slammed the bolt home.

She yanked her arm away. Blood ran from the wound, although it was shallow. She could still move her fingers. They closed on a piece of ancient skeleton.

Gasping for air, she came up to the surface. The beast threw itself at the gate. The bolt held, but she wasn't sure if the creature was smart enough to figure out how to open it, and she didn't have a way to reattach the padlock. She drove the long bone in her hand into the door's main lock. By the ancestors, she hoped that would hold.

Boruc grabbed her arm. "Let's go!"

"The lantern!"

"Forget it!" He yanked her up the stairs.

The crab-thing threw itself at the gate again. Glass shattered as it crushed the lantern with its great mass, and the stairway went dark. Jendara stumbled on an uneven riser but caught herself before she fell.

The creature banged against the steel grate, again and again, the ugly clanging echoing all the way up to the next level.

10

ROCKFALL

The stairs only went up a short distance before they paused at a broad landing. Cutting up to the right, another flight of stairs ran into the darkness. The group had paused to wait to for Jendara and Boruc.

"Everyone all right?" she asked.

Tam shook his head. "Vorrin's bleeding bad."

"M'fine," Vorrin mumbled.

Down below, the giant crab creature rattled the grate again. Jendara tightened her lips. "Tam, try to put pressure on his wound. Let's put another flight of stairs between us and that son of a bitch."

Zuna led them up the next flight of stairs. Jendara put an arm around Vorrin's waist. This close, she could hear the hiss of his breath through teeth clenched against pain. Below them, the crab-thing clanged louder. Jendara found herself repeating the same words over and over under her breath: *Please let the lock hold. Please let Vorrin be okay. Please let the lock hold. Please let Vorrin be okay . . .*

"That's not very comforting," Vorrin said weakly.

"You," Jendara mock-growled. She stopped whispering and took more of his weight on her arm.

They stumbled out into the next hallway. This one was wide, a definite street instead of a corridor. Shells crunched under Jendara's boots as she helped Tam ease Vorrin onto the floor.

Glayn knelt beside Vorrin. "Take off your shirt."

Jendara helped him get the sodden thing off. The blood came from a gash running down his arm—a long one, and deep. Boruc lit his lantern and held it close enough to show the shining mass of exposed meat.

"Oh, that's ugly." Glayn took off his pack and rummaged a moment until he found needle and thread. "Going to have to sew you up, Cap." He hesitated a moment and then, like a man ever ready to patch sails, brought out his leather thimble.

"That ain't the worst of it," Boruc said in a grim voice. "Look at this shoulder."

Jendara moved around to take a look at the second wound. It didn't bleed. Maybe it wouldn't have looked so bad if it had. Sullen purple welts showed on both the front and back side of the shoulder, deepening into swollen puncture wounds big enough for Jendara to fit a finger or two into. "Oh, shit."

"It bit hard there." Vorrin gave a pained grunt as Glayn's needle pierced his skin.

"Sorry, Cap. You've got tough hide," the gnome apologized.

"Good thing, too," Vorrin managed.

Jendara winked at him. "At least it's just your left arm."

He managed a smile. "Nothing I use, right?"

"Jendara? If you look in my pack, there's a little roll of flannel in the bottom. Could you get it for me?" Glayn asked. "Probably wet," he added in a grumble.

The roll of flannel was indeed damp, like everything else inside. As Jendara closed up the pack's top, she gave the group a careful look-ing-over. Every one of them was soaked through. Vorrin had turned a shade of pale closer to gray, and his teeth chattered, as did Yerka's. Kran leaned casually against the wall as if he were as comfortable here as in their own cottage, but as Jendara turned back to Vorrin, she caught a glimpse of him rubbing his arms. She had nothing to warm or dry him. They had to get back to the *Milady* soon. They'd start risking hypothermia if they didn't get out of the cold and wet.

She handed the roll of flannel to Glayn, who had finished his stitching. He pulled a small blue bottle out of the fabric. Jendara plucked it from his fingers. "Is that what I think it is?"

He nodded. "Picked it up in Halgrim at an exorbitant price, along with a few I stowed back on the ship. I figured you can never be too careful." He took back the bottle, cracked the wax seal, and held it out to Vorrin. "Drink up."

Vorrin eyed the bottle. "Is that brandy?"

"Healing potion," Jendara growled. "So drink it."

He reached for the bottle and raised an eyebrow. "I thought you said healing potions were for helpless assholes."

"Hey, I never said 'helpless.'"

He knocked back the bottle and shuddered as the potion burned down his gullet.

Boruc settled down beside them, notebook in hand. "I think this is the second level." He pointed at the map he'd drawn. "We dropped down when we went into the prisons. That big landing must have led into the third level, the one just above the sewer tunnels. The next flight of stairs took us up here. I'm not sure how far south we've come, though. With a little luck, we might be at the halfway point."

Jendara's forehead wrinkled as she thought about his words. "So if we can find a staircase up, we'll probably be in one of the streets intersecting the boulevard?"

He nodded. "I hope."

She tossed Vorrin his shirt. "Then let's go."

Boruc took the lead, and Jendara walked beside Vorrin again, Zuna and Kran just in front of her. Even the dog walked like it was tired.

Her mind wandered back to that prison. That creature and its larder had managed to stay inside the island when it rose to the surface, as had that seaweed monster that had lured Vorrin and Glayn away. How many other creatures had managed to find a bolt-hole while the sea sluiced out of the island's tunnels? She felt naked, walking down this hallway with Vorrin injured and two noncombatants in her party. There were so many people to protect and not enough of her to go around.

When Zuna stopped, Jendara nearly walked into her back.

"What's wrong?"

Boruc turned to face them. "Look ahead. This tunnel's collapsed."

Zuna put her hands on her hips. "We're at an intersection, right? Can we take the hallway to right? There's some rock blocking the way, but it looks like spillover from the cave-in."

Boruc frowned. "We can't be sure of that."

"Let me check," Zuna said. She turned up her lantern and began scrambling over the rocks until she was near the top of the blockage. She leaned precariously over a boulder. "Oh yeah, it's totally clear past this point."

"Then we try it," Jendara said. She felt tremendously tired. Vorrin was hurt, Sarni was missing, they were all soaked through and running out of lantern oil, and now the island itself seemed eager to turn them around and trap them. She'd rather deal with an entire pack of ulat-kini than feel lost.

"Then start shifting." Boruc hoisted a boulder and began trucking it to the far side of the tunnel.

"Don't block off the stairs," Jendara warned. "Try to pile it up next to the walls."

Zuna sat the lantern on the floor and hoisted a big rock. Jendara grabbed her own boulder and caught up with her. "Nice work."

Zuna gave her a sideways glance. "Thanks."

"This is going to take a long time," Jendara said. She hunkered down to grab a chunk of rock. Zuna just grunted and turned away.

Jendara shook her head. Zuna needed to toughen up if she was going to handle adventuring. She could be angry if she wanted to, but it didn't change the fact that her stupid hair had given them away at that ulat-kini camp. Jendara moved to the heap of rubble. They didn't have time to coddle people's feelings out in the field.

Then Glayn began to sing, not loudly, and not one of his usual work songs. There was no sound of the sea or raucous chorus for drinking. But somehow how his voice evoked the sensation of gentle breezes stirring the trees, the soft light of spring dancing on wildflowers.

"Yer a real nice singer," Yerka told the gnome. "I almost feel warmer."

The gnome beamed at her and started another tune. Everyone looked more cheerful as the music continued—even Zuna.

A few songs later, Boruc decided the side tunnel was clear enough to enter. The group huddled around Kran's lantern, waiting in silence as Boruc disappeared to explore. Without comment, Tam lit the lantern he'd kept in reserve.

The sound of Boruc's footfalls brought them all to their feet. "Well?" Vorrin asked.

"Looks clear enough," Boruc announced. "There are a few rocks down the hall, but nothing blocking the way." He patted the tunnel wall. "It's sturdier than it looks."

A sudden rumbling made Jendara leap forward, but she was too late. Rocks tumbled down from above, crashing as they closed off the tunnel a second time.

"Boruc!"

Dust filled the air. Coughing, blinded, she stumbled forward. Someone grabbed onto her.

"Give it a second to settle, Dara," Vorrin warned. A fist-sized hunk of rock tumbled out of the wall of rubble ahead of her—if Vorrin hadn't pulled her backward, she would have been brained.

Everything went quiet, except for a tiny patter of water coming down from the ceiling. Jendara had to force herself to breathe again.

"Boruc!" she shouted.

"I'm okay!" His voice was muffled, but sounded normal enough. "There's—" He had to stop to cough.

Jendara reached for Kran's lantern and studied the fall. She could see open space beyond. "Looks like the original cave-in just dropped another load of rock." She raised her voice. "Boruc, can you see anything? Is your tunnel still clear?"

He was quiet a moment. "Maybe." She could hear a little grunt. "I can't see too good. Rocks got me pinned right up against this wall. Lantern's all right, though!"

Jendara rolled her eyes. "Ridiculous man. Worried about his lantern at a time like this." She turned back to the others. "It looks clear to me, so I guess we keep hauling rocks. But be careful. Real damn careful."

They worked slowly, Jendara stopping them now and then to check on Boruc. His voice sounded more strained each time he answered. She hoped like hell they weren't going to get him crushed. There was no way to tell if moving a rock on this side of the heap might cause a rock on Boruc's to fall; it was like building a house of cards with her eyes closed and a crossbow bolt pressed to her temple. She tasted blood and knew she was biting her lip.

"This big stone is holding up a lot of loose bits," Tam pointed out. "If I can push it out of the way, we might be able to bring down half of the pile."

She studied the rock. He had a point. The rock looked smooth enough to pivot, and pushing on the right-hand side of the massive slab might make the left ease out enough to drop a massive load of gravel. The hole it could make would certainly be big enough for someone to climb through.

"Let's try it. But slow, right?"

He nodded and set his shoulder to the stone. "I'm pushing slowly."

Boruc cried out.

"Are you all right?"

"Something started pushing into my side. Scared me."

Jendara and Tam exchanged glances. Boruc had to be just on the other side of that stone. They were closer than she'd thought.

"Boruc, can you move away from that stone?"

"No." His voice was small. "It's hard to breathe," he admitted.

"Okay." She closed her eyes and thought for a second. "Okay, I have an idea. I hope it doesn't get anyone killed. Tam, give me a hand up."

Vorrin stepped in front of her. "What are you going to do?"

"We're almost through, right?" She pointed up at gravel Tam had hoped they could move. "I'm going to clear out some of those little rocks, squeeze through the wall, and see if I can get Boruc out of the way so you and Tam finish moving this big rock."

"But when you come out the other side, you'll be twelve feet up in the air."

"It'll be a jump," she agreed.

"You could bring down half the wall on your head."

"I don't think I will," she argued. She put her hands on his shoulders. "And if I do, I know you'll dig me out."

He sighed. "I don't like this."

"I know, but it's the best plan we've got right now. We need another set of hands on that far side, and I'm our best bet." She turned to Tam. "Can I climb up on your shoulders?"

He knelt and up she went. She tossed down a few handfuls of gravel before selecting a stone the size of her head. Her boots wobbled on Tam's shoulders as she worked it out. She could see through the wall now, although the hole she'd made was barely large enough for a child.

Well, it would get bigger as she forced herself through it. She grabbed onto the wall of rubble and pulled herself forward.

Everything shifted as she slid down the tumbling slope. She thought she'd catch herself on something, but she just slid down,

down, rocks tumbling and crashing all around her. She brought her arms up to protect her face and felt her boots catch on a ridge of rock. She hung for a second like a fish on a line. A rock hit her scalp, cut a gouge, and then spun off into the darkness.

Then her foot slipped and she tumbled down the last three or four feet, hitting the floor and tumbling in an awkward somersault. She lay still a few seconds and waited to see if her soul would escape her body.

"You okay?" Boruc gasped.

Her ears still worked. And she could make out a vague flicker on the rock beside her head. She blinked a few times—the faint light probably meant she could see. Now if only she could stop feeling everything. Her head pounded like a barbarian was using it for a drum and every inch of her skin stung and prickled. Her knees felt like they'd been put on backward.

"Jendara?" Vorrin's voice sounded panicked. "Jendara!"

"I'm—" She had to pause. "All right, I guess."

She got to her feet, although she hobbled more than walked the few steps toward the flicker of Boruc's lantern. As she got closer, she saw that a decorative support column on the side of the hallway had provided a bit of shelter for her friend. Most of the hallway really was clear, but rock had piled up on all sides of him, and the big slab of stone Tam had tried to lever was pressed right up against his round belly.

She pushed aside some of the debris. "I think we can get you out of here."

"Good thing," he whispered.

It took a few minutes to shift rock from the far side of him and from the back side of the column. She wasn't in any kind of shape to move quickly. Only a few years ago, a few bumps and bruises and sore muscles wouldn't have been anything she'd even notice, but those days were behind her. "I refuse to get any older than this," she grumbled.

"If our luck doesn't improve, you won't have to," Boruc growled.

She removed another rock, and Boruc let out a gasp of relief. "I can move!" He squeezed out of his prison. Jendara helped him across the debris-strewn hallway. They backed away from the wall, just to be safe.

"We're clear!" Jendara called. "Bring it down!"

The big stone slab began to pivot. The small hole Jendara had created in her passage over the wall widened, and then rock and dust rained down. Jendara had to grin a little, watching the display of destruction.

Boruc put his arm around her shoulders. She winced. "Don't even talk to me about getting old," he said. "Just tell me you've got some kind of liquor hidden in your pack."

Jendara gave a weak laugh. "Maybe our young companions came prepared."

This second tunnel proved as wide as the first, and in much better shape. The decorative columns stood tall and strong, and there was no further debris to slow the group, although here and there the top layer of stone flooring had buckled, leaving pockets for water to collect. Gardens of colorful sea anemones still waved in these pools, their tiny sticky fingers grasping for fallen bits of weed. They wouldn't live forever like this, not without some kind of wave to refill the pools and bring more food. But for now they were reminders of the beauty the sea could provide. It wasn't all crab-monsters and putrid corpses.

"This is amazing," Glayn murmured.

Jendara looked up from the pinks and greens of the anemones. The gnome wasn't looking at the tide pools; he walked with his head craned back, eyes wide. "What are you looking at?"

He pointed at the ceiling. She tipped back her head to squint into the shadows that mostly obscured the ceiling above. "More mica?"

"Tam, can you shine your light on this?" Glayn waited for the light to come close, then began to point out the constellations outlined in glittering minerals. "There. That's The Rose, I think." He broke into a half-run, splashing through the nearest pool. "And that's The Caravan. Zuna, come see!"

The navigator joined him. "Yeah, that's The Caravan, all right. I can't believe these frescoes weren't more damaged when this place flooded."

"Me, neither." Glayn ran ahead a few feet. "But look! This could be the Stair of Stars!"

Zuna strode faster to catch up with him. "It's almost like it's pointing at this—" She broke off and stabbed at the wall ahead. "Door."

They all came to a halt, staring at the massive set of double doors. The lower half of the doors was almost impossible to make out beneath the thick layer of dying anemones and shellfish encrusting them. The faint glimmer of gold showed here and there on the pale bonelike material whose carvings had once been lavishly decorated.

"They're like the Star Chapel's doors," Boruc observed.

"But not as well-preserved," Jendara pointed out. "I don't think we could open these even if we used a pickaxe."

"I can still make out some of the details." Glayn pointed to stone doorframe. "This looks like it was painted. Some of it looks like the glitter they used on the ceiling."

"More stars," Zuna interjected.

"Yes, exactly." He pointed to the top of the doors. "That's a crescent moon. And down *here*," he had to jump up to tap the midpoint of the door, "looks like some kind of procession. It's hard to make out the creatures in the procession, because the corrosion is so thick, but they're built a lot like people."

"Hey, look over there." Vorrin reached for Boruc's lamp and played it down the hall a few feet.

"That's a rib cage!" Jendara hurried toward the bones. "There are bones spread up the hallway, probably scattered by the water when it ran out." She moved to the nearest pool of water. "I'm looking at a jawbone, maybe some kind of arm bone, and—" She broke off.

She reached into the water. The sea anemones snapped shut their colors. Jendara could see the soft glint of steel sticking up from the sand and broken shells covering the bottom of the little pool. Her fingers closed on the smooth shape of a pommel. The rest of it was buried beneath the dirt, and bits of the rusted blade crumbled away as she eased it out of the water.

"A dagger," she announced.

"It looks heavy," Vorrin said, squatting down beside her to see better.

"That's why it didn't get washed out of the pool," she said. "The hilt's in pretty good shape. Could probably still be attached to a new blade."

In the background, she could hear Glayn still wondering over the doors. "That one's holding up something. I wish I could see better. Tam, could you move the light?"

Jendara tucked the dagger hilt into the small pocket of her pack just as a clatter sounded behind her.

"Tam!" Glayn shouted. Jendara spun around.

"I'm fine," Tam reassured them as he brushed himself off. "Under all the shells, this wall is in bad shape." Where he'd rested his weight on the wall, the stone showed a network of cracks, and had actually broken through in one spot, leaving a hole the size of Jendara's fist. Water must have eroded the stone on the back side of the wall, weakening it.

Zuna held up her lantern. "Good thing you didn't lean any harder on this; it looks like this wall's about to fall down." She squinted. "Is there something moving in there?"

Rock exploded from the wall as the head of a sea snake punched through and snapped shut on Zuna's arm. With a shriek, she whipped around and bashed the greenish snout with her fist.

It didn't let go, its long fangs digging into the thick leather of her coat.

She leaned back, straining to get free. Its neck looked thicker than her arm.

Jendara ran toward Zuna. Tam dropped his lantern and grabbed the beast. It wriggled and bucked.

"I can't get a good hold on it!" Tam lost his grip and stumbled backward.

Zuna bashed at the snake's head again, and then tried to wrench herself out of the beast's bite. "Somebody help me!"

Jendara unsheathed her sword. "Watch out!" She brought her sword down on the thing's exposed neck.

The tough hide blunted the blow, but at least the snake dropped Zuna's arm to focus its attention on its attacker. Blood spurted from the gash in its neck as it snapped at Jendara's face.

But she'd fought snakes before and was ready for the attack, her blade leveled at its eyes. The sword passed through its skull with a wet crunch as it skewered itself.

The snake went still.

Jendara pulled her blade free and wiped the worst of the gore off on the sea snake's green hide. She kicked the snake's drooping head, just to be sure. They were primitive creatures: she didn't trust one to die just because its brain had a hole in it. "I don't like snakes."

"Zuna, you okay?" Tam's voice was worried.

The navigator pulled off her jacket. "Anyone have a handkerchief? I'm bleeding."

"Kran's dog has mine," Boruc complained.

Vorrin handed her a spare kerchief. She hissed a little when it touched her wound. Like all their gear, the cloth was soaked with saltwater.

"Do you think it was poisonous?" she asked.

Jendara used her sword tip to lift the snake's head. She peered into its mouth. "The teeth don't look hollow, so I doubt it. Do you feel all right?"

Zuna shrugged. "It hurts. Guess I'll find out."

Jendara let out a wry laugh. Then she cocked her head. For a moment, she thought she'd heard the sea. She leaned a little closer to the hole in the wall. "Hey, Tam, come listen."

He put his ear up close. "Sounds like surf."

"Yeah, that's what I thought." She pushed some of the broken rock out from around the dead sea snake and tried to see deeper into the hole. The sound of waves came up to her, far away and somehow down, as if the sound traveled through some fissure in the ground to taunt her. "Somewhere beyond those doors, this leads to the ocean," she said.

"Or maybe another sea cave," Boruc suggested. "There's no way it's the grotto where we left the *Milady*, but who knows how many caves and fissures this island's got? The sea has a way of wearing things down."

"Yeah, if there's one thing the sea is good at," Jendara said, her voice dry, "it's finding weakness." She thought of her cottage as she said it, flooded and ruined. The sea had found Sorind's weaknesses that day, all right.

They began to follow the corridor away from the corpse of the dead sea snake and the doors that might never open. Vorrin leaned close to her. "We can rebuild, you know. Maybe we'll put the cottage on stilts."

"You knew just what I was thinking." She smiled at him, although in the dim light, he probably couldn't see her expression.

"I often do," he said.

They walked in comfortable silence for a few minutes. Then from the lead, Boruc announced: "I see a stairwell just ahead."

Jendara took a deep breath to clear her tired head. Perhaps this was finally it, the way up to the purple boulevard. It felt like days since they'd left the flooded prison, although if it hadn't been for the tunnel's collapse and their long work clearing it, they could have reached this point an hour ago.

"It's clear!" Boruc called.

Jendara's spirits rose a little.

11

THE MINDS OF PRISONERS

Jendara waved Yerka in front of her. The woman had kept quiet except for the occasional cough, and now Jendara gave her a closer look. Circles ringed her eyes and she held onto the wall as she trudged up each step.

"It's been a long day, hasn't it?" Jendara asked.

Yerka nodded. She wheezed a little as she climbed.

"When was the last time you—" Jendara paused, not quite sure how to ask. "I mean, has it been a long time since you were around humans?"

"There was another girl." Yerka paused and sniffled, making mucus rattle loudly in the back of her throat. "A few months ago. She died, though."

"Oh."

Yerka took a few more steps, then turned to look at Jendara. "Them that gets pregnant usually do. Childbirth is hard enough when it's human, ain't it?"

When it's human. The thought turned Jendara's stomach. But of course, that was where hybrids came from, wasn't it? From those kidnapped women like Sarni's mother and Yerka. Jendara forced her attention back to the woman.

"You've never borne a . . ." She searched for the right word.

"Nope. Body don't seem to work that way. Glad of it. Don't want to die."

Then she noticed: beyond Yerka's silhouette, a faint bloom of light showed. It wasn't lantern light, either, but the soft purple haze of the boulevard. "Look!" Jendara called out. "The sun's up." She felt a tired grin start to spread across her face. "Don't worry, Yerka—we're almost to the *Milady*. We can get you a nice meal and maybe a hot toddy for your cold, and hells, you can even go down and punch that hybrid bastard in the face if it'll make you feel better."

Yerka paused. "Hybrid?"

Jendara nudged her forward. "Yeah, we captured one of those half-ulat-kini. If you want—"

But they had reached the open hallway and she forgot what she was going to say in the pure excitement of seeing and feeling light. It may have been filtered through layers of grime and warped glass, but the lavender light of the boulevard felt as warm and fresh as a summer day. Laughing, Kran ran forward and Jendara left Yerka behind to run after him.

They stood together at the intersection of the two halls, reveling in the light, and Boruc joined them. "We're a bit north of the midpoint," he announced. "Between the big pool and the Star Chapel."

"I hadn't even noticed this cross-tunnel the last time we came down here," Jendara admitted.

"Neither did I." Vorrin tucked his thumbs in his sword belt, swiveling at the hips to scrutinize the length of the boulevard. "But I think there's one more headed off at the far end—we probably missed that one because we were distracted by the entrance to the Star Chapel—and I think there are two other tunnels closer to the stairs leading to the sea cave, including the one we took earlier."

Tam passed them to stand in the middle of the boulevard. "You don't really see them from over here," he said, surprised. "There's a lot of debris heaped up at the entrance to that far one."

Fylga began climbing up on the heap of debris, sniffing at the rotting sea weed and detritus. She grabbed a fragment of driftwood in her mouth and dashed down with it. Kran grabbed it from her and tossed it a few feet, as if they were on a completely ordinary beach on an ordinary day.

Jendara smiled. Kids were resilient, she had always maintained, and here was the living proof of it. They were good at making the best of things.

Then movement called her eye and she glanced over her shoulder. "Yerka? What's wrong?"

The rescued woman didn't look back. If anything, she ran faster toward the tunnel at the end of the hall.

"Is she afraid of the dog?" Vorrin asked. "Maybe she didn't notice Fylga in the dark.

"I'll get her!" Boruc called as he ran after Yerka.

"Wait!" Tam shouted, running after his friend and the frightened woman, his lantern light bobbing as he went. They disappeared into the cross-tunnel.

"I guess we go after them," Vorrin said.

Then Fylga began barking.

Jendara swiveled to face her son and his dog. Fylga's lips pulled back from her teeth in a snarl, and the hair on her back rose up in damp prickles. Kran looked around, unsure what the dog sensed.

The soft scrape of chitin against stone made Jendara turn to face the same direction as the dog: toward the tunnel they'd just left. She drew her sword.

"That door couldn't hold forever," she said.

Then the crab-thing stalked out onto the boulevard. Out of the water, it was no less terrifying. It stood a good ten feet tall, its thick, armored legs like an extrusion of the stony floor itself. Its carapace nearly blocked the entrance to the smaller side tunnel; Jendara had no idea how it had gotten through the rock falls and the stairwell to reach them. It raised its cracked pincer, clacking it menacingly.

At least its humanoid hand was too badly injured for it to use. She should have never have left it alive back there. Nothing with such evil eyes could resist revenge.

"Get Kran out of here!" she shouted and charged the beast.

Her blade slipped into the joint between its two massive leg segments, and the creature staggered a little. She darted sideways, but the beast moved faster than she expected, its claw smashing into her side. She tumbled against a heap of stone.

"No!" Vorrin bellowed. Sword in hand, he launched himself at the crab-thing.

The creature caught him by his wounded arm, flinging him out of the way like a bug. It wanted Jendara. That was all it cared about.

"Big mistake," she growled, scrambling higher up the hill of debris.

It charged her.

With a roar, she leaped off the crest of rock and landed on the beast's shoulders, sword plunging into the gap where the thing's carapace ended and its armored skull began. The creature stopped. She twisted her blade, grinning at the sick squelching it made. Green ichor welled up from the wound.

The crab-thing toppled against the rocky pile. Jendara jumped onto the rocks, ripping her sword free.

"You dead yet?"

The creature didn't move.

Jendara's pulse beat hard in her ears, the wild energy of battle cooling in her veins. By the ancestors, it felt good to finish off that thing! She climbed to the base of the heap and nudged the creature's leg with her toe. It flopped a little, but the beast was clearly dead.

Her brain snapped out of its fight-fueled bliss. "Vorrin!" She ran to his side.

"I'm fine," he said, sitting up with wince. "My arm—"

"You ripped your stitches." She helped him up. "That's a lot of blood. We'd better get you back to the *Milady* so Glayn can sew you up again."

She squeezed his bloody arm tight and led him down the hall.

"What about Tam and Boruc?"

"They'll find Yerka soon," she said, "and they know the way back." She glanced over her shoulder. "If they forget, they can just follow the blood trail."

A small white-and-yellow shape waited for them at the top of the stairs leading to the sea cave. Glayn and Tam had succeeded in getting Kran to safety, but apparently Fylga didn't follow Jendara's orders. The dog wagged her tail as the pair approached.

Jendara found herself surprisingly glad to see her, too.

Jendara screwed the lid on the jug of whale oil and put the jug down by her feet. Outside the mouth of the grotto, noon's brilliance sparkled on the water. She guessed she'd been sitting on this deck for a good forty minutes or so, waiting for Vorrin and Zuna to come back from their search for Yerka, Boruc, and Tam. She'd kept herself busy as best she could. She and Glayn had repaired and replenished all their exploratory supplies. The gnome came hustling back from the cargo hold with another roll of rope under his arm, and she waved at him from the bench she'd dragged over by the gangplank. "That's the last of the lanterns. They're all topped up."

"We'll be glad to have them," Glayn said. He picked up the nearest pair of lanterns and then put them back down. "Dara? You all right?"

She looked past him, out over the dock and the beach. Vorrin and Zuna weren't back yet. "I don't know, Glayn. This place is getting to me."

"I think it's fascinating." He sat down and laughed at her expression. "Don't get me wrong: it stinks like a fish's latrine and it's about as dark. But don't you think it's incredibly interesting? Who were these people? What was it like when they lived here?"

She shrugged a shoulder. "The buildings on the top side were pretty amazing."

"I wish I could have seen more of them. Boruc showed me some sketches he made of the ones on the hill. All those star and tentacle designs. Amazing stuff."

She thought of the skeletons they'd found down in that prison. "Not all of it's amazing. They spent a lot of effort making those prison cells—I think they even used magic on the bars."

"And did you notice how much more worn the lower levels were than the purple boulevard?"

"The lower levels were shabbier. Even the stairs were plainer," she mused. "If I had to guess, I'd say that was where the poor lived."

"Rough to have to live down here, knowing the splendor that was up above," Glayn noted.

"There are haves and have-nots in every city," Jendara pointed out. "I always think islanders are so fair, but Sarni had to steal her first pair of shoes."

"I miss her," he said. "She could always make me laugh."

"I brought her on board to protect her." Jendara bit her lip. "I haven't done a very good job protecting anyone."

"You'll find her," he said. "I know you will."

"I don't know, Glayn," she admitted. "It's like I'm fighting the island itself and I can't win. Every time we make a plan, something comes up to ruin it."

The gnome put his little hand on her knee. "You'll figure it out." Then he frowned and jumped up from the bench. "There's Vorrin and Zuna."

She sprang up, too. "Where are the others?" she shouted.

Without a word, Vorrin held out his fist, closed around the shaft of a vicious-looking trident. It looked just like the one their prisoner had used to fight off the fish-folk in the Star Chapel.

"Ulat-kini," Jendara growled.

Vorrin looked grim. "Let's go check in with our prisoner."

They prepared the galley for the ulat-kini hybrid, setting up a chair with enough room around it for a questioner to move free, and lit enough lanterns to bring a sense of daylight to the proceedings. No one had suggested they bring in so many lamps. Every one had simply found themselves setting a lantern or two into one of the galley's mirrored sconces, or finding a place for a light to hang from one of the many storage pegs.

Jendara knew a thing or two about interrogations. She just hadn't realized her crew had learned so much from her.

Jendara took her time getting ready. She studied Kran when she thought he wasn't looking. He had claimed the ulat-kini had rescued him from the fish-folk, and he looked worried as he sat on the edge of a dining table, waiting for things to begin.

Jendara had her doubts about the creature's purported heroism. Kran had to have felt overwhelmed, alone in a dark and unfamiliar place after Sarni's disappearance. It would have been easy for him to misconstrue the creature's motivations as altruistic when really it was simply trying to defend itself from the fish-folk.

Still, he was her boy. She didn't like seeing him so miserable.

Zuna swore as she and Vorrin dragged the ulat-kini out of the storage room. Kran dropped to the ground beside the dining table, huddling next to his dog.

Jendara hurried to the cupboard above the galley's tiny stove and took out a pouch. The others were focused on securing the ulat-kini's bonds. Kran pulled Fylga close, rubbing his chin on her floppy yellow ears. Jendara slipped a piece of toffee from the pouch, put it in her pocket, and crossed to her boy. He looked up at her with an anxious expression and then quickly brought his gaze back to the dog.

Jendara reached out to stroke the dog. Fylga's coat was softer than it looked, sleek and smooth and dense beneath Jendara's hand. Jendara reached for the toffee and held it out to the boy.

"Can we talk later?"

He hesitated for a second before taking the candy. Then he gave a stiff nod. Jendara smiled at him.

"Do you speak Taldane?" Vorrin asked. They'd made a plan in case it didn't, but the creature surprised them all with a nod of its head.

Jendara joined Vorrin. The ulat-kini stared back at them, its—his, Jendara corrected—face unreadable. His cheeks and chin looked very nearly human, a strange contrast to his broad, pale-lipped mouth and bulging eyes. The pale fuzz of his eyebrows against the greenish-gray tone of his skin did nothing to improve his appearance.

"What's your name?" Jendara asked.

The ulat-kini's eyes jerked toward her. "Korthax," he answered.

"Korthax," Vorrin repeated. "When we found you with our boy—those creatures you were fighting. Do you know what they are?"

Korthax nodded. He coughed. "May I have some water?"

His accent was thick and his words stumbling, but his grammar surprised Jendara. Korthax must have had regular contact with humans for his Taldane to be so good.

No one spoke while Zuna scooped a mugful from the hogshead and held it to his lips. He slurped noisily and then pulled away, water dripping down his chin.

"Thank you."

Zuna set her back to one of the ceiling supports. She pulled out her belt knife and began to clean her nails. With her height and broad shoulders, it had to be an unnerving sight for the creature.

Korthax stared at Vorrin, pointedly ignoring Zuna. "We call them 'deep ones.'"

"So, these deep ones. Why were you fighting them?" Vorrin asked.

"I think maybe they live here," Korthax said. "We did not know this before we came with Ahrzur and his crew."

"Ahrzur? Who's that?" Jendara found herself leaning in, her neck and shoulders tense.

The ulat-kini looked around at the faces staring at him. "You think I just tell you everything because I am afraid of you. You all have weapons nearby and *she*—" he jerked his chin in Zuna's direction, "already has a knife in her hand." His thick lip curled. "You make me sick."

Vorrin raised a fist. "You damned scum."

Kran stepped forward, waving his arms. Everyone stared at the boy. He took out his chalk and wrote in his clearest hand: *He HELPED me. Don't forget.*

Glayn folded his arms across his chest. "And why did you help him? Doesn't seem like the kind of thing thieves like you do."

"I—" Korthax shook his head. "I run from the deep ones. They are dangerous. They kill for their gods. Like me, the boy runs. I not let the deep ones get him. Is right to save small ones."

Jendara narrowed her eyes. "So you were just trying to save my son because he's young? It's not because you wanted to steal him like one of your people stole Tam and Boruc and Yerka?"

"Yerka?" Korthax went rigid. "What do you mean, Yerka?"

"Your people wanted her back," Jendara said. Her voice climbed with every word: "You had her locked up in a filthy boat and we saved her, and you didn't like that." She stopped and took a deep breath. Her nails were biting into her palm. It wasn't time to use violence on him yet. She had to get more information, first.

"No." Korthax shook his head again. "No, you not understand. Yerka is wife of my brother. That boat is her home. She is not locked up."

"Of course she's locked up!" Jendara snapped. "You think she would stay with you slimy things of her own free will?"

"That is how you see us," Korthax said quietly. "As things. Not people."

Vorrin sighed and held up the trident. "Let's cut the crap. I found this trident in one of the hallways beyond the Star Chapel where we found you. It's an ulat-kini's, I know it. Now tell us how your people get around on this island."

"Or what?" Korthax's eyes flashed. "You will kill me?"

"I might," Jendara said. "You've taken my friends. If I don't get them back soon . . ."

The ulat-kini smirked. He looked from Jendara to Vorrin, then back again. "My people have something you want. And you have something I want. Maybe we make a deal."

Jendara didn't like the ulat-kini's smug expression. "I don't know that you're in a position to negotiate."

"I am. I know things you want to know." He smiled, showing pointed yellow teeth. "I know how many ulat-kini on island. I know secret route that Ahrzur and his black robes shared with us. I know if black robes get their hands on you, you will be made slave like others Ahrzur getting. I think that makes me worth more alive than dead." His smile widened, and for a moment, despite the ferocious teeth, he looked so much like a smarmy merchant that Jendara could almost forget he wasn't the same species she was.

"Why would you want to deal with us?" Glayn suddenly asked. "After all, we don't even think you're *people*."

Korthax chuckled. "I do not trust you. But my brother . . . he turns our people against me." His face darkened. "I should have become leader after Father die, but with my uncle's help my brother stole place from me. I make him pay. I see him hu—humiliated like he did me. I am sure his wife took your friends."

"Yerka?" Zuna snorted. "I find that hard to believe."

"Ahrzur took the other ulat-kini—those of us who are not hybrids—to collect humans for his project. Your friends would be very valuable to him. Yerka would be rewarded."

Jendara looked from the hybrid to Vorrin and back. She didn't like how easily the creature had shared his information, but that didn't mean it was worthless. And if there were some kind of power struggle going on inside the ulat-kini community, perhaps that would make it easier to get their crew back.

"We go back to camp," Korthax said. "I take you there. You can keep me tied up. Once you see Yerka in action, you will believe. She is clever. Hungry for power. You will see."

He closed his mouth and watched them think, seemingly content to wait.

Jendara narrowed her eyes and beckoned to the others. She lowered her voice. "There's a trick somewhere in this, but I'm willing to go back to the camp."

"We don't have any other leads," Vorrin whispered, "and I'm not eager to try the route you took earlier. They'll be watching that now."

"And the sewage tunnels are out, too," Zuna added. "That last passage was too unstable for us to risk it again."

Vorrin turned back to the ulat-kini hybrid. "It's a deal," he said. "But if anything goes wrong, I won't hesitate to stick my sword through your slimy little heart."

Korthax grinned. "All hearts are slimy. That is something our species have in common."

Jendara marched to the storage room and opened the door. "Let's put him away for the night. I'm sick of listening to him."

Their eyes met, prisoner's and jailer's. Something flickered in the depths of Korthax's protruding orbs. Jendara had the uncomfortable feeling it was laughter.

12

LIFE IN THE DEAD CITY

Jendara stood on the shingled beach, watching the waves grow taller and taller, until they scraped the night sky. She knew she had to get back to Kran and warn him a tsunami was coming, but her feet had fused to the rock. She couldn't move.

Jendara! the waves called, in Sarni's desperate voice. *Help me, Jendara! Help me!*

"I promise I'll take care of you!" Jendara called, struggling to lift her feet. "I'm coming, Sarni!"

The wave rolled closer, tearing the stars from the sky until their lights burned within the depths of the sea. The star-filled wave crawled toward her, the foam on its surface drawing together into a dozen faces, a hundred screaming faces, and she knew each and every of them, and they were all begging her to help them, but she couldn't move and in a minute she would drown in all their terrible need—

Jendara sat up, breathing hard. For second, she wasn't sure where she was, and then she realized she was in her own bed inside her cabin on the *Milady*. Darkness filled the room like tepid water. She forced herself not to hold her breath.

Just a nightmare, she told herself. The wind shrieked outside the cabin's windows. She shivered. Her linen shirt had soaked through with sweat.

Vorrin snored softly beside her. She eased out of bed. Her nap was over—there was no way she could go back to sleep after that dream. Every muscle in her back and legs felt tight, and her jaw hurt. She slipped on her clothes and stepped outside without waking even the dog.

Off toward the bow, she could make out the soft glow of the lantern. The crew had all agreed they needed a few hours shut-eye before risking a trip into enemy territory, and she and Zuna had drawn straws for the two short watches. Jendara thought she'd sleep heavily when she'd finished her rounds, but apparently she'd been wrong. Perhaps it was the screeching of the wind. It certainly seemed louder now.

Jendara crossed to the bench by the gangplank and pulled her jacket more tightly around her. She couldn't help remembering that room underground where she'd heard Sarni's voice, only to realize her voice carried on a wind blowing from ancestors-only-knew where. She didn't want to think about what might be happening to the girl.

Jendara scrubbed her cheeks with her fingers. Before they'd come to this island, it would have been hard to imagine Sarni finding any kind of trouble she couldn't handle. Trouble might as well have been Sarni's middle name. Jendara had first met the girl in a tavern, stealing purses from sea captains while she lost wildly at cards. Then she got so drunk celebrating she fell off a table and lost all the purses. That girl could handle anything but herself.

Jendara gave a little laugh and stretched out her legs. The lantern approached, and she saw Zuna headed toward her. Jendara braced herself for more of the woman's bad attitude.

"Hello, Zuna."

"Hello, Jendara." The tall woman stood in front of Jendara, her lantern glaring down into Jendara's eyes. "May I sit for a moment? I don't want to shirk my duties, but I wouldn't mind resting my feet."

Jendara made room for her on the bench. "Of course."

The bench creaked a little as Zuna took a seat. Jendara sat quietly waiting for her night vision to return. The breeze shrieked and hissed in the background, reminding her unpleasantly of her dream.

"What were you laughing about just now?" Zuna put the lantern on the decking between their feet. Its glow gave the deck a sense of warmth.

Jendara shrugged. "I was thinking about the first time I met Sarni." The answer sounded curt, so she added: "She's spirited."

Zuna rubbed the toe of her boot against the back of her calf and then studied its surface. "I didn't like her at first. She was trouble."

"You're right," Jendara agreed. "But she had so much potential I had to bring her on. She's a smart kid."

"Yeah," Zuna agreed. "And she's one of us now."

It was an opening Jendara had to take. She didn't want to coddle Zuna, but she needed her. "Look, Zuna, this crew is like my family. I get pretty stupid about my family. I don't know if you've noticed."

Zuna gave a dry laugh. "Maybe a bit."

"Back there at the ulat-kini camp, I was worried about Vorrin. I shouldn't have cut you down like that."

Zuna turned to face Jendara. "You and Sarni are a lot alike. I didn't like you much when I first met you, either. I'd known Vorrin for years, worked with him on two different ships. I thought you'd get him in trouble."

"I'd put trouble behind me by the time you met me."

"That's what you say, but I think you've got some kind of magnet for trouble. You don't mean for things to happen, but they do when you're around."

Jendara couldn't read the other woman's face or her tone. "Do you think I *asked* to have my house flooded, or to come here and get attacked by fish people? If so, you're crazy, Zuna."

Zuna shrugged. "I call it like I see it. Before I met you, I'd never been attacked by a pirate or seen a goblin. I've led a nice quiet life. I go to sea, I get time off, I spend my money on my lady. But when I'm around you, all kinds of excitement breaks out."

Jendara opened her mouth to protest and then went quiet. Like it or not, her own history argued that Zuna was right.

Zuna let out a face-breakingly wide yawn. "Sorry. I tried to sleep, but I kept having these weird dreams. Spiders, mostly. By the gods, I hate spiders."

"Me, too," Jendara agreed.

"Jendara!" Vorrin shouted from the captain's cabin, his voice hoarse and urgent. "Where are you?"

Jendara sprang up and ran to the cabin door. Vorrin pulled her inside. "I didn't know what to do," he said.

By the soft light of the lowered lantern, she could see Kran crouched in the corner, clawing at the wall and whimpering. Fylga nosed at the boy, but he didn't stop. Jendara knelt beside him and stroked his cheek. "Kran? What's wrong?"

"He won't wake up," Vorrin explained. "He was walking around, knocking things over. That's what woke me. I tried to get him out of it, but he just dropped to the ground and started crawling around."

"Kran." Jendara shook the boy's shoulder. "Kran!"

The boy pulled away. His eyes stared at nothing, their pupils huge and black. His hands scrabbled before him as if he could dig his way through the air.

Jendara seized hold of his hands. "Wake up," she said, gently. "Wake up, Kran." His hands twisted in her grip, but she held him fast. "Wake up."

He suddenly jerked and blinked. He looked around himself, confused.

"Kran? Are you awake?"

He rubbed his eyes and looked around again. Finally, he nodded.

"Do you know where you are?"

He leaned to see around Jendara, the chart table, his empty cot, Vorrin and Jendara's unmade bed. He nodded again.

Jendara eased back to sit on his cot. The dog clambered up into Kran's lap to lick at his face and paw his chest. After a minute he pushed the dog away and reached for the slate he'd left beneath his cot.

His handwriting slanted tiredly. *Sleepwalking?*

"Yes," Jendara answered. "And you wouldn't wake up."

Bad dream, he wrote. *Something in a pit moving. I threw rocks but it didn't stop.* He paused a second and wiped his hand across the slate. *It wanted to eat everything. You. Vorrin. The whole world.*

"I had a nightmare, too," Vorrin said. "Something was trying to bring down the *Milady*. When you were knocking things over in your sleep, I thought it was really happening for a second."

Jendara cocked her head. "I had some bad dreams, too, and so did Zuna. I don't like that."

Vorrin shrugged. "We've been stuck on this island for two days; I'm not really surprised we're having nightmares."

"This *island* is a nightmare," Jendara agreed. She paused, looking from Kran to Vorrin. "We have to stick together here."

Kran cocked his head, not sure what she meant.

"You have to listen to me while we're here. You did a good job while we were looking for Vorrin, and I'm proud of you, but we're going to be in really dangerous territory once we go back to the ulat-kini. I don't want you to try to be a hero."

Kran tipped up his slate so she couldn't see what he wrote while he wrote it. He looked at the words for a long moment and then turned it around. *You are.*

She laughed. "I'm a lot older than you, Kran. Give it time."

He shook his head and wrote again. *Even when you were a kid.*

She sighed. "It only sounds like that in the stories. Trust me, if I hadn't had my father to bail me out, I'd have gotten myself killed by the time I was six."

Vorrin smiled at her. "I don't think you're giving yourself enough credit. I'm thinking five, tops."

Jendara laughed again and got up off the cot to stand by her husband. "I owe you an apology, too. I wasn't careful back there with that crab-monster. I wasn't thinking about what would happen if I got hurt. If we're going to be a family, I can't go off half-cocked. We're a team."

"Well, you're the one with all the experience," he said.

She stepped in closer. Vorrin's brown eyes twinkled at her, the lantern's glow softening his sharp features. He smelled of her laundry soap, the stuff she made every summer when the lavender bloomed.

Someone rapped on the cabin door. With a sigh, Jendara opened it a crack.

"Dara? Are you all awake in there?"

"Yes, Glayn." As she answered, Vorrin sighed and reached for his jacket.

"I started some food. Couldn't sleep, so I figured a bit of belly timber was in order."

She opened the door wider and frowned down at him. "You had nightmares, too?"

He nodded. "But I've got biscuits baking, so I figured I'll be fine in no time."

Jendara had to agree with him on that one.

Jendara piled the clean plates back onto the shelf. Glayn had been right: a big, hot breakfast had been just what they needed. There was nothing like a full belly and ordinary domestic tasks to clear away the fug of bad dreams. Now Kran, who had just finished the washing up, sat with Glayn at the big table working some kind of elaborate cat's cradle; Vorrin had a book out, and even the prisoner looked content as he munched a biscuit and a slice of ham.

Zuna, though, sat on her own, face covered by her long black braids. Jendara brought the last of the biscuits over and watched the other woman as she took a pair of pliers and painstakingly crushed the silver bell at the end of a braid.

"Need a hand?" Jendara asked. She held out half of the biscuit. "I could help with the back."

Zuna shook her braids back over her shoulders and then took the biscuit. "If you don't mind. I got a lot of hair."

Jendara reached for a braid. "Can we just take them out?"

"Don't have time," Zuna said. She tapped one of the shorter braids by her chin and made the bell chime. "It'd take hours to finish all the ends, and we need to be quiet."

Jendara squeezed the second silver bell between the pliers' powerful jaws. "I'm sorry." Zuna had never set out to be a fighter or an adventurer, but working on the *Milady* had forced her to become one. It wasn't fair.

Then something shiny caught in between two braids distracted her. "Hey, look at this."

Jendara pulled out a thread, long and shimmering, and held it where Zuna could see. Thicker than a string of silk or linen, the thread caught the light and broke it up like glitter.

"Shiny," Jendara mused. "Where'd it come from?"

"Was that in my hair?" Zuna squinted at the thread. "Must have brushed off of something. It's pretty."

Jendara reached for her empty tea mug. "Let's keep it. It reminds me of . . . something. I'm not sure what, but maybe it'll come to me."

With a sigh, Vorrin closed his book. "If everyone's finished, we better start gearing up."

"Oops. I'm almost done." Jendara hurried to crush the last few bells, and gave Zuna an awkward smile as she passed over the pliers. "I'll miss the sound of them."

Zuna shrugged. "I'll probably just get beads the next time I get my hair done." She turned away to put the pliers back in her pack.

Jendara wasn't sure what to make of the other woman's response, but there wasn't time to chatter. She beckoned Kran over. "Do you have some extra dried beef for Fylga? We don't know how long this will take."

He nodded. Then he reached for his slate. *You like Fylga now?*

She made a face. "Don't push me, kid. Now get up on deck and make sure everyone gets a lantern."

He hurried away, a spring in his step. He might not have gotten a solid nap, but at his age, he recovered faster than the rest of them. Jendara's limbs felt leaden with tiredness, but there was nothing for it. Boruc, Tam, and Sarni were depending on her.

She made her way up to the deck. Outside the cave, she could see the clouds jamming up in the sky.

"Rainy raids are the luckiest," Jendara murmured. Her father had sworn by that particular bit of folk wisdom. Her hand went to the handle of her belt axe. It wasn't the timeworn weapon she'd inherited from her father, but it reminded her of him anyway. He would have approved of its craftsmanship. A sudden lump rose in her throat. It had been only two days since her birthday, but it felt like a hundred, two hundred. Boruc was missing. Tam and Sarni, too. Three of her best friends, stolen from her by this island.

"Just what we need, right? Shit weather." Zuna looked in her pack. "Glad I packed a scarf."

Jendara had to smile at that. She'd grown up on these islands, but Zuna and Glayn were newcomers to this part of the world. Ice and snow were still an enemy to them. She glanced over at Glayn. He was already wearing the woolen cap she'd knitted for him a few years ago. Suddenly she felt less gloomy.

"Let's go get our friends," she said.

They made their way up to the main boulevard in comfortable silence, but once they passed the crab-thing's corpse, Vorrin pushed Korthax out in front. They'd tied a rope to his waist to make sure he wouldn't cut and run. "Which tunnel do we take?"

Korthax gave his elbow a flap; his hands were bound in front of him and lashed to his waist so he could move them no more than a few inches. "At end."

Vorrin looked back at the others. "That's where we found the trident."

Jendara's hand went to her axe. She didn't like Korthax and she didn't like his little deal. But at least they were on the right track.

They entered the cross-tunnel. This one was broader than either of the two they had explored, the floor the smoothest. Only a few puddles showed in the light of Glayn's lantern as he moved at the head of the group, Vorrin and Korthax on his heels. Jendara looked up at the ceiling, lost in the darkness above. This tunnel didn't seem like the other cross-tunnels at all. With its high ceiling and finer stonework, it had the same gloomy grace as the main boulevard.

Kran tapped her elbow and pointed to Fylga. The dog kept her nose close to the ground, sniffing hard. He raised an eyebrow.

"This is where Yerka went yesterday," Jendara mused. She watched Fylga snuffle at the first closed door. Jendara leaned close and listened. She didn't hear anything except the whisper of the wind. She gave the door a shove and felt it swing open. The heavy stone slab moved far more easily than the other doors she'd tried opening on this island.

Fylga trotted in and went immediately to the farthest wall, darting from place to place while sniffing hard. Jendara played her light around the room. "No debris."

"It's like someone cleaned it out," Zuna said. She stooped down beside the spot Fylga was examining. "I can't tell why the dog's so interested."

They left the room behind, although Kran had to urge Fylga out. Jendara eased the door shut and watched the dog move up the hallway, pausing to sniff every few steps. Jendara brought out her handaxe. It wasn't just the dog's behavior that made her feel uncomfortable and exposed. It was the strangely clean room and hallway. The tunnel felt well used and well tended, somehow horribly alive inside this rotting shell of a city.

"Wait up, Glayn," Vorrin called out.

Jendara hurried to catch up. The tunnel ahead split, one hallway bending off to the right and one staying mostly straight. The two hallways narrowed, and the ceilings descended to the height of most of the others. Their floors still looked preternaturally well maintained and clean.

"Which way do we go?" Vorrin asked the ulat-kini.

Korthax turned from left to right, clearly uncomfortable. "I only come this way once."

"Which I'm certain was a memorable experience," Vorrin said in a dangerous voice. "Which way?"

"Uh—straight." The ulat-kini took a few steps into the hallway ahead. "Yes. Straight."

Kran caught Jendara's sleeve. He jerked his head in Fylga's direction. She was nosing around the entrance of the right-hand path.

She looked from dog to prisoner. Vorrin and Glayn had followed the ulat-kini into the other hallway, and their light was already fading. "I guess we can double back if he's wrong," she said. Her gut told her to follow the dog, but she wanted to see where Korthax would lead them.

Kran raised his eyebrows. But they both followed the light and the ulat-kini hybrid.

13

STAR TAKER

The hallway ended in a set of double doors. No mollusks coated their plain stone faces, no corrosion sealed them to the floor. They looked in perfect working order. After passing so many ruined or disfigured doorways in these tunnels, Jendara had started to take for granted that most everything on the island was falling apart. These doors and the doors to the Star Chapel stood out.

Korthax paused in front of the doors. "They look different," he murmured. "Cleaner, maybe. But this is way. I am sure of it."

Zuna tested the door with one hand. "It's not locked."

"Then let's go," Vorrin said.

Zuna pushed open the rightmost of the doors. The dank smell of mold and mildew wafted out, stronger than any place they'd yet explored. Kran made a disgusted face. Glayn strode inside, his lantern gleaming amber in a dimly lit chamber with a vast, high ceiling. A kind of mezzanine ran around the room, its floors broken in several places, and the stairs were long gone. Half-dissolved metal brackets in the walls suggested where shelves must have once run around the room. A corroded ladder, still showing a glint of bronze here and there, hung at an angle against the far wall.

"A library," Glayn whispered.

Kran stepped out into the center of the room, craning his neck back to stare at the ceiling. His mouth had fallen open.

Jendara tipped her head back, too. A faint gray light emanated from the ceiling, where a hazed and milky glass allowed daylight to penetrate the aged space. Perhaps it wasn't glass at all—it could have been alabaster, she supposed, and missed Boruc more than ever.

When the island was young, this room must have been filled with light. She could imagine it: soft white light shining down into the open room, lamps brightening the areas tucked away beneath the mezzanine. There was room in this dead library for thousands of volumes, a vast storehouse of wisdom.

"Amazing," she breathed.

Kran took her hand and pointed out details around the milky skylight that she hadn't noticed: simple but beautiful golden bas-reliefs of the creatures and beings from which the major constellations took their names. Not all of the gold-leafed figures were ones she recognized; whoever had built this library had certainly envisioned the night sky in a way far different from her own people. She had to wonder what stars were contained in the octopus or the great shark. Some of the animals weren't even identifiable.

"It's so old," Vorrin said. "And all of it's ruined. Just flooded away."

Kran began to move around the edges of the room, studying the heaps of debris. Jendara joined him. While most of the stuff was unrecognizable, merely corroded metal or rotting shards of wood, sometimes she could make a guess at a thing or two: a pewter weather vane caught her eye, sticking out from beneath a heap of fallen floor tiles; a marble bowl, perhaps a mortar, sat unharmed and upright.

Kran wrote on his slate: *Science*.

Jendara shook her head. "I don't understand."

Not just a library, he wrote. *A school.*

The others' voices echoed off the stone walls around them. She frowned, and looked from the weather vane to the mortar. "How do you know?"

Kran reached for his chalk, but his eyes suddenly went wide. The slap of feet on stone spun Jendara around. A deep one lunged out of the shadows in the corner of the room, a bone-white trident leveled at her.

And behind were more of them.

She drew her sword and ran toward the hulking things. The smell of fish and dampness rolled off them in a wash of stink. Jendara's blade met the trident with a thud that vibrated up into her wrists. She wrenched the trident out of its bearer's hands and sent it clattering onto the ground. The creature's bulging eyes widened. Before it could respond, she brought her sword back around and slashed through its green belly. The deep one dropped like a stone.

Another was on her before she could even step over the dead one's blood. The deep one clawed at her with its webbed fingers, its spiky nails slicing into her cheeks. Her skin immediately burned: had it tipped its claws with poison? Jendara squeezed her eyes shut in a desperate attempt to protect them and smashed her forehead against the deep one's slimy cheek, driving it backward. It lost its grip on her face. She opened her eyes and realized the thing had slipped on its comrade's innards.

"Dara!" Vorrin cried out, but she didn't turn her attention away from her attacker. It was still too close for her to get in a good blow with her sword. Jendara drove her fist into its unprotected face and sent it reeling back a step. She made a one-handed chop at its leg and heard the gratifying splintering of bone.

The deep one went down, crying out in its gurgling language. She skewered it through the chest and then leaped away, turning to face the battle. There were at least four more deep ones in a mass. Vorrin and Zuna had gotten Kran between them and Glayn closed off one side of their group. For now their swords could keep the creatures off her son, but they were outnumbered, and Glayn lacked the reach of the hulking deep ones.

Jendara went stiff. Where in all hells was Korthax?

She spun around. The ulat-kini, still bound and now on his back in the blood of the two fallen creatures, grappled with a large, heavily muscled deep one. Its dorsal fin glistened in the pale light, and the spines jutting from it looked wickedly sharp. Korthax bit down on his attacker's gills and the thing hissed with pain.

So Korthax hadn't run. She supposed she'd have to help the ulat-kini, but if she misjudged her blow, she risked killing him.

The deep one suddenly head-butted Korthax. The ulat-kini lost his grip and fell backward. The bigger creature grinned evilly.

"Stay down!" Jendara barked and made a deep lunge. Her sword pierced the side of the deep one's head and passed straight through to the other side. The creature blinked once, and then its legs and arms began to jerk.

Korthax rolled out from under the seizing deep one. He jumped to his feet. "The boy!"

Jendara kicked the deep one off her blade and turned to follow him. The ulat-kini threw himself into the thick of battle, shouldering a willowy deep one out of his way. In the tumult, she could just make out Kran's slight figure. Over the roar of her own pulse in her ears, she could hear Fylga's angry growl.

The enemy's attention was entirely on the knot of fighters. That was their mistake. Jendara slashed through a deep one's neck. For a second she felt her sword catch on its collarbone, just as it had back in the Star Chapel, but she slid it free. She glanced around. Vorrin and Zuna held off their attackers; Zuna had cut enough holes in her adversary to turn him a new color. To her left, Glayn drove his dagger into the leg of a deep one and danced aside as a fountain of blood sprayed out.

Jendara looked up just in time to see Vorrin slash at the deep one facing him. The dead deep one collapsed, and Vorrin paused, scanning the room, then wiped his blade on the creature's shoulder with an expression of distaste. "That's the last of them. Where in all hells did they come from?"

"They came from over there." Jendara strode into the shadowy corner where the creatures had appeared. She hadn't noticed any exits when she'd first entered, but she'd been distracted. Kran moved to pass her, and she grabbed him by the arm, pulling him to her for a quick hug. She had wanted to protect him, but she had to admit she'd made the wrong choice. She'd left his side to charge into battle when she should have backed them both into a corner and let the enemy come to her.

He wriggled in her grip. She squeezed him hard enough to feel the air go out of his lungs and then let him go. The boy rolled his eyes.

"Hey," Glayn called out. "There's a set of stairs here!"

They hurried across the library to the narrow flight of stairs set into the far wall. Glayn stooped to shine a bit of light down them.

"Look at that." Zuna pointed to two rust-colored bumps set into the floor. "I bet those were hinges. This was probably covered by some kind of trapdoor that fell apart hundreds of years ago."

"A secret door," Glayn mused. "That would explain why it's so narrow."

Korthax took a step forward. "It goes down long way, to an opening by the camp. We swim a bit."

Vorrin grabbed his arm. "How far is a bit?"

The ulat-kini looked around the group, his round eyes profoundly froglike. "You can all swim, can't you?"

Vorrin narrowed his eyes at him.

A clinking sound distracted Jendara from the incipient argument. Kran was still behind the group, and she knew before she even turned around that he had been poking at the heaps of debris.

"What did you find?"

He half turned from the heap he knelt beside and waved her over. As she got closer, she could see the remains of what must have been a stone bench built into the wall. Broken bits of flooring from the mezzanine overhead had fallen onto it, but a crack ran down the stone front, and now Kran pried at the crack with his dagger. Jendara squatted beside him.

"It's hollow, huh?"

He nodded. He'd already broken off a bit of the stone, widening the crack. Jendara reached for the lantern on her belt and lit it while Kran broke off another bit of rock.

Jendara held the lantern close to the crack. "Can you see anything?"

His eyes widened and he nodded rapidly. Jendara glanced over her shoulder at the others. Korthax was sketching in the silt on the floor, maybe drawing some kind of map for Vorrin. No one was shouting, which was a good sign. She turned back to her boy and nudged him aside. "Let me try."

Once the bench had probably opened from the top, but there were enough mineral deposits from its years underwater to seal it shut. Kran's idea of prying open the crack was probably the best option, but his little dagger wasn't long enough to get any good leverage and she knew he'd never risk the new treasure of his seax. Jendara slipped the handle of her handaxe into the crack and hesitated. It was new, after all, and if Boruc had been there, he would have hated to see her scratch up the beautiful engravings. She sent him a mental apology and pulled back on the axe with her full weight.

The stone front didn't even grumble as it broke free from the bench's walls. Jendara toppled onto her backside and Kran rushed in to see what she'd found. Jendara pushed aside Fylga's concerned licking and brushed herself off while the boy rummaged through the debris.

"Find anything good?"

Kran brought out a small box, possibly made of lead, since it looked heavy and unaffected by water or corrosion. He opened it to reveal a string of lustrous black pearls.

"Wow." Jendara blinked at the treasure. "Do you know how rare these are? They're worth a lot."

He tucked the pearls in his belt pouch and then returned his attention to the hollowed bench. He removed a flat object that had once been wrapped in some kind of heavy canvas. The canvas had rotted into an orangish slime over the centuries, and Kran pulled it off in handfuls. Fylga sniffed at the stuff and shook her head. The pungent smell didn't discourage Kran in the least.

He wiped off the last of the rotten fabric and held up a shining bronze disk. He made a questioning face.

Jendara reached for the disk. Like the bars in the prison below, someone must have taken great pains to preserve the thing; it showed no signs of water damage or any kind of age. It could have been wrought yesterday. She brushed her fingers over the tiny engravings that ran around the thing's edge. Another, smaller disk covered the top half of the larger one, its own edges engraved with unintelligible symbols, and a bronze bar, something like a handle, lay over the two pieces. A center pin secured the three layers. The bar had been fashioned with a sea snake's face at each end, and their conjoined tails met in a complicated knot at the center. She tried turning it and found it still moved easily.

"Glayn?" she called. "Can you come take a look at something?"

The little gnome joined them. "Find something?"

"Kran found it. Does it look familiar?"

Glayn nodded. "I think it's an astrolabe." He saw Kran and Jendara's faces and shook his head. "Not the kind we use on the ship for navigation. The kind that shows what stars are in which alignment." He turned the sea snake bar. "This is probably a pointer for the outer ring. The inside disk probably adjusts in accordance with the date, or perhaps some other astronomical occurrence that interested these people. But these symbols mean nothing to me."

"May I see?" Zuna asked. Jendara hadn't noticed her arrival. Glayn put the astrolabe in the other woman's hand. She turned it over. There was something like a flattened tube on the back, as if perhaps the astrolabe had been designed to mount on a post. "Do you think they hung it on a wall or something?"

"It reminds me of something," Korthax said. He started to reach for the bronze thing, then whipped his hand back. "I'm not sure what," he added, quickly.

Kran jumped to his feet, waving a hand to catch their attention as he scribbled: *Star Chapel!*

Jendara shook her head. "What about the Star Chapel, Kran?"

Symbols on disk, he wrote, *like symbols in chapel.*

Glayn nodded. "If it's an astrolabe, that makes sense. And the stars seem to be important to these people."

Jendara remembered the huge templelike structures on the surface level of the island. She wished Boruc and his notebook were here. He'd sketched the buildings and some of the details from their remaining artwork. Maybe there was some clue as to the symbols' meaning hiding in his notebook.

"Well, whatever it is," Vorrin said, "it looks valuable. Good find, Kran." He nodded toward the stairs that Glayn had discovered. "In the meantime, we've got some friends waiting for us."

Kran slipped the astrolabe into his pack and he and the others made for the staircase. Jendara caught up with Vorrin.

"I wish we could figure out what those symbols mean."

He gave her an odd look. "We're here to save our friends, not solve mysteries."

"I know—there's just so much here we don't understand. It would be nice to *know* something for once." A narrow landing broke up the staircase, and Jendara paused. "How much farther?"

"Not much," Korthax assured her. "After this, there is just a short corridor before we reach the exit." They pushed on after the ulat-kini. The narrow and uneven stairs continued down into the darkness, far steeper and longer than any of the stairs they had taken before. Jendara had to imagine this was some kind of back door, a secret bolt-hole. The society that had built this city built beautiful things, but the prison and this staircase suggested it was a community with secrets and a suspicious nature.

They emerged from the stairs into a faint light. "This is it— this hole in the rock," Korthax explained. "There is climbing to get down to the water, but like I told the others, it's not too hard."

Jendara put out her light and tucked it into the depths of her pack. She hoped the oiled leather still protected her things as well as it had her last swim. She was tired of getting soaked, but at least her gear was holding up.

Zuna led the descent into the water, and Korthax went down between Glayn and Vorrin. Fylga dove into the sea as confidently as if she'd been a seal. Jendara eyed Korthax as she paused on the rocks above. Even with his hands bound in front of him, he had no problem treading water, and he paddled beside Kran, making some quiet comment that made the boy smile. She still didn't trust the hybrid, but she had to admit he had helped Kran back there. She just wasn't sure why. She made her way down the slick rocks and swam for her son's side, watching Korthax the whole time.

"There." Korthax pointed with his chin. "Camp is just around those rocks."

The group began to swim for the camp, and Jendara realized why they hadn't seen this other entrance on their first trip. Not only were there rocks, but the spray from the waterfall they'd discovered blocked the view of this spot. If the ulat-kini were used to using this entry point, they might not have seen the humans moving behind the spray.

But now she could see the ulat-kini camp. The ugly, make-shift boats were still gathered around the dock, but this time she saw far more of the full-blooded ulat-kini. They floated in little groups out in the water. Their air-breathing hybrid relatives looked paler and more spindly than the aquatic ones. She made a mental comparison between the ulat-kini and the deep ones. They shared a general resemblance to fish, although this group of ulat-kini reminded her far more of herring, while the more solidly built deep ones reminded her of anglerfish, all big jaws and needle teeth. The ulat-kini's hands were more like hands and less like flippers, too.

"If we come up behind this boat, I don't think they'll see us," Zuna pointed out, so they swam around to the far side of the nearest ugly vessel, which stank of tar and spoiled fish. Zuna swam into the boat's shadow, then pulled herself up onto the dock. Zuna took Korthax's lead rope from Vorrin and reeled him close to her side while the others pulled themselves up onto dry ground.

"Where are they?" Vorrin whispered.

Korthax looked around. "Yerka's scow can lock. It is the only one." He pointed at the boat when Jendara had found Yerka. Jendara's lips tightened. Earlier, he had claimed the vessel was Yerka's home, but it sounded more like a prison.

The group followed him quietly. But before they reached the scow, another hybrid scrambled up onto the dock. "Korthax!" It babbled something in its awkward-sounding language, and then its golden eyes went big. It reached for Korthax's bindings, suddenly realizing he was a prisoner.

Vorrin grabbed the hybrid and clapped his hand over the creature's mouth. "If you want to live, you'll take us to your prisoners."

The hybrid shook his head wildly, sending off droplets of water.

Korthax frowned. "He tries to tell us something." He leaned closer. "Tharkor, do not scream. Otherwise, we are both dead."

The smaller hybrid whimpered.

Kran frowned. Jendara knew he had to feel sickened by the threats to the two ulat-kini. He had never seen Vorrin or Jendara in any position other than the defensive, and now his parents were the attackers. But he had to understand that this was an ugly situation, and it called for ugly measures. She reached for the boy's hand and gave it a reassuring squeeze.

"Can we get on board the scow?" Vorrin said in a low voice. "I'll uncover your mouth when we're inside."

Tharkor nodded and Vorrin pulled him on board the vessel. Jendara readied her axe. Out here on the deck, they were dangerously exposed. She nearly held her breath as Zuna opened the door to the scow's cabin.

"There's no one inside." Surprise colored Zuna's voice.

"Get in," Vorrin hissed. They all hurried inside. Vorrin pulled his hand from Tharkor's mouth. "If you scream, I'll slit your throat," he warned.

Tharkor cringed away from the man. In the close space, Jendara could feel Vorrin's arm trembling. Vorrin had faced down plenty of enemies, but there was a difference between self-defense and an execution. But he was worried for Tam and Boruc, and she knew he would do anything for his friends.

They squeezed into the foul-smelling cabin. Some of the stink of urine and unwashed bedding had faded, but Kran still looked sickened by the stench and squalor. Jendara pulled him closer to the wall, away from the hybrids and Vorrin.

"Where are our friends?" Glayn growled.

"And no lying," Vorrin warned him. "I'll break your neck if I think you're lying."

"Not know," Tharkor whimpered. He flinched away from Vorrin's raised hand. "No lie!"

"Tharkor, *tell* them," Korthax pleaded.

"I see nothing. Please!" Tharkor shuddered. "Korthax, please." He burst out in his native tongue.

Jendara stepped forward. "Speak Taldane, ulat-kini."

Tharkor shivered. "Things bad here. Leng men not come back. Some of us missing. Korthax first, but now many. Full-bloods, hybrids, even Yerka."

"How many?" Korthax leaned in closer to the other hybrid.

Tharkor's fishy lips worked as he silently added up the number. "Nine," he said. "No, eleven."

Jendara frowned. "Eleven of your people have gone missing."

Tharkor nodded vigorously. "Leng men not going to be happy."

"Leng men?" Jendara asked.

"The black robes. Them that raised the island!" Tharkor's eyes gleamed. "We help them, they take us with them to Leng. We live like kings. Soon, Skortti use star scepter to wake the Sea Lord. Then we all go to Leng."

Jendara tried to make sense of the creature's words. The people on the black ship had made the island come up out of the sea? That spoke of some serious magic.

Glayn folded his arms across his chest. "What in Desna's skirt does that even mean? Star scepter? Sea Lord? Leng Men?"

Vorrin narrowed his eyes at Korthax. "Why don't you explain? Seems you left a few things out of your original story."

Zuna gave Korthax's wrist bonds a twist. "Spill it, scum."

The cabin door burst open, letting in a torrent of enraged babbling in the ulat-kini tongue. Everyone spun to face the new speaker.

From the doorway, an ulat-kini wearing an ornate miter leveled his trident at Korthax. He narrowed his eyes. "I do not know who you are, but if you are with Korthax, I will kill you all."

14

THE POLITICS OF THE SHORE

Jendara stepped sideways, subtly placing her body between the new ulat-kini and her son. "You're just one frogman up against four well-armed adventurers. I don't think you're in any position to make threats."

In the dim light of the cabin, mother-of-pearl shone on the ulat-kini's miter. The headdress had been shaped from what appeared to be white shell and carved to resemble lace patterned with bits of mother-of-pearl and threads of shining silver fish skin. She recognized it from her initial observation with the spyglass. Its wearer ignored her. It growled something else in its own language.

Vorrin glared at the newest ulat-kini. "Drop your weapon before you get yourself killed."

The ulat-kini looked from one crew member to the other. The confidence slid off its face, and it dropped its trident with a clatter.

"What you want?" it croaked.

"We're looking for—"

Korthax cut Vorrin off. "Heretic! You sell the star scepter to the black robes!" He lunged toward the other ulat-kini, but hit the end of his rope with a hiss.

Zuna reeled him backward. "We don't have time for this."

"You are not strong like your father." The other ulat-kini smirked. "The people have judged you!"

Korthax spat. "If I were not tied up—"

"But you are." The older ulat-kini turned to Vorrin. "Drylander. Why you come to this sacred place?"

"We don't want to get in the middle of your fight," Vorrin said, his voice calm, almost friendly. "We don't want to interfere with your people at all. We just want our companions. We assumed you took them, but Tharkor here insists our friends are not here."

Skortti took his attention off Korthax. "You are not working with the traitor?"

"I am not traitor!" Korthax shouted. "You, Skortti! You and Fithrax! You agree to give star scepter to the black robes of Leng!"

"Shut up," Jendara snapped. "Skortti, don't listen to him."

Vorrin said carefully: "We found Korthax in the tunnels and took him prisoner, assuming he could help us."

Jendara shifted uncomfortably. They'd been lucky to grab Tharkor and keep this Skortti under control. If any more of their kind arrived, it would mean a fight. She glanced at Kran. They'd been able to keep him safe back in the library, but in these tight quarters, he'd be in far greater danger.

Skortti drew himself to his full height. The miter nearly scraped the roof of the cabin. For the first time, Jendara realized he was taller than Korthax. His shape was pure ulat-kini: webbed fingers, bandy legs, back hunched beneath a fairly substantial dorsal fin. Korthax was mostly human with ulat-kini qualities, while Skortti showed no hybridization. Moreover, he had a prosperous plumpness about him, and his fish-skin belt was ornamented with what appeared to be fish-bone scrimshaw.

"If you not work with Korthax, then you not our enemy. You first of your kind I see on this island. Leave now, and we let you go."

"I think he's telling the truth," Glayn said.

"He is!" Tharkor blurted.

"Quiet, Tharkor," Skortti growled.

"Then where are our friends?" Jendara demanded, of no one in particular.

Kran's chalk squeaked on his slate. Jendara's lips tightened. She had hoped to keep him out of Skortti's attention. She couldn't say why, but she didn't like the pompous ulat-kini, and she definitely didn't trust him.

Kran held up his slate. *Deep ones.*

"It makes sense," Vorrin admitted. "The deep ones made that pit trap."

"They already try and get your little one," Korthax reminded him.

Skortti frowned. "The deep ones claim this island. They will not trade with us or Leng. I do not know their plans."

Jendara frowned. She had assumed the deep ones had found the island when it arose just as she and her crew had, and were here to explore and gather treasure. But she'd assumed the same about the ulat-kini, and it sounded as if they had some strange ritual planned that would help both their species and the mysterious black-robed people of Leng.

Leng. The name was vaguely familiar, but it meant nothing to Jendara. It must be a very distant land, perhaps an island out of ordinary sailing range. The black ship the robed and turbaned people had piloted certainly looked sturdy enough to manage long-distance sea voyages.

She brought her attention back to Vorrin, who was quietly consulting with Glayn. He nodded at Skortti. "I believe my people have no fight with yours. As long as you don't interfere with our exploration of this island, which we will leave as soon as we find our companions, then I think we can leave you in peace."

Skortti studied his face for a long moment. Then the ulat-kini nodded. "Your deal is accepted. I will tell our people."

Vorrin released Tharkor and turned to Korthax. "I'll have your bonds cut in a moment."

He began sawing at the heavy rope. Korthax looked from Vorrin's blade to Skortti's sneering face.

"May I stay with you?" Korthax asked, his voice tense.

"What?" Vorrin stopped cutting to stare at the hybrid.

"I have no place among ulat-kini. If I stay, they kill me."

Vorrin slashed through the last strands of hemp. "I don't trust you much, Korthax. I'd never take you on as crew."

"No!" Korthax shook his head. "I pay! Pay to get to nearest port. I would join another tribe of ulat-kini."

"How would you pay?" Jendara scoffed.

Korthax reached into the pouch slung on his belt. "I found this," he admitted, holding up a thick gold coin inset with a chip of diamond. "And I mend fishing nets," he added.

Vorrin took the coin. It looked ancient, the design on the front like some kind of sea star. "I suppose that might cover a short journey."

Jendara urged Kran toward the cabin door. Skortti stepped aside for them to pass, but blocked Korthax's path with a thick, finned arm. Jendara watched them, her axe held at her side, but ready.

"You truly are a traitor," Skortti murmured. "Pray that you are far away when I raise the Sea Lord tomorrow."

Korthax made an unpleasant smile. "You have the star scepter, Skortti, but the black robes only use you." He ducked under Skortti's arm, then passed Jendara and stared up at the cliff as he brushed bits of rope off his wrists.

She watched him carefully. He may have just bought passage on their ship, but she wasn't sure what he was really up to.

"Come on, let's get out of here." Vorrin put his hand on her shoulder. "I don't like the way this place smells."

She thought about sharing her misgivings about Korthax with her husband, but noticed the worry lines digging into the skin between his eyebrows. Vorrin had enough on his mind, including the deal he'd just made with Korthax. She decided to give him a smile, instead. "From now on, Captain, you can arrange our trade deals."

He shot her a look as they crossed the dock. "What?"

"You did a good job negotiating back there. You got us out before we got hurt, and Skortti even seemed pacified. I'd say you were a natural." She lowered herself into the water. "Ughh. Are you as tired of being damp as I am?"

He joined her in the water. "Extremely. I'm supposed to be on my nice dry ship. Swimming is not an acceptable means of transit."

Korthax pulled himself onto the rocks below the tunnel entrance they'd used to leave the island. Fylga leaped up beside him.

"Wait a second!" Jendara swam faster. "Let's use ropes for the ascent. I don't want anyone getting hurt."

Zuna waved Korthax back into the water. "I'll go up first. I can anchor the line, just in case. Korthax, you come up after me."

"Kran, you next," Jendara said. "Glayn and I will be right behind you."

Zuna moved up the cliff face faster than Jendara could have. Fylga followed right behind. The tall woman leaned out of the tunnel opening and made an "all right" sign at the rest of them. Korthax hurried up the cliff face, ignoring the line Zuna had taken up. It wasn't a difficult ascent, or even particularly high, but Jendara worried about cold fingers on slippery handholds. She wasn't about to see Kran getting his brains bashed out on these rocks.

Fylga barked at the boy from above, and the lad began to climb. He made it halfway up and then paused, looking for the next handhold.

"Slow and steady," Jendara called up to him. "There's a good handhold to your left."

The boy reached out.

Fylga barked. Korthax, nearly to the top, turned to see what was wrong and saw the stone give way beneath the boy's hand.

Kran dangled by the rope wrapped around his waist. Jendara felt her heart stop.

"Kran!" she shouted. "Don't move!"

Oh ancestors, what if the rope gave way or he slid down too quickly? She began to free climb toward him. There was no way she could reach him in time if Zuna's anchor broke loose, but she had to do something.

A rain of gravel sifted down on her. Korthax was moving down the cliff face, his webbed hands and feet finding purchase where boots never could. He caught the boy's arm and stopped his swinging. For a second, Jendara saw Kran's face, a white oval with dark holes where the mouth and eyes should be. Any other boy would be screaming in terror, but that wasn't an option for her son.

Korthax pulled the boy close, and Kran grabbed onto the ulat-kini's waist. Korthax began to slowly move back up the wall.

Jendara's mouth had gone dry. "Are you doing okay?" Her voice sounded more like a croak than a call.

"We are fine," Korthax shouted back. He caught the edge of the tunnel entrance.

Zuna reached for Kran's hand and swung him up into the tunnel. Korthax hugged the cliff side for a moment. Jendara was only a few yards below him now. She could see his sides working as he struggled to catch his breath. Then the ulat-kini scrambled up over the rim of rocks and disappeared inside.

In a few moments, Jendara joined them inside. Kran was scribbling on his slate, his face bright as he wrote. Fylga licked at the ulat-kini's hands. Kran showed Korthax whatever he'd written and then clapped the ulat-kini on the back. Korthax smiled at the boy.

It was a pleasant scene, but it pained Jendara to see the hero worship written across her son's face. The boy shouldn't have had to be rescued by some frogman; she should have been there for him. Her stomach tightened around itself.

Puffing, Vorrin made it inside the tunnel and moved to stand beside Jendara. "Thank the gods Korthax was there. Thank the gods."

"Yes," Jendara agreed. "I'm very thankful."

Korthax couldn't read, but that didn't stop Kran from trying to communicate with him. He drew pictures as they walked up the long flight of stairs, borrowing Jendara's lantern to show Korthax what he'd drawn. He made hand signs that grew broader as he struggled to explain what he meant. It was a valiant effort. Jendara watched the two together, the frog-lipped ulat-kini and the human boy. She supposed she could understand why Kran was trying so hard. The creature had saved him, after all. Twice.

For his part, Korthax seemed genuinely interested in the boy. Maybe he just liked children; she didn't know much about ulat-kini, but she hadn't seen a single child when she'd spotted the group of them approaching the islands. For all she knew, the ulat-kini had a boy of his home back at home, and spending time with Kran was some kind of comforting experience. She scowled at Korthax's green back anyway. He didn't need to be so greedy of the boy's attention.

They entered the ruined library and Vorrin clapped to get their attention. "How about we take a break to eat and make a plan?"

Jendara smiled at him. She could use a rest after the long walk up the uneven stairs and the hurried climb up the cliff face. She found her water skin and drank deeply. The water tasted faintly of the oak casks they'd carried it in, but also tangy and fresh, the crisp mineral flavor of Sorind's well water. The taste of home.

She sat down on a slab of fallen rock. Home. How were Morul and Leyla doing? Was Oric's arm healing all right? It had been only a few days since they had left the island, but she missed it fiercely, perhaps because she'd left it in such a terrible state. Her father had taught her to help others when they needed it, not run out on them when things got rough.

"What's wrong?" Glayn asked, holding out a cheese sandwich.

She took it and looked at it for a moment. "This came from the baker at Sorind. His bread is delicious even when it's stale. Tangy."

"He inherited his yeast from his grandmother," Glayn said. "She claimed to have gotten it from her own grandmother, and that's why it tastes so good."

"I didn't know that." Jendara took a bite. "Do you think he's okay?"

"Of course." Glayn patted her arm. "I know things looked bad when we left, but the town's been through worse. The people can take a little flood."

Jendara sighed. "I just wish we were back there to help. This trip sounded like a good idea, but . . ." She shook her head.

"We've all found a few good things," he reminded her. "We'll get our friends back, then stop and sell our artifacts in Halgrim, and when we get home, we'll have a shipload of lumber and necessities. People will be glad for them."

She smiled down at him. "How can someone so small have such a big brain?"

"I need it to keep track of you lot," he said with a grin. The grin faltered a little. "I sure wish we'd find Tam."

Jendara squeezed his hand. "We will. Don't worry."

Vorrin wiped his mouth with a square of cloth from his pack. Jendara often teased him about his proper manners, but today it was nice to see him bringing a bit of civilization to this decrepit place. "So, we need a plan."

Kran, seated beside Korthax, wrapped his arms around his knees and rested his chin on them. He looked thoughtful.

"It seems pretty clear that the deep ones stole our people," Zuna said. "They're attacking the ulat-kini, too."

"I'm forced to agree," Vorrin said. "I don't know what brought those creatures to this island, but they obviously don't want to share it."

Kran raised his hand. He already had his slate on his knees, and he was writing as he waved at Vorrin.

"What do you think, Kran?"

The boy held up the slate so they could all see. *Maybe they live here.*

Vorrin frowned. "I don't know. This island sure seems abandoned."

Kran shrugged. He crammed in another line: *Seem to know it.*

Jendara nodded, slowly, thinking of the pit trap. If the deep ones had arrived after the island rose to the surface, then they couldn't have reached the island much before Jendara's own group arrived—so how had they had time to both build a pit trap and find their way around the island? The tunnels were a labyrinth.

"If they don't live here," she said, "then I think they've been exploring the island for a long time." She shrugged. "They live underwater, right? They could have already been on the island when it came up to surface. We don't know."

Vorrin looked around the group. No one said anything for a minute. No one liked the ramifications of what Jendara had just said. If the deep ones knew the island, they had a tremendous advantage over both the ulat-kini and the human arrivals. The island suddenly felt like enemy territory.

Jendara caught Korthax's eye. "You know more about them than we do. What do you think?"

He shifted uncomfortably. "I do not know much about deep ones, only what they told Ahrzur and his black robes. They say island sacred." He spread his hands, a gesture Kran often used like a shrug. "Maybe you are right."

"I think we should leave." Zuna pulled her arms in close around her stomach. "Right now."

"Not without Tam," Glayn snapped.

"Or Boruc or Sarni!" Jendara narrowed her eyes at the other woman. "How can you even suggest leaving them?"

"No." Vorrin shook his head. "No, we're not going to leave until we've tracked them down. I think we should make our way down to that lower level where you found me and Glayn. There were deep ones down there."

Zuna turned her head away. "I just want to get out of here."

Jendara stared at Zuna. The navigator sounded like she was going to break into tears. Jendara hadn't always liked the woman, but she hadn't pegged her for a coward. She opened her mouth to say as much.

Before she could speak, Kran got to his feet and went to Zuna. He put his arms around her shoulders—a stretch, since she was so tall—and squeezed her. He didn't reach for his chalk.

Zuna sniffed. Jendara winced at the sound. But of course Kran had the right idea. She felt in her belt pouch for a clean handkerchief and then stepped to Zuna's side. She pressed the handkerchief into Zuna's palm. "We're going to get out of this. It's okay."

Kran stepped back from the navigator and stooped to rub Fylga's head. He brought a few strips of dried meat out of his belt pouch and fed them to the dog. Zuna watched him.

"He's not scared," she said. "He's just a kid, and he's not scared."

Jendara let out a dry laugh. "Kran? He once rescued a bear from a pack of goblins. He got kidnapped by shapeshifting cannibals. He tried to kill an armed lunatic with a slingshot. I don't think he's a very good judge of danger."

Zuna stared at Jendara for a moment and then threw back her head and howled with laughter. "Look who's talking!"

Jendara and the others joined in.

15

TRACKING THE DEEP

Zuna took the lead as they left the library. Kran followed behind, his infatuation with Korthax apparently satisfied for now.

Vorrin fell in beside Jendara. "How do you think we can find them? Boruc had the map. I don't even know how you got down to that level in the first place."

"We got in there from the cliffs by the ulat-kini camp, but I don't think we should try to go that way again," she said. "I don't want Kran climbing up and down those cliffs. These hallways might be dangerous, but I *know* those cliffs could kill somebody. I won't see him slip again."

"Then what do we do?"

"Maybe . . ." She paused, thinking back. Yerka had run down this same hallway when Boruc and Tam had come after her. There had to be a connection.

Her thoughts were interrupted when she nearly walked into a distracted Fylga. She gave the dog a dirty look. She knew dogs relied on their noses as much as she did her eyes, but the dog's constant sniffing didn't make walking any easier. She took a diagonal step to avoid the yellow-and-white animal.

Then she stopped in mid-swerve. Vorrin walked into her with a rattling of his teeth.

"Fylga!" She shook her hands in frustration. "This place is so strange, I stopped thinking straight. We've got a dog. Damn it all, we can track them! Kran!"

The boy hurried back to her side.

"Remember how Fylga was so interested in that other hallway? Do you think she smelled Boruc and Tam?"

He shrugged, then nodded.

Jendara squatted to look in the dog's eyes. Too small to pull a cart or help bring down a boar—ever since Kran had brought Fylga home, she'd been waiting for the dog to prove itself useful. "Now's your chance, dog," she said. "Show me you're not just a lazy sack of fur." She screwed up her face, thinking hard. "I wish I had thought of this back on the *Milady*. I need a shirt or something, something that smells like one of them."

Kran caught her eye, tapping his temple.

He untied the makeshift bandage Boruc had wrapped around the dog's leg—Boruc's handkerchief, Jendara remembered—and held it out to the dog. He snapped his fingers. Fylga sat up straight. Kran leaned closer and let the dog get a good noseful of scent. Then he made a series of odd clicks with his tongue. The dog stood and hurried up the hallway, headed for the junction.

"That was amazing," Vorrin murmured as they followed behind boy and dog.

Jendara watched Fylga sniff the ground around the entrance of the second hallway and then hurry around the corner. "I never thought about him training her. I just assumed they played together and loafed around. Any good behavior she had, I figured was luck."

"Me, too," Vorrin said. "I'm ashamed to admit it. I know how smart and strong Kran is, but sometimes I guess I underestimate him."

"I do, too." Jendara smiled. "He really doesn't let anything hold him back."

Vorrin put his arm around her shoulders. He kissed her cheek.

Up ahead, Glayn had stopped to examine something sitting on the floor. He picked it up and turned to show it to Vorrin. "I think we're on the right track."

Jendara leaned down to get a better look. The gnome had found a small glass bottle, its top broken off and its sides salt-stained, that held a faint blue-green blob.

"Glow weed," Vorrin said.

"Drying out, but definitely the same stuff." Glayn shook the jar and made the hunks of weed flop around. A thin rime of salt showed at the bottom of the jar. "I'd guess they put a little water in there to keep it fresh, but it looks like the water dried up."

Jendara played her lantern's light over the ground. "There's a bit of glass here. Whoever was using this as a lamp must have dropped it and left it behind."

"Pretty sure it was deep ones," Zuna said from a few feet ahead. She held out a piece of something pinched between her fingertips, and the trio hurried to see.

Jendara's nose crinkled at the rank smell of spoiled fish. "Is that a fin?"

"I think it's part of one." Zuna dropped the bit of flesh and wiped her hand on her pants.

Kran caught Jendara's eye. He pointed at the fin and a scuff on the floor, then waved back at the spot where she'd seen the broken glass. Then he pointed down at the ground again and motioned her over. Jendara hunkered down to see more clearly. A faint trace of blood caught her eye.

"A footprint," she said. "Not human."

Kran nodded. He brought up three fingers, hesitated a moment, then raised a fourth.

Excitement built in Jendara's chest. "Three, probably four deep ones. They found Boruc, Tam, and Yerka here in this hallway. Then they fought, and the deep ones won."

Kran nodded. He pointed down the hallway.

"And they continued down the hallway—" She squinted, catching another faint scuff mark on the ground. It was hard to make out a track down here. When they'd first entered these hallways, she'd gotten the sense that someone had cleaned these halls, and that sense had only grown stronger as they'd continued exploring them. Now she knew why. The deep ones were using this hallway as their major thoroughfare, and they didn't want anyone to track them. "They must have been dragging one of the prisoners in an upright position. Those marks look the toes of someone's boots being rubbed along the ground."

Kran grinned and bobbed his head. She smiled back at him. "Nice work, boy." She knew he'd been learning a lot about tracking from Yul, but this was amazing work. Most adults she knew couldn't have read this scene as well as her boy just had.

Vorrin studied the empty hallway ahead. "So this is the right way."

"Yes." Jendara helped Kran to his feet and watched him take the lead with Fylga. Jendara couldn't stop beaming.

The hallway continued, just as clean as ever: no dead and dying creatures to crunch underfoot, no mud or debris to show tracks. It must have taken a big crew a long time to clear out the hallway this much. Jendara bit the inside of her cheek, trying to work out just how big and how long.

They hadn't passed any doorways since they left the junction off the first tunnel, but now doors began to appear. The cleaners had concentrated their efforts on the floor, leaving the usual encrustations that sealed shut the doors of the island. Whatever religious item interested the deep ones, it wasn't tucked away inside this hallway.

She wondered just what they had found. What could make a place sacred to creatures like that? She wasn't even sure what gods they might worship.

Fylga's bark of warning cut through Jendara's musings.

"Kran!" she shouted, pulling out her sword as she broke into a run. She couldn't see a thing in the darkness beyond the boy, but she knew something was wrong.

Then she could hear the slap of webbed feet striking stone. As she reached her boy, her lantern caught the green frog-face of an ulat-kini. She shoved her lantern into Kran's hands and brought up her sword.

"Get back!" she shouted at him.

Fylga snarled and sank her teeth into the ulat-kini's leg. The frogman shrieked, but there were a half-dozen more at his side. Jendara parried the injured creature's awkward stab with its trident. Where had they come from? She tried to scan for an open doorway, *something*, but the ulat-kini lunged again. Wounded or not, the damned thing was eager to kill her.

But he'd overextended himself and exposed his entire side. She drove her blade into his ribs and felt the bones shatter against the force of her blow. His face went suddenly still. Jendara drove her palm into his chest to clear her blade. There were too many of the bastards to risk getting her sword hung up in anyone's spine.

Somewhere another ulat-kini shrieked in pain and fear, but Jendara stayed focused on the ones in front of her: two ulat-kini with sturdier tridents than the one she'd just fought. Vorrin was keeping them at bay, but he couldn't keep up his pace for long. She glanced over her shoulder and saw Kran with his back pressed against the tunnel wall, his seax at hand and a snarling Fylga at his feet. There were no ulat-kini nearby—for the moment, he was safe enough.

Korthax grabbed her arm. "Wait!"

She shook him off. She wasn't going to go easy on these scum just because one of their kind had bought passage on her ship. Jendara charged at the nearest ulat-kini and sent it sprawling.

"Help!"

That was Zuna's voice, sounding strained. Jendara kicked the fallen ulat-kini in the head and felt it go limp. She risked a quick glance around to find Zuna.

Zuna had managed to disarm her opponent, but now the big ulat-kini had wrapped its hands around her throat. She clawed at the creature's webbed fingers. If Jendara didn't do something, Zuna would be dead in seconds.

"No!" Korthax shouted. "There's something—"

And then a cloud of white webbing covered Zuna and her attacker. For one moment, they stood frozen together, and then the netting went taut and the package of Zuna and ulat-kini flew sideways and disappeared into the darkness.

"Zuna!" Vorrin shouted. He shoved his attacker aside. "Zuna!"

Another sheet of webbing shot out, just missing Vorrin to land on the floor. The ulat-kini Jendara had stomped groaned and tried to push itself upright. Its hand touched the webbing. The ulat-kini tried to pull away, but the webbing was too sticky.

The web went taut. With its free hand, the ulat-kini caught Jendara's leg and held tight. She kicked at its ribs, but the creature didn't loosen its hold. Her boots began to slide across the floor.

"You bastard," she growled. She kicked it again, but then a wet ripping sounded and the web pulled away from the ulat-kini's palm as its skin gave way. With a screech, the ulat-kini scrambled away, clutching its hand to its chest. One of its kind pulled it to its feet and the pair raced away.

"Is everyone all right?" Jendara called. Kran ran to her side, patting her shoulder and arm with his free hand. She grabbed his chin and made him look in her eyes. "I'm fine. Are you okay?"

He nodded.

"Zuna's gone," Vorrin said. He pointed at a dark hole in the wall. "There's a staircase right here. The ulat-kini must have been coming out of it."

"They were running away," Korthax said, his voice hollow. "They were afraid, and they were running away, and you killed them." He pointed at three dead ulat-kini lying on the floor. "You did not even talk to them."

Jendara tightened her lips to hold back angry words. She'd done what the situation had demanded. She had to protect her family. It was her first duty.

"The one with your friend," Korthax managed to say. He trembled as he spoke. "That was my brother, Fithrax."

Vorrin stared into the dark stairway. There were no sounds whatsoever. Nothing to encourage them on. "We've got to go after them."

"Yes," said Korthax. He pushed past Vorrin and raced into the dark.

16

CLEARING COBWEBS

No one spoke as they made their way down the stairs. The island had so many, many staircases, some narrow, some broad, some long enough to stretch from the top floor down to the lowest tunnel, and others that only connected the bowels of the place to its lower levels. The people who had made this city must have spent most of their lives moving from level to level, from one dark hallway down to the darker. So many stairs, and not a single one was built for someone with a human-sized foot. Jendara glowered at the dark stones beneath her boot. Her legs hurt.

Fylga pressed against her as they walked. The dog had never expected Jendara to pet it or feed it or do anything beyond open the door so it could go outside to relieve itself, but now Fylga want to be right next to her. Maybe it was just Kran's closeness. He always carried himself with independence, but now he, too, walked as closely behind Jendara as physically possible. She could feel his warm breath against her shoulder and smell the odd combination of laundry soap and dog that made up his scent these days.

If she could have clung to someone, perhaps she would have. But she needed both hands free to carry her axe and her lantern. She'd rather have her sword out—if they came upon whatever shot those webs, she wanted to inflict damage from as far away as possible—but she knew the axe was a better choice in this narrow stairwell.

"There's more of the web stuff," Glayn murmured.

Vorrin and Glayn gave the web a wide berth as they passed, but Jendara paused to take a closer look. This webbing didn't look like quite like the white material that had shrouded Zuna. This was a long silky strand with an opalescent gleaming. Jendara had seen it before—stuck to Zuna's hair. Her stomach sank as she realized she'd seen it before that, even. Back on Sorind. It was the stuff that had trapped Oric and Fylga on the rocks.

She made sure Kran avoided touching the web and stayed quiet until they reached the landing below. She caught Vorrin's arm and quickly told him about the shimmering threads. He grew more uncomfortable as she spoke, but didn't open his mouth until she had finished.

"On Sorind? You're sure?"

She nodded.

"I don't like this," he admitted. "That means that whatever is making these webs isn't limited to this island." He shook his head. "Do you think something could hitch a ride on the *Milady*?"

"That thread is about a thousand times thicker than a regular spider's web. I'm sure we would have noticed a giant spider."

"Vorrin and Jendara? Do you see this?" Glayn held the lantern higher.

The hallway they had just entered looked very much like the other second-level tunnel they'd explored. It was quiet enough Jendara could hear the faint sound of feet splashing in the distance—probably Korthax, running up ahead of them.

Everything felt damp down here. When the island had been submerged, this level had certainly been filled with water, and every surface was overgrown with seaweed and crustaceans, now very dead. But the big black box leaning up against the nearest support column was completely clean. It sat in the midst of some broken and dirty spider webs, a structure that reminded Jendara of an abandoned bird's nest.

Vorrin rapped his knuckles on the front of it. "What's this made out of? It's not metal, that's for sure."

"I don't care much what it's made of." Glayn edged away from the thing. It was nearly as tall as he was. "Look at all that web stuff inside. It's like it was part of a spider's nest or something."

Recognition struck Jendara. "It *does* matter what it's made of." She squatted down to study the strange black stuff more closely. She ran her palm across it. Not a single scratch marked its surface. "Remember when we first saw the ulat-kini and the black ship? They were unloading those really big black crates."

Vorrin nodded. "The crates were full of the pieces they used to build the floating dock."

"Right." Jendara stood back up. "But what if there was something else inside one of them? What if they had a stowaway?"

"Shipping crates make good places for vermin to hide," Glayn pointed out. "Plenty of bugs and spiders get hauled around on ships."

"But what kind of spider shoots a web big enough to snare two human-sized creatures?" Jendara asked.

Kran's chalk tapped on his slate. They all turned to watch him hold up his slate. *Are there spiders on Leng?*

Jendara frowned at him. She had no answer for her son.

Somewhere in the distance, someone screamed.

The hallway sloped downward as they ran, and Jendara's boots slipped and slid on the damp sludge of rotting seaweed and mud. A faint breeze stirred the fetid air, bringing with it a charnel stink: not the usual pungent stench of fish and crustaceans, but the darker reek of death.

In the corridor ahead, something gleamed. Jendara slowed, trying to make sense of the dazzle of light. Fylga gave a sudden excited bark and picked up speed, leaping over heaps of broken shells as she went.

Realization hit Jendara. "Kran! Stop!"

In mid-jump, Fylga hit the wall of webbing and yelped with fear. Kran tried to stop, but the floor was too slick. Fylga flailed and whimpered.

Vorrin stumbled and caught himself. "Kran!"

Jendara and Glayn reached the web. "Are you okay?" she asked.

Kran looked up at her and nodded. He and Fylga were tangled together in the sticky stuff. The dog's struggling had done nothing to loosen her. Kran was in better shape, because Fylga's furry body had come between his legs and the web. But his right hand, the one carrying his lantern, had thrust into the gap between two of the thicker strands so that his entire right shoulder and rib cage were stuck fast. He had to hold his neck stiff to keep his head free.

"Don't touch anything," Glayn warned unnecessarily. Everyone was thinking of the ulat-kini who had lost his skin to the powerful stickiness of the web.

The little gnome moved closer, frowning. "A spider web isn't sticky all over," he pointed out. "Otherwise the spider would be trapped like the bugs it catches. Some of its strands are made out of a different kind of thread."

Fylga stopped flailing, but her whimpering grew louder. Vorrin reached out to stroke the top of the dog's head. "Don't worry, girl. We'll get you out of this."

Jendara stooped so she could make eye contact with Kran. "We'll have you loose in a second, okay?"

Kran smiled and waved his free hand in a show of unconcern. Jendara tried to smile at him, but her face didn't want to work properly. He couldn't even talk to her, not with his slate caught in the web.

She had to stop looking at him. "Okay." She looked up at the web. "Okay," she repeated. "How do we know which strands are sticky and which aren't?"

Glayn stared up at the top of the tunnel, where coarse strands of silk joined with the ceiling. "Those ones, there," he pointed out. "Those are definitely for structure."

"There must be threads like that at the bottom." Jendara lowered her light.

"One of them doesn't actually go down to the tunnel floor," Vorrin noticed. "It goes off to the side and down the hall. It almost looks like a trip line." He paused. "Like on a snare."

Fylga stopped whimpering and began to growl.

"Do you hear that?" Glayn whispered.

A tiny sound, barely audible over Fylga's growling, came from the darkness beyond the light of Kran's lantern. A tiny click-clicking, like the tap of some hard point against stone. Jendara raised her lantern so its light shone on the ceiling just beyond the web.

Four gleaming orbs reflected back at her.

"Shit!" Jendara almost dropped the lantern.

The clicking hurried toward them. Jendara pulled her handaxe from her belt and chopped at the thick cord of web on Kran's right side. For a horrible moment she thought the blade would stick, but with a faint squeak, the fibers parted. She tried to find the next structural thread, but Fylga was struggling again, and the whole web bucked and twisted along with her.

"Can you calm Fylga down?" she begged Kran. What the hell was the spider doing? Was it just *watching* them?

"Watch out!" Glayn yelled.

Vorrin threw himself sideways just in time to miss the silk-and-rock bolas that launched his way. It hit the wall with a nasty thud.

This was no ordinary spider. Its body filled the roof of the tunnel, its many legs gripping the walls on either side. And it wasn't just huge, it was smart enough to make weapons. Jendara chopped at the next strand of the web, watching the creature from the corner of her eye. She could just see Glayn slicing away at the strands around Fylga.

The spider dropped to the ground, and Jendara could see it fully now. Each of its eleven legs was close to twice as long as Jendara was tall, and its bulbous purple belly glistened faintly in the lantern light. Its mandible-like mouth parts opened and shut with a cold snicking sound.

Fylga snarled at the thing. With a twang, the main structural thread beneath her broke under Glayn's slashing, and the dog fell free. She rushed at the spider, strands of web trailing out behind her. The spider raised a massive spiky leg and batted her aside as if she were a gnat.

The dog struggled to get to her feet, but the sticky webbing caught and stuck to the floor. She barked angrily and the spider raised its clawed foreleg above her, poised to strike.

Kran's hand moved faster than Jendara could have expected. He'd drawn his belt knife while Jendara worked to cut him loose. The knife flew true, driving into one of the spider's eyes with a squelch. The spider hissed.

Glayn squeezed beneath the bottom of the web, the sticky stuff catching his pack for an instant before he pushed through. His short-bladed gladius sliced through the bottom third of the spider's leg. Blue-green blood sprayed out. The spider reared back on its remaining legs, exposing its mottled black spinneret.

"Help me," Jendara called to Vorrin. She nearly had Kran free.

He grabbed Kran's shoulder and began pulling at the boy as she chopped at one last strand. Vorrin and Kran tumbled backward. Through the veil of the web, Jendara saw a shimmering as the spider began to play out a length of silk. It chittered at Glayn. His attack on the spider had been brave, but now he'd drawn its ire, and there was no place for him to run if the spider tried to net him.

An idea hit Jendara.

"Glayn—the broken leg! Throw it to me!"

He grabbed the sheared-off spider leg and tossed it through the gap beneath the web. It felt cold and strange in Jendara's hand, a weirdly smooth substance that reminded her of the material of the black packing crate and the floating docks. No stone or metal or wood had ever felt like this. The hair spikes on the inside edge of the leg bit into her palms as she hefted the thing. It was only about three feet long, but it weighed a tremendous amount.

She struck at the web, tearing at its threads with the leg's three sharp claws. The web ripped easily under the touch of its maker. "Come on!" she shouted at Vorrin. She threw aside the leg as she ran.

Her axe bit into the spider's nearest leg with a crunch. She pulled back to chop again—

And suddenly faced a wall of ice. Snow blew into her face— not the powder-soft wet snow of late autumn, but the dry shards that whip off glaciers in the worst windstorms. She had to shield her eyes from the biting bits of ice.

"Kran? Vorrin?" She couldn't see anything. The wind shrieked and screamed. She took a step back and then froze. She stood on the knife edge of a mountain peak. The summit reared above her, a needle of black stone and slick ice. Rocks fell away beneath her in steep slopes like she'd never seen. She wobbled and almost fell.

"Kran!" she shouted.

"Jendara!" Vorrin's voice echoed from nearby, but she couldn't see him. She turned, very slowly, so as not to overbalance and slide down the face of the icy mountain. Where was she? Where was everyone?

"Glayn?" She narrowed her eyes. Was that Glayn, behind that broken bit of ice? She took a cautious step forward.

A rock the size of Jendara's fist whizzed past her head and hit the ground, bursting into shards. From behind the hunk of ice, Glayn shouted in surprise. Jendara may have found him, but now they were under attack. Another rock struck Jendara in the shoulder, hard enough to send shock waves of numbness down her arm. She nearly dropped her axe.

Her mind struggled to make sense of it all. She'd been in an underground tunnel fighting a gigantic eleven-legged spider and now she was on top of an icy mountain. She'd never seen any place like this. The mountain rose up above a gray expanse, empty and unreadable. No trees, no buildings, no meadows, no farms. A barren waste.

She didn't have time to get her bearings. Another rock flew past her, falling short. On any other surface, Jendara would have rushed her attacker, but she didn't trust her footing. It would be all too easy to slide right over the side of the steep cliff. She'd be dead in a heartbeat.

Jendara tucked her axe in her belt and drew her sword. Her best hope was that whoever had thrown those rocks would try to move in closer, coming within range of Jendara's blade. She set her feet in the best stance she could and readied herself for someone to come out from around the rock spire.

The edge of a figure appeared: a ghostly figure, a floating cloud of white fabric. Was it an elemental? Some kind of a spirit? Jendara narrowed her eyes. It had to have a body to throw stones.

The figure took another slow step toward her, its labored breathing audible. Beneath the white shroud, Jendara made out messy brown hair and a pair of dark eyes.

Jendara shook her head. It couldn't be. It looked like Sarni, but it couldn't be.

The figure raised its arm, preparing to launch another stone. The arm wavered and shook as if the muscles were tasked to their utmost. The figure's mouth opened and closed, but made no sound.

Then Glayn threw himself at the figure. They stumbled backward, going right through the wall of stone to slam into the ground. Jendara stood frozen. Glayn and Sarni—if it was Sarni—twisted and grappled. The icy wind stirred up, and a sheet of snow nearly obscured the fighters.

A shimmering cord shot out of the snow and twisted itself around Jendara's ankles. She went down hard. She should have rolled down the mountain face, but she simply lay flat on the ground, her legs hanging out over what should have been empty space. Something was terribly wrong with all of this.

Kran was suddenly by her side, hacking at the bolas tied around her ankles. The boy perched on what looked like thin air. She stared around herself as he worked, her mind spinning. Off to her right, she could see Vorrin blindly hacking around him at the rocks, the occasional spatter of blue announcing his hits.

She squeezed her eyes shut and reopened them. No, there were no rocks. There was no snow. It was all an illusion, a screen pulled up to block the spider from their sight.

But the shroud-wrapped Sarni was entirely real. Glayn slammed his fist into her face and she went limp. Jendara felt her ankles come free and jumped to her feet, grabbing onto Kran's arm. For a second she saw snow again, but then she was truly free of the illusion. A huge leg drove down in front of her, cutting her off from Glayn and Sarni.

Jendara slashed at the leg with her sword. Her aim was too high and the blade ricocheted off the leg's tough shell. Moving faster than any huge creature ought to, the spider twisted around, snapping its cruel mandibles shut on her arm. Her heavy jacket miraculously kept them from biting into the flesh, but she could feel bone and muscle crushing in that punishing grip. She lost her hold on her sword.

A crunch came from nearby, and the creature made a sudden surprised hiss, the sound muffled by Jendara's arm. Vorrin shouted something, but she couldn't make it out. The pain in her arm made it impossible to concentrate on the world. Her left hand fumbled at her belt for her handaxe. The spider shook its head, making her legs go out from under her. All her weight hung on her aching arm.

Then Kran shoved past her, her own lost sword in his hands, and drove the tip up under the spider's chin. The spider shook and jerked. Jendara fell hard and lay on the ground, clutching her arm for a second. But she couldn't just lay there. The spider hadn't fallen yet, and her boy was in the fray.

She forced herself upright and took her axe in her left hand. The spider snapped at Kran with the two short "arms" that framed its nasty fangs. The boy had no weapon. Her sword was caught in the spider's skull. Blue-green blood ran down in it rivulets, but the spider showed no sign of slowing.

Two more of the spider's severed legs lay on the ground between Jendara and the beast, but it was still balancing perfectly well on the other eight. Only the luckiest hits could pierce its thick hide. Jendara studied the creature for another moment. Kran had the right idea, she was sure of it. If they could pierce the spider's brain, they could kill it.

Vorrin lunged at the spider and it brought down a pair of legs to block him. It was her moment.

Jendara raced toward Vorrin and leaped up onto the second joint of the spider's leg. Before it could respond, she found the spiky hairs on the inner surface of the leg and used them as handholds, hurrying up the leg like a ladder. The spider tried to shake her off, but the hairs were too large and her grip too strong. Vorrin gave a happy shout and drove his sword tip into the spider's other foot.

It was the perfect distraction. The leg went still long enough for her to pull herself up onto the creature's back. Her boots skidded on its slick carapace, but she had enough momentum to keep moving forward. Her right hand's fingers closed on the handle of Kran's knife, still sticking out of the creature's eye. Her grip wasn't strong enough to use it as a handhold for long, but she didn't need much time. With her strong left hand, she brought her axe down beside the handle of the knife.

The spider screamed as her axe smashed through its eye. It bucked and twisted, but she kept her grip on the axe handle and the knife and didn't fall. She wrenched free the axe and drove it in at an angle, taking out a wedge of the spider's shell. A fissure opened up that ran down the front of the creature's face, and she brought the axe down again, passing through tough muscle and striking the soft brain in a burst of gray sludge.

The spider collapsed on the floor. Jendara slid down off its back.

"Kran." She flung her arm around her son. "Vorrin."

Vorrin pulled the two of them close. "Are you all right?"

She tried to move her right arm and winced. "I think my arm's messed up."

Vorrin pulled back. "Broken?"

She forced her fingers to move and shook her head. "Just bruised pretty bad." She looked around. "Where's Glayn?"

"Here." The gnome groaned as he ducked under the fallen spider's leg to join them. Blood ran down his face in streams.

"What happened?" Vorrin asked.

The gnome felt around in his pocket and came up with a hand-kerchief. He mopped away blood, revealing a wicked cut running through his eyebrow, but no other signs of damage. "I had Sarni, but she suddenly went all stiff and then threw me off her. I hit a rock with my face. When I got up, she was gone."

"She threw rocks at me," Jendara said. "I don't understand why she'd try to hurt us."

"I don't think she recognized me." Glayn found a second hand-kerchief and pressed it to his wound. "It's like she wasn't herself."

Jendara watched as Kran pulled the knife out of the dead spider's eye and wiped it on his pants. He looked so matter-of-fact, so grown up. It shook her almost as much as seeing Sarni acting like some kind of zombie.

"Let's keep going," Vorrin said. "Sarni and Korthax both went down this hallway. Whatever we're looking for, it's down there."

Kran caught Jendara's eye. He finished writing and studied his words for a moment before holding up his slate. *Are there more spiders?*

17

A WEB OF HORRORS

Jendara stared down the hall. In the dim light cast by the fallen lanterns, she could see sheets of spider webbing lining the walls, giving everything a faint otherwordly shimmer—a reminder that this creature was nothing like the ones that lived in her own garden. It had been smart, and it could make illusions, and it had somehow turned Sarni into its own slave.

She had no idea how that kind of magic worked, but she had a horrible feeling that once the spider controlling her died, Sarni ought to have returned to normal. Jendara turned and wrenched her handaxe out of the dead spider's brain.

"Sarni didn't come back," she said. "I think—" She broke off, repulsed by gray goo dripping off the blade of her axe. With a grimace, she scrubbed it off on the bloated purple creature.

"You think that means there's another one." Glayn had balled his bloody handkerchiefs in his fist, and the cut on his forehead looked raw and puffy, though it no longer dripped.

"Yeah," she agreed.

"What if it has Tam?"

She squeezed his shoulder. "We'll get him back. Tam, Boruc, Zuna, Sarni—we're going to get them all back and get the hell out of here."

Kran began gathering the lanterns and redistributing them. Jendara had mixed feelings about the lights. She wanted to be able to see what they were getting into, but she knew spiders were less dependent on their eyes. Even the common house spider had a remarkable sense for vibration and heat. These freakish things? They could have super-hearing and see through stone walls for all she knew. She felt a sudden urge to punch the tunnel wall. She was up against something huge and terrible, something she barely understood, and her sword arm was practically useless. And even if they fought off the next spider and found the team, they were little better off than they had been before. The team had come to this island to find a fortune, and instead they were trapped underground with giant spiders and the enmity of the deep ones.

But her crew needed her.

Jendara raised her lantern to study the hallway up ahead. "Let's get moving."

She took a step forward and felt the ground drop out from under her feet. Glayn screamed as he plummeted down beside her.

She bounced off something soft and then tumbled down a long drop. She hit ground hard and lay there gasping.

"Dara!"

"I'm okay." She sat up.

Vorrin got to his hands and knees beside her. He made a little hissing sound and brought his wrist close to his chest, rubbing the joint. The lantern hung above them, caught in a tangle of web. Glayn hung from a handhold a few feet above it. Jendara reached for the lantern and sat it down on the ground.

"Kran?"

Fylga barked in reply. She could just make out the outline of boy and dog, leaning precariously over the edge of a long tube of spider web. It had to be a good twelve feet up.

"A trapdoor," she growled. The damn spiders must have camouflaged the trap with gravel and rock.

"Can you get me down?" Glayn asked.

"Yeah, just a second." She touched the silk with one cautious fingertip. "This is a different kind of silk—slippery. It's going to be a real pain to climb back up."

Fylga whimpered.

Kran gave a sharp intake of air.

"What is it?" Jendara squinted up at him, but he was already throwing Fylga down. He launched himself down the slippery wall, sliding several feet before he caught himself.

Jendara heard a soft scraping above. "There's another! Get out of here!"

Vorrin grabbed Glayn and they raced away from the trap. They had landed in another tunnel, its walls sheathed entirely in webbing: a tight funnel of stretchy, sticky stuff. Jendara had to turn sideways to keep it from touching her. The walls caught and held the lantern light with an eerie opalescence.

And then the tunnel opened out into a cavern that rivaled the *Milady*'s grotto in size. Jendara lowered the flame on her lantern and beckoned to the others. They were alone here where the tunnel joined the cave, but faint sounds warned her they would not be alone for long. Over the faint whisper of the wind, a strange tapping and rustling echoed within the cavern.

Walls of webbing cut the cave into a long open space with smaller chambers opening off the sides. From where Jendara stood, she could see all the way down to the far wall, where a web-veiled window about her own height let daylight filter into the room. Despite the opening in the rock walls, the air felt much warmer here than anyplace else in the underground labyrinth. The spiders had created a snug fortress for themselves.

Movement to her right made her spin to face an attacker, her injured arm bringing up her lantern as if it were a weapon. A terrified gasp made her stop before she smashed the lantern into a familiar face.

"Korthax!" she whispered.

He nodded and struggled out of the pocket of webbing where he'd been huddled. It clung to him, but he wasn't immobilized by stickiness.

"I did not think we see each other again," he whispered. His pupils were huge, as if he were in shock. "I saw . . . a spider, making a web . . ." His speech trailed off. He was shivering, Jendara realized. However he'd gotten past that spider, he hadn't yet recovered from the sight of it.

"It's okay," she murmured. "It's dead now."

Vorrin leaned in. "We have to find Zuna," he said in a low voice. "Korthax, have you seen her?"

The hybrid ulat-kini shook his head, hard. "I think she is in here. I do not know. I had to hide from the spider."

Jendara raised a hand to stop him. "There's another spider in here?"

"I saw it on ceiling, by that window." He looked like he was going to be sick for a moment. Kran gently touched Korthax's shoulder. The ulat-kini looked down at the boy and forced a deep breath. "I am afraid of spiders."

"You keep watch, then," Vorrin said. "You and Kran can keep an eye out for any spiders on the ceiling, or if anything comes out of the tunnel. We'll go get Zuna."

"And Fithrax," Korthax said, quickly. "Please do not leave him."

Jendara met Vorrin's eyes. She didn't want to put herself on the line for a slave-taking ulat-kini, but she didn't want Korthax upset. They'd already made enough noise talking out here as it was. "We won't leave anyone behind," Vorrin said. "Not if we can help it."

Korthax nodded. Some of his color had returned, but his pupils were still huge.

Jendara stooped so she could murmur in Kran's ear without Korthax hearing. "I want you to keep your blade handy. If a spider comes, I don't know if you can count on Korthax to help you."

Kran nodded. He brought out the long seax and held it in an easy grip, like he'd been fighting with it for years.

"Let's leave all but one of the lanterns," Glayn said. "We can see well enough here."

Jendara spared Kran one last glance over her shoulder and then crept into the nearest chamber. Her eyes roved the walls and ceiling, searching for spiders.

She had never felt so tense, not in any dungeon she'd escaped or facing down any enemy. Every flicker of shadow made her ready her axe. The damn spider could be anywhere, behind any silken wall. It could be right on top of her and she might not even notice because the bastards could make her see things that weren't there.

Glayn made a tiny terrified sound, and she spun to face the far corner. A dark form hid behind a thick wall of webbing, its long legs outlined blackly against the shimmering silk.

"It's not moving," Vorrin whispered. "It hasn't seen us yet."

Jendara couldn't tell if it was as big as the spider they'd found in the corridor. Its long curled legs were pressed against the sheets of web, obscuring its body, and the spikes on the foreleg looked as long as her hand. The edges gleamed in the light. If one of them touched her flesh, she knew it would slice right through skin and muscle. But it didn't move.

She took a cautious step forward, wishing she could hold her axe in her right hand and not her left.

"Why isn't it moving?" Glayn could barely whisper. He stared at the thing as if rooted to the floor.

Jendara moved closer. She heard nothing. The creature didn't even twitch. It could be a trap. If it was, she'd be dead the instant it lashed out at her. But if it wasn't—if the thing really slept this deeply—she could have it dead before it could bring its weapons and venom into play.

"Don't get so close," Vorrin begged.

She pushed her axe blade against the web. The spider didn't move. She could see its fangs now, a dull black that stood out against its purple underbelly. Jendara leaned closer, frowning at that horrible face with its many eyes. She got closer, really looking into the dull surface of the nearest orb.

"It's just the shell," she said. "Like a crab or a garden spider—it grew and molted." She leaned back, taking in the full size of the creature. It couldn't have grown much, though. The husk was shriveled and flattened, but the legs looked just as long and thick. And underneath it, she saw another smaller form, the husk of a spider no larger than Fylga.

She thought back to the empty shipping crate. When crabs and spiders molted, it took time. They hid in the dark for a long time, waiting for their old exoskeletons to slip away and the new to grow. The shipping crate would have been the perfect way to bring a group of molting little spiders onto the island.

How many of them were there?

"Jendara?" Glayn tugged on her elbow. "I only see nine legs. Didn't the one in the tunnel have eleven?"

A gurgling scream interrupted any answer she might have made. Vorrin raced out the chamber faster than Jendara had ever seen him run. She raced after him.

"What was that?" Glayn asked, his shorter legs making him fall behind.

She nearly slammed into Vorrin. He had stopped in place at the entrance of an upward-curving tube of spider webbing. In the darkness beyond, she could make out panicked voices babbling in fear. Someone moaned.

"I think it's Zuna," he said. "But I don't know how we can get to her."

Jendara touched the end of her axe handle to the wall of the tube and gave it a tug. "It's the sticky kind."

She peered into the gloom. The muted sunlight barely penetrated the thick walls of webbing, casting the room beyond in shadows. She tried to guess at the room's dimensions, but the space went back a long way, winding off to the right and upward.

"It's all spider webs, isn't it?" Glayn whispered. "A whole room made out of spider webs."

"I'll bet only the entrance is sticky," Jendara mused. "Whatever's in there is something they want to protect. No point wasting sticky stuff on the walls—it'd just make it dirty and harder to move around." The spiders seemed immune to their own sticky threads, but if they had to maneuver other items, like food or gear, they wouldn't want to get them stuck. Or so she hoped.

Leather scraped against stone behind her, and she spun around to face Kran. "What are you doing here?" she snapped, keeping her voice quiet with some effort. "I told you—"

He waved a hand to cut her off, then tapped his temple.

"You had an idea?" Vorrin asked.

Kran held out the bowl he used to give Fylga water. It was full of crushed chalk—no doubt one of the pieces he carried for use with his slate. He smeared some on his palm and then patted the webbed wall beside him. His hand didn't stick.

"Of course," Glayn breathed. "I use sawdust to coat my caulking gear so it's not sticky."

"Good idea." Jendara said. Then she rapped her knuckles on the top of Kran's head. "Now get back to the entrance and hide like I told you."

Glayn took the bowl of chalk dust and began to toss handfuls on the floor and walls of the tube. Someone sobbed in the room beyond, and Jendara had to bite down on the side of her cheek to keep from calling out reassurance. She wanted to slash through the spider webs and charge in to the rescue, but she had no idea how the room was constructed. One wrong slash could drop the floor out from under Zuna and whoever else was in there. If she was already injured, a fall could kill their friend.

Glayn dropped to his hands and knees, testing the surface. "It's not too bad," he whispered. "But the roof's sticky, so stay low." He shrugged off his pack and began crawling.

Jendara and Vorrin left their own packs at the mouth of the tube, and then she followed Glayn inside. The silk creaked around her, the threads stretching beneath her palms. The dust had coated the top layer of strands, but she could feel the stickiness of the stuff below as their movement exposed it. The way out would be worse, she realized.

"Careful," Glayn gasped, and she paused to see what had startled him.

She stared around herself. Perhaps her eyes had grown accustomed to the dim bluish light that made its way through the webs. Glayn hung a few inches below her, clinging to the wall as he tried to make his own sense of the place.

The tube they had crawled through was like a straw stuck in the side of a hollow gourd. The curved floor of the gourd-shaped chamber lay at least twelve feet below the tube, and the ceiling stretched above at least thirty feet more. Thick strands of spider silk ran up the side walls, serving as support beams for the lighter-weight wall material. Each silk cable was the thickness of Jendara's leg, and its surface shimmered softly with that purple, alien sheen.

In the center of the room, a series of these cables ran down from the ceiling to support a massive disk of spider webbing. Another set of cables connected it to the back wall. It all supported the beginnings of a strange structure made up of smaller silken tubes, and as she studied it, she was suddenly reminded of the beehives in her yard. The bees built a framework of wax where they stored young larvae, placing each egg tenderly inside a chamber before sealing it off and building the next layer around the sleeping baby bee.

Here the silken structures were not small hexagons, but tall boxes that looked terribly like a bank of open coffins standing side by side with open fronts. Inside the row of silken boxes, she could see five humanish shapes, one per box, with Zuna and Fithrax at one end and three larger, misshapen ulat-kini beside them. Jendara wished she couldn't see those three tormented creatures with their bloated and bulging bodies.

"What do you see?" Vorrin whispered, and she realized she blocked his view. She hesitated a second, then gingerly touched the wall off to her right. As she had hoped, it wasn't sticky. She pulled herself out of the way, clinging to the wall like a frightened monkey clinging to a wall of vines.

Jendara's eyes crept back to the three sickening ulat-kini imprisoned in their silken coffins. They stood upright, a few coarse strands of silk binding them, finer webs gluing their hands and feet securely into the walls of their otherwise open prisons. She had no way to guess how long they'd been inside.

A flicker of movement caught her eye, and Jendara stifled an instinctive shriek. A massive spider hung from the ceiling above the silk coffins. Jendara held her breath, but it didn't seem to have noticed them.

The ulat-kini beside Fithrax groaned and writhed. His bloated body bucked. Jendara wished she could look anyplace besides the sickening bulges that pulsated on his chest and torso. The ulat-kini beside him slept.

The faint shushing of spider legs moving against silk warned that the spider moved. Its pendulous body twitched as it slowly slid down the largest of the support cables. The structure in the center of the chamber vibrated softly.

Zuna gave a frightened shriek and thrashed against her bonds, but her hands were swallowed up in silk. Thicker strands secured her waist so she couldn't wriggle too strongly.

Jendara scanned the room. The horror that had gripped her fast when she first saw the spider subsided a little. She pointed out a support cable that ran around the belly of the chamber. Longer and thicker than the others, it looked wide enough for them to follow around the side of the room.

Vorrin nodded and began to creep toward the cable. Glayn realized what Vorrin was doing and followed him cautiously. Jendara closed her eyes and sent a desperate prayer to the ancestors that the spider wouldn't see them or feel their movements vibrating through the silk strands. She risked another look at the most bloated ulat-kini.

Suddenly the ulat-kini shrieked, louder and longer than before. It was a scream of pure terror, of absolute pain, and it broke off with a squelch. Blood geysered from his mouth as he jerked. A groaning, crunching, crumpling sound came from his body.

And then the skin covering his ribs ripped open.

Blood and yellow pus boiled out of the wound and a pair of slender legs appeared, scrabbling on the slippery surface of the ulat-kini's chest.

Jendara couldn't move. She couldn't even breathe as the first fist-sized spiderling emerged from the ulat-kini's body. It perched on the dying ulat-kini's shoulder, rubbing its spiky legs in his blood.

She wrenched her eyes away. Vorrin was halfway across the chamber, one hand gripping the wall and the other out for balance. Glayn moved behind him cautiously. Jendara lowered herself down to the biggest cable and paused, thinking. If the spider noticed them, she was far enough behind the men that she wasn't sure she'd be able to help.

She glanced up at the spider. It had picked up speed and had nearly reached the cells that held the trapped prisoners. Its eyes were focused intently on its goal.

Jendara began to hurry along the cable in the opposite direction from the one Vorrin and Glayn had taken. Splitting up felt smart, and in a situation like this, she had to trust her gut. She moved quickly, keeping her balance without touching the silken wall, but ready to grab it if she needed. She'd spent most of her life on a ship. Walking this cable was easy.

Fithrax gave a startled yelp, and Jendara paused to check why. One of the spider's huge legs bore down on the layer of webbing that formed the top of his prison cell. The leg sank deeper into the web as the massive spider slowly repositioned itself. It adjusted its other legs to hold its great weight as its bloated abdomen slowly rolled to point down at Fithrax. Jendara glanced at the other ulatkini and the second spider crawling out of its torso. She had a horrible feeling she knew what was going to happen to Fithrax.

The spider's abdomen rippled. From the tip of the spider's abdomen, just below its spinneret, a flexible tube squeezed out. The spider's flanks gave a spasm, and the tube slowly extended. The tip glistened with a yellowish fluid. The spider tightened its grip on the cable, then drove its claw down through the web, coming down on the top of Fithrax's head hard enough to snap his forehead back. Yellow slime spurted over his exposed face.

Fithrax shrieked in terror.

18

MOMMY LONGLEGS

The spider's massive body obscured Fithrax from her view, but Jendara had seen enough. She leaped onto the support cable tethering the massive web platform in place. For the first time, the spider noticed the movement. It twisted around to stare at her with its ruddy eyes. At the edge of her vision, Jendara saw a flicker of movement as Vorrin climbed onto the far side of the platform. She had to serve as a distraction as he and Glayn freed Zuna and Fithrax. It might be their only chance.

She chopped at the wall of the coffinlike cell closest to her, sending out a shock wave of vibrations. The baby spiders—three now, and a fourth pulling itself up out of the dead ulat-kini's mangled chest—froze in place, staring at her with the same blood-red eyes as their mother. One of the little beasts flexed the armlike limbs on either side of its mouth.

The mother spider hissed.

Jendara grinned. "Better come and get me."

The flexing baby spider scurried down the dead ulat-kini, running far faster than its newborn legs ought to move. At the last second, it leaped into the air, soaring like a missile launched from some infernal catapult.

Jendara was ready for it.

The side of her axe caught the spiderling and sent it flying. It struck its mother's belly with a satisfying crunch. The mother spider shrieked in rage. Its spinneret pulsed and a long strand of sticky silk shot out at Jendara.

She managed to sidestep it. A sudden tugging on her pants leg made her realize another spiderling had approached while she was distracted. It raced up her leg, and she slapped at it. The sharp claws scored the side of her hand, ripping the flesh. She shouted in surprise and disgust and slapped it again, knocking it to the ground. She stomped on it, but the web beneath it absorbed most of the blow. The spiderling chittered and burrowed deeper into the platform.

A soft grunt made her glance away from the creature. Vorrin and Glayn had cut through the webs securing Zuna's limbs and were now trying to pull her away from the sticky back wall of her cell. They still had a lot of work ahead of them.

A silken cord just missed Jendara. She leaped backward, realizing even as she moved that she'd freed the smaller spiderling. She couldn't keep fighting two opponents, not when one moved with such uncanny speed—and she had no doubt the thing's bite was poisonous. The spiderling jumped at her and she spun sideways, slamming into the web coffins.

The third spiderling scrambled up over the dead ulat-kini's face and scurried along the top edge of the structure, headed straight for Jendara. She could hear squelching as the fourth spiderling finished emerging from its host.

Screw being a distraction. It was time to get rid of these nasty bugs.

Jendara kicked out, the tip of her boot catching a spiderling underneath its belly and sending it up into the air. A reel of silk shot out of its spinneret, but caught on nothing. Jendara swung her axe up underneath the spiderling, and it exploded in a cloud of blue goo and purple shards.

The other spiderling jumped, expecting to land on her face, but Jendara was already dropping into a crouch. She didn't pause, instead straightening up before the spiderling had a chance to regain its balance. Her bleeding right hand caught one of its nine legs and sent it flying into its mother's belly. It hit the surface hard and fell, stunned.

Jendara swept it off the platform with her boot. She flexed her hand. It bled a little, but at least she was regaining feeling and function in her right arm and fingers. If that first spider had known her, it would have bitten off her arm instead of just trying to crush it.

Then she saw the mother spider's head turn and stare down at Vorrin, who was helping Zuna cross the support cable to far side of the web chamber. The spider made a near-growl.

"Shit."

Jendara had to distract it before it shot down Vorrin and Zuna. The spider was still too high for Jendara to reach, and she wasn't sure the top layer of the web coffins would hold her if she tried to climb on them.

And then she had an idea.

"Watch out!" she shouted at Glayn, who knelt at Fithrax's feet, slashing at the ulat-kini's bonds. The gnome twisted aside as she charged.

Her axe bit into the spider's abdomen, and the spider screamed. Its legs flailed, stabbing down into Fithrax's shoulders and ripping at the coffin walls. Jendara reached out for the ulat-kini.

A leg speared down through the sheet of web, nearly skewering Jendara. She bobbed aside. "Is he free?" she shouted.

"He is now," Glayn grunted.

She grabbed Fithrax's shoulders and pulled hard. The sticky web of the back wall clung to him, ripping at his flesh. Jendara pulled harder.

Fithrax fell against her. His mouth opened and closed as he gulped for air. A thin ribbon of blood dribbled off his lip.

"You don't get to die," Jendara said. "I told Korthax I'd bring you back."

Fithrax coughed out a fine spray of blood. But he put his hand on her shoulder and took a wobbly step.

"Come on!" Glayn shouted.

Something struck Jendara between the shoulder blades. Hard little knives dug into the flesh of her shoulders. Jendara doubled over. There was no way she could reach whatever was biting into her back.

"Help!"

The gnome's knife flew through the air. The spiderling shrieked as the knife drove it back into the web coffin, pinning its body to the wall.

Glayn shoved Fithrax toward Jendara. "How in all hells are we going to get him across to the other side?"

"Take my sword," Jendara ordered.

"What?"

"Just take it!"

The gnome pulled the sword from Jendara's scabbard and stared at her. She pushed Fithrax down onto the support cable and wrapped one arm around him and the other around the cable.

"We all hang onto each other," Jendara explained, "and you cut the cable. Fast!"

The spider mother's spinneret twitched and sprayed out web as she worked to build the net that was rapidly filling the top of the chamber. The second she dropped that thing, they'd all be trapped inside with her.

"Cut it, Glayn!"

Gripping the sword in both hands, he slashed at the cable. Then he grabbed onto Fithrax's belt and gave the cable one last awkward chop. With a *twang*, the cable split. The three swung through the air and hit the wall. Jendara reached up to grab the main support beam, the one that Glayn and Vorrin had followed around the side of the chamber.

"Get up there, Fithrax." She grunted as she pushed him up past her, shoving his arm into the deep white fluff that made up the wall. It wasn't sticky enough to hold him up, but he managed to get a grip and bring his feet up onto the cable. He stopped moving for a second, coughing hard. A fine mist of blood spattered the white wall.

Jendara glanced back at the center of the room. The spider had stopped weaving her net and now turned to face them, realizing they were about to escape.

She caught Glayn's hand and yanked him up onto the cable. "Hurry! Go!"

They raced along the cable. Up ahead, Vorrin and Zuna were just scrambling up into the web tunnel. Jendara urged Fithrax and Glayn forward. If the spider caught them, they were dead.

Fithrax struggled to pull himself into the tunnel, and Glayn gave his backside a shove. Jendara didn't wait for the gnome to start climbing; she hoisted him up ahead of her. "Hurry!"

Fithrax crawled faster. Zuna and Vorrin were a dark blot at the end of the tunnel.

Jendara twisted around. The tip of a huge black leg appeared at the entrance of the tunnel, the biggest claw stroking the silk tenderly. It was feeling for vibrations, she realized. Feeling for them. She turned back around and felt her shoulder catch in the sticky stuff.

"Shit."

Glayn stopped. "What's wrong?"

She glanced back over her shoulder. Now there were two spider legs. "I'm a little stuck." She wouldn't say anything about the spider, not yet. "It'll just take me a second. Crawl faster."

She dug her toes into the spider web and threw herself forward. Her shoulder pulled free with a ripping of silken threads—thank goodness her sheepskin jacket was tough—and behind her, she heard a thin, high-pitched screeching that sounded all too horribly of delighted laughter.

"Hurry up!" she screamed, beyond the ability to keep calm, beyond feeling anything but the blind need to run. There was sudden light as Glayn wriggled out of the tunnel and she shot forward.

Her hands touched rock at the same time something tightened around her right ankle, and her leg yanked backward hard enough to make the joints scream with pain.

"Help!" She clawed at the stones, but her body slid backward inexorably.

"Jendara!" Glayn grabbed her wrists.

She gasped as her body snapped tight, held fast between her friend and the spider. "It's got me!"

"Hold on to her, Glayn!" Vorrin pulled out his sword. He slashed at the web that made up the roof of the tunnel, trying to make enough space to reach the line pulling on her ankle.

Glayn's boots skidded on the floor and Jendara let out an inadvertent shriek.

Then Kran was there, throwing his arms around Glayn's waist. Jendara tightened her grip on Glayn.

Vorrin swore softly as he chopped at the tough, sticky fibers. "Got it," he grunted and gave the sword one last swing. Jendara's ankle came free and she fell forward.

Glayn dragged her to her feet. "Are you all right?"

Fylga let out a volley of barking as the mother spider broke through the wall of the chamber, her tough leg spikes tearing free of the web as if it were wet paper. The wall beside it sagged and buckled, revealing more of the cavern's true shape. Where she and the others stood, the stone floor ran straight and true, but from that point left, erosion had worn away the stone. A rip between the egg chamber's wall and the floor revealed what she couldn't see before: the spiders had spun their web rooms over a hole in the ground. A salt breeze wafted up, carrying with it the sound of waves.

A sea cave. Jendara's mind spun. That was probably how the spiders had gotten inside the island—they'd simply floated inside, no different than riding the *Milady* into their own little grotto.

"We can get out down there!"

The others stared at her.

"Don't you hear the sea?" She point at the rip. "It's just down there!"

And then the spider mother knocked Jendara off her feet.

19

THE BITTEREST POISON

Jendara slid across the stone floor. A rock gouged into the meat of her chin as she went, and then she saw stars as her head smashed into the ground. She lay still a second, clutching her face. Her chin bled, a lot, but she didn't think the jaw itself was injured. She got to her feet and nearly toppled over backward as the rock crumbled beneath her feet. Desperate, she lunged forward and caught solid ground.

The spider snapped at Vorrin, venom dripping off its black fangs. He sidestepped the thing, his sword slicing through the air as he moved. The blade sheared through the tip of one of its mouth parts, and the spider reared back, more surprised than hurt.

Jendara looked around herself for something that might do more damage. This spider was huge, bigger than the one they'd faced back in the tunnel. She'd gotten lucky with that one, finding a weak spot in its armored hide. She might not get so lucky with this one.

An idea hit her. This time they weren't trapped in a tunnel. This time, they were perched on the edge of a crumbling cliff, and if she had to guess, that spider weighed a lot.

"Go for the face again!" she shouted.

Vorrin dropped to the ground as a length of silk shot over his head and came up with his boot dagger in hand. He launched it. The dagger soared through the air and drove into one of the spider's eyes. The creature took an inadvertent step backward over the edge of the cliff. Its front legs caught the rocky edge, but its great weight was too much for the weathered stone, and the wall crumbled beneath it. A length of silk caught for a second, and then another slab of stone sheared off the side of the cliff.

For a moment, no one moved, afraid the rest of the floor would follow. Then Jendara moved to the rim of the precipice, peering down into the darkness. Down below she thought she saw waves. There was no movement along the walls and no opalescent gleam of spider web, but she was ready for the thing to climb back up at any second.

"I heard a big crunch."

Jendara had almost forgotten Zuna, but the woman knelt on the floor beside her, gripping the edge tightly as she looked down into open space.

"I think it's gone," Zuna added. "We'd see it if it were going to climb back up. The rocks must have crushed it." Her voice was soft and horribly dry.

"Are you all right?"

Zuna shook her head. "I don't think so." She sank back into a seated position, and Jendara could see the effort it had taken Zuna to kneel.

Jendara hunkered beside her. "Your leg is bleeding."

"It hurts like demons are in it. But at least I can see again." Zuna rubbed her eyes. "Everything was colors, even sound. Ripples of strange colors like nothing I've ever seen before."

Vorrin touched Jendara's shoulder. "We have to get her back to the ship." He shook his head, his eyes dark and unhappy. "There's no way to know how much damage the spider's bite did, or what it's poison is doing to her."

Jendara got to her feet. "No one else got bit, right?"

She looked around at the group. Glayn and Kran shook their heads. A few feet away, Korthax knelt beside Fithrax, whispering in his ear. She squeezed Kran's shoulder as she passed him. Korthax whipped backward as she approached, as if embarrassed to be seen comforting his brother. Fithrax looked bad.

"Fithrax? Would you like some water?" She held out her canteen. Fylga paused to sniff at the three of them and then trotted away, disinterested.

"Here." Korthax took it. He sprinkled a few drops of water on his brother's lips. Up close, Jendara could see that Fithrax's face was wider and more froglike than Korthax's. He still showed hybrid features—there were a few threads where he might have once sported eyebrows, and his legs were longer than other ulat-kini's—but he looked more aquatic than his brother. Perhaps that was why the ulat-kini had chosen him as their leader, and not Korthax.

He coughed a wracking cough that sent pink froth spraying out his mouth. Korthax reached into the pouch at his waist. Something shiny slipped from his hand and he drew out a scrap of seaweed, which he wiped Fithrax's mouth with.

"What was that?" she asked on instinct.

"What?"

"That metal thing you just put in your pouch."

Korthax withdrew a bit of mother-of-pearl. "Our father's. I asked—" he broke off. "I do not think he has much time left."

"I'm sorry. I hope you can make him comfortable." She left her canteen with him and went back to look over the edge. There was no sign of the giant spider, and no way down to the water below except to lower themselves down by rope. She bit her lip. She had no idea how they were going to get Zuna back to the ship.

Kran waved at her. He tapped his ear and cupped a hand around it, miming listening hard. She paused to listen and heard only her own breath.

"What is it?"

He shook his head. But he kept his head cocked as if he still heard something. Then Jendara stiffened as she heard it, too. A tiny whisper.

"Somebody's trapped." She stared at the remaining web rooms. She didn't want to go into them now that she knew they hung over open space. Spider silk might be tough, but she didn't want to trust it with her life.

Kran raised an eyebrow and reached for his slate. *We don't weigh a tenth of what that spider did*, he wrote, as if reading her mind. He paused, listening again. Then he added: *Fylga*.

He didn't need to clarify. Jendara remembered the way the dog had sniffed around so purposefully when they first entered this chamber. Fylga had found something. Or someone.

Her heart climbed in her chest. Maybe the dog had found Sarni.

Jendara ran to nearest web chamber. "Fylga!" she called. "Fylga!"

She stopped in the entryway and covered her nose with her hand.

"Don't come in here, Kran," she warned, but too late. He was already beside her.

The walls of the chamber were lined with silk-wrapped bundles roughly the shape of small sea creatures. Black goo dripped from one bundle, and a charnel stink came off the foul puddle below. She was standing in the spiders' larder, and they needed to clean out the pantry.

Jendara caught Kran by the shoulders and steered him out. He spun around to wrap his arms around her, burying his face in her shoulder like he had as a little boy. She couldn't blame him.

Fylga barked again, and Kran pulled away. His cheeks were dry, his mouth set and hands curled into fists at his side. For a moment, she saw her father in him—her father and herself.

The dog stood in the doorway of the next chamber, her tail held high and ears pricked. If there was a spider inside, Fylga didn't smell or hear it. Jendara took a step inside, more than a little nervous. With every step, she expected that gigantic mother spider to burst up through the floor and grab her. If there was one thing she'd learned from that crab-thing, it was that she needed to make sure things were dead before she stopped worrying about them.

"Dara?"

The tiny voice came from deep inside the room. Jendara broke into a run. "Sarni?"

"Where am I?"

This room's walls were unbroken spider web, its lumps even larger and stranger. Kran tugged on her arm, gestured to the room and then the previous one, then made a gesture that meant *Same?*

"I don't think so." She poked at one of the lumpy spots and felt it resist the tip of the stout ash axe handle. She ripped back a hank of silk.

A deep one stared back at her, goggly eyes filmed over and dried. Its mouth opened and closed, but no sound came out. Jendara ripped at the fabric again, trying to make out its chest. It looked normal, not bloated like the chest of the ulat-kini who had been filled with eggs. Only its arms and legs looked strange, the skin black and cratered like a frostbite victim's. The deep one stared back at her without sight, its mouth opening and closing, opening and closing.

"Jendara?" Sarni whispered. "Where are you? Where am I?"

Jendara wrenched her eyes away from the deep one. "I'm right here, Sarni." She squinted hard, and could just make out Sarni's brown cap of hair above one of the silk-covered lumps. She went immediately to the girl's side, tearing silk away from her face.

Sarni stared around herself with the same blind, frosted gaze as the deep one. Jendara tugged the sheet of cobweb out of Sarni's fingers. "I've got you," she murmured. She put her hands under Sarni's arms and pulled the girl to her feet.

The stench hit her before realization did. Sarni's misty eyes rolled weakly in her head. Up close, Jendara could see the silken threads pinning the lids open. Fine strands of silk covered her nose, her ears, her mouth. Every surface of her had been meshed over, pulling her skin tight in places.

But not tight enough. Beneath Jendara's hands, she felt Sarni's skin sliding away, sinking into the gooey layer beneath the flesh.

"Oh gods," Jendara whispered. "Kran, get Vorrin."

The boy ran.

"Dara, I'm sorry."

"Sshh," Jendara said, easing the girl toward the doorway. She had to get her out of this place.

"I thought the danger was in the water, but it was on the cavern ceiling all the time. The *Milady*—" Sarni broke off with a little gasp of pain, and Jendara felt a hot trickle run out over her hands.

"Don't talk," she warned the girl.

"I woke up a couple of times. I was like a puppet. My body was moving, but I couldn't control it." Sarni began to weep. Her tears beaded up on the silk and then soaked through the fabric, making it sag.

Vorrin met them at the doorway and reached out to take Sarni's elbow. He stopped when he saw the black goo running down her sides where Jendara's hands dug into her rotting flesh. "Oh, sweet Desna. What happened?"

Jendara hesitated, not sure if she ought to try to keep Sarni upright or if her grip was doing more harm than good. The girl's legs buckled beneath her, and Jendara eased her to the ground. Skin and meat sloughed off with trickles of stinking black liquid.

"It sounds like she was some kind of a slave," she said. "Under the spiders' control."

Glayn came to kneel beside the injured girl. "Her whole body looks like Zuna's wound. The spider's bite is . . ." He trailed off, shaking his head. "We've got to get Zuna back to the *Milady*."

"I know," Jendara said. She squeezed her eyes shut against tears. "I don't think Sarni's going to make it back with us."

Sarni let out an anguished groan.

"It's okay," Jendara murmured. "We're here."

Blood welled up in the corners of Sarni's eyes, and a black rivulet trickled out of her left nostril. "It hurts so bad," she gasped. She gave a little shriek. "Oh gods!"

Jendara stared down at the girl. Stretched out flat like she was, Sarni's wounds were apparent: the spider silk had held her together, but only barely. Tarry goo wept out her pores, stinking of rotten flesh, and her skin was cracked and buckled. They'd never get her back to the *Milady*'s sick room in time to stop whatever vile poison was doing this.

Jendara had promised herself she would take care of Sarni. She had promised she would help the girl find a better life, a good life. And now Sarni lay here dying. "I'm so sorry."

Sarni's back arched with pain. "Make it stop!" she screamed. "Please!" Blood bubbled up on her lips. "Please, Dara. Please."

Jendara reached for her belt knife, tears making her vision blurry. "I'm so sorry," she repeated.

Vorrin reached out to stop her hand. "Jendara?"

Jendara blinked away the tears. "I promised myself I'd take care of her."

And then with clear sight she slashed the knife across Sarni's throat, and everything went silent.

Glayn put his arm around Jendara's shoulders. "We should go."

Jendara nodded. The melting husk that had been Sarni looked crumpled and hollow now. There was nothing left of the girl here. She let Glayn help her up.

She looked around the cavern. Korthax still knelt beside his brother. Kran and Fylga huddled together. Zuna sat propped against a rock. A huge weight settled into the pit of Jendara's stomach. They had come to find treasure, and it had all gone so wrong. Boruc and Tam, missing; Zuna, hurt; Sarni, dead.

She shook her head, as if she could shake away the feelings of despair that held her fast. "Korthax." Her voice was nearly a croak. She cleared her throat. "How's your brother?"

"Not good," the ulat-kini answered, without looking at her. "I do not think he will last much longer."

Jendara hunkered down beside the brothers. Fithrax's breathing made a horrible gurgle in his chest, as if something vital had broken inside him. She searched for words. She ought to reassure the creature, give him some kind of comfort. But she didn't have it in her to lie right now.

She reached for her canteen. "Are you thirsty?"

Fithrax shook his head, eyes rolling wildly in their sockets. He squeezed them shut, and then reopened them to fix his gaze on Korthax. "Yerka," he managed to say.

"I'll find her, don't worry."

"No." Fithrax stopped to cough. He drew a deep, wet-sounding breath. "She brought the black robes. For long time, she . . . watched us. For them."

Korthax stiffened. "I don't understand."

"They want something," Fithrax gasped. "Yerka . . . told me . . ." He closed his eyes, fighting for air.

Jendara leaned closer. "Korthax, what does he mean?"

"I don't know." His eyes narrowed as he spoke. She could see him thinking hard. "He shut Yerka up in the boat. I did not know why. I thought—to protect her? But perhaps he caught her spying for the black robes."

A thought struck Jendara. All signs had pointed to the deep ones as Yerka, Boruc, and Tam's kidnappers. But maybe there was more to it than mere capture. "Fithrax, does all this have something to do with the deep ones? Why did they argue with the black robes?"

"Deep ones—their god—" He stiffened, fighting against some deep pain. "Should have listened to you, Brother. Should have used . . . star scepter as you planned."

"Fithrax," Korthax whispered. He murmured something in their harsh language that made the other creature's features soften.

Then Fithrax burst into a coughing fit, his body doubling up as he fought to breathe. Finally, he coughed up a glob of bloody flesh. He lay back in Korthax's arms, limp. After a moment, he opened his eyes. "Tomorrow is the night to summon the god. The stars are right."

Korthax shook his head. "Don't talk anymore, please."

Fithrax fought for his next words. "Protect . . . our people. Do not let the black robes break their word." He gasped with pain and then went still, his eyes empty.

Korthax lowered his brother to the ground. "Fithrax?"

Jendara reached out toward the fallen ulat-kini, pausing for a second, unwilling to touch his green flesh. Then she put her hand on his arm. It was warm. It didn't feel remotely like a human arm, but it was still warm. There was no pulse. "He's dead."

"Yes." Korthax got up.

Jendara followed. Her joints were stiff. Her arm hurt, even if she could wiggle her fingers again. Her chin felt as if someone had inflated it and kicked it around like a ball. Her eyes were dry and puffy. "We've got to get out of here." Even her voice sounded tired and worn.

Vorrin helped Zuna to her feet. "And quickly. Zuna's getting weaker."

"Kran." Jendara looked around for the boy, who had followed Fylga away from the group and the spider web chambers. She hadn't paid much attention to that end of the cavern, where a few sheets of spider web hung like tent walls, obscuring much of the space. She pushed between them to watch her boy.

The way he climbed over the huge boulders and slabs of rock, intent on his footing, he could be back on Sorind, happily exploring. It made her smile to see him like this, as ordinary as could be, just a boy and his dog and their ever-present curiosity.

Even with the wind keening at her, she felt a little better watching him.

"Kran!" she called. "It's time to go!"

Fylga looked back at her and barked twice. Kran stood up straight and waved his arms hugely. Jendara put her hands on her hips, trying to figure out what he meant. He beckoned at her.

She made her way toward them. With the ground strewn with fallen rocks, it wasn't easy. "What is it?"

Kran cupped his ear and pointed at the wall ahead.

Jendara strained to hear whatever he did. All she heard was the wind, muttering and hissing to itself. She straightened up. They didn't have time—

Fylga scrambled up on a shelf of rock and began to paw at the wall, raking away loose gravel and mud. Kran jumped up beside her and set his shoulder against the wall. Rock groaned and scraped.

"Be careful!" Jendara shouted and raced to catch up with him just as Fylga fell through.

20

THE STARS OBSCURED

Jendara grabbed Kran by the back of the jacket as he wobbled on the edge of the rock shelf. "Vorrin! Help!" She hauled backward, her heart pounding.

Kran looked back at her, his face split in a wide grin. He shook his head.

"What?" she snapped.

Fylga barked, the sound resounding off the rocks. Jendara let go of Kran to rub at her ears. He wasn't falling. Fylga hadn't fallen, either. She leaned around Kran to peer into the gap they'd opened in the wall.

On the far side, another slab of rock stuck out, this one canted at a steep angle. Fylga stood a few feet below the tilted slab, her tail wagging as she balanced on top of another massive boulder. Huge rocks stood all around her, evidence of previous rockfalls and cave-ins.

Kran waved his hand in front of her face. Jendara frowned at him. "What?"

He crooked two fingers at his eyes, his gesture for "look where I look," and then stabbed them out into the darkness.

But it wasn't entirely dark. Beyond the massed boulders, a faint gray light reflected off rippling water. It had to be sunlight. The spiders' cavern must have once been joined to this larger one, until some ancient cave-in and subsequent rockfalls had separated the two spaces. "A sea cave," she mused. She patted his shoulder. "It's some find."

He pushed her hand away and pulled out his slate. *Nearly sunset. Western light?*

She read the words twice, her mind still focused on the cavern behind her. Zuna was in bad shape, and Fylga was already making her way to the next boulder. It was hard to pay attention to her son's cryptic notes when all she wanted to do was grab the stupid dog and get out of this damned cave and back to the *Milady*'s grotto.

Kran underlined the last sentence, looking at her questioningly.

Western light. But there hadn't been any other open sea caves when they'd circled the island—just the big grotto on the west side of the island.

Jendara grinned at him. "Yeah, I think you're right."

"Jendara? Kran? You two all right?" Vorrin called from behind them.

Jendara spun to face him. "Kran found the *Milady*'s cave!"

Jendara waited on the rocky shore for the dinghy to reach them. It had pained her more to watch her son and his dog swim away from her than it had to rip open her chin, but as Vorrin pointed out, Kran was the best suited for the job. Glayn was a slow swimmer, and with Jendara's injured arm still so awkward, she couldn't have made it across the cavern.

That logic hadn't made it any easier to turn her back on her boy and go help Vorrin bring Zuna out of the spiders' cavern. Fylga was a good swimmer, but if there was anything lurking in that lake—a group of deep ones or even an ordinary sea snake—Jendara knew the dog was no protection. She made Glayn stand with her and watch the boy's every stroke while they were separated.

But here they were, boy and dog, rowing to their rescue. He'd even had the presence of mind to grab a lantern.

Vorrin put his arm around her. "He's a fine boy, Dara. Strong and smart and level-headed."

She rested her cheek against his shoulder. "I don't know how we got so lucky."

"He gets it all from his mother." He pulled back, his eyes dancing. "Well, at least the first two."

Jendara swatted his arm. "Thanks a lot!" Then a thoughtful look came over her face. She nodded at Glayn, who was offering Zuna water from his canteen. "But in all seriousness, the whole ship raised Kran. Everyone helped. And you've always been there for him."

"I've always loved Kran," he said in a soft voice.

Then he hurried into the shallows to hold the dinghy steady for the boy. Kran gave the man an absentminded hug and then scrambled up on the shore. The moment made Jendara's heart float.

But a ribbon of chilly steel tethered her heart inside her rib cage. To love, she had learned over the years, was to risk loss. And today she'd lost Sarni just when she was starting to really get to know her.

By all she held holy, she promised herself, she wasn't going to lose any more of her loved ones to this damn island. And anything that came between her and her people would find that out the hard way.

Glayn entered the galley and Jendara jumped to her feet. "How's Zuna?"

Kran and Vorrin looked up from their card game with anxious expressions. Only Korthax ignored the gnome, lying on the floor with his face covered.

Glayn sank onto a bench. "Better, I think. With the healing potion and a little sleep, I think she'll be mostly herself tomorrow.

The worst was bandaging the bite. I just kept thinking of—" He broke off and rubbed his palm across his face.

Jendara swallowed down the lump in her throat. "Let me get you some dinner."

She brought him a dish and sat down beside him. "We've been making some plans," she said. "We'll set out first thing in the morning."

"Sure."

"I'm not leaving this island without Tam, Glayn. He's like a brother to me. But none of us are in any shape to go out tonight."

"I said 'sure,'" the gnome said in a dull voice. "So let me be until morning."

She got up from her seat, stomach twisting around what she'd eaten earlier. She strode over to Vorrin and leaned close to his ear.

"I'm going above. Do a little scouting, just to make sure we didn't miss anything in that far corridor."

"I'll come with you." Vorrin started to his feet, but she pushed him back into place.

"No, I need you to keep an eye on things. You know I can handle myself."

"I know, but I don't like it."

"I won't be long." She shrugged on her sheepskin jacket and hurried off the ship. She jogged up the stairs as quickly as her human-length strides could take her.

The boulevard unfolded in quiet gloom: with the sun so low, the glow from the skylights was faint, but the open doors of the Star Chapel spilled out a soft amber glow. Jendara broke into a run, eager to reach the chapel. She could check it over and catch the last of the sunset.

Inside the chapel, a few bloodstains marked the spot where they'd fought the deep ones, but besides that minor token of violence, the room was filled with peace. A breeze wafted in through the broken windows, and peach and pink tones fanned across the horizon joyfully.

Jendara leaned her forehead against the cool stone, breathing in the clean fresh air and letting the last rays of sun play over her skin. As a pirate, she had seen the world. Much of that world was dark and unpleasant, with petty crooks and vicious creatures eager to prey upon anyone weaker than themselves. Ancestors knew, she'd been one of them once. But wherever she'd gone, the sweetness of nature had always revived her. Fresh air and clean water were things she could always count on.

But not here. The island's long sojourn beneath the waves had corrupted this place, corroding even the inner wholesomeness of the stone itself. She wondered if that corruption came not from the sea—the sea had been Jendara's constant companion since the day she was born on a small island—but from the people who had lived here before and died in the island's drowning. From the prison cells in the island's depths to the horrible staring eyes in the ruined paintings staring down from the boulevard's walls, this place was saturated with foulness and despair. She had run down the boulevard, she realized, not just to reach this last bit of sunshine before it could fade away, but to escape the evil around her.

Who had lived in this place? Why had they built it? The questions felt vital. There was a reason the black robed denizens of Leng had been so interested in this place. The deep ones knew it, even if the ulat-kini didn't—they had their own connections to this place.

She had a hunch that whatever had brought all these creatures here, it had something to do with the evil she could sense at the heart of all of this.

"I thought you might come here."

She turned to face Korthax. His face looked less strange than it had the first time she'd seen him, here in this same room. She couldn't decide if that was because she'd grown accustomed to his fishy, froggy looks, or if she had simply seen so many odder faces. She found herself unsurprised to see him. After what they'd just been through, he must have needed to be alone as well.

"I'm sorry about Fithrax."

He crossed to her side so he could lean out the window. "Do not be. He was a—" He made an unintelligible sound, but his face conveyed plenty.

"Even if he was a real bastard, he was still your brother."

He glanced at her. "Yes." He paused, looking for the words. "But he was too hungry for power. It is his fault we work for black robes. If I had become leader, everything would be different."

"What do they *want*?" Frustration colored Jendara's voice. The black-robed folk of Leng, with their black ship and their strange building materials, were not like any of Golarion's people that she had ever known.

"They ask us for help, ask us to join them and free Leng from evil spiders. They say they admire us for our lives on the sea and under it." Korthax gave a disbelieving snort. "Fake talk. Too showy."

"False flattery or not, if there are spiders like that on Leng, I'm not surprised they came looking for help."

Korthax leaned far out the window, his face darkening. "You see that?"

Jendara shifted to see out farther. The bulk of the island cut off her view, but she could just make out a black dot moving in from the far northwest.

"Is that the black ship?"

He squinted. "But it is not alone."

Jendara watched the black shape become a cluster of dots. The massive black ship from Leng led a group of smaller longships. None flew a flag. They could hail from any port in the Ironbound Archipelago, or even from the mainland. There was nothing northwest of this island, not even a tidal atoll, but Jendara knew that meant nothing. The rocky shoals off the northeast side of the island meant any craft wanting to approach the ulat-kini's docks had to come from the northwest.

Her lips tightened. Her easy-come, easy-go treasure mission was getting even more crowded.

"Let's go tell the others," she said.

Korthax kept staring as if he hadn't heard her.

"Korthax?"

He pulled his head back inside and blinked at her for a second. The last fingers of sunlight cast a ruddy stain across his green cheek.

"Yes," he said, finally. "The others should know."

Jendara opened her eyes. The cabin was quiet. Even the wind had died down, and yet she couldn't sleep. When she'd been on watch, she could hardly keep her eyes open. Only the sounds of one of the crew members thumping around down in the storage room had kept her from dropping off with her head on the deck railing. But somehow now that she was in bed, the act of closing her eyes felt repugnant.

She rolled over, trying to enjoy Vorrin's warm bulk beside her on the mattress. In the dim closeness of the cabin, she could hear Kran's easy breathing. The boy had spent the last few hours of the evening playing some ridiculous string-weaving game with Korthax, and now he slept the peaceful sleep of the young. She owed Korthax for that, she supposed. After the horrors of the day, the boy needed time to play and be silly to clear his mind and settle his thoughts.

She sighed. If she kept thinking about it, she would never go to sleep. Jendara forced her eyes closed and listened to the soft sounds of her family's breathing.

She fell

down

down

into the well of sleep, where far above the black velvet of the sky turned behind a veil of unchanging diamond pieces.

Stars. Her thoughts echoed off the walls of stone around her. The great weight of them pressed down upon her and she clawed at the walls, unable to rip her eyes from the sky above for even a second. The stars. The stars. She had to reach them. They burned brighter and brighter, bearing down on the world like fierce, angry eyes.

Her fingers slipped and skidded on the damp stone. Something was wrong, something was terribly wrong, she wasn't hearing just the sounds of her thoughts and the sounds of her own flesh slapping against the stone, but some other terrible sound—

a screaming

—she batted the thought away, of course no one was screaming, she had to get to the stars, no matter what happened—

And now the light of the stars was bright enough to bring a grayness into the very depths of the well itself, and she glanced around her and realized she was floating, floating on a thick liquid whose level was rising, rising, terribly rising even as the volume of the screaming grew louder and louder—

And then a face broke the surface of the liquid, and it was Sarni, her face bloodstained and swollen and another face emerged, so bloody Jendara couldn't name it for a moment, but it was Leyla, and then Morul, and then all the faces of the people of Sorind and she was swimming in *their* blood and the level was rising, rising, rising—

Taking her toward the stars whose gaze she could no longer meet, but could feel drilling into her flesh and another face came up from the depths of the blood, an utterly familiar face—

she tried to wake up, but she couldn't pull herself up out of the well of sleep—

she had to wake up before the eyes opened and it was really him—

Kran's eyes opened and blood washed over her head and she was drowning and—

"Jendara, wake up."

Jendara's eyes flew open.

Vorrin shook her shoulder again. "Wake up."

"I'm awake." She shuddered and sat up. Someone had lit the lantern beside the bed, and Kran stood beside it, his eyes huge and darkly circled. "What a nightmare."

Kran nodded. She could see him tremble even at this distance. She reached out for him and pulled him to her. "A horrible nightmare. So horrible."

Vorrin folded his arms around them both. "Me, too. Blood, and stars, and I was trapped."

Kran went stiff in Jendara's grip.

"What did you say?" Her voice was a whisper.

"My dream." Vorrin pressed his cheek against hers. "I was in some kind of pit trap and there were these horrible stars in constellations like I'd never seen before."

"And a lot of blood," Jendara said.

Kran pulled away, his eyes wide and terrified as he nodded.

Jendara dug her fingers into the edge of the mattress. "What in all hell were we dreaming?"

Haggard and drawn, they dressed and made their way to the galley. Fylga greeted them at the galley door, her tail pressed low to her legs. Jendara brewed tea and moistened some dried meat for the dog. They could all use a bit of a treat this morning.

Zuna trudged into the galley, bundled up in an old quilt. Jendara offered her a cup of tea. "You all right?"

Zuna shook her head. "Bad night. Gozreh keep me from dreams like that ever again."

Jendara stirred oats into her pot of hot water. "You worship Gozreh?" She felt strange asking. Zuna had served as the ship's navigator for years. Jendara should have known such a basic fact about one of her crew members, but Zuna was a private person, and Jendara . . . well, she had to admit that she hadn't tried very hard to get to know her.

Zuna pressed the hot mug against her bandage, the tired lines of her face softening. "My mother raised me to believe. I'm not a good follower, but I make offerings when I remember."

Jendara could understand. She opened her mouth to explain her own feelings, but the galley door swung open and Glayn came in, looking even worse than Zuna.

Vorrin looked up from his mug. "Bad dreams?"

Glayn's lips tightened. "Bad's not the word for it." He joined Jendara beside the stove and she put a mug of tea in his hand. "Thanks."

"I had a feeling." Jendara rubbed her dry eyes. She could make tea and start porridge as if it were just another morning, but it wasn't. She squared her shoulders. "What kind of place gives a group of people the same evil dreams? What does that?"

Kran's chalk scuffed across the surface of his slate. He held it up. *I keep having nightmares. Don't want to sleep.*

Vorrin patted the boy on the back. "I know, Kran. You must be exhausted."

Glayn put down his tea. "Do you think it's just us? I mean, do you think Korthax had those dreams?"

Zuna stretched and yawned. "He's humanoid. I guess."

"Well, I'm going to ask him." Glayn strode out the door.

Jendara brought down bowls for everyone, moving at what felt like half speed. They had to find Tam and Boruc today. She couldn't imagine another night like the last one.

The galley door burst open.

"Korthax's gone." Glayn paused to catch his breath. "I checked everywhere, and he's just gone."

21

STAR TAKER

Zuna squeezed past Glayn and Jendara to reach for the crock of sugar. She pulled out a lump. "He probably just changed his mind about leaving his tribe. After all, with Fithrax gone, he could take over as leader."

Vorrin frowned. "Wouldn't he have asked for his fare? Ulatkini still like gold."

Gold. Jendara suddenly thought of the thumping that had kept her awake on her watch. "Who was in the storage room last night?"

Vorrin shook his head. "I was trying to sleep before my watch."

She looked around at the others. "Did anyone else come back to the storage room last night? When I left the galley for my watch, it was just Vorrin in the kitchen and Kran and Korthax at a table, playing games."

Kran sat up straight. Jendara moved away from the stove to face her boy. "What happened?"

He wrote very slowly: *Got tired. Korthax was eating, so I left him here.*

Jendara strode to the storage room door and flung it open. "Not locked." She gave the lock a cursory glance. "The metal's all scratched up. He must have picked it."

The others crowded into the small space. Their stores of flour and ham were untouched. Jendara checked the shelves, trying to see what, if anything, was missing.

"Oh no."

She turned to face Vorrin.

"I put Kran's pack in here," he said. "Just to get it out of the way while he was playing. I knew he'd put that astrolabe inside, and I didn't want it to get stomped on." He pointed to an empty hook on the back of the door. "I put it right here."

They filed out of the storage room. Jendara tried to remember what else Kran kept inside his pack, but she couldn't imagine Korthax being interested in such ordinary items as a canteen and a bowl for watering the dog. Only the astrolabe stood out. But what could Korthax have wanted with the thing? It was beautiful and likely valuable, but not nearly as valuable as the statue Zuna had found. There was certainly more money to be made collecting gold leaf from the tops of the island's towers than from hawking an ancient brass astronomical device.

Jendara ate her breakfast beside a frowning Kran. He had liked Korthax, and the ulat-kini had stolen from him. She could understand if the boy was hurt.

She pushed a bowl of dried apples toward him. "You okay?"

He reached for his slate but didn't write anything for a long moment. He looked around for Fylga and snapped his fingers, calling her to his side. The boy stroked his dog for a moment, and then, still rubbing at the dog's ear, began to write:

Astrolabe. Stars. The dream.

Jendara's skin prickled as she read the words. Kran studied her face to make sure she had read them all and then added:

Fithrax said the stars are right.

"But right for what?" she asked. "They kept talking about their god."

He scrubbed the words off slowly, working his lip between his teeth. He tapped his chalk against the slate and then wrote: *In my dreams—had to reach the stars. Had to get out of a deep pit.*

Jendara remembered the desperate compulsion she'd felt to pull herself up to those scorching stars. "Yeah, me too."

What if ulat-kini's god needs to get to them?

She met his eyes. "You think Korthax stole the astrolabe to take it to the ulat-kini. For whatever this ritual is."

He shrugged, then nodded.

Something else he said made her pause. "Kran, did you say, 'in your dreams'? Like, more than one? You dreamed about the stars before this?"

He nodded.

Jendara beckoned Vorrin over. "I think I have to go talk to the ulat-kini again."

He folded his arms across his chest. "Why?"

"I think there's something they're not telling us about this ritual, something that might affect us." His expression didn't change, so she pushed on. "I just have a feeling, Vorrin. That dream we had last night? About the stars? Kran had it before. I think that means something."

"The people who built this place were obsessed with stars," Glayn reminded them. "Maybe there's some connection between the stars and what happened here before."

"By the gods, I hope not," Vorrin said. "I'd like to think this island sank from purely natural causes."

Jendara's eyes widened. "But what if it didn't? What if there's some star-planet alignment thing going on, and the island sinks again? We can't stay here if the ocean is going to come drown us all!"

Vorrin sighed. "Okay, we go talk to the ulat-kini again."

"Not we," Jendara said. "Just me. The rest of you need to keep searching for Boruc and Tam. That tunnel we found yesterday led somewhere. We saw tracks, we saw a broken lantern. We know someone took Boruc and Tam and that they went that way. Maybe you'll find them today."

"No," Vorrin said. "We don't split up. It's a bad idea."

"Vorrin."

They all turned to face Zuna, who stood cupping her mug of tea in her hands. "We have to. If Jendara's right, we don't have much time. Splitting up makes the most sense."

"I'll go fast, I'll get in, I'll get out, I'll be back before afternoon. My pack's all ready. I can leave now."

Vorrin leaned down, bracing his hands against the table. "I don't like this," he murmured, too low for the others to hear. "If something happens, I want to be there to help you."

She leaned her cheek against his shoulder. "I know. But you're the captain, and you have an obligation to your crew."

"I have an obligation to my wife."

She pulled back so she could see his face. "I love you," she whispered.

"I love you, too."

Jendara gave him a quick kiss. "I'll be back before you all know it," she announced. "Kran, you and Fylga had better find our friends, okay? We're depending on your skills."

She stopped in the doorway and looked back at them: Vorrin, frowning after her; Glayn, tiny, and for once, unsmiling; Zuna, the skin under her eyes puffed with tiredness, but an encouraging look on her face; and last, her little boy, the only one who wasn't watching her leave, but instead crouched beside Fylga, his face bent close to the dog's yellow ears.

Her people. She wasn't about to let anything happen to them, stars or no stars.

Jendara set her back to the stone support column and listened hard. Ever since she'd entered this hallway, headed toward the ancient library, she thought she'd heard someone behind her, but every time she'd glanced back over her shoulder, the hallway had been dark and empty. If it was someone—some deep one, perhaps— making for the hallway where they'd found Boruc's, Tam's, and

Yerka's tracks, then it must be alone and not eager for a run-in with a lone human.

She hesitated.

The most pressing issue was the astrolabe. Whatever the ulat-kini planned to do with their god and the stars, she had to know more. She had to protect her people.

But if there was a deep one skulking along behind her, maybe she could get it to take her to Boruc and Tam right now. She could have them all back to the ship before Vorrin could even get his gear together.

Jendara lowered the flame on her lantern and left it tucked behind the column. Her boots didn't make a sound as she crept across the floor the deep ones had so thoroughly cleaned.

A tiny scuffing sound warned her that her prey was nearly upon her. She reached for her belt knife. Her arm was good enough today for her to use her sword, but she didn't want to kill the creature—just snare it. She stalked forward a few steps and then launched a kick at the form she could barely see in the gloom.

Her kick went over its head as the creature dropped to the ground, rolling across the stone. Jendara launched herself at it, grabbing its narrow shoulders and pinning them to the ground. She reared back, ready to head butt it into submission.

Then sense struck her.

"Kran, what are you doing here?"

He patted blindly at her face. She realized she'd terrified the boy, and she caught his hand in hers. "It's okay," she said, as gently as she could under the circumstances. "It's just me."

She led him back to her lantern and turned up the light. He held out his lantern. Jendara reached in her belt pouch. "You left without lighting your lantern or grabbing a flint striker. Let me guess. You didn't bring water or food, either."

He hung his head.

"Going out unprepared will get you killed." She lit his lantern and then folded her arms across her chest, studying him. At least he'd had the presence of mind to replace his belt knife with something from the stores. "What was so important you had to chase after me?"

He brought out his slate and wrote for a second, pausing to dig in his pocket for a fresh stick of chalk. *Skortti has star scepter.* He paused, then underlined the word "star."

She looked from the words to his face. An idea began to bubble in the back of her tired mind. "You think there's a connection between this star scepter and the astrolabe?"

Kran nodded vigorously.

Jendara began to walk. "So Skortti's his uncle, and Skortti's obsessed with the star scepter. Maybe Korthax wants to give Skortti the astrolabe to win him over."

Kran tugged on her arm. He scribbled: *Skortti made Fithrax leader.*

"Good point. With Skortti's help, maybe Korthax could become the ulat-kini's new leader. If—"

She broke off, hearing feet on the floor behind them. She spun to face the sound.

And then stopped.

Not because she wanted to stop, but because her body might as well have been made of wood. She stared at the creature in front of her, its soft pinkish flesh making it look like nothing so much as a hairless bear. But its face was no bear's face. Instead of a snout or a mouth or even eyes, it had only thick, fat tentacles that wriggled and writhed like snakes seeking out its prey.

And worse than all that was the horrible mocking laughter resounding inside Jendara's mind.

22

MOON-βEASTS AND MINDS

Jendara had been knocked out more than once in her life. She was familiar with the feeling that came before losing consciousness, the strange hollow, metallic ringing in the ears and the distant sensation that took hold of the body. If she could have summoned up those feelings and used them to actually pass out, she would have.

But instead she remained sickeningly awake even as her body began to move against her will. A thickset ulat-kini bound her hands, and she simply followed after him without any kind of struggle. She wanted to rage. To vomit. To close her eyes and wake up and find it was all a dream.

Her body followed meekly, with Kran trotting along beside her.

The pink beast stepped aside as they approached, although she had no idea how it could sense them. There were no signs of any sensory organs on its hideous head. She couldn't hear its laughter any longer, but she could still *feel* its presence within her somehow, like a heavy hand pressing down on the inside of her brain. The pressure came with a sensation of oily heat that cut her in half— her thoughts lay on one side of the hot divide, her frozen legs on the other, and any attempt to cross made her thoughts slip and slide away from her grasp until that heavy weight pressed them back down into an inert block.

She couldn't even force herself to take the deep breaths that might have given her calm. She could only batter her thoughts against the pink beast's revolting presence and then regroup them, tired and desperate to return to their ordinary connection to her body.

As the group moved back down the long hallway, she considered the strangeness of the entire experience. If anyone had asked, Jendara would have maintained that her mind and her body were two very separate entities, and that she controlled both of them with the force of her will and personality. Now, observing her mind's struggles to reconnect with her physical being, she wasn't so sure. Her thoughts were so feeble and weak without the strong support of her senses. While she could see and hear well enough— although distantly, as if the information came to her down a long, echoing tube—she had almost no sensation of movement or balance or touch. She drew up her will and struggled to wiggle a finger, twitch a face muscle, anything at all.

Pain and pink light filled her head, and for an instant, Jendara did not exist.

When she was able to think and focus again, her body and the rest of the group had already marched down into the depths of the island. She had no idea where they were. But the bindings on her mind and body had now loosened a little, giving back her eyes and ears. In her peripheral vision, she could see Kran stump along, chin down and face unreadable. An ulat-kini led them both, but ahead of the ulat-kini walked two squat, black-robed figures, their faces veiled.

It was the first time she had gotten to see the people of Leng up close. She studied them closely. They were stocky folks, shorter than herself and much broader, with no definition of waist or hip. Though they moved easily enough, Jendara noticed a number of lumps and bumps along their backs, strange protrusions their robes didn't cover. Weapons, perhaps. Their feet struck the ground with the click-clack of a sheep's hooves.

She wished she could move her head to get a better view of the Leng folk and her surroundings. One of the ulat-kini carried a lantern, but most of the light around her came from the faint blue glow of phosphorescent seaweed. Its cold light provided a soft gloom that made it harder to see, not easier. Blue shadows added a strange dimension to everything.

"Be on the watch for the spiders," one of the Leng people snapped at the nearest ulat-kini. "And make sure the prisoners' weapons are free so they can guard our backs."

"But—" the ulat-kini began, and the black robe cut him off. "They're completely under the moon-beasts' control. Like puppets. Or do you want a personal demonstration of the moon-beasts' power?"

One of the other denizens of Leng gave a nasty laugh. If Jendara could have moved, she would have knocked its teeth out.

The hallway turned a corner and the overpowering stink of old urine, unwashed bodies, and rotten fish washed over her. The ulat-kini stepped aside and Jendara saw what she smelled: a large group of people crowded into a room with a vast open hole in the floor. One man hung over the edge, dangling from the black ropes binding his wrists to the woman beside him. He did not move. He said nothing. And although his weight pulled her nearly over the edge of the pit, causing the rope around her wrist to bite deeply into her swollen, purple flesh, the prisoner beside him said nothing, either.

The only sound was the faint damp rustling that came from far below.

Jendara stared at the nearest prisoner, and he stared back at her. Only his eyes moved, wide and horrified in his filthy face. How long had all these people been standing here, immobilized by that tentacled creature?

"Put her in the back," a cold and somehow metallic voice announced, and the ulat-kini captor marched Jendara and Kran to the narrow aisle left between the prisoners and the wall.

Now Jendara could see that the orderly columns and rows of frozen, silent humans stretched nearly the full length of the room—a massive cavern nearly as large as the spiders' cave. A few more of the pink-tentacled creatures—moon-beasts, they'd called them—circled the room, and there were at least two dozen ulat-kini guards, as well as several denizens of Leng.

There were at least a hundred people here, if not more. Half-paralyzed as Jendara was, it was hard to get a look at the full expanse of them. The first man she had seen was filthy, his face mostly obscured by a smear of dried blood and hugely swollen broken nose. The woman behind him looked injured, too, a deep cut on her forehead showing the bone. The moon-beasts may have taken control of these people's bodies, but some of them had gotten a chance to fight before they'd been captured.

Jendara strained her eyes as far to the side as she could, wishing she could turn her head to make out these brave faces. These people had to have arrived on the longships she'd seen yesterday from the Star Chapel. The ones she could see wore simple wincey or woolen garb, the same homespun fabrics in the same rich colors the people of her own island wore.

A pebble shifted underfoot, and Jendara stumbled sideways, for the first time tilting her body toward the center of the great room. A bearded face leaped out of the crowd, the thick red hair all too familiar. Morul stared back at her with panicked eyes.

The ulat-kini dragged her back in line.

Morul! Had she really seen him? Jendara's heart sank. Sorind sat apart from the other inhabited islands of the archipelago, easily reached without interference from the more heavily armed islands of Battlewall or Flintyreach. If the people of Leng were looking for prisoners, the island would have been a tempting destination.

The ulat-kini shoved Kran sideways, his bindings dragging Jendara along. The boy slammed into the arm of the nearest prisoner, a heavyset old woman that Jendara recognized by her posture and simply braided gray hair. It was Chana, the healer and wise-woman of Sorind. Behind her, a bored-looking ulat-kini snapped to attention.

Out of the corner of Jendara's eye, she noticed a narrow doorway at the very corner of the room, the tunnel beyond unlit. She felt the ulat-kini's webbed hands dig into her skin as it lashed a tough rope of seaweed around her arm. It knotted the rope to the bindings of the prisoner in front of her, then quickly secured Kran in the same fashion, adding a second rope running from his wrists to Chana's.

Jendara squeezed her eyes shut. Her people, *her* Sorinders, captured by these loathsome fish-men. And why? Why would they steal an entire village of innocent people and hold them captive in their horrible sea cave? What did they want with them?

A familiar voice came from her right. Skortti said: "Has the device been taken to the Star Chapel?"

"It will be there when we need it." This was the same speaker with the cold, metallic voice that had sent her and Kran to the back of the room. Jendara's eye muscles trembled from straining to see farther to the right. She could just see Skortti emerging from the dark doorway, and moving toward him, one of the black robes of Leng.

"The offering will keep the god calm enough for travel," Skortti warned the denizen of Leng, "but it will still be dangerous. The god has been sleeping a long time. It will not be easy to control."

"The moon-beasts will be more than its match," the denizen of Leng answered.

"So you have said, Ahrzur. But the people of this island worshiped this creature. Their whole city worked to keep the creature happy. If such superior beings could not keep the god under control, I worry that a few pudgy pink beasts can handle it."

Was Skortti right? Had the entire island civilization existed just to control some sleeping god? And if so, what had made the civilization fall? Jendara struggled to move her hands. She had to get free and find Vorrin. There was no way she was going to risk staying on this island with a rogue god that may have already destroyed an entire society.

She missed Ahrzur's reply. The man seemed to be the leader of the denizens of Leng, or at least their representative to the ulat-kini. Though she couldn't hear his words, his condescending manner was unmistakable.

Ahrzur's answer seemed to rankle Skortti. "Yes," the ulat-kini snapped. "I *am* certain of the calculations. Not only have I been studying the scepter since Fithrax gave it to me, I've also done extensive study of the Old Ones' library since our arrival on this island. The scepter's symbols are clear: tonight is the best time for the ritual. Beginning before moonrise would be foolhardy."

The two leaders moved away, still discussing the ritual. Jendara wished she could follow behind them and learn more. What would happen during the ritual? What kind of device was going to be moved to the Star Chapel?

The ulat-kini who had tied up Jendara stepped away. A black robe joined him. Jendara couldn't quite tell, but she thought they were the only guards at this end of the room.

"The god seems restless," the black robe mused.

"I hope we have enough humans to satisfy it," the ulat-kini said.

The two guards disappeared into the dark tunnel.

Jendara could only widen her eyes, although she wanted to scream. That was it, then—Skortti was going to kill them all, a sacrifice to his god. A hundred people were going to die for the ulat-kini's deal with the denizens of Leng.

A sharp tug on her wrists brought her tumbling down to the ground. Kran pulled her face so she could look into his eyes. Whatever had held them immobilized no longer seemed to work on her son.

He held her gaze for a long moment, his huge brown eyes filling her vision. She had to get free. For him. Her mind struggled in its prison. For a moment, a horrible squeezing sensation filled her head.

And then, somehow, she could move.

Kran pulled out his belt knife and cut her bonds. She had no idea how he'd gotten free of both his ropes and his mind control, she was just glad their guards had left them their weapons in case of spider attack. Jendara glanced around. The nearest exit was the doorway that Skortti had used. She had no idea where they were on the island, and the ulat-kini had taken her lantern, but it was better to be free in the dark than trapped in here.

She jerked her head toward the doorway, but Kran held up a hand. He pointed to his left, toward the edge of the pit. Jendara frowned. She hadn't been able to turn her head and look down inside the pit before, but now she might be able to get a glimpse. She wondered what Kran wanted her to see.

Easing around Chana, she peered down into the dark pit. She thought she could hear the faint sound of waves coming from far, far below, but she saw very little. The walls of the chasm gave off a blue-green glow that filled the pit with an eerie gloom. She squinted.

Something moved in the deeps, something huge and moist and horrible. Just looking at it made her remember her nightmare the previous night, as if the endless screaming of the stars still resounded in her head.

Jendara wrenched her gaze away, feeling blessed silence fill her skull. What in all hells was down there? She didn't want to stick around to find out.

She seized Kran's hand and hurried toward the doorway. Suddenly, Kran's hand was ripped out of hers and she stumbled forward.

"Hey, that kid's getting away!"

Jendara realized she hadn't been seen, and was now hidden in the doorway—but Kran stood completely exposed, as still as a statue under the moon-beasts' renewed control. An ulat-kini guard burst into view. Jendara shrank into the shadows. The guard grabbed her son's frozen figure and dragged him back toward the others.

Every instinct screamed at Jendara to charge the bastard, but she could hear more guards running their way. She backed away, holding her breath. If she was seen and paralyzed again, she couldn't help anyone.

She had to leave her boy behind if she was going to save him.

23

IN THE DEPTHS

Somewhere behind her, ulat-kini shouted at each other. They had caught Kran, and now someone had finally realized Jendara was gone.

Jendara didn't dare run in the dark tunnel. She remembered all too well the rotten stone walls and floors she'd encountered throughout the island, and found herself whispering pleas to the ancestors as she groped her way along the nearest wall. If she died, no one would know about the people trapped in that horrible room behind her.

Her prayers were answered by sudden empty space beneath her hand. She fumbled around, trying to feel if it was a doorway or just a crack in the wall. It was impossible to tell. The shouting sounded louder and nearer. Desperate, Jendara wormed her way into the opening just as torchlight appeared at the end of the tunnel.

Her foot slipped on slick rock, and for a moment she teetered on open space. Then she dropped like a lead fishing weight.

Jendara twisted and clawed at the rock wall, bashing her elbow on an outcropping. She bit down on a curse and clamped her arms around her head as she tumbled.

She hit bottom in a spray of water and lay still for a moment, making certain all of her was intact. Her head protested the thumping ride, as did her elbows and tailbone. She was somehow, miraculously, in one piece.

She rolled onto her hands and knees. A trickle of water ran over the floor around her, only about an inch or two deep. The wall she'd slid down felt wet, too. Maybe it had served some kind of drainage function, or perhaps it had been a sewage sluice in the island's good years. She used the damp wall to pull herself to her feet. Sewage sluice or not, it had been a thousand years or more since anyone had flushed a chamber pot down that thing. That was more than clean enough for her.

The tiny sound of water trickling over stone was not loud enough to obscure the low voices she could hear off to her left. Jendara hesitated. There was something familiar about them.

Slowly, she made her way through the darkness. Her hand struck a stone wall, a dry one this time. But the voices came clearly from a point a few feet away. She followed the sound to another narrow opening in the wall, just wide enough for her to squeeze through. It mirrored the one she'd stumbled upon in the tunnel above. The people who'd built this island had needed to access their sewage system, but they certainly didn't want to see or smell it any more than they had to.

She wiggled out into another tunnel, this one faintly lit up with a submarine glow. Every twenty or thirty feet, a jar of phosphorescent seaweed sat on the floor giving off a little cold blue-green light, just bright enough to reveal the open doorway across the hall from Jendara. All she could make out inside the room was the far wall, as if the room had been built with its own narrow entry hallway. The rest of the space stretched out to the left, a mystery.

But she was certain that was where the voices had come from. She crept forward into the room. On her left, a limpet-encrusted divider a little taller than herself formed the edge of the entry hall. She peered around it.

Several jars of seaweed surrounded the space, bringing this room close to brightness. Three humans sat on the floor, bound tightly together. An ugly gash ran across Boruc's forehead, but Tam and Yerka looked mostly unharmed. There were no guards.

Jendara ran around the divider and dropped to her knees beside her friends. "Thank the gods and ancestors!"

"Dara!" Tam stared at her. A bruise covered his cheekbone and the bridge of his nose, and his nose sounded stuffy—probably broken. "You found us!"

She began sawing at the coarse green ropes biting into his wrists. "How did you wind up down here?"

"A bunch of deep ones got the drop on us," Boruc answered.

Jendara cut the last strands of Tam's ropes and moved on to Boruc. Tam shook out his hands, trying to get some circulation back into his fingers. "They think we're part of whatever the ulat-kini are doing. I'm sure they'll be back any minute to question us again." Tam pointed at the far corner, where their belts and gear were heaped. "If you hand me my dagger, I can help."

Jendara brought their gear over and was glad to see a lantern in the heap. They'd need that if they were going to get out of here. She went back to work on Boruc's ties.

"I'm sorry," Yerka began, and broke off coughing. She twisted her head to wipe her mouth on the shoulder of her shabby tunic. "I didn't mean for any of this to happen."

"Why'd you run away?" Tam asked. "You can't want to go back to the frog-faces." He reached out to cut the woman's ropes.

Jendara caught Tam's hand. "Don't." She stared into Yerka's dirty face. "Fithrax said you were working for the denizens of Leng. What did he mean?"

"I don't know!" Yerka shook her head angrily. "And if I was, the denizens of Leng are the ulat-kini's *allies*. They're all friends."

Jendara dragged the woman to her feet. "I don't think so." She caught Tam's confused looked. "Let's keep her hands tied for now. I want to keep an eye on her."

Boruc and Tam hurried to buckle on their belts. Boruc patted the scabbard of his sword lovingly, which Jendara fully understood. Being unarmed and captive was nearly unbearable.

Tam, with the lantern now lit, stepped out into the hallway and announced an all-clear. Boruc made a lead for Yerka and he steered her out of the room. Jendara followed behind.

"Where are we?" Boruc asked. "They covered our eyes coming here—lost all my sense of direction."

"I'm not sure," Jendara admitted. She briefly explained what had happened to the rest of the crew since the two had been taken, and then gave them a more detailed account of what had happened to her since she left the ship this morning. Telling the tale made her realize the depth of their difficulties. She had no idea how long her mind had been hazed over by the moon-beasts; she couldn't even guess what time it was.

Tam nodded grimly. "This is bad. Our friends and Kran, captured for sacrifice. Enemies that can turn your mind against itself. And the captain has no idea what he'll be walking into once this ritual begins."

Jendara stopped walking, horrified that she hadn't thought of this herself. Deep down, she'd clung to the hope that of all the crew, Vorrin was the safest. She had told herself she had to save Kran. She had to save Boruc and Tam. Vorrin, though—he could save himself.

But he was in just as much danger as the rest of them.

Yerka broke into a coughing fit that doubled her over. Even Jendara was feeling the chill through her damp layers. This far down, the moisture clung to everything and resisted evaporation.

This far down. Jendara thought about the island's tunnel system. She might not know exactly where she was, but she knew she was in one of the lower levels, and that the very lowest level served as the sewers, which dumped refuse into the sea. If they could just get down to *those* tunnels, they could find their way to the outside. All of the *Milady*'s crew were good swimmers. They could swim for freedom.

She kept her plan to herself as they walked along. Yerka's defense against Fithrax's accusations not only rang hollow—she'd practically agreed to them. If Yerka was a spy for the denizens of Leng, Jendara didn't want her on board the *Milady*.

A second tunnel joined their hallway, and Tam paused in front of its dark open mouth. "What do you think?"

Jendara peered into the darkness. No jars of glowing seaweed broke the darkness, and the floor here at the entrance was covered in an untouched layer of grayish silt and broken shells. Nothing had passed down that hallway since the sea had drained from this level of the island.

"Let's stay on this path," Boruc suggested. "The lights have to lead somewhere."

"We can always double back to try out the other tunnel," Jendara said.

Yerka shook her head. "Do you really want to stay in this hallway? Who do you think put these lights here? This is enemy territory."

Boruc turned to face the woman. "Why are the deep ones *our* enemies? We're just looking for treasure."

Yerka pressed her lips tightly together.

Jendara resisted the sudden urge to shove her into the wall. "Typical spy," she spat. "You'll sell your information to the highest bidder, but you won't give it away to protect your own hide."

Yerka didn't answer. They moved forward, Jendara's words heavy inside each of them. This was deep one territory. The fish-folk had scoured clean the hallways and even lit them up. The deep ones may have been interested in the island for religious purposes, but it seemed as if they wanted to colonize it as well.

Jendara couldn't understand why the creatures would want to. She didn't know much about deep ones, but they seemed more at home in the water than on the land. The ulat-kini were shallow-water creatures with no females of their own kind, totally dependent on islands and beaches to bring up their air-breathing hybrid spawn. The deep ones inhabited the deep waters of the open seas—hence the name. Jendara had never even seen the secretive creatures until she'd come to this place.

With their broad skulls and large fins, the deep ones were quite different from the ulat-kini, much more like the remains Jendara had discovered in the flood prison two days ago. Had the deep ones' ancestors visited this place? They certainly hadn't built it. The strange, uneven stair treads would have been no easier for the deep ones to navigate than they were for humans.

Tam raised his hand to stop them. "Someone's coming."

"To the other tunnel," Jendara ordered. "Quick!"

They raced back toward the other tunnel. Yerka gasped for air, but Jendara yanked her along by the elbow. She wasn't about to leave her behind to talk to the deep ones. They skidded into the tunnel, their footsteps crunching slightly on the dirty floor.

Tam turn his lantern down to the faintest bit of light and then shielded its glow with his body. "Do you think we lost them?" he whispered.

Jendara held her breath, listening. There were voices out in the tunnel, their foreign words meaningless to her ears.

"They didn't see us," Yerka whispered. "I think they're on their way to interrogate us." She paused and listened for another moment. "They brought along something called 'the Elder.'"

"You speak the deep ones' tongue?" Jendara asked.

"It's not much different from the ulat-kini's ceremonial language. I can get a little."

"We'd better get moving," Tam warned. "They'll realize we're gone any moment."

They moved faster. Tam uncovered the lantern but kept the wick low. This tunnel was narrower and colder, as if the heat were being sucked out into the bedrock of the island.

Except that Jendara was starting to wonder if this island even *had* bedrock. It seemed to float upon the sea like a giant stone ship. Which meant if the cold came from anywhere, it came from the ocean, and this tunnel led to it.

Jendara opened her mouth to tell Tam, but a roar from behind cut her off. The floor beneath her boots began to tremble.

If the deep ones were coming, they were bringing something huge and angry with them.

"Run!" she shouted.

The lantern wasn't bright enough for them to run safely, but run they did. Jendara smashed into the wall when the tunnel took a sharp turn to the left. The floor began to slope down, and a cold breeze rushed up it, carrying the fresh tang of the sea.

"I think I hear the ocean!" Tam shouted, and ran ahead. He hit a nearly invisible line at waist-height and toppled over, striking the ground hard.

"Tam!"

Jendara stopped short, but Yerka kept running. She jumped over the now sagging line and looked back over her shoulder to make sure no one was following.

She didn't see the spider on the ceiling until it dropped on her.

Jendara grabbed Tam and pulled him to his feet. His mouth fell open as he stared at the spider, its purple hide nearly black in the low light. Its bulk filled the tunnel, blocking their path. It closed its armlike graspers around Yerka, lifting her toward its glistening fangs without taking its gaze from the humans on the ground.

No, not the humans. Just one.

Jendara.

With a sinking heart, Jendara studied the creature. Yellow spattered one of its legs, and dripped down onto the floor: the same yellow as the stuff that had sprayed down on Fithrax's face.

She should have known Mommy Longlegs wasn't dead.

Yerka shrieked as the creature's fangs pierced her chest.

"Shit." Jendara spun around, dragging Tam behind her. "Back to the other tunnel!"

"But the deep ones," Boruc protested, gasping for air as he ran. He wouldn't have asked if he'd seen the rage burning in the spider's eyes. He wouldn't have asked if he'd faced one of their kind before, with their eerie mind tricks and hideous cunning.

They rounded the corner and saw the blue light of the deep ones' lanterns. Jendara drew her sword. Her right arm still felt a little stiff, but the muscles would work well enough for this job.

She charged into the first deep one, skewering the creature before it could bring up its spear. The fishman's mouth opened and closed, but she knew it was dead the moment she'd hit it. She slammed the heel of her hand into its shoulder to force it off her blade.

Boruc skidded to a stop beside her. "Merciful ancestors," he breathed.

And then she registered what she was seeing.

By the ancestors, it was big—probably three times as tall as the other deep ones, and twice as broad, surrounded in a strange mist of rainbow colors. Its eyes were two black beads in its sagging green face, the eyes of a creature brought up from the darkest, foulest depths of the sea. Jendara's head hurt from the pulsing shroud of colors.

Tam began to whisper, but it was just a stream of incoherent sound. Jendara kicked aside the dead deep one and stepped into a fighting stance. She'd fought ogres and giants. She could handle a giant fish-man.

One of the ordinary deep ones rushed forward, a spiked club in its hand. Boruc sidestepped and punched the creature. It went stumbling down the tunnel. Good. Jendara didn't need them distracting her from the Elder.

The Elder roared, and Boruc went stiff, as if the sound had frozen him. Jendara darted in, slashing into the meat of its massive thigh. The creature raked out at her, and she ducked just in time to hear its claws screech on the stone walls. A net of spider silk shot over Jendara's head, wrapping the Elder's clawed hand tight. A second passed her by, and a third shot out to wrap around the nearest deep one like a sticky purse seine net. The deep one toppled over, its arms and legs sealed to its side. One of its comrades dropped to its knees to help free it.

Jendara cursed under her breath. The small distraction Yerka had provided was over. This was the worst sort of battle, caught between two gigantic enemies. They had to get beyond the Elder before the spider could catch any of them.

Then a chest-high wall of water whooshed down the tunnel, sending her staggering. The cold nearly made her drop her sword. She gasped for air as water sprayed up into her face.

The Elder laughed, a bass rumbling. The tunnel was filling fast, and the gigantic deep one would be in his natural element.

"Tam!" She paddled one-handedly. "Boruc!" She couldn't see them anywhere. They had to get out of this tunnel before they drowned.

Tam bobbed up to the surface. "The spider," he gasped. "Can it swim?"

She didn't know. The spiders she knew of were all land creatures, but this one was too alien for her to guess anything about. Ants could live a long time underwater. Why not spiders? But getting to the ocean was still their best chance. They had to risk passing the spider.

"Try to swim under it!" Tam shouted. He and Boruc dove beneath the surface of the water.

Jendara forced herself under. Tam and Boruc lay on the bottom of the tunnel, wriggling and kicking as if weighed down by lead weights.

"Help!" A weak hand grabbed Jendara's pant leg. Yerka pulled herself closer, pressing her bleeding body against Jendara. A trickle of blood ran from the corner of her mouth.

Jendara blinked at her stupidly. How in all hells was Yerka even alive? They were underwater, and yet she was talking and breathing as if everything was normal. The blood didn't even cloud the water.

"Help me," Yerka begged, and realization dawned on Jendara.

"This is all an illusion!" Jendara stared around herself. Tam and Boruc were struggling to swim down the tunnel. The last of the deep ones was trying to swim, but the Elder stood unaffected, its eyes fixed on the tunnel ceiling and the spider making its way along it.

The spider flailed as if it had been hit with a wall of water. Then with a shriek of what sounded like rage, the spider shot forward along the ceiling. It dropped onto the Elder's back and drove its fangs deep into the beast's thick neck. The Elder screeched in pain and grabbed the spider's nearest leg. There was a sickening pop as it ripped free. The spider reared back in pain and then drove its fangs down again.

Boruc sat up, no longer caught up in the illusion of drowning. He shook Tam.

The Elder staggered to his feet. The spider's carapace groaned as it ground into the stone ceiling. The spider hissed and its legs jerked. A strand of silk shot out, catching on the tunnel wall. The spider flew off the Elder's back.

Black, rubbery tentacles burst out of the floor, closing around the spider. With a wave of the Elder's hand, the tentacles yanked the spider back into the Elder's grip, the spider struggling mightily. The titans were completely absorbed in their own battle.

Yerka pulled at Jendara's leg, nearly toppling her. "Listen to me," she whispered.

Jendara dropped beside the woman and glanced from her to the monsters grappling in the hallway. "We've got to get out of here."

"I won't make it." Yerka said weakly. The spider's poison, Jendara realized. It was beginning to take effect. "I killed Bothrax—Fithrax's father. Bothrax would have never let the denizens of Leng use the star scepter. The gods will judge me for his death, but the denizens of Leng forced me."

"You chose to work for them," Jendara said.

Yerka made a humorless smile. "You believe that? They make slaves. That's what they do. You felt what it was like."

The tunnel shook. The Elder rammed the spider into the tunnel wall again, and the spider shrieked, an otherworldly sound that made Jendara's ears ache. Tam and Boruc scrambled to Jendara's side.

Jendara jerked her attention back to Yerka. "Tell me more about them."

"They are not of our world," Yerka whispered. Her eyes rolled up in her head.

"I don't understand." Jendara shook the woman. "They'll kill us, Yerka. All of us! Just to get the ulat-kini's god."

"Don't you wonder what they could do with that god?" Yerka's voice was nearly inaudible. "They are not of our world," she repeated. And then she went limp.

The Elder choked as a loop of silk closed around its throat. The spider closed its massive legs around the creature.

Boruc grabbed Jendara's shoulder. "The wall is crumbling," he warned. "The whole tunnel could cave in."

She scrambled to her feet. "We've got to get to the sea."

Bones groaned as the spider squeezed the Elder tighter and tighter. The two beasts all but filled the tunnel. But their attention was on each other.

"Come on!" she shouted and broke into a run. Rock pattered down from the ceiling. The vibrations of their boots were finishing what the goliaths had started.

Jendara saw a space between the bottom of the spider's carapace and the floor and launched herself into it. She hit the ground and skidded. A boulder smashed down just inches to her left, but she was through. She could smell the sea breeze in the dark ahead of her. She jumped up. "Hurry!"

They ran down the hallway. Rock smashed and clattered. The Elder roared.

And then a bolt of spider silk wrapped around Jendara's middle, yanking her backward.

24

SALTWATER

For a moment, Jendara hung in open space, clawing and kicking at air. Then she smashed against a massive block of stone that had once been part of the ceiling. She slid to the ground, the air knocked out of her. Her sword lay just out of reach.

"Jendara!" someone shouted, but the only light came from a broken jar of seaweed, casting more shadows than blue-green light. The line of spider silk sagged on the ground beside a tendril of the luminescent stuff.

The spider's claw suddenly shot out from behind Jendara, raking across her leg, ripping open fabric and drawing blood. Jendara found her breath. The stone slab at her back had saved her life. Now it alone stood between her and the spider, giving her just a little room to maneuver. She threw herself forward to reach her sword.

Her fingers closed on the hilt just as the silk thread went tight, dragging her sideways around the big boulder. She twisted around and hacked at the silk.

Now she could see the spider. The falling rocks had closed off the tunnel and half-buried the monster. Its blood spread out in a blackish lake around its forelegs. It yanked on the thread of silk, drawing Jendara closer.

She slashed at the thread. With the spider's back half buried, it couldn't spin out more silk. It struggled to free itself, but Jendara knew it didn't have much life left in it.

It tugged again, pulling Jendara very nearly into its face. Its forelegs curled around her, the claws biting into her back and legs. The creature's eyes flashed.

It had caught her, and now it was going to punish her.

"No way," Jendara growled, and drove her sword into one of its four red eyes.

The sword sank in up to the hilt. Blood burbled out of the wound. The spider bucked and shrieked and twitched, and Jendara threw her weight into the blade, enlarging the hole in the creature's head. It made one last high-pitched shriek and then went still.

"Dara!" Tam shouted. "You okay?"

"Yeah." She pulled her sword free and slashed at the silk binding her. Even the blade's hilt was covered in gore.

"Let me help you." He ripped off a hunk of the silk wrapped around her waist. She took a handful and wiped off her hands, and then her sword before sheathing it. "The lantern broke," he added.

"We can use seaweed," Boruc called. He gathered up the stuff. "It'll help a bit."

Somewhere behind the wall of rubble, more rock tumbled and crashed. "Let's hurry," Boruc warned. "The whole thing could collapse."

They moved as quickly as they could. With their adrenaline ebbing, they all moved slower, their aches and pains becoming apparent. The grade of the tunnel grew steeper, and they had to fight to keep their footing.

Then Boruc's boot skidded on the gritty floor. Jendara caught his arm and reached out for Tam to steady her, but he moved too slowly. Boruc tumbled down, and his weight pulled Jendara down after him, rolling down the steep hill.

And then there was no tunnel floor, only falling.

Jendara hit water with a tremendous splash. She sank a long time, but she was already swimming for the surface. Her gear was an anchor, but she swam harder. She could see a faint glow off to her right and fought to reach it.

Her lungs protested, but she forced onward, moving always upward and to her right. Her vision grew spotty, and then suddenly she broke the surface of the water and was breathing again.

Tam came up beside her, gasping and choking. "Boruc?"

She wiped water from her eyes and looked around. They had come out beside the rocky outer wall of the island, the water darkened by late afternoon shadows. They must be on the island's southeast side, with the bulk of the land between them and the low afternoon sun. "Boruc!" she called.

He burst out of the water in an explosion of spray, gasping and flailing. "Gods damn!" he managed to choke.

She had to laugh a little. She blinked away salt and looked around again. Yes, they were on the east side of the island, but now she could see that the tunnel had dumped them out very near the southernmost tip. They just had to reach that little promontory of rocks, and they'd be nearly to the *Milady*'s grotto.

"Come on," she said, and swam for the shore.

No one met them on the ship. They changed into dry clothes and ate a quick meal of bread and cheese in worried silence. Every bite stuck in Jendara's throat as if it were made of thistles.

She cleared her throat. "I have to get Kran back," she said. "I don't know where Vorrin and the others are, and this goes beyond anything I'd ask of my crew. I want you two to stay here and ready the *Milady*. If we don't come back, the ship is yours."

Tam put down his mug. "Are you telling me to leave you and the captain behind?" Tam reached across the galley table and crushed her hand in his. "Are you crazy?"

Boruc shook his head. "We'd never leave you, Dara. Not you two and not Kran. You're family."

Tam got to his feet. "Plus, you're forgetting that Glayn's out there. I'm not leaving without him, and that's that."

Jendara swallowed a lump in her throat that wasn't bread. "We could all die."

Boruc shrugged. "You can die any day. What's new?"

Jendara shoved her sandwich aside. "Then let's go. Sunset's not for another hour or so. We might be able to find Vorrin before the ulat-kini start their ritual."

Jendara half expected to see Vorrin standing beside the stagnant waters of the pool in the boulevard, or if not there, then striding out of a corridor, eager to see her. She *needed* to see him. Tam and Boruc would help her, but she wasn't sure she could go up against moon-beasts and the black robes of Leng without Vorrin at her side. She was no coward, but those things frightened her.

She caught Tam and Boruc both glancing around as if they, too, had hoped to find Vorrin up here. They didn't say anything, but she had known them too long not to predict their response. She tried to find something encouraging to say, and settled for just walking faster. With or without Vorrin, she was going to have to reach the Star Chapel.

Her footsteps didn't sound quite right as she walked, the noises somehow muffled, as if a heavy fog swallowed them up. She didn't like it. Every other time she'd walked down the big boulevard with its purple skylights, the space had echoed with the empty sound of an abandoned mausoleum.

She rubbed at her arms. She'd changed out of her wet coat, but this one still felt clammy. The fog must be moving in, she supposed. That was all. The fog.

Boruc tapped her shoulder. "Look. The chapel doors are closed."

He was right. Up ahead, the great gold-leafed doors had been shut tight. That end of the boulevard stood dark and unwelcoming. Jendara didn't like that, either. She hadn't realized how much she had been counting on a moment or two of clean sunlight before all of this began.

"I guess we have to go check it out," she said.

"Someone's coming down the far tunnel," Tam said.

His hearing was better than hers. "I don't hear anything."

He cocked his head. "It was faint. Like a shout. Or maybe—"

"A bark!" She laughed. "Tam, that's Fylga!" Jendara raced toward the sound.

The two men hurried to catch up with her. Far up ahead, a bobbing yellow dot of light reassured her. Yellow, not the blue of the deep ones' weed lights.

"Vorrin!" she called.

With a happy bark, Fylga threw herself against Jendara's legs, licking at her hands and arms. Jendara caught the dog's collar. "You wonderful mutt," she grumbled, rubbing the dog's ears and chin.

"Dara?" Vorrin's voice echoed off the tunnel walls. She could see him now, running full out. "Get back to the boulevard! Run!"

She loosed the dog and did as ordered. Whatever chased her husband and friends had them scared.

That didn't bode well.

She hit the end of the tunnel and made a hard left. Jendara glanced around and then led them into the next tunnel intersecting the boulevard. It had been safe yesterday, and it was narrow enough she thought their crew could hold it if it came down to making a stand. She brought up her lantern and was glad to see the space looked empty.

Jendara set her back to the wall and waited for the others. "What happened?"

"Deep ones," Vorrin gasped. "Lots of them."

"They came out of nowhere," Glayn added. "We were in the library after we left the ulat-kini camp."

"There was no one at camp," Zuna added. "The boats were all gone or scuttled—"

"One of the scuttled boats was a longship," Glayn interrupted.

"And we thought you were gone," Zuna finished.

Vorrin pulled Jendara close. "I'm so glad you're all right," he whispered.

She let herself press her face against his shoulder for one weak moment. Then she pulled back to face them all. "The ulat-kini have Kran," she said. "And most of the village of Sorind."

"What?" Vorrin stared at her. "How?"

"They have creatures that can control your mind," she explained. "You're like a watcher trapped behind your own eyes as they puppet you around."

"But . . . why?" Glayn shook his head. "I don't understand."

Jendara hesitated, trying to remember what Yerka had said and put it together with what they'd gleaned from the ulat-kini. "The people of Leng are fighting a war against the spiders," she began, "but they want more power, and more of these mind slaves."

Vorrin looked thoughtful. "They want the sleeping god to help them fight the spiders."

"Right." Jendara leaned back against the wall. She had caught just a glimpse of the slithering thing down in that pit, but it had been enough. Enough to know that whatever slept beneath this island was huge and horrible and evil enough to make the stars themselves scream in fear. "The god, the ulat-kini, the black robes—they're all evil."

"But why did they want the Sorinders?" Zuna asked. "Are they just the newest bunch of slaves?"

"They're going to be sacrificed," Jendara explained. "As a *treat* to make the god behave. Like taming a feral dog."

"Merciful Desna," Boruc whispered.

Vorrin rubbed a palm over his face. He took a deep breath. "All right. What do we do now?"

Tam frowned. "You said there was a big group of deep ones behind you. So how come it's so quiet?"

Vorrin frowned. "Zuna caught sight of them first. I just assumed they were after us, but maybe we were wrong. Maybe they're just on the move—or organizing an attack on . . . someone else?"

Jendara began moving back toward the boulevard, Fylga at her heels. "But attacking who?"

Out in the boulevard, nothing moved. The sun had sunk too low to penetrate the skylights, and now shadows ruled the great hallway. Jendara crept out behind a heap of rubble. The soft rumble of voices came from behind the closed doors of the Star Chapel.

She fixed her gaze on them. The ulat-kini and denizens of Leng were already inside, preparing for the night's terrible ritual. Vorrin hunkered down beside her and gave her hand a quick, nervous squeeze.

Jendara glanced around. The boulevard was empty, but it was easy to imagine deep ones and pink-tentacled moon-beasts in every shadow.

Then a black-robed figure raced out of the far tunnel—the tunnel that led to the ulat-kini's camp, the tunnel where she had just found Vorrin—and pounded on one of the chapel doors. Jendara leaned in, wondering what was going on.

The door swung open. For a second, Jendara could see inside the chapel, which was crowded with human prisoners and milling ulat-kini. Then Skortti emerged, accompanied by three denizens of Leng. Skortti was dressed for ceremony. He wore his usual fishbone and mother-of-pearl miter, but also a cloak made of shimmering fish skin. A rope of black pearls hung down over his chest.

"The ritual can *not* be interrupted, Ahrzur!" Skortti snapped. "My people are busy tending to our sacrifices. Your scout discovered the attack party—*you* handle it."

Ahrzur waved a hand. "The deep ones are a minor inconvenience. Your warriors can handle them while you and your assistants prepare for the ritual. My people must prepare the portal device."

Skortti clasped his hands, clearly about to try a new approach. "Even just one moon-beast could stop the deep ones. My warriors would put themselves in real danger fighting such beasts. You do not want to weaken your allies before you even arrive on Leng, do you?"

Ahrzur's casual manner vanished. The veil obscuring his face twitched, as if the flesh beneath had given a spasm of irritation. There was something strange about the shape of his face, Jendara realized. She wanted to snatch off the veil and see just what hid behind it.

"The moon-beasts prepare to control the god. They are the ones who will protect us from his rage when he wakes." Ahrzur's voice was harder and colder than ever. "We made a *deal*, ulat-kini. You will wake the god, and your people will keep the deep ones from interrupting the ritual."

Skortti took a step back. "It will not be easy," he admitted. "When Bothrax stole the scepter the deep ones hid in the sunken city, he knew they would do anything to get it back. They worship the sleeping god. They are zealots."

Jendara sat back on her heels. The deep ones—they had searched the island so intently because they wanted the scepter the ulat-kini had stolen from them!

"Bothrax was as big a fool as his sons. We tried to make a deal with him, but he insisted on keeping the scepter for himself," Ahrzur said.

Skortti narrowed his eyes. "Then I guess it was lucky for you that Bothrax, our finest hunter, somehow encountered a sea serpent too fierce for him to kill. Korthax was always suspicious about his father's death."

Ahrzur gave a mirthless chuckle. "I suppose you were lucky as well when that idiot Fithrax won the bid for the tribe's leadership.

Things would be very different for you and for us if Korthax had taken the leadership—and the scepter."

Skortti folded his arms across his chest, beaten. "I will send out a unit of our best warriors to wipe out these deep ones. But remember: we dare not allow anything to interrupt the ritual."

Ahrzur nodded, and then they all slipped back behind the doors.

Jendara jumped to her feet. "They're sending out their best fighters. The moon-beasts will still be in there, but I think this is our best chance."

Vorrin made a thoughtful face. "The moon-beasts are the biggest threat. We can't help anyone if we're captured."

"Kran—" Jendara paused, thinking. "Kran was able to get control of his body somehow. Then he helped me. Maybe if we can free the Sorinders' bodies, Kran can help us get enough people's minds free to attack the moon-beasts. There has to be some way to hurt them, some way to keep them from using their powers."

The great doors opened again and a large group of armed ulat-kini hurried out.

Vorrin yanked Jendara down behind the heap of rubble. "So that's our plan?"

She didn't hesitate a second. "That's our plan."

She sounded confident even to her own ears.

25

DEAD MOON RISING

Jendara slipped inside the Star Chapel and dropped into a crouch. Vorrin and the others barely made a sound as they came in behind her. She had expected guards by the doors, but the remaining ulat-kini were gathered at the windowed wall, deep in discussion with Skortti. Perhaps they were regrouping after losing their warriors.

She motioned for Zuna, Tam, and Glayn to circle around to the left side of the great space. She and her remaining crew moved into the shadows of the right. A few torches burned at the front of the room, but the Star Chapel was mostly dark. Through the window the last smudge of sunlight showed at the edge of the overcast sky. The air felt heavy and thick.

Jendara studied the room. The prisoners were crowded between the worn and broken stone pews. A few hung from their bindings—if not dead, then unconscious. She searched for Kran, but the room was too crowded to make out one dark-haired boy amid the mob.

Beside the knot of ulat-kini, the denizens of Leng and their loathsome pink beasts gathered around a large plinth made of the same slick black material as their floating docks and packing crates. It stood about waist high, and it supported a smaller block of the black stuff with a glowing blue orb set in the middle. The block and the orb vibrated and hummed loud enough to make the hairs on Jendara's arms prickle. She was glad she'd tied Fylga up in the other tunnel—the sound would have made the dog howl for sure.

Jendara ducked behind the nearest prisoner, thinking about the strange device as she scanned for Kran. Ahrzur had mentioned a portal device; the humming black box had to be it. What kind of portal would it open? And where would it lead to? Where could Leng be if, as Yerka had said, it wasn't of their own world?

She squelched her uncomfortable thoughts and crept forward to the next row. There he was. Just another row forward, his head turned a little so she could see the hint of a frown sketched on his face. Kran's mind was back in control of his body, and he wasn't doing a very good job hiding it.

Falling in behind him, she risked a whisper: "Keep your face blank as I untie you." She began picking at the knots. "We've got to get everyone free before this ritual starts. Can you help with their minds?"

The rope came undone. Kran looked around and nodded very slightly.

Jendara squeezed his shoulder. It was a long shot, but the best one they had.

"Skortti!" Jendara turned to see Ahrzur snap his fingers at the ulat-kini. His nails were long and hooked, more talons than fingernails. "The sun has fully set. Why haven't you begun the ritual?"

"We wait for moonrise," Skortti said. He raised up a bronze staff, its surface covered with complex symbols. "The instructions on the scepter are clear."

Ahrzur strode toward the ulat-kini. "Our power source will only last a few more hours. We'll need every second if we're going to get the god and all our people through the portal. Now begin!"

"Not until moonrise!"

Ahrzur lunged at the nearest ulat-kini, his black-robed arm lashing out with preternatural speed. Jendara barely caught the flicker of movement as his free hand drew a dagger out of his robe and then drove it into the ulat-kini's throat. Blood sprayed over Skortti's silver cloak.

Ahrzur pulled the blade free and kicked the dying ulat-kini aside. His veil had come loose and now hung open, revealing the flesh beneath. Jendara gave an inadvertent gasp.

Where his lips should have been, a mass of tentacles twisted and writhed around a mouth filled with glossy black teeth. Behind those cruel teeth, a pair of fleshy organs like the mouth parts of some primitive intertidal creature wriggled and danced.

"Begin the ritual," Ahrzur commanded. He ripped off the damaged veil and tossed it on the ulat-kini's corpse.

Skortti trembled as he nodded.

They were running out of time. Jendara drew her belt knife and slashed the ropes holding Chana. Kran was already working on the ropes of the man in front of him. He finished and gently turned the man's face toward him. It was Norg, the baker with the amazing bread. Jendara felt a pang as she remembered all the times Norg had given Kran a fresh roll, hot out of the oven. He wasn't just some strange man that needed to be rescued: he was her neighbor. Kran smiled at the man and patted his cheek.

She moved to the next captive and sawed at his ropes, still watching Kran and Norg. Suddenly Norg went stiff. He blinked a few times. Kran mimed for the man to be silent and Norg nodded. He stared around himself, clearly searching for a way out. Jendara grinned. They had at least one ally. She hoped the others were as lucky.

She scanned the room and frowned. An ulat-kini at the front of the room had turned around. The creature peered out over the group with a suspicious expression.

Jendara shoved Kran down. "Don't move!" she breathed, and hoped Norg heard it. The baker froze in place.

The ulat-kini left the group and walked toward them. Jendara stood straight and motionless. She knew it had looked at her, but

Kran was short enough he might have gone unnoticed. She tried to remember how her face had behaved while she'd been under the moon-beast's control. Had her mouth sagged open? She forced her muscles into a peaceful expression and hoped she wasn't overdoing it.

The ulat-kini gave her a hard look and then turned back to the others. Jendara pulled Kran to his feet.

"We have to hurry," she whispered.

He nodded and turned to the blank-faced Chana. Jendara cut the ropes of the next prisoner. She could see the rest of her crew moving throughout the room. A few of the prisoners were looking around themselves, awake and alert. She had no idea what made a person gather their will and throw off the moon-beast's control. She couldn't remember doing anything other than just *looking* at Kran, but that had somehow been enough.

She slashed the bonds of the next person. She was almost to the end of this row. At the front of the room, Skortti's six acolytes had lit more torches. Their ruddy glow flickered and danced as an evening wind blew in through the broken windows. Twilight had ended. Without the torches, it would be entirely dark.

The acolytes clasped hands and began to chant, their voices melding into a hollow drone.

Skortti raised high the bronze scepter. "Awaken, O sleeping one," he intoned. "Awaken, O child of the stars."

The chapel doors burst open. Fylga rushed past the ulat-kini in the doorway, barking furiously. Jendara cringed, ready for the moon-beasts and ulat-kini to attack the dog.

But the figure in the doorway distracted them. Korthax marched inside the chapel, Tharkor at his heels. He strode toward the startled Skortti, holding the stolen astrolabe before his chest. "You dare awaken the sleeping god without this."

The stones beneath Jendara's boots gave a little lurch. She caught herself on the shoulder of the prisoner in front of her. She looked around. No one else seemed to have noticed the minor earthquake.

Skortti lowered the scepter. "I have no need of your petty bauble."

"My father observed the ritual of the deep ones. He was the one who saw what power the sleeping god could give us." Korthax stopped at the midpoint of the chapel's broad aisle. "At the time, he thought the scepter woke the god, and the astrolabe was only a tool for measuring the moment when the stars were right. But I have learned otherwise." Korthax paused, his face bending in a triumphant smile. "The astrolabe taps the power of the stars so that the god may be controlled!"

"Get it," Ahrzur snapped. A black robe charged at Korthax.

The floor began to shake. A crack split down the aisle, separating the left group of prisoners from the right. A horrible sound came up out of the crack, a shrill whisper that clawed at Jendara's eardrums.

A huge green-gray tentacle broke out of the floor and sent the black robe flying.

26

FALLING STARS

The woman beside Jendara shrieked and fell over, pulling down the man in front of her and the little girl beside him. Jendara grabbed the woman's arm.

"Calm down," she ordered the woman, hacking at the rope that connected the prisoner to the row of captives in front of her. She caught a glimpse of Boruc helping another group of prisoners run toward the shadows on the far right-hand side of the room. The moon-beasts must have lost control of the humans, too distracted by the giant tentacle breaking through the floor.

The woman gasped and Jendara brought her attention back to her. "Hold still," she snapped.

"Where am I? What's happening?" The woman burst into tears. "Jona!" she screamed. The knife parted the last strands of rope and the woman stumbled sideways, out into the aisle. "Jona!"

"Wait!" Jendara shouted, but too late, as a terrified man slammed into the woman on his way toward the still-open chapel doors. She stumbled backward, her right foot going into the crack in the floor. The chapel shook and lurched, and the woman sank down to her waist, wedged into the crack.

"I'm coming!" Jendara called, but the crowd shoved her aside in its mad dash toward freedom. Jendara caught herself on the remains of a pew. She could just see the trapped woman, her screams overpowered by the roar of the crowd.

The woman's right side suddenly jerked and sank deeper into the floor. Her torso went rigid. Her mouth opened and closed, and then blood fountained up out of her lips.

There was a crunching loud enough to be heard over the panicked shrieks of the mob. And then the woman vanished into the crevice. Jendara could only stare at the spot where the woman had been.

Someone yanked on Jendara's arm, forcing her to turn. It was Kran, wide-eyed and pale. He tugged her toward the door.

"No." She had to shout to be heard over all the terrified voices. "We'll get trampled."

Then the voices changed from shouts to screams. The crowd pushed back from the doors as armed deep ones, dozens of them, hacked and slashed their way inside.

"To the windows," Jendara ordered Kran. She shoved him toward the front of the room. With the deep ones serving as a distraction, maybe she and the others could find a way to lower people down to the sea.

The floor shook again, harder. The walls and ceiling rattled. A huge slab of stone crashed down in the center aisle, sending people racing back into the pews. A woman shoved Kran aside, ripping his hand out of Jendara's grip.

"Kran!"

But a trident caught her in the side of the arm. She twisted away. It was a glancing blow, but the tines stung where they cut into the flesh. The deep one lunged at her.

This time she wasn't distracted. Jendara stepped aside and let the creature's sloppy attack take it past her, driving her knife into its exposed spine, just above the fin. It dropped without making a sound.

Jendara spun around, but Kran was gone. And she'd been driven back into the center aisle, just inches from the crack in the floor. A stench wafted up from it like rotten fish and death. The stink of the sleeping god's pit.

"Out of the way," a voice shouted, and Korthax pushed past her. He scrambled over the huge slab of stone and then broke into a run. With a snarl, he slammed into Skortti and toppled the older ulat-kini. They grappled together on the floor. The acolytes kept chanting, but they looked ready to run.

Jendara looked around herself, desperate for a glimpse of her son. The ground rumbled and lurched beneath her. The sleeping god was about to rip its way into the Star Chapel.

"Dara! Where's Kran?"

Vorrin had found her. He grabbed her by the shoulders, turning her to face him.

"I don't know," she shouted. Panic hit her. "I don't know!"

He stared at her, as scared as she was. The chapel was chaos and their boy was lost in it.

The portal device's humming, so constant that Jendara had stopped even noticing it, suddenly grew louder. Jendara felt her teeth buzzing in their sockets. A brilliant blue light filled the room.

Jendara squinted as she searched for the source and saw that the light poured out of the portal device. The denizens of Leng must be readying to open the doorway back to their own land, wherever that was. As her eyes adjusted to the glare, she realized Ahrzur was not among the massed denizens, and she pulled her gaze away from the device to search for him. He was the one who had set the moon-beasts on them in the first place, the one behind all of this.

She saw him moving behind the still-chanting ulat-kini acolytes, toward the brawl. Skortti suddenly cried out, and Korthax dragged himself to his feet, holding both the astrolabe and the scepter. With the grin of a madman, he brought them together, the end of the scepter sliding neatly into the tube on the back of the astrolabe. He pulled something like a shining bronze key from his belt pouch—the same metal object she had seen him take from

Fithrax in the spiders' cave. The symbols on the two ancient brass relics burst into white light.

Ahrzur lunged at Korthax and ripped the starry scepter from the ulat-kini's hands. Korthax swiped at the denizen of Leng, but Ahrzur knocked him aside as if he were no more significant than a fly. The ulat-kini fell to the floor, stunned.

Ahrzur took position in front of the portal device. Blue light outlined his stocky figure, and the starry scepter glowed. Jendara could barely stand to look at him, but she had to see what he would do next. She glanced away for a second to ease her aching eyes, and noticed Skortti's battered shape crawling across the floor. He had lost his proud miter and silver cloak; his eye had swollen shut, and blood trickled from his nose. But he kept dragging himself toward Ahrzur. He stretched out his hand for the scepter.

Then the portal device's humming changed. A long peal ran out. The walls of the chapel began to vibrate. The stones behind the portal device began to glow and shimmer with their own blue light.

"What's happening?" Vorrin shouted.

"They're opening the portal!" Jendara bellowed. Tiny shards of stone rained down from the ceiling. It felt like the whole island could shake apart. "We have to find Kran!"

She spun around, searching for the boy. She saw Zuna with Glayn at her side, fighting a group of deep ones. On the far side of the room, Boruc carried Chana in his arms as he urged a group of anxious Sorinders toward the exit.

"He's with another boy!" Vorrin shouted. "There, in the front row. They're trying to get to the windows."

She could see Kran now, with Oric in tow. Jendara drew her sword. "We'll have to cut our way through the ulat-kini."

The scepter's light surged brighter. Ahrzur raised it over his head, and a beam of white light shot out onto the shimmering chapel wall. The ground flung itself sideways. Jendara and Vorrin grabbed at each other as they slid down the suddenly tilting floor.

Salt spray erupted from the crevice, which had more than doubled in width. The ancient beams beneath the floor groaned, and on the far side of the gash in the ground, an ulat-kini warrior screamed as one of the huge floor tiles broke loose and plummeted into open space. Within the crack, something with a faint luminescence struggled to writhe its way upward.

The deep ones rushed the front of the room. Humans and ulat-kini no longer mattered to them: they cared only for the scepter that controlled their god. They threw themselves at the denizens of Leng and the fleshy moon-beasts.

Jendara scrambled up the sloping floor. "We've got to get to Kran," she warned Vorrin, reaching backward for his hand. She grabbed the edge of a crumbling pew and pulled them onto safer ground.

This part of the chapel, just moments ago packed with terrified people, was mostly clear now—but the spaces between the pews were filled with fallen rock and the dead and injured of several species. Jendara didn't have time to pick her way carefully across the debris. She jumped on top of the pew. The stone back of the bench wobbled beneath her boots, and she jumped to the next one.

A huge deep one, nearly the size of the Elder, rushed past her.

"It is not time!" it bellowed. "The stars are wrong!"

Roaring as it ran, it flung itself at Ahrzur. They slammed into the portal device. The denizen of Leng was momentarily stunned. The huge deep one grabbed Ahrzur's limp arm and began to tug. The denizen of Leng struggled in the beast's grasp, but his arm stretched taut for a moment and then ripped free. There was no blood, no screaming, no nasty exposed bits of tendon and snapped arteries—his arm was simply no longer attached to his body. The hulking deep one gave a hoot of delight and flung the limb, star scepter and all, up into the air.

The scepter flew free of Ahrzur's hand and hung for a moment, its glow fading. Then it spun end over end out the open window and was gone.

Ahrzur's arm fell to the ground and lay there, a dead snake of a thing. The denizen of Leng lashed out with his free hand, slashing open the deep one's chest with his black talons. The deep one stumbled backward, clutching at the shredded flesh. Ahrzur drove a kick into the creature's torso and sent it flying backward. The beast hit the end of the crevasse in the floor and pedaled for traction, but it was too close to the edge. The deep one fell back into the opening.

A tentacle whipped up out of the crack, the massive deep one wrapped tightly in its coils. It squeezed the fish-faced creature, and blood ran out of the beast in rivulets. The tentacle gave one last squeeze and then tossed the creature down into the depths of the pit.

The tentacle hung motionless for a second, its tip pointed like a dog's nose fixed on a scent. Then it slithered forward, groping along the ground until it reached the spattered blood left by the injured deep one. It rubbed itself in the gore, its surface seeming to drink it up.

Jendara turned away from the sight. She had to find her boy. "Kran!" she shouted. She was close, she knew it.

"Jendara!" a young voice screamed, and she saw Oric at the front of the room, waving, frantic to get her attention.

"No!" Vorrin roared, and Jendara realized what he saw: the denizen of Leng bearing down on the boys. The creature snatched up Oric and leaped over the debris that separated them from the end of the crevice in the floor.

Kran ran after his friend.

Time seemed to stand still for Jendara. She saw her son's enraged face, the knife in his hand. She saw the denizen of Leng holding up Oric as it shrieked jubilantly and raced toward the blood-hungry tentacles. The boy was a lure, she realized. The damned denizen of Leng still thought it could lure the sleeping god through the portal, using Kran's best friend as bait.

Kran threw his dagger and it flew true, slamming home in the denizen of Leng's shoulder blade, the shoulder of the arm that gripped Oric. Oric tumbled to the ground and rolled to his feet.

The tentacle lashed out, sweeping the denizen of Leng down into the crevice. The entire chapel rumbled and shook. The floor beneath Kran and Oric tipped sideways, down the aisle and away from Jendara. The ground groaned, and the far end of the crevasse opened wider. It now threatened to swallow up the chapel's back wall, and the boys were sliding right toward it.

"Kran!" Vorrin yelled, and then he was off. Jendara spun around to catch up with him. He was headed for the huge slab of roof that had fallen across the aisle and now spanned the crevasse like a bridge. He scrambled up onto the rock, hoping to grab the boys as they passed below.

Something rose up out of the pit, huge and leathery like the wing of some gigantic bat. A film of phosphorescent algae clung to it so it glowed a pustulant green. The wing twitched, sending out air currents that sent everything around it flying.

Including Vorrin.

27

THE SLEEPING GOD

Jendara's boot caught the end of the nearest pew and she crashed to her knees. Her son. Her husband. She couldn't save them both.

A hand brought her upright. "Look," Tam shouted in her ear. "Just look!"

Fylga, her white coat outlined dark against the green glow, stood half-on and half-off the slab of fallen stone, her teeth clamped shut on the back of Kran's jacket. His arms were wrapped tightly around Oric, whose boots were jammed against an outcropping of stone. It and Fylga were the only things keeping the boys from plummeting over the edge.

Tam and Jendara ran to the crevasse.

"Help!" a voice shouted from far below. "Help me!"

Jendara's eyes widened. "That's Vorrin!" She dropped onto her belly, peering into the gloomy depths below. She could just see him, clinging to the end of a broken support beam a good two floors below.

"I've got the boys," Tam said. "Go find something to lower to the captain!"

"But—"

"Trust me!" he bellowed.

She ran to the pews where she'd cut through so much green rope. She found several short lengths before she found one of the longer pieces. Her fingers trembled as she knotted them all together. Would it even hold? She dropped to her stomach and tossed it over the edge. It dangled a good four feet too short.

"Shit, shit, shit," she breathed.

Zuna threw herself down beside Jendara. "Is that the captain down there?" She didn't wait for a response. "Boruc! Send those survivors to the *Milady* and get over here!"

She yanked off her belt. "I'm going to lash this around your feet," she announced.

"What?" Jendara blinked at her stupidly. Vorrin, Kran, they were both going to die. She didn't care if she slid over the edge after them.

Zuna tightened the belt around Jendara's ankles. "Boruc, grab onto me," she ordered, as she wrapped the end of the belt around her own muscular forearm. "You bring him back," she commanded.

Jendara finally understood. She pushed herself over the edge and watched her makeshift rope hang down beside Vorrin's face. "Grab on!"

He reached out for it with one hand. For a second, he hesitated. Once he let go of that support beam, his life would hang on Jendara's makeshift line.

A patter of rocks rained down on his head. Jendara risked a glance upward. Tam had a hold of Oric. By the gods, the boys were going to be all right.

Vorrin yanked on the line. "What are you waiting for?"

"Pull!" Jendara shouted. She rose slowly up the cliff's face.

In the corner of her left eye, something glimmered. Jendara didn't want to look, but she knew she had to.

Something huge gleamed below her, something that for a long moment her brain refused to recognize. It rolled wildly at her, a vast black orb whose depths showed the madly dancing stars. That orb, she felt—she *knew*—meant the end of the world and the beginning of eternal nightmare. It beamed pure raw evil straight into her heart.

It was the sleeping god's eye.

"Jendara!" Vorrin shouted.

She snapped her attention back to him. The muscles in her hands and arms screamed. She was nearly out of the crevasse, but she didn't know if she could pull him up.

Maybe it would be a blessing to just let him go. He would die quickly, instead of drowning in the madness the god would wreak upon them all. She stared down at him, memorizing his face, his hair, the shape of his knuckles gripping the rope.

"Jendara," he repeated, softer. She blinked hard. What was she thinking? She couldn't let Vorrin go!

"Help me!" she shouted, and with a lurch, she was suddenly back on the ground. Boruc and Zuna were reeling Vorrin back up over the cliff. Jendara lay still for a moment, just breathing and wishing that horrible eye would disappear from her memory.

Someone laughed, the happy laugh of a child, and she sat up to see Glayn and Oric nearly dancing beside the crevice. Kran knelt beside him, hugging Fylga. But Tam was standing far too close to the edge. Her heart gave a sudden swoop of horrible certainty. The god had seen her and called to her, and she had denied him his tribute.

"Tam." But her voice was only a tiny whisper, not nearly loud enough to reach him as the tentacle appeared behind him.

Fylga barked a warning, but she was too late. The tentacle wrapped around Tam's ankle and pulled him over the brink.

Glayn rushed forward and dropped to his knees, staring down into the darkness. He cried out in wordless despair.

"What happened?" Vorrin asked, still pulling himself over the wall.

"We've got to get out of here," Zuna snapped.

Vorrin rolled onto ground, breathing hard. "Is—" he had to stop and catch his breath. He tried again: "Is everyone all right?"

"No," Jendara said. She freed herself from Zuna's belt and tossed it back to the other woman. She hurried to Glayn's side and knelt beside him. "We have to go."

He refused to look up at her, shaking his head wildly. "Not without Tam."

"Come on," she said, her voice rough and thick. "Come on!"

"No!" he shouted. "We saved Vorrin! We saved *your* son! Why not my Tam?"

"It'll get us all," she said. "It wants us all!"

Zuna shoved Jendara out of the way and scooped the gnome up into her arms. "Hush now, Glayn. We've got to get out of here."

The floor shook and Zuna stumbled a little. Something deep inside the island groaned, and a slab of rock slammed down beside the group. Without looking back for the others, Zuna broke into a run.

Boruc raced after her, pulling Oric along by his unbroken arm. Fylga gave a worried bark and dashed ahead of them.

Kran tugged on Jendara's arm and pointed back at the portal device. Behind it, the wall of the chapel was gone, replaced by a black doorway outlined in eye-searingly bright blue light. Jendara pulled Kran closer as they watched the last of the moon-beasts run through that horrible gate.

Horrible was the only word for it. The world beyond was a gray wasteland of rock and sand and mountains so sharp they cut the sky and made it weep black, angry tears. Stars like none she'd ever seen wheeled and spun in the ink-stained heavens, their coruscating lights making her head ache. She realized she was holding her breath and had to cough to find air.

An ulat-kini—no, not *an* ulat-kini, but Skortti, bleeding and battered, darted for the doorway. Only a few of the denizens of Leng remained at the portal, and one spun around to face the ulat-kini wiseman. The denizen drew a black scimitar from its belt.

Skortti dodged away from the creature's slash. For a second, Jendara thought he would make it: that the ulat-kini would cross into the realm where he'd been promised all the power and glory their own world had denied him. But the scimitar flashed in the air and Skortti stopped at the very edge of the doorway, clutching his throat in startled agony.

His body had come up short, but momentum propelled his severed head across the boundary between worlds. His eyes widened and then the life went out of them. Skortti's head struck a big charcoal stone and bounced off it, coming to a stop upon the gray sand, his olive-toned flesh the only color in all that world.

"Jendara!"

She spun around to see Vorrin beckon to her. The stones around them grumbled and smaller fissures began shooting out from the edges of the great gash in the floor. She and Kran ran as hard and as fast as they could toward the bronze doors of the chapel. They leaped over one last fissure and then they were out in the nearly empty boulevard.

The whole island shook and shuddered as they ran down the dark hallway. No starlight or moonlight penetrated the great skylights; nothing lit up the debris-strewn boulevard except for the faint bobbing light of Zuna's lantern in the distance. The light jerked right and vanished.

"Zuna, wait!"

Zuna had found the staircase. Jendara could only hope that she and Vorrin could do the same. The dark pressed down on her as if it had its own mass. It filled the air and made it hard to breathe, and when the island shook, its velvety, unpleasant folds wrapped around her like a damp blanket.

A bark, just a few feet ahead, shook off the weight.

"Fylga!"

The dog barked again and Zuna's light reappeared. "Hurry up!"

Jendara raced toward the light, Fylga panting along beside her. To her right, stained glass shattered as it hit the floor. The island was shaking itself to bits. Kran sped ahead, and the dog kept pace with him.

"Come on!" shouted Zuna. She waved her free hand wildly.

They all rounded the corner and launched themselves down the stairs in less a run than a barely contained fall. The strangely shaped stairs jerked and twitched beneath their boots, but no one tripped. Jendara hit the beach and felt a new strength enter her legs. Boruc had already dropped the *Milady*'s gangplank, and was waving a crowd of haggard Sorinders on board. Jendara saw Leyla and Morul in the crowd, and her heart stirred.

She slowed to a stop. There was another craft behind the *Milady*, a smaller longship that looked like it was struggling to get away from the shore. The sail was still furled, and no one had put out oars.

"That ship's from Sorind," Vorrin said. "If we could get some hands on board, we could lighten the *Milady*'s load."

Boruc shook his head. "It's not abandoned. I saw an ulat-kini cast off just before the first villagers hit the beach."

"That son of a bitch," Vorrin spat. "We ought to capture that boat and throw the scum overboard."

The ground lurched and the gangplank bucked. A stalactite smashed on the end of the dock, just inches from Kran.

"We don't have time!" Jendara shoved a woman onto the gangplank and urged her forward. "This island is breaking apart."

And the island, Jendara realized, was the only thing containing the sleeping god. The scepter was gone. The moon-beasts were gone. There was nothing that could control that monstrous thing.

She rubbed the back of her left hand, where the ancestors' mark blazed across the tendons. They had saved her before, but she had no idea if their spirits could do anything against the might of a god. She didn't bother looking at the skull and crossbones inked on her right hand. Even if she still worshiped Besmara, the pirate goddess wasn't likely to stand up for one unimportant ex-pirate.

No, she was on her own.

"We've got to get out of here," she warned.

Vorrin nodded. They hurried on board and stowed the gangplank. Vorrin began barking orders to the fisherfolk he recognized from Sorind, pressing them into duty. Jendara eyed the out-of-control longship. Its bow spun slowly around. In a minute or two, it would hit the cave wall and grind to a halt. A longship could sail with a small crew, but it was nearly impossible for one this size to be sailed by one person alone.

Jendara frowned. Hadn't Zuna said all the ulat-kini's boats and the longships that had brought in the Sorind prisoners had been scuttled or cut loose? So how had this one gotten inside the cave? It would have had to run against the current.

She saw a small figure at the mast, fighting to get the sail up. It looked more human and less stocky than most ulat-kini, and realization hit her.

Korthax.

Korthax had stolen this longship because, as a hybrid, he couldn't just swim away from the island once he woke the sleeping god. He had to breathe, after all. He'd gotten rid of the ulat-kini's other boats because he needed to make sure the others wouldn't follow him away from the island. He'd known the ulat-kini would never accept him as a leader after confronting Skortti and the denizens of Leng. He'd planned to escape on a ship with the sleeping god following behind him like a pet.

Now he was on his own and failing. Moreover, he hadn't taken the time to disable the *Milady*. He had probably expected the other ulat-kini to wipe out all their prisoners, and what remained would have certainly gotten picked off by the angry deep ones.

Anger stirred heat into her cheeks. He hadn't thought much of her and her crew, had he? By the gods, she'd be glad to watch the island swallow him up.

A horrible grinding sounded overhead, and Jendara snapped her gaze up at the ceiling. The roof was splitting. A slab of stone splashed down beside the ship, sending up a massive wave that immediately drenched Jendara. She grabbed the deck railing as the ship rocked hard.

She smelled mold and rancid seaweed, and caught a glimpse of something black unfolding from the ceiling. Seawater filled her eyes, and as she blinked it away, the huge blackness swung down and slapped her hard enough to break her grip and send her overboard.

She hit the water and sank into the boiling surf.

28

STARSPAWN

Jendara surfaced gasping. Rock rained down around her, sending up spurts of water that obscured the line between sea and air. She couldn't see the *Milady*; she couldn't see the beach; a shard of stalactite hit the side of her head and the world went gray for a moment. She sank like an anchor beneath the water, arms and legs no longer getting messages from her brain. Then a sharp yank on her sleeve pulled her back up into air.

Something warm and wet slapped against her face and she blinked awake to find Fylga licking her worriedly. Another chunk of stone hit the water and nearly swamped the pair. Jendara began to tread water, searching around her for the best course of action. The cave was dark now, and she realized the *Milady* and her lanterns were already slipping out of the cave's mouth.

No one but the dog had noticed her go over the side. She was going to have to swim for it.

A soft crunching caught her attention, and she realized the stolen longship had broken free of the cave wall. It slid forward a few inches, moving inch by inch toward the cave's opening. A seam ran along the water behind it: the long trail of a dangling mooring rope, its end only a few yards away.

Fylga and Jendara paddled toward the ship. Jendara grabbed onto the rope with one hand and then reached out for the dog. "Good thing you're small." She pulled them closer. It was a longship, after all, and low to the water. Jendara hoisted the dog up onto the gunwale and gave her butt a shove. Then she braced her legs against the ship's side and hauled herself up and over the side. She landed hard in the bottom of the boat.

Korthax looked up from the rudder with a snarl.

"You should have made sure I was dead before you double-crossed us, Korthax." Jendara got to her feet. "The only thing I don't understand is why you were so nice to Kran the whole time."

He bared his teeth. "I knew you would not hurt me if the boy liked me."

Anything he might have added was swallowed up by a booming roar that shook the walls of the cavern. A surge of water shot the longship out of the cave's mouth, grinding its side against the rocky wall all the way. The longship moved fast, but not so fast that Jendara couldn't see, looking over her shoulder, the enormous figure wriggling out of the demolished back wall of the cave. The sleeping god had finally pierced through the shell of the island.

The ship moved west into open water. Waves rocked the longship and an icy wind whipped at Jendara's hair. After weeks of warm weather, winter had announced its arrival with a fury. Thunder crashed, and Jendara, still looking backward, saw the entire island silhouetted against a flash of lightning that must have struck the tall towers on its surface.

The rock at the mouth of the cavern sagged to the right. Something inside the cave, some integral bit of stone, groaned sadly. Rocks jiggled and jolted down the cliff face and plunged into the ocean, faster and faster, larger rocks and entire chunks of the cliff shearing off. The waves battered the longship and Jendara grabbed onto the gunwale.

The island split open, revealing the terrible glory of the sleeping god.

The sound of the stars screaming filled Jendara's ears as if it came from inside her head and vibrated out through the bones of her skull. She struggled to breathe. The air was air no longer, but some thick moldering substance that drained the life from anything that inhaled it. She couldn't take in the entirety of the creature before her—it undulated before her eyes, parts swelling to unimaginable sizes and then shrinking down to something she could almost compare to ordinary creatures. Only its eyes remained absolute, vast and all-seeing and lit from within with an evil flame.

"The starspawn," Korthax breathed. She wondered how she could hear him over the sound of the universe's terror.

The god spread its leathery wings and gave a luxurious flap. Water spouts broke out on the surface of the sea, spinning off in wild directions.

Jendara loosened her grip on the ship's gunwale. The pressure in her head abated a little. The water spouts raced past her, and she realized the longship and the *Milady* weren't alone out here in the sea. The sharp fins of the deep ones sliced through the water all around them as the strange creatures raced away from the crumbling island. She saw an ulat-kini swim past as well.

The towers on the surface toppled, their spires tumbling down over the cliffs and smashing into the sea. Fissures opened on every cliff face. Water that had been trapped inside closed-off chambers and hidden caves poured out of the cracks and crannies that opened up as the island shook itself to pieces. Another flash of lightning lit everything up a startling white, and Jendara saw a golden figurine of something not quite octopus, not quite human, slide down the eroding rock, its priceless curves winking in the light.

That alone would have rebuilt Sorind and allowed Jendara to quit working forever. It hit the water with a tremendous splash. Gone, destroyed, like all the majesty of this strange and ancient place.

Fylga began to growl.

Jendara had nearly forgotten the dog and the ulat-kini who shared the longship, and it was a struggle to wrench her attention back to the ordinary world. Destruction and despair had nearly swallowed her whole.

If she had to guess how Korthax had escaped the Star Chapel, she would have assumed he crept out the front doors while everyone's attention was on the drama of the blue portal, but she could see now he had not. He had taken the other route to freedom, the route she had suggested to Kran. Korthax had followed the star scepter out the open window—and reclaimed the magical device.

Now he held it up to the dark sky and chanted something in a mysterious language whose very syllables made the hair rise on Jendara's neck:

Ph'nglui mglw'nafh Cthulhu R'lyeh wgah'nagl fhtagn!
Iä! Iä!

The symbols on the star scepter began to fill with a creamy light, and the same brilliant glow appeared at the heart of the astrolabe. The sleeping god snapped open its wings and screeched loud enough to pierce the clouds.

The star scepter. The astrolabe. Jendara's head spun. It was almost impossible to concentrate. The god's thoughts, so huge they escaped its tentacled head, filled her mind with rage and disgust. This world disgusted it. The beings of this world disgusted it. It was time for it to sleep, time for it to draw together its powers and wait for its priest-king to send the orders for all destruction.

She suddenly remembered the huge deep one in the Star Chapel as it made its attack on Ahrzur. "The stars are wrong," Jendara whispered.

"It's obeying!" Korthax laughed wildly. "I can make it do whatever I want! *Iä! Iä!*" he roared.

The sleeping god—no, Jendara realized, that was wrong. What Korthax had called it? The starspawn?—the starspawn took a giant step toward them, sending out waves huge enough to nearly swamp the longship.

Fury began to boil in Jendara's chest. This was where all her trouble came from. This was where the tsunami had come from— the rising of the island had displaced that great wall of water and sent it crashing down over Sorind. All the damage, all the trouble, all of it came from the denizens of Leng and their desire to control this monstrous being.

Lightning crackled off the starspawn's massive domed head, and as if her thoughts had summoned them, she saw the sleek dark shape of the Leng ship, creeping away toward the rest of the archipelago. She had thought they'd all escaped through the portal, but enough had stayed to pilot their evil vessel.

Korthax saw it, too. He pointed the scepter at the Leng ship and roared something unintelligible. The scepter burned brighter in his hands.

The starspawn turned, just a little, sending huge ripples across the surface of the sea. Its eyes fixed on the black ship of Leng. A tentacle shot out, impossibly long, impossibly powerful, and pierced the side of the alien ship.

Korthax shrieked with delight. He raised the scepter again. But whatever he planned to do, Jendara knew she couldn't let him do it. Rage boiled off the starspawn in palpable rays. The star scepter might control the god for now, but the starspawn's mind was still mostly asleep. If it awoke—really and truly awoke—nothing in the world could keep it under control.

She threw herself at Korthax. They hit the deck hard, and she drove her fist into his face. He writhed underneath her, claws slashing at her sides. She slammed her forehead down on his, momentarily stunning him.

She reached for her belt axe.

The longship flew up into the air as a giant wave flung it away from the island. Jendara tumbled sideways, smashing into the base of the mast. Something crunched inside her. She lay still a moment, clutching her side.

Korthax rushed at her, the star scepter readied like a spear. Jendara tried to get up and felt her legs go out from under her.

Fylga sank her teeth into the ulat-kini's leg. He screamed in pain and Jendara pushed herself upright. She brought up her axe.

The ulat-kini kicked the dog aside. He leveled the star scepter at Jendara. "*Iä*," he began, but her axe struck him in the forehead. His eyes rolled up in his head, and he collapsed.

Jendara crawled to his side and pried the scepter from his fingers. Every movement hurt. Just breathing felt like her insides were on fire. She'd broken ribs before, but this time she thought she might have done real damage. But she couldn't let that thing out there wake up.

She forced herself to her feet and turned to face the starspawn. She could feel its mind bearing down on her, crushing her will—not just her will to fight, but her very will to exist. The world was a place of darkness and evil. Everything would be so much better if she just laid down in the bottom of the boat and closed her eyes. Everything would be so much better.

Jendara forced her arms above her head. She didn't know the ancient language that Korthax had used, but she'd heard enough. "*Fhtagn*," she said, her voice barely a whisper. But the scepter's glow brightened. She squeezed shut her eyes, wishing she could remember. "Sleep," she begged it. "Just go back to sleep. You know the stars are wrong. Just—sleep."

The starspawn pulled in its wings and stared back at her with its ancient alien eyes. The stars whimpered in her mind. All of time looked down at her and into her and she knew she was crying. All she wanted was to close her eyes and sleep.

The giant eyelids drooped. The island shuddered and began to sink down around the starspawn, and the creature began to sink with it, slowly at first, then faster and faster.

Jendara's arms shook, but she didn't lower the star scepter. She trained its light on the starspawn's closed eyes and prayed to the ancestors and any god that could hear her that she was right about the stars.

Fylga barked, and Jendara turned to see what the dog saw: the clawed hand gripping the gunwale. Jendara dragged herself across the boat, spinning the star scepter so it faced the newest enemy staff end first. The deep one lashed out at her with its free hand, and she slammed the butt of the scepter into its face. It clung on tenaciously.

"Why are you attacking *me*? I'm worse off than you." Her legs wobbled beneath her.

"Jendara!"

"Vorrin?" She peered out into the darkness, searching for the *Milady*'s lights on the dark sea. A tiny flicker caught her eye: the soft glow of a lantern sitting in the bottom of a dinghy. Vorrin was coming for her.

"Look behind you!" he shouted.

She turned again, slowly, unwillingly, and saw the whirlpool. The denizens of Leng's great black ship was caught up in it, circling wildly around the sucking maw at the center of the maelstrom where the god had sunk beneath the waves. The starspawn was gone, and only the very tip of the island's tallest spire still showed above the water. A deep one struggled to escape the downward pull, and then a chunk of debris slammed into it and drove it beneath the water.

The island's hollow core was going to swallow them all.

"Get out of here, Vorrin!" Jendara screamed, or tried to scream, but it was harder to breathe every second. She dropped to her knees in the bottom of the boat. She could feel it surging toward the whirlpool, caught up in the island's death.

The deep one clinging to the side stared back at her, panic flickering across its bulbous eyes as it realized she had no control over the longship, and that the boat could provide no safety. It threw itself backward into the sea. She felt a bit of pity for it. The deep ones had tried to keep the starspawn from waking. They could have been allies if things had been different.

"Jendara! Jump down here right now!"

The dinghy had pulled up right beside the longship. Fylga leaped over the gunwale and landed beside Vorrin. They both looked back at Jendara, expectant. Jendara pulled herself to her feet.

"Get away," she whispered. "Too dangerous."

"Get in here!" Vorrin ordered.

She shook her head. She didn't have the strength to jump, and if Vorrin waited for her, he was going to get caught up in the whirlpool and die, too.

The dinghy bumped the side of the longboat. "You're not going to make Kran an orphan, are you?"

Kran. Jendara forced herself to breathe as deeply as she could. Her boy was nearly grown, but he still needed her.

She fixed her eyes on Vorrin's face and jumped.

It was more of a tumble, but the two boats were close enough she still made it inside, even if her side screamed and gray spots swam before her eyes. The star scepter dug into her shoulder, but she couldn't sit up. Vorrin threw himself down and began to row hard and fast. The longship pulled away from them, hurrying toward the maelstrom. The dinghy stayed in one place, Vorrin's rowing and the whirlpool's powerful suction canceling each other out.

But there was no way he could row like this forever. A flailing ulat-kini shot past them, and then a scrap of shimmering silk, a final remnant of the giant spiders' nest.

"What . . . are . . ." Vorrin's face was red and he gritted his teeth, "they . . . waiting for?"

With a twang that Jendara heard over the wind and the rushing water and the shrieks of the drowning, a rope sprang tight at the prow of the dinghy. The dinghy shot backward a few feet and then slowly began to crawl away from the foaming maelstrom.

Lightning flickered in the distance, and she could see the *Milady*, its sails high and full-bellied as they caught the winter wind. It towed the dinghy along in its wake. They nearly flew across the water, speeding toward safety.

Jendara managed to sit up and look over her shoulder. The black ship of the denizens of Leng was gone, and Korthax's longship stood tilted up on its nose, caught in the tug of the whirlpool. Its timbers groaned, and for a moment Jendara thought she saw a body tumble out into the water. It seemed somehow right that Korthax should join the ocean without any vessel to shelter or protect him.

She coughed and tasted blood, but she didn't take her eyes off the whirlpool. It spun tighter and tighter, growling and gurgling like some angry beast. She sagged against the gunwale, watching the evidence of the island's horror circle the closing spiral, and the scepter dug harder into her side.

Jendara tugged it out from beneath her. In a flash of lightning, the bronze device gleamed. If she didn't know better, it could have been any kind of astronomical device, just a tool to measure the transit of the stars—not a powerful magical apparatus for controlling an ancient, powerful being.

She had just enough energy to hoist it above her head. "It's your problem now, starspawn."

The star scepter soared over the debris to splash into the whirling foam at the edge of the maelstrom. For an instant, she felt that terrible, ancient mind touch hers, and she shuddered.

There was a gurgle, and a whoosh, and the whirlpool closed on itself, leaving the water flat and quiet, with only a stained blot of foam to remind anyone that there had ever been a whirlpool or an island or the lost and angry spawn of an abysmal star.

THE DREAMER IN DARKNESS

Jendara awoke in her own bed on the *Milady*. Weak sunlight trickled in through the porthole, suggesting early morning. She had slept only a few hours, but she felt a thousand times better than she had last night. She lay still a few minutes, enjoying the gently painful feeling that came from breathing. She patted her side and felt a stiff layer of bandages.

A clean set of clothes sat on the chart table. She eased herself out of bed and wriggled into them, happy to find her water-skin tucked underneath. Her mouth tasted like bitter herbs and scorched earth, the flavors she'd most associated with a healing potion. Glayn had saved her, then, even if she hadn't saved his Tam.

She pulled on her boots and opened the cabin door. For a moment, she wanted to simply crawl back in bed and sleep for a day or a week or a month, but she needed to know how her people were doing. She walked outside. The air smelled like snow.

The deck was full. She counted at least twenty folks sitting with idle hands, and a full complement of sailors were at their posts. She recognized all the familiar faces: the baker and his wife; Kaleb, the owner of Sorind's one tavern; Chana and Leyla chatting as they sat with a pile of mending. Her heart gave a squeeze. This wasn't all that was left of Sorind, was it? They hadn't lost all the other villagers?

Kran raced past her, Oric and Fylga on his heels. Only Fylga looked back at Jendara. The boys were too caught up in their merriment. It made Jendara feel a little better. If the boys could act like things were normal, then she could, too.

She found Zuna in the galley, brewing up a pot of tea. A crowd of villagers filled the space, some sitting in the pained sorrow of those who had lost everything, others playing cards or eating or simply talking in quiet voices. There was none of the laughter that came in a typical village gathering. Jendara caught Zuna's eye and joined her at the stove.

"You all right?" Zuna asked. Unbidden, she pulled down a mug and filled it for Jendara.

Jendara nodded. "Right enough." She looked out at the people crowding around the tables. "Is this everyone? All the . . . survivors?"

Zuna shook her head. "The ulat-kini didn't get everyone," she said. "Most folks had holed up inland after the wave, waiting for things to dry out."

Jendara sagged with relief. There was hope, then. Hope enough to ask: "How many died?"

"At least forty," Zuna said. "We'll have to do a head count when we get back to Sorind." She paused. "You just missed the captain," she said. "He went up on deck."

Jendara squeezed Zuna's shoulder, and the navigator clapped her on the back, the blow as solid as Boruc's or any other islander's. Then Jendara went back up top.

She paused for a moment, thinking about how she had handled Zuna back on the island, how she had handled the entire expedition. It wasn't the way her father would have handled things, she knew. But then again, her father had never faced anything like the thing sleeping in that pit.

She rubbed the spot on her hand. The ancestors could only give her guidance. She had to find her own way to do things.

It was time to find Vorrin.

Her steps were slow as she walked to the stern of the ship. She knew where she would find him and who he would be with. She was in no hurry to face this last test.

Vorrin leaned against the stern railing, looking out to sea. Glayn stood beside him, head bowed.

"Hey," she managed.

The men looked up at her. Vorrin looked serious, and sorrow had etched itself across Glayn's face. The happy gnome who had played the hurdy-gurdy for them when they first set out from Sorind was gone.

A tiny speck of white swirled in the air in front of her and then settled on the railing to melt. Winter had arrived in the islands.

"Glayn—" she began, and stopped, blinking hard. She didn't know what to say to him.

"Don't," he said. "Tam was my everything. I'm two hundred years old, and I've never known anyone like him, not ever. Gnomes don't give their hearts easy, but I gave him mine."

The wind blew into their faces, carrying a sharp edge and the kind of snow that stings and sticks. Jendara shivered. She'd left her coat in the cabin.

"But," Glayn continued, "I'm still a part of this crew. And Tam wasn't my only friend, just my best one."

Jendara stared at him, not quite sure whether to believe his words. He had looked at her with such misery back there in the Star Chapel. He had blamed her and resented her and maybe even hated her. But she saw none of that in the gnome's eyes now. Sorrow, yes. Recrimination, no.

"So what do we do now?" she asked.

"We keep going," Vorrin said. "We found enough treasure to take on a couple more crew. We're sailors. We'll find a way to make ends meet."

"But our cottage," Jendara said. "Our home . . ."

Glayn shook his head. "We're sailors. Our home is right here." He spread his hands, taking in the ship and the sea and even the clouds that spit snow into their faces. The wind ruffled his green curls and he looked a little more like himself.

"You're right," Jendara agreed. She leaned her head on Vorrin's shoulder and studied the sky. It was good to feel clean air on her skin. It was good to see sunshine, even filtered through heavy clouds. She would like to keep the sun and the clouds between herself and the sky for as long as she could.

Because beyond the clouds, the stars were up there, someplace in the dark, turning and dancing and crying to themselves. Crying because they knew that in the darkest depths of the world, something slept and dreamed and *waited*.

Waited for the stars to be right.

ABOUT THE AUTHOR

Wendy N. Wagner grew up in a town so small it didn't even have its own post office—or worse, cable. Forced to read for entertainment, she was doomed to walk a literary path. A Hugo Award-winning editor as well as a writer, she has over thirty short stories in print and currently serves as the Managing/Associate Editor for the genre magazines *Lightspeed* and *Nightmare*. Her first novel, *Skinwalkers*, is also a Pathfinder Tales adventure about Jendara and her family, who first appeared in the web fiction story "Mother Bears," available for free at **paizo.com/pathfindertales**.

Wendy lives with her very understanding family in Portland, Oregon. An avid gardener and board gamer, she can be found online at **winniewoohoo.com**.

ACKNOWLEDGMENTS

Massive thanks go out to the crew at Paizo. There are just too many fantastic people working there to thank properly—but I hope they know how great they are. Big hugs to James Sutter, my terrific editor, who said yes to a Lovecraftian novel and had the wicked idea to make it about Cthulhu.

A huge shout-out to the staff of *Lightspeed* and *Nightmare* magazines, who put up with me while I worked on this book. John, Christie, Robyn, Erika, Lisa, Dana, and Melissa: you are the best! I promise I'll be less distracted now that I'm not trying to put a starspawn back to sleep.

This book could not have been written without the assistance of the finest writing group known to humanity: the Masked Hucksters. Thanks for helping me outline this project and wrangle all the monsters. You are the best and bravest of friends, so mask tip to you, Jen, Rebecca, and Dale.

My family took the brunt of the madness while I summoned up this book. A big apology to Jak, for dropping the ball planning my campaign—you're the best GM in the world, and I'm just lucky you let me hang out with you. Fiona, thanks for making all those great dinners so I could work. And John . . . well, there aren't enough words to express my gratitude for your love and support.

Last, I must thank Howard Phillips Lovecraft for gifting writers everywhere with your Mythos. I will always be in your debt.

Ph'nglui mglw'nafh Cthulhu R'lyeh wgah'nagl fhtagn.

GLOSSARY

All Pathfinder Tales novels are set in the rich and vibrant world of the Pathfinder campaign setting. Below are explanations of several key terms used in this book. For more information on the world of Golarion and the strange monsters, people, and deities that make it their home, see *The Inner Sea World Guide*, or dive into the game and begin playing your own adventures with the *Pathfinder Roleplaying Game Core Rulebook* or the *Pathfinder Roleplaying Game Beginner Box*, all available at **paizo.com**.

Absalom: Largest city in the Inner Sea region, located on an island far to the south of the Ironbound Archipelago.

Avistan: The continent north of the Inner Sea.

Besmara: Goddess of piracy, strife, and sea monsters.

Boneyard: Pharasma's realm, where all souls go to be judged after death.

Cheliax: A powerful devil-worshiping nation located south of the Ironbound Archipelago.

Chelish: Of or relating to the nation of Cheliax.

Deep Ones: A race of aquatic humanoids that worship alien entities.

Desna: Good-natured goddess of dreams, stars, travelers, and luck.

Forest of Souls: A forested area on the Isle of Ancestors where ancestor spirits linger to support the living.

Giants: Race of humanoids many times larger than humans.

Gnomes: Small humanoids with brightly colored hair and strange mindsets, originally from the fey realm of the First World.

Golarion: The planet on which the Pathfinder campaign setting focuses.

Gozreh: God of nature, the sea, and weather. Depicted as a dual deity, with both male and female aspects.

Great Beyond: The planes of the afterlife.

Halgrim: Capital city of the portion of the Ironbound Archipelago controlled by the Linnorm Kings. Seat of power for the Linnorm King White Estrid.

Inner Sea: The vast inland sea whose northern continent, Avistan, and southern continent, Garund, as well as the seas and nearby lands, are the primary focus of the Pathfinder campaign setting.

Ironbound Archipelago: Network of cold islands off the coast of Avistan. The largest population center in the Steaming Sea, though the residents are rarely more organized than local villages. Partially independent, with the northern islands controlled by the Linnorm Kings.

Isle of Ancestors: Island where heroes from certain islands in the Ironbound Archipelago go to commune with their ancestors and become wisewomen and shamans.

Leng: A distant, inhospitable realm on another plane of reality, hedged in by titanic mountains and home to creatures that occasionally travel to the Material Plane to collect slaves.

Linnorm Kings: Warrior-chieftains who together rule a nation that includes part of the Ironbound Archipelago, each of whom must defeat a linnorm to claim a throne.

Moon-Beasts: Strange tentacle-mouthed creatures capable of controlling the minds of others.

Ogres: Hulking, brutal, and half-witted humanoid monsters with violent tendencies, repulsive lusts, and enormous capacities for cruelty.

Pharasma: The goddess of birth, death, and prophecy, who judges mortal souls after their deaths and sends them on to the appropriate afterlife; also known as the Lady of Graves.

Pharasma's Boneyard: Pharasma's realm.

Seax: Type of short sword or dagger typically possessing a curved and notched blade.

Skinwalkers: Shape-changing humanoids who can magically take on the forms or aspects of particular animals.

Sorind: Small island in the Ironbound Archipelago, devoted mainly to farming and fishing.

Taldane: The common trade language of the Inner Sea region.

Trolls: Large, stooped humanoids with sharp claws and amazing regenerative powers that are overcome only by fire.

Ulat-Kini: Race of fishlike, aquatic humanoids incapable of reproducing without human partners.

Varisian: Of or relating to the region of the frontier region of Varisia, or a resident of that region.

Varisians: Primarily nomadic human ethnic group often characterized as tinkers, musicians, and dancers.

Wizards: Those who cast spells through careful study and rigorous scientific methods rather than faith or innate talent, recording the necessary incantations in a spellbook.

Turn the page for a sneak peek at

shy knives

by Sam Sykes

Available October 2016

1

INTRODUCTIONS

S haia Ratani."
This wasn't how I wanted to be introduced.

"Approach."

My chains rattled as I shuffled slowly across the floor on bare feet. Despite the multitudes of burning candelabra stretching down the hall on either side of me, the tattered rags I wore failed to ward off a chill. Even I hadn't been walking the length of a hall so grand and drenched in opulence, I would have felt small.

"That's close enough, thief."

I stopped. The shackles around my wrists seemed heavy enough to pull my eyes to the ground. In the reflection of tile so polished you'd pay to eat off it, I could make out a face looking back at me, black hair hanging in greasy strands before a face covered in grime.

My face.

"Shaia Ratani," a deep, elegant voice said. "You are accused of a thousand crimes against the aristocracy of Taldor, the most heinous of which include larceny, fraud, extortion, assault, assault with a deadly weapon, assault with intent to murder, unsanctioned use of poison, trespassing, public indecency . . ."

I was hard pressed to think of any legends that began like this.

". . . and consorting with deviant powers."

Hell, I couldn't even think of a good tavern story that began like this.

But it was bards who were concerned with how stories began. In my line of work, you learned early on that it's only the ending that matters.

"You may look up, thief."

Bold, commanding words from a bold, commanding voice. You'd think, upon looking up, that they'd belong to a bold, commanding man.

Those were not the first words you'd think upon seeing Lord Herevard Helsen. They *might* have been the thirty-second and thirty-third ones, if you were generous.

Tall and thin as a stalk of corn and with ears to match, the aristocrat that stood upon a raised dais at the end of the hall seemed an ill fit for his fancy clothes. Hell, he seemed a poor fit for his own home.

While his hall was bedecked with tapestries and servants standing at attention and portraits of strong men and women with strong, noble features, Herevard, with his weak chin and shrewd eyes, shifted uncomfortably. Like he could sense his ancestors' disapproval emanating from the portraits and was already imagining what they'd say if they could see him now.

I never knew them, but I imagined they probably wouldn't be pleased to see a filthy Katapeshi girl in shackles dirtying up their halls.

"Understand this, Miss Ratani." Lord Helsen spoke down an overlarge nose at me, as though the dais he stood upon wasn't high enough to separate us. "I have had you brought from my private dungeons at the behest of another. A mission of mercy that relies entirely on your ability to be civil. Do you understand?"

That would have sounded significantly more authoritative, I imagined, if his face weren't beaded with sweat. I chose not to call attention to that, though. I merely nodded and received a nod in exchange.

Lord Helsen glanced to his side.

"She was captured not two months ago. My guards found her robbing my study. She's been serving penance in my dungeons ever since, my lady."

"Penance?"

Another voice chimed in. A lyrical birdsong to his squawk: soft, feminine, gentle.

I wasn't sure how I hadn't noticed the woman standing beside him before, but the moment she spoke, I couldn't see anything else in the room.

Had Lord Helsen not addressed her as 'lady,' I might never have guessed her to be a noble. She certainly wasn't what you'd think of when someone mentioned the word, let alone what I'd think of. Her dress was a simple thing of white and blue linens, easy to move in and functional—two words that make aristocratic tailors cringe. Her brown hair was clean and washed, but not styled with any particular elegance. She didn't look especially rich.

Pretty, though.

Or at least, she might have been. It was hard to tell, what with the massive spectacles resting upon the bridge of her nose.

"Penance, my lady." Lord Helsen nodded to the woman. "As you know, Yanmass' laws are rather . . . archaic when it comes to crimes against the gentler class." He chuckled. "Why, I'm told that Lady Stelvan, upon finding a vagrant in her wine cellar, appealed to the courts to have him walled up inside and—"

"*Please!*" The woman held up a hand. "Er, that is, Lord Helsen, I do not need to be privy to the details."

"Of . . . of course, Lady Sidara." Lord Helsen made a hasty, apologetic bow. "Regardless, I couldn't let her walk away freely. Time to reflect upon her misdeeds in the dungeons seemed adequate." He glanced back toward me. "I suspect that she will be ideal for your purposes."

"Purposes?"

I hadn't intended to sound quite so alarmed when I spoke. I hadn't intended to speak at all. Lord Helsen hadn't intended me to either, judging from the annoyed glare he shot me.

"Yes, thief. Purposes." Herevard shot me an annoyed look. I bowed my head. "The Lady Sidara has need of someone with particular . . . talents."

I nodded, head still lowered. Somehow, I figured it was going to be about this.

The three things nobles hated most, in order, were losing money, bad wine, and being reminded they had the same needs as anyone else. No matter how big your house was or who you paid to wipe your ass, eventually, everyone needed a treasure stolen, a throat cut, or something set on fire.

They might have used words like 'talents,' but nobody needed dirty work done more than a noble.

And they didn't come nobler than they did in Taldor.

"She is firmly bound, my lady, and no danger at all." Herevard gestured to me with one white-gloved hand. "You may inspect her at your leisure."

Lady Sidara cast him a nervous look before glancing back at me. I was, at that moment, keenly aware of every inch of grime on my skin, every ounce of weight in my chains, every tear in the raggedy shirt and trousers I wore. Something about this woman, with her drab dress and giant spectacles, made me feel naked. Vulnerable.

Unworthy.

Still, she wasn't the first person to do that to me. Certainly not the worst person, either. I kept my head respectfully low, my body reassuringly still as she approached me.

One dainty hand reached out as if to touch me, but she seemed to think better of it and drew it away. I averted my gaze as she studied me from behind those big round spectacles.

"You're not Taldan," she said. "From the south, maybe?"

"She's Qadiran, my lady." Lord Helsen spoke from the dais.

I stiffened at that. My hands tightened into fists, only relaxing when Lady Sidara spoke again.

"Not Qadiran, Herevard," she said. "Her features are a little too fine." She hummed a moment before her face lit up. "Ah! Of course. You're from Katapesh."

"Same thing," Herevard yawned.

Still, I couldn't help but raise an eyebrow. Not a lot of people from Taldor appreciated the difference between us southern nations, let alone a noble.

"You poor dear," she said, eyeing the sorry state of my dress and hygiene. "Listen. I know this might seem . . . unorthodox. It certainly wasn't my first choice. But I have . . . an issue." She glanced around, as though wary of who might be listening. "An issue that Herevard said you might be able to help with."

I cast her a sidelong look, but said nothing. As if embarrassed, she turned away and readjusted her spectacles.

"I can't give you the details here," she said. "Nor can I promise it will be easy. But I can promise you'll be adequately rewarded. I'll see you safely exonerated of your crimes and granted a handsome sum, besides, in exchange for your assistance." She drew herself up, fixed me with a hard look. "Of this, you have my word, Miss Ratani."

Funny how words, common as they were, seemed to mean an awful lot to some people. Nobles and their heritages, wizards and their spells, paladins and their oaths—words meant a lot to the kind of person who woke up one day and heard a higher calling.

I once heard that calling.

Then I put the pillow over my head and went back to sleep.

People like me, we don't put much stock in words. We know how cheap they are. We know how quickly they spin on glib tongues and how swiftly they scatter on the floor. People like me, we needed firmer stuff.

"I know this must sound odd," Lady Sidara said. "Is there . . . is there anything I can get you? To help you make up your mind?"

I took a breath and spoke softly.

"A drink."

Lady Sidara nodded and made a gesture to Herevard. Herevard, in turn, gestured to a nearby servant. The servant ran to a table set up against one of the hall's walls and, in a few moments, came rushing up to me with a goblet upon a tray. I took it, nodded my gratitude, first to him and then to her. I closed my eyes and took a long, slow sip of cold, refreshing liquid.

And immediately spat it out.

"What the hell is *this*?" I snapped at the servant.

"W-water!" he replied, holding up his tray like a shield.

"Well, did I *ask* for water, Cecim, or did I ask for a gods-damned *drink*?"

"S-sorry, Shy!" he cried out, cowering. "Sorry, mistress!"

"'Shy'? 'Mistress'?"

It wasn't until I looked and saw Lady Sidara, her mouth wide open in puzzlement, that I realized I *might* have just ruined things.

"What did you call her?" The noblewoman glanced from me to Cecim, the servant, and the puzzlement turned to irritation. It was a full-blown scowl when she whirled upon Lord Helsen and saw the thin nobleman quaking upon the dais, the sweat on his face having gone from beads to big as moons.

"What did he call her?" she demanded. "What's going on here, Herevard?"

"Uh, well . . . that is . . ." Lord Helsen's tongue seemed two sizes too large for him at that moment, and he fumbled over his words. "You see, Lady Sidara, when . . . when we make mistakes and . . . and things are said . . . and we try to make them right and . . ."

"Ah, give it up, Herevard," I said. "Whatever excuse you're choking on, it's obvious she's not going to buy it."

Lady Sidara turned to me, shock wrestling with outrage on her features as she watched me unfasten the shackles around my wrists and drop them to the floor.

I looked up at her, blinking. "What?"

"You . . . you're not a prisoner at all!" She pointed a finger at me that would have been accusing had it not been so dainty. "You *lied* to me!"

"If you'll recall, good lady," I replied, holding up my liberated hands in defense, "I didn't say ten words to you. Any lying came specifically from *that* man."

Lord Helsen squirmed under my finger, flailing as though he could pull an excuse from thin air. But instead, all he did was thrust a finger right back at me and let out a rather unlordly screech.

"She was *blackmailing* me!"

"I was not!" I shouted back. "I asked you *specifically* what the information was worth to you! *You're* the one that came up with the number!"

"Oh, don't you turn this on *me,* you lying Qadiran—"

"*Katapeshi!*"

"*ENOUGH!*"

To look at her, you wouldn't have thought such a little lady could come up with such a bellowing voice. But it seemed Lady Sidara, breathing heavily, holding her hands up in a demand for silence, was a woman of more than a few surprises.

"No more lies." She split her scowl between me and Lord Helsen. "And no more blaming. The truth. Now."

The nobleman and I exchanged glances for moment—or rather, *I* exchanged a glance and he gave me a look that suggested he might soil himself. At that, I just rolled my eyes and sighed.

"All right, fine," I said. "What I did might, in some countries, be construed as blackmail." I waved absently toward the dais. "I got some information on Herev—" I caught myself; didn't want to rub salt in the wound. "On Lord Helsen and asked him what it was worth to him to keep it quiet."

"And what *was* it worth?" Lady Sidara asked.

"Two months in a nice bedroom at his manor," I replied. "Waited on hand and foot by Cecim here." I shot a glare at the servant. "Who should damn well *know* by now what I mean when I say I want a drink!"

Cecim squealed and scurried off, still holding his tray up. I sighed and looked back to Lady Sidara.

"Anyway, when he said you had a job that needed doing, we made up this bit about the private dungeon." I gestured to my clothes and grime. "Though, had I known it would turn out like this, I wouldn't have bothered painting so much dirt on myself."

Lady Sidara frowned.

"And what information did you have to make . . ." She gestured over me. "*This* seem intelligent?"

"Well, I—"

"You *swore* you wouldn't tell!" Lord Helsen piped up, his face a red-hot contortion of embarrassment.

"Herevard, what good do you think *not* telling her would do?" I looked back to the noblewoman and sighed. "I found out about his mistress. A lovely little halfling woman who visits his chambers every other night." I shot her a wink. "Herry likes his short women."

Lord Helsen's mouth hung open. His eyes looked like they were about to roll out of their sockets. If I could have read his thoughts, I had no doubt that they'd be mostly my name attached to variations of the word 'strangle.'

Frankly, I wasn't sure what the big deal was. I always thought they looked cute together.

Lady Sidara, for her part, didn't seem particularly upset, either. She slowly turned a sweet, sad smile to Lord Helsen.

"Oh, Herevard," she said. "We've all known about Noma for years now."

"W-what?" Lord Helsen said. "Everyone? All of Yanmass?"

She nodded gently. He made a soft whimpering sound.

"Even Lady Stelvan?"

"She was the first to know, Herry."

"Well, then." I kicked off my ankle shackles and sent them skidding across the hallway. "I guess we've all learned an important lesson about honesty today." I began wiping the painted-on grime from my skin. "And it seems my time with Herry is at an end. Give me a couple of hours to have a bath and I'm all yours, my lady."

"What?" Lady Sidara looked at me, anger flashing across her features. "You assume I'd still hire you now, after . . . after . . ."

"Oh, what? You were happy to have me when you thought I was a thief, but now that I'm an extortionist, you're too good for me?" I rolled my eyes. "A touch hypocritical, don't you think?"

"It's not that! It's just . . ." She rubbed the back of her neck, helpless. "This . . . this is a delicate operation, one that I am intent on seeing carried through. I need people I can trust."

"Liar."

She looked at me like I had just slapped her. "What?"

"If you needed people you could trust, you would have found a knight or a brave warrior or some lovesick noble. What you *need* is someone who can get the job done, and the fact that you're here tells me that the people you can trust simply can't do that."

She fixed me with a long, methodical stare. And though it made me feel every bit as naked as it had the first time, I held my ground and my smile like a sword and shield.

"And can you get the job done?" she asked.

"Are you still going to pay?"

"I will."

"Then I can." I turned to walk away toward the hall's exit. "But, as I said, let me get a bath first. I'm not going to talk business covered in filth."

"Yes, fine, whatever." Lady Sidara stalked behind me. "Glad to be doing business, then, Miss . . ." She paused. "Is your name even Shaia?"

"Of course it is." I glanced over my shoulder, spared her a wink. "But my friends call me Shy."

As a young woman, Jendara left the cold northern isles of the Ironbound Archipelago to find her fortune. Now, many years later, she's forsaken her buccaneer ways and returned home in search of a simpler life, where she can raise her young son Kran in peace. When a strange clan of shapeshifting raiders pillages her home, however, there's no choice for Jendara but to take up her axes once again to help the islanders defend all that they hold dear.

From Hugo Award winner Wendy N. Wagner comes a new adventure of vikings, cannibals, and the ties of family, set in the award-winning world of the Pathfinder Roleplaying Game.

Skinwalkers **print edition: $9.99**
ISBN: 978-1-60125-616-4

Skinwalkers **ebook edition:**
ISBN: 978-1-60125-617-1

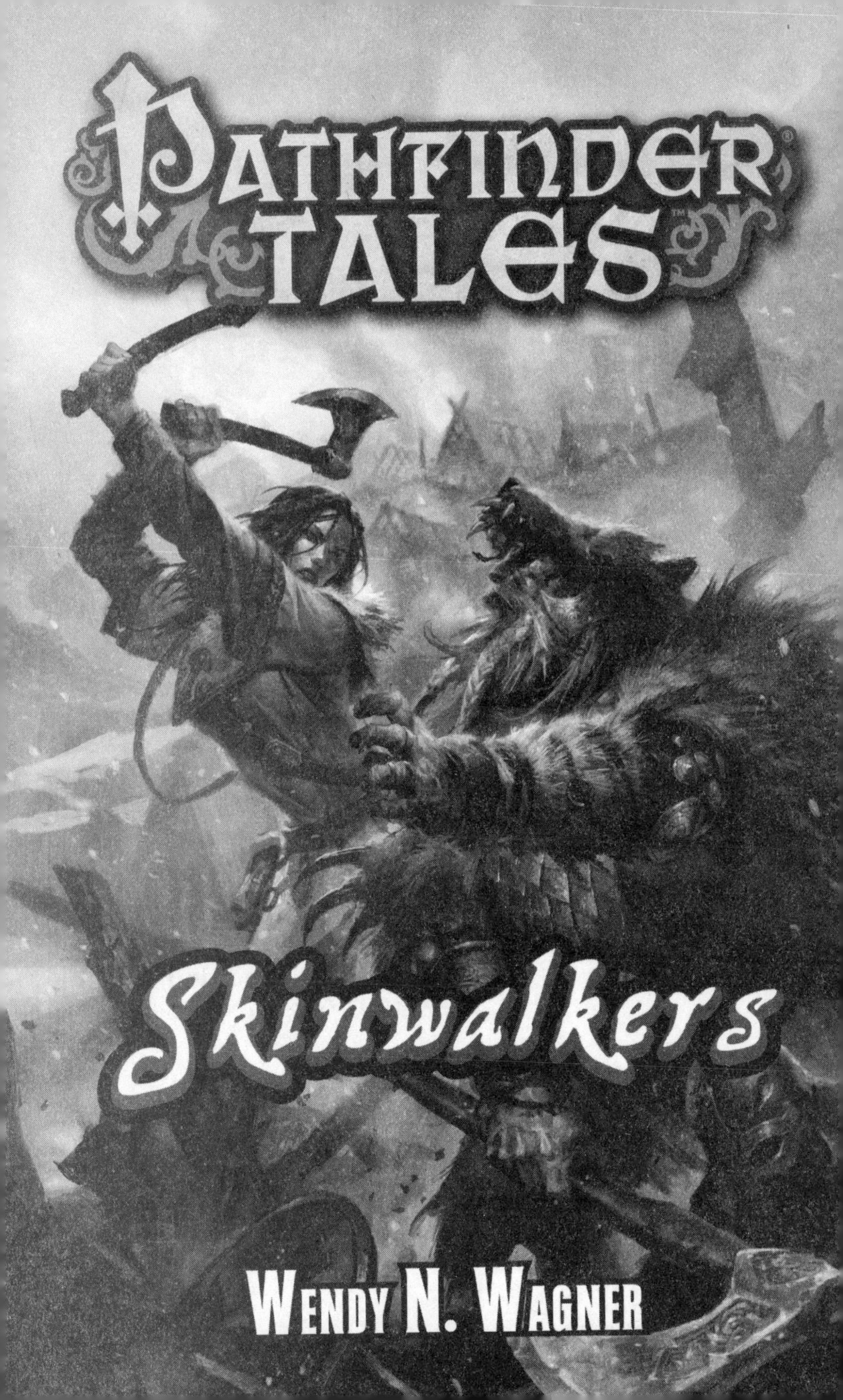
Pathfinder® Tales™
Skinwalkers
Wendy N. Wagner

When caught stealing in the crusader nation of Lastwall, veteran con man Rodrick and his talking sword Hrym expect to weasel or fight their way out of punishment. Instead, they find themselves ensnared by powerful magic, and given a choice: serve the cause of justice as part of a covert team of similarly bound villains—or die horribly. Together with their criminal cohorts, Rodrick and Hrym settle in to their new job of defending the innocent, only to discover that being a secret government operative is even more dangerous than a life of crime.

From Hugo Award winner Tim Pratt comes a tale of reluctant heroes and plausible deniability, set in the award-winning world of the Pathfinder Roleplaying Game.

Liar's Bargain **print edition: $9.99**
ISBN: 978-0-7653-8431-7

Liar's Bargain **ebook edition:**
ISBN: 978-0-7653-8430-0

PATHFINDER
TALES

LIAR'S
BARGAIN

A NOVEL BY Tim Pratt

The Hellknights are a brutal organization of warriors and spellcasters dedicated to maintaining law and order at any cost. For devil-blooded Jheraal, a veteran Hellknight investigator, even the harshest methods are justified if it means building a better world for her daughter. Yet things get personal when a serial killer starts targeting hellspawn like Jheraal and her child, somehow magically removing their hearts and trapping the victims in a state halfway between life and death. With other Hellknights implicated in the crime, Jheraal has no choice but to join forces with a noble paladin and a dangerously cunning diabolist to defeat an ancient enemy for whom even death is no deterrent.

From celebrated dark fantasy author Liane Merciel comes an adventure of love, murder, and grudges from beyond the grave, set in the award-winning world of the Pathfinder Roleplaying Game.

Hellknight print edition: $14.99
ISBN: 978-0-7653-7548-3

Hellknight ebook edition:
ISBN: 978-1-4668-4735-4

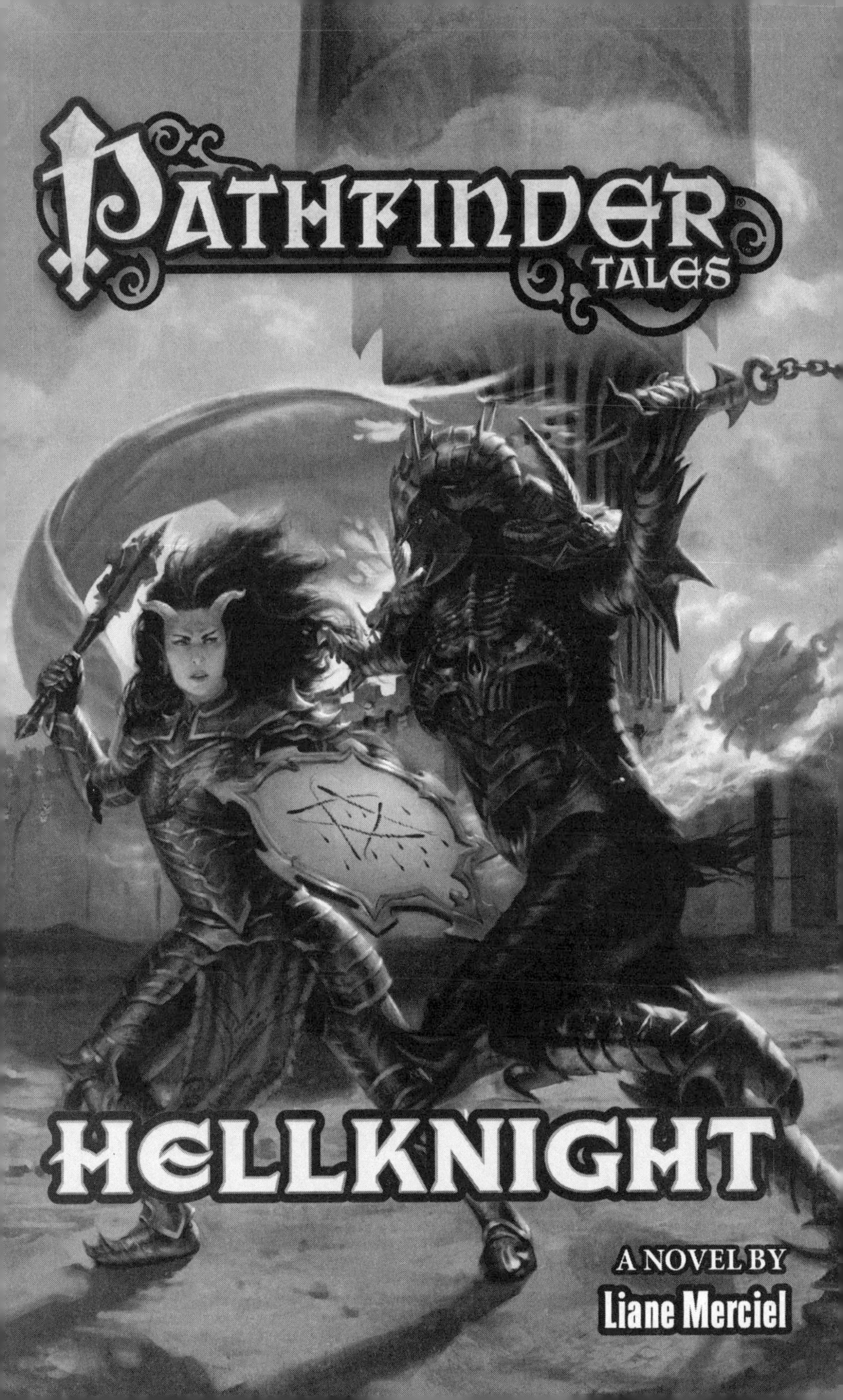
Pathfinder®
Tales
Hellknight
A Novel By
Liane Merciel

Captain Torius Vin has given up the pirate life in order to bring freedom to others. Along with his loyal crew and Celeste, the ship's snake-bodied navigator and Torius's one true love, the captain of the *Stargazer* uses a lifetime of piratical tricks to capture slave galleys and set the prisoners free. But when the crew's old friend and secret agent Vreva Jhafe uncovers rumors of a terrifying new magical weapon in devil-ruled Cheliax—one capable of wiping the abolitionist nation of Andoran off the map—will even their combined forces be enough to stop a navy backed by Hell itself?

From award-winning novelist Chris A. Jackson comes a tale of magic, mayhem, and nautical adventure, set in the vibrant world of the Pathfinder Roleplaying Game.

Pirate's Prophecy **print edition: $14.99**
ISBN: 978-0-7653-7547-6

Pirate's Prophecy **ebook edition:**
ISBN: 978-1-4668-4734-7

PATHFINDER
TALES

Pirate's
Prophecy

A NOVEL BY
Chris A. Jackson

Larsa is a dhampir—half vampire, half human. In the gritty streets and haunted peaks of Ustalav, she's an agent for the royal spymaster, keeping peace between the capital's secret vampire population and its huddled human masses. Meanwhile, in the cathedral of Maiden's Choir, Jadain is a young priestess of the death goddess, in trouble with her superiors for being too soft on the living. When a noblewoman's entire house is massacred by vampiric invaders, the unlikely pair is drawn into a deadly mystery that will reveal far more about both of them than they ever wanted to know.

From Pathfinder cocreator and award-winning game designer F. Wesley Schneider comes a new adventure of revenge, faith, and gothic horror, set in the world of the Pathfinder Roleplaying Game.

Bloodbound **print edition: $14.99**
ISBN: 978-0-7653-7546-9

Bloodbound **ebook edition:**
ISBN: 978-1-4668-4733-0

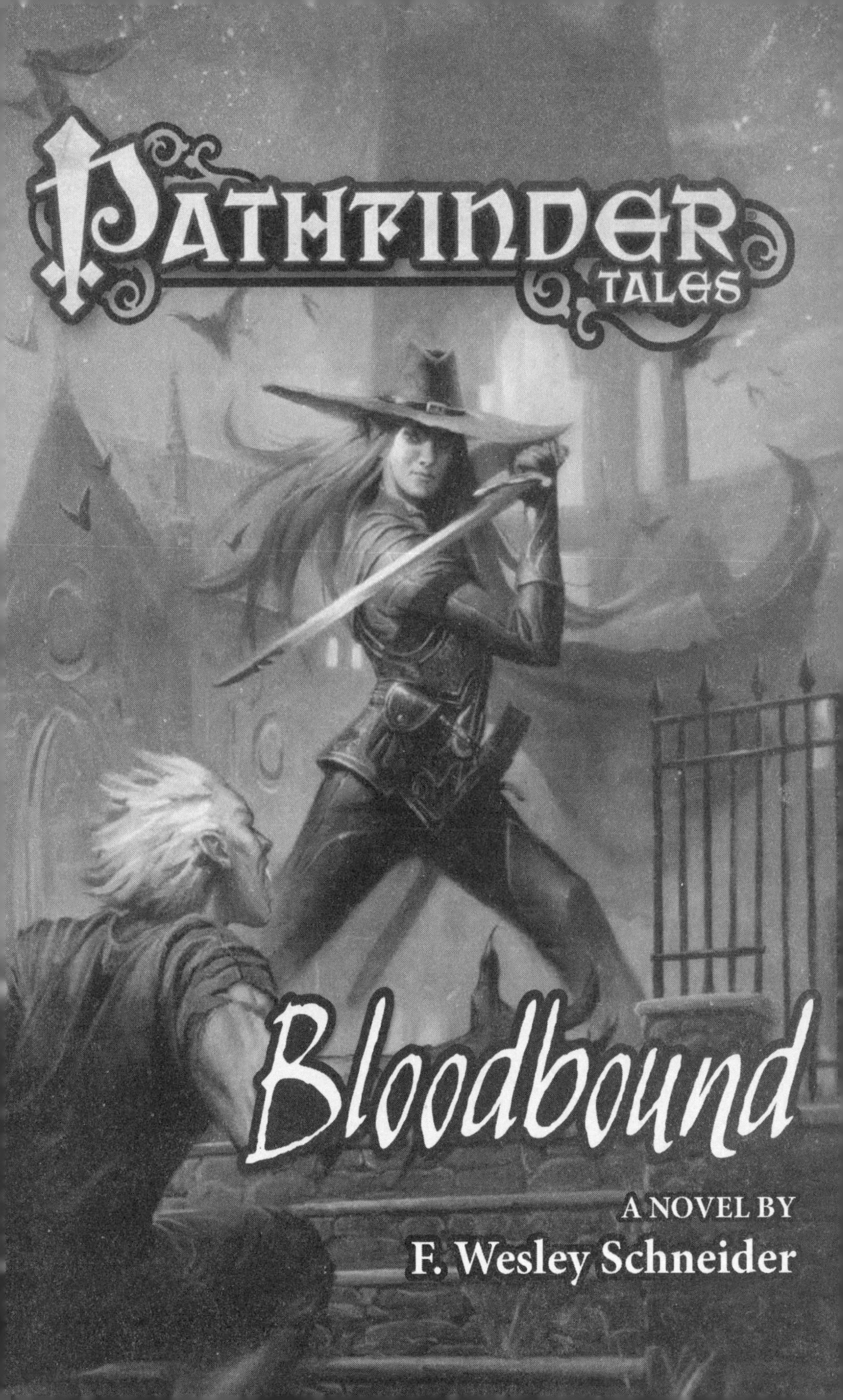
Pathfinder Tales
Bloodbound
A NOVEL BY
F. Wesley Schneider

Mirian Raas comes from a long line of salvagers—adventurers who use magic to dive for sunken ships off the coast of tropical Sargava. With her father dead and her family in debt, Mirian has no choice but to take over his last job: a dangerous expedition into deep jungle pools, helping a tribe of lizardfolk reclaim the lost treasures of their people. Yet this isn't any ordinary dive, as the same colonial government that looks down on Mirian for her half-native heritage has an interest in the treasure, and the survival of the entire nation may depend on the outcome.

From critically acclaimed author Howard Andrew Jones comes an adventure of sunken cities and jungle exploration, set in the award-winning world of the Pathfinder Roleplaying Game.

Beyond the Pool of Stars **print edition: $14.99**
ISBN: 978-0-7653-7453-0

Beyond the Pool of Stars **ebook edition:**
ISBN: 978-1-4668-4265-6

Beyond the Pool of Stars

A NOVEL BY Howard Andrew Jones

Rodrick is con man as charming as he is cunning. Hrym is a talking sword of magical ice, with the soul and spells of an ancient dragon. Together, the two travel the world, parting the gullible from their gold and freezing their enemies in their tracks. But when the two get summoned to the mysterious island of Jalmeray by a king with genies and elementals at his command, they'll need all their wits and charm if they're going to escape with the greatest prize of all—their lives.

From Hugo Award winner Tim Pratt comes a tale of magic, assassination, and cheerful larceny, set in the award-winning world of the Pathfinder Roleplaying Game.

Liar's Island print edition: $14.99
ISBN: 978-0-7653-7452-3

Liar's Island ebook edition:
ISBN: 978-1-4668-4264-9

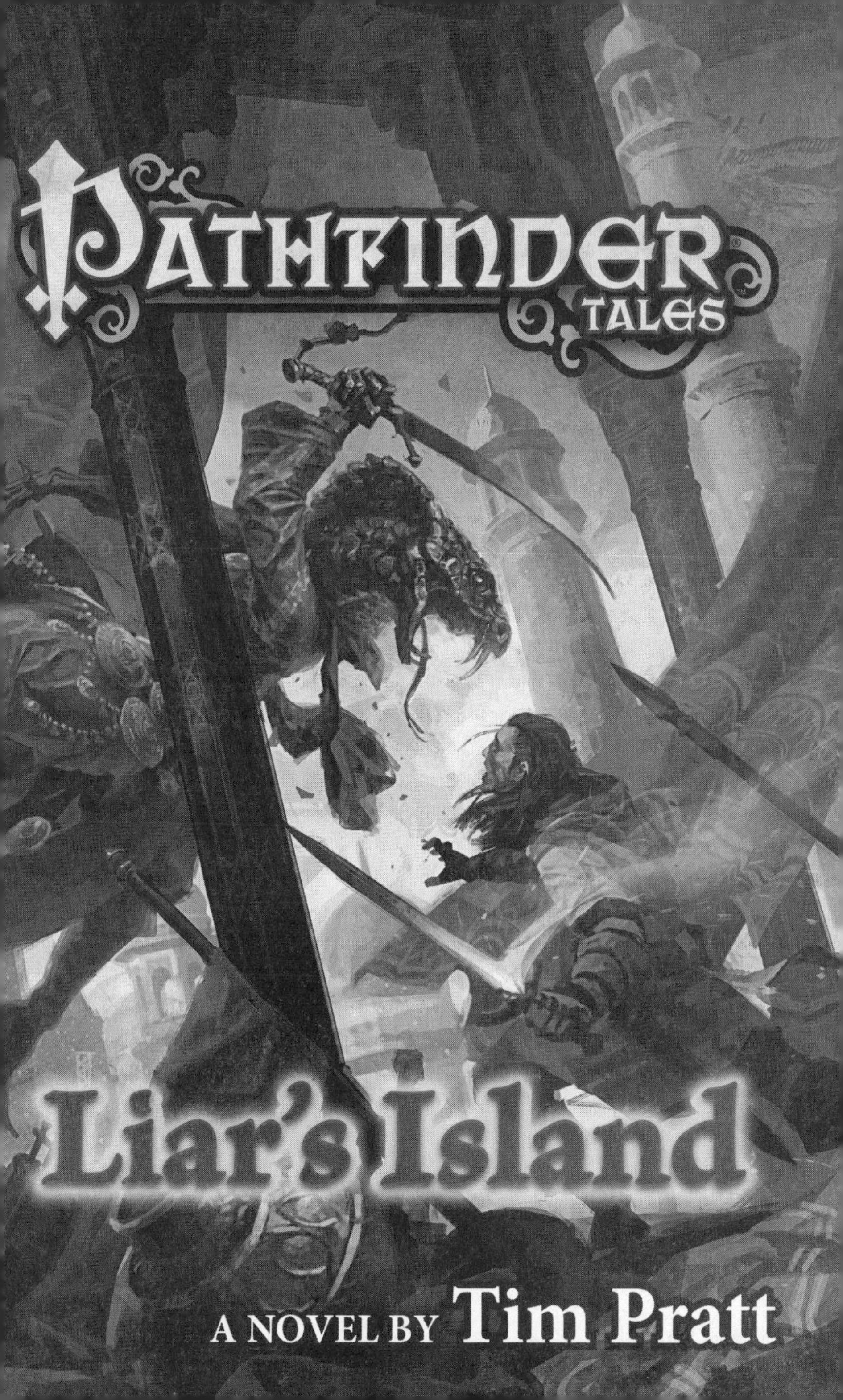
PATHFINDER®
TALES™
Liar's Island
A NOVEL BY Tim Pratt

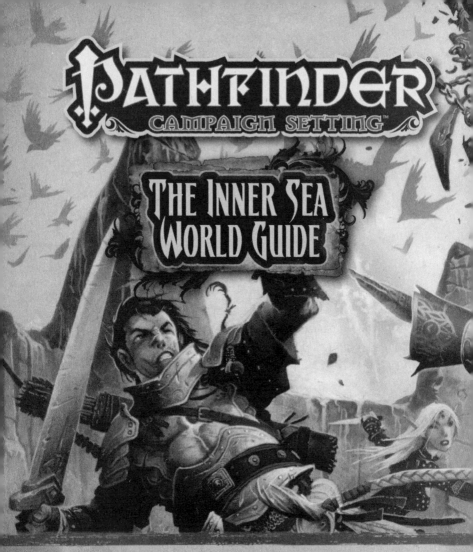

PATHFINDER®
CAMPAIGN SETTING™

THE INNER SEA WORLD GUIDE

You've delved into the Pathfinder campaign setting with Pathfinder Tales novels—now take your adventures even further! *The Inner Sea World Guide* is a full-color, 320-page hardcover guide featuring everything you need to know about the exciting world of Pathfinder: overviews of every major nation, religion, race, and adventure location around the Inner Sea, plus a giant poster map! Read it as a travelogue, or use it to flesh out your roleplaying game—it's your world now!

EXPLORE YOUR WORLD!

paizo.com